MOUNTAIN VIEW

Up in the Arizona mountains, Johnny Ringo had a lot to look back on.

He could remember Lucy, the first love of his life, and all the other women after her. He could remember riding with Quantrill's Raiders—and learning how to cut down enemies and odds with icy nerve and flaming guns. He could remember the lightning raids and deadly duels that had made him a Western legend.

But right now he didn't have time for the past—not with the law closing in. The only way Johnny Ringo figured on seeing the future was through a gunsight. . . .

"GRITTY AND HARD-EDGED"
—*San Jose Mercury News*

"Aggeler spins a fascinating and completely credible yarn from the tatters of history."
—*The Salt Lake Tribune*

CONFESSIONS OF
JOHNNY RINGO

GEOFF AGGELER

A SIGNET BOOK

NEW AMERICAN LIBRARY

A DIVISION OF PENGUIN BOOKS USA INC.

PUBLISHER'S NOTE

This book is a work of fiction. Names, characters, places, and incidents either are the product of the author's imagination or are used fictitiously, and any resemblance to actual persons, living or dead, events, or locales is entirely coincidental.

This is an authorized reprint of a hardcover edition published by E. P. Dutton. The hardcover edition was published simultaneously in Canada by Fitzhenry and Whiteside Limited, Toronto.

SIGNET TRADEMARK REG. U.S. PAT. OFF. AND FOREIGN COUNTRIES
REGISTERED TRADEMARK—MARCA REGISTRADA
HECHO EN DRESDEN, TN, USA

SIGNET, SIGNET CLASSIC, MENTOR, ONYX, PLUME, MERIDIAN and NAL BOOKS are published by NAL PENGUIN INC., 1633 Broadway, New York, New York 10019

First Signet Printing, April, 1989

1 2 3 4 5 6 7 8 9

PRINTED IN THE UNITED STATES OF AMERICA

*For Shirley Donovan Aggeler
and, as always, Sondra*

*With special thanks to the
Camoin-Barber-Rosenthal-Battin-Roberts-
Shapard-Thomas-Woodward-Kevorkian Circle*

PREFACE

For John Ringo the present is 1882. Alone in his retreat in Arizona's ghostly Dragoon Mountains, he recalls his past, and the fragmentary recollections he sets down, scenes of his youth in Texas, the war years in Missouri and Kansas and his subsequent adventures in Texas and Arizona, are an attempt to explain to himself how a well-bred youngster with elements of a classical education eventually became a feared and hated outlaw chief in Arizona.

The historical John Ringo, upon whom this figure is partly modeled, appears in virtually every historical or fictional account of his famous enemies Wyatt Earp and Doc Holliday, but he remains a very mysterious figure. It is known that he carried the Greek and Roman classics in his saddlebags and read them in the original when he wasn't taking part in various underworld operations with Curly Bill and the "Cowboys." He had received part of his education at the William Jewell College in Liberty, Missouri, and was a school official in Texas before he became involved in the so-called Mason County War. The nature of his relationship with his cousins the Youngers and the Jameses is a matter of some dispute. It is believed that he rode with them during the Civil War as a member of Quantrill's guerrilla raiders, though his record as a guerrilla has not been documented.

Ringo's activities in Arizona are well documented, including the challenge of Wyatt Earp and Doc Holliday to single combat and the standoff at the San Pedro bridge. He was known for his chivalry to women, his loyalty to friends and his reckless courage, as well as a capacity for savagery that manifested itself in such actions as the Skeleton Cañon massacre. He spent his last few weeks in the Dragoons and died with a gun in hand: he was found sitting in a hand-shaped oak tree with a bullet through his brain. Though his death appeared to be suicide, the absence of powder burns near the wound in the temple suggested murder. Three different killers have been suspected—Wyatt Earp, Buckskin Frank Leslie, and one Johnny-Behind-the-Deuce. While there is good reason to suspect any one of these men, I found the testimony of Wyatt Earp's mistress, Josie Marcus (*I Married Wyatt Earp*), most persuasive. According to her, Earp returned secretly to Arizona and killed Ringo.

Because everything about Ringo is so mysterious, it may never be possible to write a connected biography. But the mystery that hampers the historian can liberate the novelist. This book does not pretend to be anything but a novel, and its treatments of historical characters who interact with wholly invented figures are fictional. On the other hand, any reader who has ever camped in Cochise's former stronghold in the Dragoons or has visited other scenes depicted here or has perused the memoirs of John McCorkle and other former guerrillas with Quantrill may find the ring of authenticity. What Ringo was doing during his last days in those still ghostly mountains, no one can say. He was certainly capable of setting down his memoirs and leaving them for someone who would tell his story, as Augustus Appler told the story of the Youngers (*The Younger Brothers, their Life and Character*). If Ringo didn't leave me as much material as the Youngers left Appler, he still left enough for a fictional account that is in harmony with what is known about one of the more fascinating, enigmatic figures of the old Southwest.

—GEOFF AGGELER

ONE

MEETING COCHISE

"It is the goddamnedest, infernalest place that red devil could have found to hole up in. Like ridin' into hell it is. No place for a white man."

That's how old Striker describes the Dragoon mountain haven of Cochise. And when John Ringo finally sees it for himself, two years later, he will have to allow that maybe old Striker has a point. He and Striker and another man are on their way to Curly Bill's headquarters at Roofless Dobe Ranch, riding south along a trail that winds over the main divide of the Chiricahua Mountains. Having relieved a Wells Fargo coach of the strongbox it was carrying from Globe to Tucson, they've been riding hard. At Camp Bowie they helped themselves to some fresh mounts, the best they could pick out in a hurry, and this brought out a squad of troopers to join the posse that was already trailing them.

The pursuers, military and civilian, are not two miles behind them, but as the sun begins to drop behind the Dragoon range they rein up and dismount for a few moments to let their animals breathe. Fifty miles away, across the Sulphur Springs Valley, the towers and turrets of the Dragoons loom malevolently, like the fortress of some cruel and hated garrison. As the sun drops behind them, the highest peaks glow molten scarlet.

"It's right inside that notch that's sort of like a gunsight. See it?" Ringo sees it clearly, a jagged break in the range, carving through it from Sulphur Springs to San Pedro.

"When Cochise had his camp back in there, waren't nobody could get him out. Time we tried to get in there to rescue a trooper they'd captured, they damn near et us alive. Poured lead on us from every rock while they tortured that poor sonofabitch and made him scream for us to hear."

11

Striker was a scout for the army before he joined Curly Bill and went into the business of, among other things, rustling army stock. A lean mournful-eyed hound of a man, he goes on:

"Still Indin mountains sure as hell, even if most of them red devils is penned up at San Carlos. You won't never get me near 'em again. I care too much about this old skin." The black gobbet of tobacco juice splattered against a boulder emphasizes the point.

"That's the difference between us, Striker," Ringo murmurs, "one of 'em anyway." With a few whiskeys under his belt, he would probably quote his favorite character in literature, who didn't set his life at a pin's fee. What does it matter if old Striker has never heard of either the character or his creator?

He stands beside Striker and gazes across the valley, a big brooding man who can, when the mood is on him, look as forbidding as the Dragoons themselves. The fire is dying out on the last high peak, leaving the whole range in darkness, and he feels himself strangely, unaccountably drawn to the place.

Not much longer. I can't put it off much longer, surely, he promises himself silently. If he said it aloud, the last word might come out "sho'ly," for he often tends to sound like his southern relations, people who always keep their promises.

But before he can keep his promise, two more years pass, two more years as Curly Bill's lieutenant and chief planner, coordinator of everything from large-scale rustling raids in Sonora to stage holdups and the ambushing of Mexican smuggler trains, chief strategist and champion of the "Cowboys" in their war with the Earps and Doc Holliday. A good life for a man, he often tells himself, free and natural, satisfying in its challenges, its risks and its simplicity. It surely beats hell out of inspecting schools in Burnet County, Texas. Yet sometimes during those years, between raids and holdups, or run-ins with the Earp faction, as he sits quietly in the Crystal Palace in Tombstone or Evilsizer's Saloon in Galeyville, with a glass and a tall bottle of the house poison in front of him, his fun-loving outlaw comrades can see that he is in no mood to enjoy their company, that he is in fact liable to draw one of his ivory-handled .44s against anyone who disturbs him.

"Jest leave him alone," Curly will mutter to the others. "Whatever it is, he'll drink his way out of it. Too goddamn many books's the trouble. . . ."

Curly keeps his voice low, so that Ringo can't hear him, but this usually isn't necessary. When Ringo enters the dark world within himself, he is barely aware of the sounds around him. It isn't his reading that gets him into this world, and as for drinking his way out of it, it is whiskey that leads him deeper into himself, or seems to.

". . . Ain't nothin' in books, is there, boys? We oughta do him a favor and burn 'em. All that readin's no good for a man. Takes all the funnin' out of him. What he needs is a woman. One of his chippies. Beats me, tho', how a man can keep his pizzle up with all that crowded into his head."

A woman can help, sometimes. Curly is right about that. Sometimes, if the whiskey lets him, he will lever himself up out of his chair, straighten up to his full six feet two inches and make a stiffly swaying progress to the door. Rarely, as he stalks out, he may acknowledge his comrades' presence by mumbling a word of farewell or raising his hand. Usually he says nothing, as he gets up and moves past or through the crowd of drinkers at the bar, a big drunken man who holds himself as rigidly erect as an Indian and seems not to see those who happen to be in his path, who always move aside quickly to let him pass. Once outside, he will point himself in the direction of the nearest crib.

In Galeyville, in Charleston, in Tombstone, and a couple of the little hells in between, as well as a couple of the little towns down in Sonora, Ringo has his favorite crib girls. He is a man who cannot long endure being without the company of women, and whose attitude toward womankind in the abstract borders on the worshipful. The particular women he seeks out are, or seem to be, nearly always pleased to see him, no matter how whiskey-sodden his condition. For he is always generous, paying freely for whatever he receives, and he is always a gentleman.

His favorite in Tombstone is a Mexican girl who calls herself Elena, who works at Irma's Place, a house down near the south end of town, within earshot of the Contention mine. It is while he is lying in her bed one evening late in the spring of 'eighty-two that he makes up his mind finally to keep his long-put-off promise to himself.

The evening is warm and fragrant. Faint smells of the desert in bloom and the pungent odors of the street drift in to mingle with the smells of the woman. Ringo loves the smell of a woman's sweat, this woman's especially, as it breaks out and makes her smooth olive skin glisten like burnished metal. He wishes that she wouldn't seek to conceal her woman's smell beneath perfume that is just a mite too sweet.

"You like me, *hombre?*" she asks in a husky whisper, grinning down at him, knowing and confident in her mastery of his body. Ringo does not answer, does not have to. She is a girl who enjoys her work, when she is with a man who can appreciate her skills and who can let her feel his pleasure. As Ringo lies beneath her, he feels himself being peeled like a bronc, his rider twisting and clasping in perfect rhythm with his passion. Gazing up at her through half-closed eyes, he loves the way her soft masses of black hair frame her delicate high-boned Spanish-Indian features and tumble about her gleaming shoulders. When she pauses for a moment in her riding, he murmurs softly:

"Sho'ly no wonder that the sons of God saw the daughters of men that they were fair and took them. No wonder atall."

"You like me, *hombre?*" she asks again, flashing nearly perfect teeth in the darkness. "*Dígame, hombre,* how can I give you pleasure? *Dígame,* Juanito Reengo," she demands in an urgent whisper, and he knows that she doesn't expect an answer in words, though he speaks her own language like a native. For an answer he shuts his eyes and pushes his head back against her pillow, chuckling a little and wanting to laugh out loud, joyfully lost in pure animal sensation, one with his passion, freed for the moment from the bondage of his own dark thoughts and rememberings. Freed from thought, he surrenders to her and to himself, the part of himself that only a woman can release.

Afterward, as he lies beside her, peaceful and tamed, all the stallion heat gone out of him, he begins to think again. It is during these moments that he is able to think most clearly, when a woman has succeeded in draining him for a little while of all his rage and bitterness and memories. When he was a boy, a Catholic priest told him about exorcism, about how a priest can drive the devil out of a man. Now that he is a man, Ringo believes, devoutly, that it takes a woman to truly exorcise a man.

This time, he begins to think again about the task he has set himself and put off so often. That "infernalest place," as Striker called the fortress of Cochise, is not very far from Tombstone. If he rides hard, he can reach it in a day and a half. He has in fact decided more than once that he is ready to go there. But there has always been something to prevent him:

"What're we gonna do, Ringo?" he remembers Ike Clanton whining. "Them goddamn Earps is goin' to arrest Curly. We gotta stop 'em." And Ringo stopped them that time, without any help from Ike or anyone else, turning them back with a rifle at the San Pedro bridge. He was always ready to stake his life in any contest with them. It is one of his most intolerable regrets that he missed out on the O.K. Corral fight.

Another time when he was ready to retreat for a while into the Dragoons, Curly heard about a smuggler train being outfitted down Hermosillo way for a trip up to Tucson.

"Thousands in silver, John! Thousands them greasers is packin'! If we can get hold o' that, we can quit everything else for a while. You gotta help us plan it at least."

And he did help them plan it, convinced them to lay the ambush in Skeleton Cañón, in the Peloncillos. He was also with them when the Mexicans arrived in the cañón. The memory of what happened that afternoon has been haunting and tormenting him in his vulnerable moments for nearly a year, a fouler and more persistent fury than any that followed him from Lawrence, Kansas, with Quantrill, or Mason County, Texas. It is only now that he thinks he might be able to endure being truly alone. And now that Curly has disappeared and the gang is breaking up, there is no one to talk him out of it.

"You are going away soon, Juanito?" It is the woman asking.

"*Sí*, for a little while anyway. How did you know this?"

"Because you have stayed already here in Tombstone as long as you ever stay. You will be careful?"

Ringo can't really believe that she cares a lot, but her expression of concern still gratifies him. It is one of the things he pays for gladly and generously, the illusion of a woman's concern.

"I'm always careful, milady," he replies, lapsing out of Spanish. "You know that."

"*Sí*, I know." She smiles and then frowns a little as she traces with her finger a fairly recent scar that runs through the mat of hair across his left breast, souvenir of a handkerchief duel he'd nearly lost down in Janos and a reminder that his speed at almost forty, even when he is fairly sober, is not what it was even a few years ago.

Perhaps it is only to prove that he hasn't lost much besides speed that he makes love with her again. Or perhaps there is something more he wants. In his own mind he is no longer just a bronc of a man being peeled, and she becomes, for him, for the moment, something more than his strong-thighed rider mingling her sweat with his mansweat. At the highest point of his passion, he whispers: "I love you, Margaret."

The woman Elena is puzzled and might even be a little annoyed if she let herself forget that Señor Ringo is just another customer, more considerate than most, but still a customer only. She is a little moved, though, in spite of herself, when she strokes his cheek and encounters a wetness that is not sweat. And it is not entirely because he is a generous customer who will pay her well for the whole night that she lets him drop off to sleep with his head pillowed upon her breast.

The next morning he awakens first and leaves her bed as quietly as he can, slipping on his trousers and padding barefoot across the room to a washstand that holds a blue pottery basin and pitcher. On the wall above the washstand hangs a large oval mirror in a wooden frame. Ringo regards himself for a moment, then looks away quickly.

"Jesus," he mutters, trying to exorcise the ruined image that has just confronted him. All the color has gone out of his lean face, leaving it the shade of wet wood ash. Furrowing the gray flesh, the deep, bitter lines are etched so much more darkly than they are when his face assumes the normal red bronze that drink and weather give it. The gray of his features is matched by the streaks that riot through his tousled mass of wavy auburn hair. Someone, a woman, told him once that he looked like Byron, only his eyes were deepset, not protruding like Byron's. Now, as he forces himself to look into the hollows out of which his dark blue eyes show redly, he wonders if Byron, who happens to be one of his favorite poets, ever looked like this.

When he has splashed some water on his face, he is able to look into the mirror again. Below his face and the muscular sun-browned neck, the ruin is less obvious. The white-fleshed, heavily haired muscles of his chest and belly are still hard, but he has the feeling that maybe his whole hard muscular body has had enough and is ready to go soft on him. He can almost feel sorry for it, when he looks at the long knife scar he acquired just a few months before and the pocklike indentations of two old bullet wounds picked up in Missouri during the war. One of those just missed his lungs and the other smashed a couple of ribs. Not visible at that moment is the mark of still another Yankee slug that went into his right thigh and stayed there to plague him on cold mornings, one of his "miseries."

"Good morning, Juanito." It is the woman greeting him. He could feel her eyes on him as he bent over the washbasin. Toweling himself dry he can see her in the mirror. She is sitting up in the bed, naked but partly covered by her long dark hair. Seeing him watching her in the mirror, she smiles and brushes back her hair as she reaches up to stretch her smooth brown arms. The pleasure of watching her fine young breasts rise with her movement is for Ringo mixed a little with the pain of longing, longing that is not simply a desire to enjoy her again. There will be plenty of time for that, he tells himself, when he comes back into Tombstone. What he longs for at this moment, as he regards the woman's flesh, is some way to preserve its exquisite beauty— imagining how its ripened gold will be withered and dried in a few years, if not ravaged hideously before then by the diseases of her trade.

The sons of God saw the daughters of men that they

were fair. A lot of good it did them, Ringo thinks sadly. No matter what the sons saw, God himself, if He exists, sees only corruption. The end of all flesh is come before me.

"Qué hombre," the woman murmurs appreciatively. She has come up behind him to clasp him round the waist and lay her head against his broad back. Feeling her body molding itself to him, he is prompted to ask her something he meant to ask the night before but just didn't get around to:

"Do you think I look like Byron?"

"Sí, hombre," she answers with perfect conviction.

Ringo grins and reaches back to brush her flank with his fingers. I guess she's wondering, he thinks, where Byron deals cards or maybe what outfit he punches cows for. What does it matter? I believe her all the same. I believe anything she wants to tell me.

He feels himself being drawn backward by the smooth brown arms. The fortress of Cochise is waiting for him, but he decides that it can wait a little longer.

2

Ringo leaves the woman most of what he picked up in two nights of serious poker at the Crystal Palace, keeping just enough to pay for his supplies. The supplies he packs into his saddlebags and the panniers on a rented pack mule include a little food and enough whiskey to fire up a pretty sizable war party at the San Carlos reservation, if he were inclined to pursue that mischievous trade. But in fact his ample supply is solely for his own consumption or that of any white visitor who might happen by his Dragoon mountain retreat. Remembering, though, what old Striker said about the fortress of Cochise, he doesn't expect many white visitors to "happen by."

He allows himself two days to reach the canyon, two days of hot, dusty, wary riding. It is a time to ride warily in this country, for although most of the Apaches have accepted reservation life, there are still small bands of hostiles and the odd "bronco" operating alone on both sides of the border. In April there was a battle over in the Steins Peak Mountains of western New Mexico, between Chief Loco's band and the army, and it has been just a year since the bloody affair up on Cibicu Creek. And though Ringo places little value on his life, he has as little taste as any man for the forms of death the Apaches are known to contrive.

So he rides warily across the low rolling hills and washes of the San Pedro Valley, scanning the ground carefully as he threads the washes and avoids the ridgetops. Riding along the San Pedro, Ringo can see pin-tailed ducks and herons, hawks and eagles soar above him from their craggy perches on distant mesas. At one point, as he follows an arroyo up from the riverbed, he rounds a corner beneath a high ledge and knows that he is being watched. Looking back, he encounters the yellow-green eyes of a cougar stretched out in the shade at rest after a night's hunting. The cat is enormous, and Ringo is suddenly inclined to give more credence to the tale he has heard and scoffed at, about the wounded trooper with General Crook who wandered away from the scene of a fight with the Apaches and was dragged off by one of the supposedly shy beasts.

He seeks to calm his big gelding when a whiff of the cougar is brought down to its nostrils on the canyon breeze. "Easy, dammit. He only eats Yanks for supper." Then to the cat, "Right, painter?"

For an answer, the animal rises to its feet, whirls and bounds up the rock wall behind the ledge. Ringo thinks again, with little twinges of longing, of Elena's wet golden flesh. Is there any beauty like the brute beauty of the flesh? Is there any other beauty?

He rides on up the arroyo, scanning the ground in front of him, as well as the ledges and ridges above him, noticing how the various kinds of reptiles blend faultlessly with the multicolored sands as they scurry or slide out of the way of his horse's hooves. Weird forms of cacti surround him—prickly pear, ocotillo, niggerhead, the irksome choya, and what the Mexicans call maguey, among others. Ringo knows that two of these plants at least, the niggerhead and the maguey, or agave, can be drunk. Ringo himself has never drunk niggerhead juices, but the distilled juice of the maguey, fiery mescal, is another matter.

It takes a few hours of riding in the sun for his head to clear itself of the crapula left over from drink and all the long nights at the smoke-clouded cardtables in the Crystal Palace and the Oriental. Once it is cleared, though, he can respond to the beauty of the desert in bloom, the ocotillo's scarlet blossoms and the pale flowers of the giant saguaro. And the Dragoons, vertical walls that appear from the west to be without any route of ascent, seem to beckon him.

Few white men live in the Dragoons: At Sulphur Springs there is one station of the Overland Stage route, and along the lower reaches of the eastern slopes there are a few ranches, including one operated by a Mexican from whom Ringo has appropriated the fine big buckskin gelding he is riding. But no white men are living near the fortress of Cochise. Ringo has a little trouble at first finding the old Indian trail that leads up into the mouth of the canyon. Skirting the northwestern corner of the range, he makes camp for one night in Dragoon Gap. The next morning he passes through the Gap, turns south and rides for about twelve miles to where a beautiful grove of live oaks marks the lower entrance to the fortress. Entering the grove, he finally picks up the trail.

As Ringo approaches the fortress, he remembers another time when Striker was with him, leading some men back up from Mexico by way of the Pedregosas. The ex-scout persuaded him to turn into a ravine, where he promised to show him some Apache handiwork. He showed him a skeleton staked out in the sand and the nearby skeleton of a tethered rattler. They couldn't figure out if the man had been able to keep his head wrenched in that painful position until he died of heatstroke or had just given up and let it roll back within range of the fangs.

Touching his big gelding's flanks lightly with his spurs, Ringo moves ahead through the entrance at a slow walk. "Abandon all hope." The poet's greeting to the damned rings through the outlaw's mind as he thinks about the Apaches' human playthings and thinks about himself as well. There is no hope of rescue from most of the hells men create. That's what the poet really meant.

But as his eyes flick over the walls ahead of him, he puts away thoughts of Dante. The low whistle of appreciation from his lips is that of the ex-guerrilla who can imagine himself in the enviable place of the defenders of this stronghold. Looking up at the giant boulders resting on the ledges above him, he pictures sharpshooters raining their fire on blue-uniformed attackers. If they ran out of ammunition, the boulders themselves could be toppled off to roll like juggernauts down the narrow trail.

When he has passed through this deadly corridor, Ringo finds himself in still another one that winds beneath layers of ascending rocks providing innumerable unassailable positions for the defenders. Some attackers might be lucky or crazy enough to get through the first passageway, but none would get beyond this one.

"Give me twenty good men," he reflects aloud, "and I could hold off two or three companies of bluebellies at least, even if they brought in artillery. Damned if I couldn't!"

He is also thinking, and not for the first time, that he has a lot more in common with the "red devils" who have held up the progress of "civilization" in places like this than with the white men confining them on reservations.

"They're the cruelest bastards on earth," Striker said, after they had viewed the skeletons of the man and the snake. "Ain't human. Like a bunch of goddamn animals!"

"They're free," Ringo replied shortly, and the other man had looked at him with his puzzled hound's eyes, expecting him to say something more, but he said nothing. He was thinking, though, that whether that kind of cruelty makes men less than human or something more depends on how you look at it. Staking out your fellow humans next to tethered rattlesnakes or boiling their brains out over slow fires was surely what most folks who read the Good Book would call cruel. But what can you say about a God who destroys with fire and brimstone all the flesh He's supposed to have made, just because it behaves like flesh? He's almighty cruel, if He exists at all, and that's mainly how He shows His power, even in the Good Book. Cruelty is a way of showing your power, showing the world that nothing can stop you. The Apaches, as near as he could figure, were just showing the world that they could do as they damn pleased. They were also, according to Buckskin Frank Leslie, a bartender at the Oriental who, like Striker, had been a scout with the army, trying to increase their power by their cruelty:

"Yeah, John, that's what they believe," Leslie said, pouring Ringo another whiskey. "That if they get a good man in their power, somebody who's been a great fighter, they can get it out of him, the spirit or whatever it is that made him what he was. So they torture him till there's just nothing left. Then they ride on and strike again, feeling all the stronger on account of all the new spirit they've picked up."

Hell, maybe they're right, Ringo thinks. Maybe they're just trying to be like their gods. He doesn't know anything much about Apache gods, but he figures they probably aren't all that different from the ones the Greeks made up or God in the Good Book. They can probably do what they damn please with mortal men and not have to worry about any consequences. Men can suffer anything imaginable, and their gods won't feel a thing. Whatever they are like, they make sense to the Apaches, and they're probably a shade more consistent than God in the Good Book. Ringo envies the Apaches, as he has envied other savages, mostly white, he's actually known in the past. There are times, he thinks, when I'd rather be one of the wildest, cruelest Apaches who ever lived than Johnny Ringo.

Beyond the second rocky corridor, Ringo finds himself entering another grove of live oaks. The trail winds between fat gray trunks and the branches meet above it, so that surprisingly little sunlight is allowed to penetrate, and he does not see the creature that leaps across the trail to block his passage until he is almost on top of it. Suddenly, as the gelding skips a little sideways and lets out a nervous snort, he makes out the form of the wolf. For a second or two, he looks into the animal's large slanting yellow eyes, as he looked into the eyes of the cougar. Its mouth is open, and it pants and grins at him in a doggy way. Then it turns and lopes away through the woods, trailing its great gray plume of a tail. What'll I see next? Ringo wonders. Probably one of those big spotted cats that come up from Mexico every once in a while, that are something like a leopard. In this place, nothing would surprise him.

He is surprised, though, that very afternoon.

Having passed through the dim woods, Ringo enters a

basin that is surrounded on every side by towering granite walls, beyond which naked peaks thrust themselves against the painfully bright blue Arizona sky. The basin itself is mostly meadow, heavily carpeted with rich grama grass and shaded here and there by clumps of oak. It isn't hard to see where the Apaches put up their wickiups. The grass has grown over the area, but the charred marks of their fireplaces are still visible. He rides slowly around the entire meadow looking for the right place to set up his camp. Finally he stops where a little spring that doesn't look as though it will last out the summer seeps up between some boulders. It is shaded by a reaching limb from a giant oak, and he decides to pitch his tent beneath this limb, where it will be partly protected from the midday sun. The tent, made of heavy white canvas, has its former, and still rightful, owner proclaimed by a broadly stenciled *U.S.A.* across the doorflap.

When he has the tent set up, he returns to his panniers and draws out several bundles, most of them roughly square in shape, wrapped in pieces of oilskin. These he carries into the tent and begins to unwrap carefully his personal library, brought all the way from his cabin at Roofless Dobe Ranch, fat volumes bound in worn morocco that he has collected over the years, read and reread. He piles them carefully in the shadiest corner of the tent, stacking Homer and Euripides upon Shakespeare, Montaigne and Marlowe upon Horace and Dante, Milton and Tennyson upon a Vulgate Bible and a King James, Byron and Keats upon Cervantes. Aside from Montaigne and *The Divine Comedy*, which is in Longfellow's translation, the two Bibles are the only books not in their original languages.

Ringo has brought his books from the outlaw headquarters because he doesn't want anything to happen to them. With the gang breaking up and no big money coming in from raids and holdups, somebody surely would have stolen them to sell to the nearest trader for a few bottles of whiskey or a little ammunition. Now, he reflects, those sonsofbitches can find something else to steal and somebody else to tell them how. He knows what some of them think of him and his learning, and he only wishes that they had the *cojones* to say it out loud.

Since he has the books with him, he figures he might

do a little reading, but this is hardly his reason for coming all the way into this lonely retreat. Wedged in with the books is a package of writing materials—pencils and a thick stack of clean foolscap. He has also stuck a board in one of the panniers to enable him to turn his knee into a writing desk. Picking up the foolscap and the pencils, he starts out of the tent, thinking he will fetch the board and maybe a bottle to prime him a little in his undertaking. What he sees as he emerges from the tent, however, makes him damned thankful that he hasn't yet unpacked any of his whiskey.

How they managed to ride up on him without making any sound whatever he cannot understand. There are six of them, five young bucks and a very old man sitting their mounts in a row in front of his tent, each with a carbine cradled in his arm or resting across his pony's withers. Apparently they've been there for a few minutes, waiting while he fussed with his things inside the tent. Except for the old man, they are, in Ringo's eyes, indistinguishable from each other—small brown men with the bright black eyes of wild things, each wearing a faded hickory shirt, breechclout and knee moccasins, and having his long black hair bound back from his eyes by a strip of flannel.

Ringo's Spencer is leaning against the giant oak trunk, well out of reach, but he is wearing his .44s. If I fill both hands, he thinks quickly, I can take two, maybe three of them. He feels no fear then, only the familiar excitement of an impending fight in which the odds are poor but not impossible. Then the old man, as though he can read Ringo's thoughts, hands his carbine to the young fellow on his right and dismounts. He comes over and sticks out his hand.

"Buenos días," he says, in a voice surprisingly deep coming out of such a withered throat.

"Buenos días." Ringo takes the hand, a small brown paw that time has mummified.

"We are hunters from San Carlos," the old man explains in Spanish. "Our agent has permitted us to come up here to hunt the deer."

"The agency beef does not fill Apache bellies?" Ringo asks, knowing that he is making a bad joke. He relaxes a little, but he is still ready, keeping his eyes on the young

ones. The old man chuckles at his question and does not
reply to it. Everyone, it seems, even the "white eyes"
who live elsewhere, knows what it is like at San Carlos
and why the young men still leave it to follow the war
trail. Ringo goes on: "If one of your men can make me a
fire, I have coffee."

The old man smiles and flings a command in Apache at
his companions. All five dismount, and while three of
them relieve the ponies of their riding pads and meager
baggage, the other two set to work building not one but
three cook fires. Ringo goes to his panniers and draws
out a sack of coffee, along with a heavily charred pot,
being careful not to reveal the ample supply of whiskey
he has crammed into the panniers.

When the fires have been built and the coffee pot has
been set over the one nearest the tent, Ringo and the old
man hunker down on either side of it. Then the young
men draw out of their saddlebags what Ringo guesses are
pieces of horseflesh and set them on planted sticks to
roast. Ringo draws out his tobacco sack from a vest
pocket and hands the makings across the fire to his
ancient guest. It is good fragrant Mexican tobacco, and
the old fellow rolls himself a smoke without spilling a
flake. He lights it with a glowing twig from the fire and
fills his lungs gratefully. When Ringo has rolled one for
himself and drawn deeply, it is time to open conversation:

"Tell me, *viejo*," he begins, "why is it that a man of
your years must exert himself and follow the hunting trail
with these youngsters?"

Before he replies, the old man regards him closely for
a moment with bright black eyes that seem not to have
aged with the rest of him:

"I am what you white eyes call a medicine man. I must
come here with them so that they may speak with Cochise.
Cochise will tell them where to hunt."

The old fellow's Spanish is clear enough, but Ringo is
not sure that he has heard him correctly.

"No comprendo, viejo."

"Of course not, young man," the medicine man replies
with a smile that shows his few teeth, barely lodged in their
ancient gums. "The white eyes do not believe that they
can speak with the spirits of those who have left this land."

"Some do," Ringo murmurs, remembering a séance he attended once with his cousin Cole Younger in Louisiana.

"I did not know that. Well, anyway, there is a cave near here where the spirit of Cochise abides. We must go there and speak with him before we hunt. The white eyes believe that he has gone forever, but his people know that they may always come to him for counsel."

Ringo draws thoughtfully at his cigarette and gazes into the flames before him.

"Is it possible," he asks finally, "that a white man could be introduced to the spirit of the great Cochise?" Ringo is a skeptic, but he is also curious, wondering if perhaps the old fellow can put on a more convincing show than what he saw in Louisiana.

Before replying, the medicine man hesitates for several moments. He looks sharply at Ringo with his bird-bright obsidian eyes, then he looks into the fire. Again Ringo draws his nearly full tobacco sack out and tosses it across the fire.

"*Por usted,* grandfather."

While the old man considers, he looks at the sack in his hand and draws hard at what remains of his cigarette. The furrows in his ancient brow deepen beneath a ragged headband that is faded nearly as white as his wispy hair. Finally he nods and puts the sack into a pocket of his shirt.

When the Indians have had their midday repast, the medicine man stands up and says to Ringo simply, "Let us go now." Snatching up his rifle, Ringo follows as the old man sets out from the camp on foot, and four of the others fall in after him. One man remains behind to watch the horses.

The old fellow sets a brisk pace up and over a ridge and into a ravine that leads for several hundred yards to an enormous wall of sandstone, in the middle of which there is a narrow fissure. Here the Indians pause to fashion torches out of sagebrush roots and twisted grass. Then the medicine man, small of stature and withered slight by his age, wriggles through the crack with the quickness and ease of a lizard. Ringo, with his broad, powerful shoulders, has considerable difficulty following, and once inside the fissure he finds his height a real liability. Gradually the fissure widens until the torches reveal that they are in a cave approximately fifty feet in circumference, but the ceiling is still too low for Ringo, and he hunkers down with his back to the wall and his rifle across his knees. Now they've got me in here, he reflects, maybe they'll want to make an acceptable sacrifice and fill a trough with my blood for their chief to refresh himself when he comes across from the underworld. He strokes the breech of his rifle.

But the Indians ignore Ringo, at first anyway. The medicine man plants his torch in the middle of the floor, and the five of them form a circle around it. They begin then to utter a mournful incantation that would, Ringo suspects, be unintelligible even to a white man who knew the Apache language. "Hee nah hay! Hum hooyay!" or something, goes its eerie refrain. Soon they begin to move into a kind of shuffling dogtrot around the flickering torch, uttering the same incantation, only now more rapidly.

"Hooh!" This sharply barked command from the medicine man brings them to an abrupt halt and silence. Then the old fellow suddenly whirls toward Ringo and points at a section of the cave's wall just beyond reach of the torchlight.

"*Ojos blancos, mira!*" he shouts. But Ringo's "white" or rather blue eyes see nothing besides the pitchy darkness beyond where the torchlight flickers against the ocher-colored cave wall. Nevertheless, he feels the hair on the back of his neck beginning to rise, and his thumb tightens against the hammer on his rifle.

There is little Ringo fears. In fact, his reputation for being "absolutely fearless," "recklessly brave," "game as hell," "crazy reckless," depending upon how the describer happens to regard him, is well founded. But as everyone knows, even those who use admiringly the adjective *fearless*, there is no sane man who is truly without the capacity to fear. Ringo, like any man, is prone to fear what he does not understand or what he doubts he can handle. In matters of the supernatural, though he is a skeptic, he is also ready to be convinced. What convinces him now and causes an icy trickle in his lower innards and an equally chilly sweat to break out on his forehead and upper lip is the old medicine man. Still pointing at the wall, he begins to utter sounds—screeches and shrieks that are deafening within the confines of the cave and utterly unlike anything one might expect from a human being. His eyes roll in his frenzy, and, after nearly a minute of this has passed, he gives one final agonizing scream and falls to the ground, where he begins to thrash about, like an epileptic in the throes of a seizure. Ringo expects the four young men around him to render some assistance, but they stand still where his command has halted them, all with their heads bowed reverently toward that same patch of darkness.

So Cochise is with us, Ringo thinks. He strains his eyes to glimpse the apparition, but the great chief will not reveal himself to the white-eyed intruder. After another minute has passed, the old medicine man's violent transports end in what seems to be a kind of trance. As he begins to come out of it, the other four squat down around him and carefully lift him to his feet. The chief it would seem, has returned for this brief visit with his children, but now he is gone.

Ringo needs a drink. Without waiting for the Indians, he makes his way back out through the fissure and returns to his camp. A short time later, the Apaches come into the camp and stay there just long enough to pick up their horses. Then they move on to another canyon, directed there presumably by the chief himself.

After they have gone, Ringo draws a bottle of whiskey out of a pannier and fills his tin cup half full. Squatting down Apache-fashion before the embers of his fire, he reflects upon what he has, or has not, seen, and why he wanted to meet the shade of Cochise. It was only partly a matter of curiosity and more, he sees now, a genuine desire to commune with the dead. Was it because so many of his comrades in the Curly Bill gang, and perhaps Curly himself, have recently been killed and he sees his own turn coming soon? Partly. He is nearly forty years old, has lived well beyond the reasonable expectancy for a gunfighting gambler, especially one who lives habitually outside the law and makes mortal enemies of the likes of Wyatt Earp and Doc Holliday. He has survived a wartime stint with Quantrill's Raiders, a range war in Texas, countless forays into Mexico after cattle or whatever might be plundered and finally, during this last year, more than one nearly fatal run-in with the Earp faction.

He guesses he is overdue to, as they say, "cash in." The Earp faction has moved on, left the territory, but they have, in their bloody fashion, effectively accelerated a process that means the end for men like Johnny Ringo, for whom the constraints of civilized law are intolerable. Not much longer will he be able to count on such lawmen as Sheriff Johnny Behan and Deputy Breakenridge to wink at his activities outside of Tombstone on the reasonable condition that he behaves himself in town. That affable type of lawman is, Ringo can see, going to be replaced by more of the Earp variety, who will, as they say, "clean out" the territory.

Ringo stares down into the cup in his hands. When the whiskey is still he can make out his image there looking back up at him from alcoholic depths. The ever-climbing odds against him are, he realizes, in no way diminished by his drinking habits. Curly and all of his men were heavy topers, but no one drank as Ringo drinks. Like his enemy Doc Holliday, he can accommodate enough whiskey to render most men unconscious and yet have his wits about him at the cardtable. At both faro and poker, he is a most skillful dealer, and his mastery of the indispensable companion arts of gun- and knife-play seems unimpaired, or so the shades of two victims who had criticized his dealing might testify.

But Ringo knows that drink is taking its toll. Thanks to years in the saddle, he still maintains a hard physique, but when he practices with his .44s, which he seldom does anymore, he can see that his reflexes and his accuracy are going. A gunfighter who cared at all about his survival would practice religiously and maintain at least some degree of temperance. Ringo's indifference is obvious. Curiously, this very indifference has served as an advantage in mortal-combat situations: He has faced more than one antagonist with a coolness that is itself unnerving, and in the midst of circumstances that would terrify most men, he is capable of reasoning clearly and objectively. It was for this capacity especially that Curly Bill valued him as a lieutenant.

Now, he reflects, he has a much better reason for both maintaining a cool head and curbing his thirst. The task he has set himself he wants very much to complete before "cashing in." Tossing down the remainder of his drink and promising himself that he will hold off awhile before having another, he rises to his feet and walks over to his army tent. Although he has pitched it in the shade of the giant oak, it is intolerably warm inside, the late afternoon sun having heated up the canvas. He reaches inside the doorflap and draws out the package of writing materials. Then, having picked up his writing board, he goes over to a large boulder beside the spring and settles himself against it as comfortably as he can.

Smoothing out a sheet of the foolscap on the board, he pencils in the date: April 28, 1882. He is about to begin writing, but then he hesitates, still thinking about the meeting with Cochise he has just witnessed. I envy that old bastard, the medicine man, he admits to himself. He looks to be as old as Tiresias, and still he can believe in something. I wonder if his faith will put any venison in his wickiup. And I wonder what Cochise could have told me. Maybe that life is worth hanging on to a little longer? That he'd rather be a poor dirt farmer raising hogs for some *patrón* down in Sonora than chief of all the dead? The old man must have the answer, if there is any. And maybe he could tell me a few more things I need to know. Like how I'm going to find my way back across the wine- and whiskey-dark sea of memory. Where do I begin? Where *did* I begin? He chuckles bitterly to himself. Does it matter?

Then he begins to write:

"My name is actually Ringgold, John Ringgold, and . . .

TWO

BEGINNING

. . . if you look at a map of Georgia, at Catoosa County, you'll see that Ringgold is a county seat. I've never been there, but I've been told that folks in Catoosa County and thereabouts have a high regard for the Ringgold family. Before the war, it seems, they had everything people needed to be respectable in those parts—land, slaves, money. Now I guess they've got nothing much left besides their name. That's something, though. Enough reason for this Ringgold to stay away from Georgia.

"Not too many miles south of the town of Ringgold is where they fought the battle of Chickamauga. After the war I talked to one of my Georgia cousins who was in it, and while I've always enjoyed a good fight, I'm not sorry I missed that one. At the time it was being fought, I was out in Missouri doing what I could for the South as one of Quantrill's Raiders. With me were some other relations who have, like my kin in Georgia, made a name for themselves, though of a somewhat different kind. I guess by now everybody's heard of Frank and Jesse and the Youngers. And I guess everybody's supposed to breathe easier now that Jesse's dead and poor Cole and Bob and Jim are locked up for life in some Yank prison up in Minnesota.

"I got word to my Younger cousins through their sisters that I'd like to try and break them out, but I guess they don't have much faith in my jailbreaking talents. They're going to be 'model prisoners' and try to get themselves paroled. Personally, I couldn't last that long without a woman, and I wouldn't have thought Cole could either. Belle Starr surely isn't the only lovely lady between Jackson County and Fort Worth who'll be missing him.

"Maybe now he'll get around to writing that book he

was always talking about. He was going to tell the world all about his 'romantic adventures.' I'd laugh out loud every time he brought it up. Not that he hadn't had the adventures or didn't know how to dress up a good story. But I just couldn't imagine him sitting still long enough to write a book. He was always too busy living his adventures to write about them, and in between adventures he was busy enough just being a natural man.

"Which is what somebody might say about me, I guess, if he were inclined to speak kindly. I've been so busy for so long being Johnny Ringo that I've damn near forgotten how he came to be or whatever happened to somebody by the name of Ringgold. I guess I like to think of Ringgold as somebody who didn't survive the war, who died more or less honorably as a 'good ol' rebel' and was buried by his bushwhacking rebel comrades somewhere back in Missouri or Kansas. In a way, it's true, and I could almost believe it, if I didn't have to bring him, or at least his name, back to life every once in a while when I have to write a letter to my dear little sister out in California.

"Writing those letters is the hardest damned thing I've had to do since I gave up honest work. For one thing, I've got to keep all my lies straight and remember from one letter to the next what I've told her. But that's not the worst of it. All the time I'm writing I have to be somebody I'm not, somebody I never was or ever wanted to be. I've got to be Mr. John Ringgold, prosperous, upstanding Arizona cattleman, member of the Arizona Stockmen's Association, contributor to the fund that will pay two thousand dollars to any bounty-hunting sonofabitch who can bring in the head of Johnny Ringo.

"Having written so many letters from him, I've actually got a pretty clear picture of that fine upstanding rancher I'm not. I can almost make out the man himself standing right here in front of me, looking down on this good-for-nothing reprobate cowboy, regarding him with the kind of scorn that's only decent and proper from a man of his 'substance.' You see, we just don't have a whole lot in common, besides being the same age and standing six and a couple. He's such a solid citizen. You can see it in that firm roll of tallow he's packing around his hips, about where I wear my gunbelt, and that thick dewlap

BEGINNING 33

under his chin, like the neck flesh on one of those prize whitefaces he's just imported from England. He eats well, drinks nothing but the best imported whiskey, has a standing order for shipments of cigars from Cuba.

"That roll of fat is all he ever packs on his hips, most of the time. He has enough men on his payroll to do all his fighting for him. And since he has a reliable foreman, a good ramrod and a crew the size of the garrison at Fort Apache, he doesn't have to spend a lot of time in the saddle. He can leave things in the hands of his good capable foreman while he goes into Prescott to confer with the politicians he's bankrolled to help him get his ranges extended.

"Stockman Ringgold. Sounds like a real pillar of the territory. I only hope to God that little sister never comes to Arizona to visit him. She'd roll into Tombstone on the stage from Yuma and ask somebody to direct her to my ranch. 'You see, he's in the cattle business,' she'd explain to somebody. Then somebody else overhearing her would figure out that she was looking for me. 'Beggin' your pardon, ma'am,' he'd say, when he finally got his laughing fit under control, 'but you see, Ringo, or Ringgold, as you call him, is what we call a . . .'

"Jesus, don't let it happen. Let her believe me when I promise her I'm going to visit her out in California just as soon as I 'get my affairs in order.' Funny how a man can still seem to pray, even when he can't believe in anything.

"In a way, telling her I was in the cattle business wasn't too much of a stretcher. I've helped Curly Bill run off enough stock to make more than one good-sized spread. We also did well in horses. Hit every army post in this part of the territory at one time or another, and it always did my heart good to even the score a little for all the horseflesh the bluebellies drove away from my cousin Harry Younger, using the war as an excuse.

"Now I guess maybe that's all over. Curly's disappeared, it seems. That pompous big-balled sonofabitch Wyatt Earp claimed he killed him over at the Iron Springs waterhole. Eighteen buckshot in the chest. Jesus, I hope it isn't true. Maybe Earp made it up. Maybe Curly has finally left these parts, as he always planned to, and gone down into Sonora or Chihuahua to start a new life. I hope that's how it is, with Curly getting fat lying in the shade on the porch of his own big hacienda while a pretty señora rubs his back and he dreams about the kids she'll bear him. Bright kids they'd be, full of mischief as baby bobcats, with dark, laughing eyes like old Curly's. God, I hope Earp and company didn't get him. But I'm awfully afraid they might have. They were damnably efficient when it came to killing. Still are, I imagine, wherever they are. Wish it were hell.

"Speaking of hell, I've been wondering lately if there is such a place, some kind of eternal torture pit, located maybe out somewhere under the Sonora Desert, where God or the Devil has pressed some Apache bucks into service to see to it that sinners who haven't had enough misery in this life will get their fair share in the next. Stands to reason there should be such a place, I suppose. If I could believe that anything in this world stood to reason, I could believe in that. When you've had the kind of good Christian upbringing I had, it's a mite easier to believe in hell than heaven, easier to believe you've been predestinated to feel the wrath of God than any of His mercy on whom He will."

Ringo pauses for a few moments in his writing to recall a Sunday morning twenty-four years in the past, when he and his brother Clayton and their sisters were going with their mother into San Antonio to attend a prayer meeting. His mother and little sister Mary were on either side of him as he drove, and he remembers the slow, jolting progress of the wagon as their two old horses pulled it across the flat, treeless land along the hard-baked gray ruts that widened randomly into deep potholes muddied by the previous day's thundershowers. With each of the more severe jolts came laughter and loud squealing complaints from the rear of the wagon bed, where Clayton and the two other girls sat with their feet dangling above the ruts.

Next to him his mother sat, small and delicate, yet perfectly, rigidly erect, her back unbent by even the hardest spine-rattling bumps. When the prairie breeze blew back the sides of her bonnet he could see the delicate outline of her features, the fine high-bridged nose, wide forehead, full but firmly set mouth. The bonnet almost completely concealed her graying but still bright auburn hair, which tumbled down like a stream of molten copper well below her waist when she combed it out each night. The stiff high-reaching collar of her Sunday dress concealed the white, graceful curve of her still youthful neck.

With a kind of fierce hunger in her beautiful gray-green eyes, she was staring ahead along the miles of ruts grooved across the prairie. The boy was used to seeing that same yearning hunger in her eyes at times when they were home and she looked up from the open Bible in her lap to stare across the room, not seeing anyone in it, not seeing even the walls, he guessed, but looking well beyond them out to God, and God only, knew where. Now the small white hands resting in her lap were clutching a small black hymnbook.

"Can't you hurry us a little, John?" she was urging him.

"The wagon might not take it well, Mama," he replied. "I know Bessie and Frank won't, and we've got to use them to plow the upper field tomorrow."

"Brother Mitchell's preaching this morning. I do so want to hear him."

"You will, Mama, don't worry about that. Even if we're a little late, he'll still give us an earful." Immediately he regretted letting on how he felt about Asa Mitchell's sermons.

"John, you must speak respectfully of Brother Mitchell. He's a man of God. His word will do you good."

"Yes, Mama." The boy didn't dare ask her whose word she meant, didn't want to hear her say right out that God spoke through Asa Mitchell.

They finally arrived at the outskirts of San Antonio, at the place where the Methodist congregation they belonged to was planning to break ground for a new church. In place of a church then, there was simply a platform upon which Mr. Asa Mitchell performed as preacher and hymn leader.

"If you had any doubts about the wages of sin," Ringo writes, "Asa Mitchell would set you straight. Either that or see you swing. He was a sawed-off dumpy little fellow, not much to look at when you met him on the street. But I imagine that when he was mounted up and had his vigilance committee behind him, he looked impressive enough, at least to sinners receiving their wages. And when he was up there on that platform of a Sunday morning, roaring down at you as though he'd just come down off some holy mountain all full of inspired rage, he did command your attention. Whatever inspired his sermons, besides rage itself they were, I must admit, memorable."

That particular Sunday morning, as his mother feared, they were late: the rest of the congregation was already assembled and the preacher was leading them through the opening hymn, "Lead, Kindly Light." At the conclusion of the hymn, Judith Ringgold led her children in as close as they could get to the platform, and Brother Mitchell, seeing her, beamed with pleasure for an instant. Then his round, florid face reassumed the sternness appropriate to the text he had chosen.

Before he began to preach, however, Asa Mitchell called upon his congregation to join with him in beseeching the Almighty to lend him the aid he needed.

"Let us pray, my brothers and sisters in Christ," he commanded them, as he went down on his knees on the platform next to where he had set his big white hat. All eyes dropped to the ground beneath clasped hands, save Brother Mitchell's eyes, bulging bright blue orbs that rolled up toward heaven. "O heavenly Father, hear me, Your sinful instrument that dares in the abominable filth and ignorance of his manhood to speak of Your justice. Lend me the wisdom to teach my fellow Christians here what it is You would have us do that Your justice may live here as it does in heaven . . ."

John Ringgold could guess more or less what was coming and was determined to hear as little of it as possible. Already the anger was rising in him, the anger he always felt as he listened to the Word according to Asa Mitchell and looked around him to see the effects it was having on others. Next to him his mother had her head bowed in prayerful submission to the preacher's command. In a moment she would be gazing up at him, shining-eyed, raptly attentive to every word that came from his mouth. That would be enough in itself to fill the boy's heart with rage, but what would make it well-nigh intolerable would be the undeniable effects he would be feeling himself. He wished that he could ignore Brother Mitchell's words altogether, but there was a part of him that simply could not.

". . . Amen."

Having concluded his prayer, the preacher rose to his feet and walked over to the edge of the platform. His bright bulging eyes swept over the congregation and back up to heaven for an instant, as though looking for a signal. Then he began:

"Fellow Christians of San Antonio, I greet you this morning with a fearful warning: 'The wages of sin *is* death . . .' "

This text, the first half of the twenty-third verse of the sixth chapter of Paul to the Romans, was one he favored especially, had preached on more than once when the Ringgold family was in attendance.

"When you heard Brother Mitchell preaching on his favorite text," Ringo remembers, "you had the idea that that was really about all Brother Paul had to say to the Romans. He never bothered to mention the other half of the verse, which, if you can believe it, is a shade more comforting: '. . . but the gift of God *is* eternal life through Jesus Christ our Lord.' I guess maybe he was afraid that we'd be distracted and not get hold of what he had to say about sin and death, figuring that was more important for good Christians to think about. And maybe he was right. Maybe the fear of sin is the beginning of wisdom. . . ."

"How much longer do you think the Lord will withhold His hand . . ."

The boy tried desperately to shut his ears without actually using his fingertips. He looked around him for someone or something upon which he could concentrate all of his attention. A few feet away stood Lucy McMaster, next to her father, the wealthiest horse rancher in the area and a God-fearing man who never missed a meeting. Though the sermon had begun, the girl's head was still bowed in a prayerful attitude and her face was hidden by her bonnet, so that the only portion of her flesh that was visible was the back of her neck. Upon its pure smooth whiteness some dark blond pin curls were stirred by a little prairie breeze that also cooled the boy's face.

". . . from wreaking just punishment upon the sinners of this community?"

The words fell from the platform like the blows of a fist, but he could ward them off—almost—if he could just concentrate hard enough on that smooth untouchable whiteness, imagine himself stroking . . .

". . . His work of vengeance into the hands of . . ."

Suddenly she raised her head and turned to look at him, her violet eyes wide with curiosity, neither trusting nor fearful but wondering, like those of a young doe that has never been hunted or an unbroken filly watching her would-be rider approach her for the first time in a corral. Must have felt his eyes on her, he thought, felt a little of his warmth as he imagined his trembling boy's fingers stroking, ever so gently. . . .

". . . beareth not the sword in vain. But I ask you, What if the magistrate beareth not the sword as he ought to?"

It was in a corral that she'd first noticed him, he guessed, when she'd come out of the house to watch him try to break one of her daddy's mustangs. He'd noticed her of course, plenty of times, while he'd been forking manure out of stalls, polishing harness, helping the blacksmith and whatnot, whatever he could do to bring in a little of the extra money the Ringgolds needed to survive on their dirt farm. Seeing her climb up to rest her elbows and her ripe young bosom on the top rail, he damn near forgot to listen to what an old waddy was telling him:

". . . and don't forget to jam both your feet full forward in the stirrups. Otherwise . . ."

Otherwise, you caught it all in your thighs and crotch. Jam your feet full forward and the shock ran up your legs.

Mr. McMaster was not an overly generous employer. He paid John Ringgold next to nothing for the work he did, and the boy had asked him how he might earn another dollar or two. Mr. McMaster, a tall stoop-shouldered man whose hard, thin-lipped mouth and hawklike bony features seldom relaxed in a smile, had grinned at him in a strange, warmthless sort of way.

"Sure, sonny. There's something you can do."

There were always broncs to be peeled, including some that his own men wouldn't go near, "half-rattlesnake-half-grizzly" demons that would spread a rider all over a corral if they could. On one of these, a fiddleheaded beast with a dark stripe along its back, he had begun his career as a bronc peeler.

As he grasped the reins and a handful of black mane in his left hand, placed his left boot in the stirrup and started to swing up onto the animal, thoughts of Lucy McMaster quickly vanished. He was so frightened he was numb, almost too numb to hear what the four punchers holding the bronc were telling him.

". . . an' you got to keep hooking an' raking him with them spurs."

He had never worn spurs before, was wearing a borrowed pair that he'd nearly tripped over walking across the corral.

". . . an' if he goes for the fence, remember . . ."

The boy never heard the rest. He barely managed to settle himself in the saddle before the bronc released itself from the restraining hands of the four punchers.

After one long forward jump, which nearly sent him over its head, the bronc went straight up into the air, kicking out with its hind legs so that the boy's head was snapped back and his hat flew off. When they landed, he caught the shock full in his crotch and felt it run right up through his body, along with a terrible nausea. He could see nothing clearly, only the brown blur of ground rising and falling beneath the dark plunging thing he was clinging to with both hands, but somehow he knew, sensed, that they were headed for the fence.

When they reached it, the animal turned sharply and the boy lost his hold altogether. He would have been rolling in the dirt, but the fence was in the way, and he felt something hard across his chest, like a well-swung ax handle or a club. It was the top rail, and without thinking, he wrapped both arms around it. At the same time his lower belly encountered the next rail down, and for a few moments all the breath was knocked out of him. When he began to breathe again he also began to vomit.

Heaving over the rail cleared his head some, and he was able to look back and see what the bronc was doing. Which made him a lot sicker. The animal had thrown itself on its side in the middle of the corral, and as the boy watched, it rolled over on its back, scrambled to its feet and went on bucking, trying hard to throw the saddle after the rider.

He was so absorbed in watching the killer bronc perform that he hardly heard the whooping laughter of the men watching.

"Want to try him again, sonny?" McMaster was asking. His thin, nearly lipless mouth was still set in that cold grin, and he chuckled a little, as though he'd made a joke. The other men laughed along with him. In fact, everyone was laughing, laughing at the boy who'd thought he was man enough to be a bronc peeler.

The only one who wasn't laughing was Lucy McMaster. He noticed that she seemed a little paler, and in her wide violet eyes was something a boy might take for sympathy, or, more likely, pity, the condescending pity a poor dumb farm boy might expect from a rich man's lovely daughter when he'd been humiliated in front of her.

As he climbed shakily down from the fence, he saw his vomit on the rails and some on his shirt front as well. He could feel his face warming red with shame and rage.

"How about it, sonny?" McMaster was asking again, wanting to make the most of the boy's humiliation, assuming he'd back down and say he'd had enough.

Hearing the laughter of the other men, feeling the girl's pitying eyes on him, he felt the rage growing inside him, till it seemed to fill him right up and there was almost no room left for fear. He wiped his mouth with the back of his hand, then said to McMaster, in a voice that was just a little shakier than he could help:

"Sure, I'll try him again."

He climbed on the bronc six more times that afternoon. Twice again he was thrown into the fence. Twice he was unloaded head first in the middle of the corral, and during his fifth try the animal threw itself down and tried to roll over on him. Finally, he managed to stay aboard.

"You got sand, sonny, I will admit that," McMaster said, handing him a dollar and a half, twice his usual pay for a day's work. "If you live till next year I'll put you on the payroll regular."

Some of the men were still laughing, but one of them pounded him on the back by way of congratulations. "You got the makins," he said.

The boy looked over to where Lucy McMaster had been watching. She was gone, having left after he'd scrambled out from under the rolling bronc. She hadn't been there to see him stay on top.

"How long, my brothers and sisters in Christ . . . ?"

She had never spoken to him, had generally ignored him when she and her daddy passed by where he was working. But now she was regarding him with what seemed to be curiosity. Shyly, the boy managed to smile at her, thinking maybe she would return the smile. But then, apparently, she felt the hard stare of her father, who was looking sideways at her and beyond, suspiciously, at the boy he'd tried to humiliate. Or maybe it was the relentless hammering of Asa Mitchell's sermon that made her turn away and look up toward the platform, blushing a little as she did.

"How long, I ask you, will the Lord withhold His wrathful hand . . . ?"

The preacher was warming to his subject. So much so that his red face glistened with sweat, and he reached down into his big white hat for a handkerchief to wipe it away.

"Is it not the duty of good faithful Christians to . . . ?"

Suddenly the women gasped. Hearing this and noticing that Brother Mitchell had paused, John Ringgold looked up at the platform, just in time to see the preacher drop the end of a length of rope back into his hat, letting it go quickly, as though he'd accidentally grabbed a snake. His florid face became the color of raw beef.

"I damn near laughed out loud," John Ringo writes. "Who else would have a length of rope coiled up inside his hat?"

He glanced over at his brother Clayton, grinning a little as he restrained an outright laugh, and his little sister Mary gave him a hard dig in the ribs. "Mama'd never forgive you for laughing at Brother Mitchell," she said to him later.

"The rest of that sermon, as I recall, was to the effect that San Antonio was likely to suffer the fate of Sodom and Gomorrah if we, the God-fearing elect of that sinful community, did not take action to see that the reprobate received their due. He didn't say right out that all prosperous law-abiding God-fearing folks should join his vigilante band, but everybody there knew what he meant. In fact, a good many of the men there, like Lucy's daddy, were known to be members already."

He remembers walking past the San Antonio jail about a month before Asa Mitchell preached this sermon and noticing a crowd of men gathered around a chinaberry tree next to the building. Taller than most of them, the boy looked over their shoulders and saw the man they had just cut down. Though hideously swollen and discolored, the face was recognizable as that of Old Man Franks, accused murderer of two Mexicans who had come to purchase horses at his ranch. " 'Jest a couple o' greasers, goddammit,' was his last words," one of the men was saying. "It's what I'm told anyway," he added hastily.

"The wages of sin was death in San Antonio," Ringo writes. "No question about that. Brother Mitchell spoke for his congregation. I only wish I'd felt like laughing at him more often. Maybe I could have, if he didn't have such a goddamn hold on Mama's thinking."

He remembers the Sunday afternoons when Brother Mitchell came to call, and he can see the two of them, his mother and the preacher, in the front room, seated on the elegant plush-cushioned sofa that was the only fine piece of furniture Judith Ringgold had left of all she and her husband had tried to bring out from Missouri. Usually she had a Bible open in her lap, and she would ask the preacher what he thought about this passage or that. While she was looking down, reading the passage aloud, his bulging frog eyes would rove over her in a way that the boy could barely endure to watch. The rage he felt as he listened to Mitchell's sermons was nothing compared to what he felt watching the man look at this small pretty woman who was his mother.

"Well now, that's a mighty interestin' verse, Sister Ringgold," he'd say, no matter what verse she'd read out to him, and as she looked up from her Scripture he would lift his frog eyes from her breasts up to heaven, coughing a little as he worked out an impressive-sounding commentary.

And Judith Ringgold listened to him, so intently the Good Book itself might have been speaking, her beautiful yearning eyes inspiring him to new heights of speculation about the great mysteries of God's plans for His elect and how the rest of His creatures in their abominable manfilth fit into the scheme of things. Listening, the boy would burn with his rage, but for some reason he didn't understand himself, he went on listening, even when he was free to leave the house.

"A good, God-fearing man," Judith Ringgold said one day, as she and her son watched the preacher-vigilante leader ride away from their farm. The boy did not reply, and she, troubled by what she saw in his eyes and what she, as a mother, could feel, sought to admonish him:

"John, don't ever let your heart be hardened. The Lord punishes hard hearts."

She had said this to him once before, and he had tried to reassure her that he didn't think his heart was hardened. But now he replied:

"I don't guess I have a whole lot to say about it, Mama. Any more than Pharaoh did, when the Lord hardened his heart for him. I just can't figure how it was right for Him to punish Pharaoh for having a hard heart when He made it that way."

"His ways are mysterious, John. We must simply accept and believe that it's all part of His great plan. Just like Brother Mitchell tells us, He hardens the hearts of some so that His great purposes may be fulfilled."

"But it don't seem fair, does it?"

She smiled that weary, patient smile of hers and put her arms around him.

"Just like your daddy. Always asking questions about everything. That's why he wasn't happy." The sadness came into her eyes then, the sadness she always showed when she spoke of his father. "The smartest, wisest man I ever met," she called him, "and the biggest fool."

"I'll admit," she went on, "there are things in the Good Book that don't *seem* fair. If you're a good Christian, you don't ask questions about such things. You just accept the Truth, that everything *is* fair from the Lord's point of view and you put your trust in Him. He is just, but He is also forgiving and merciful."

"Why didn't He forgive Pharaoh?"

"Because Pharaoh's heart was hardened, John. He wouldn't repent."

"I loved my mother too much to push this any further," Ringo writes, "or to ask her about other things that were vexing me, such as why the Lord loved Jacob and hated Esau, even before they were born, or why one of His miserable manfilthy creatures didn't have the right to ask Him straight out, 'Why hast Thou made me thus?' I didn't want to start her worrying about my soul, the way she'd worried about my father's soul, and was still worrying about it, on account of the way he died."

Because he didn't want her to worry, he said nothing about peeling broncs for McMaster. She believed him when he told her that McMaster had just suddenly become a shade more generous with his part-time help. And because he didn't want her to worry about his soul, he didn't tell her about certain of his other activities at the McMaster ranch that were potentially a lot more dangerous than bronc peeling.

The day after Asa Mitchell pulled the rope out of his hat, the Ringgolds began spring planting, and this prevented the boy from returning to the McMaster ranch for nearly two weeks. When he did finally ride over to the ranch, he was set to work in the tack room mending and polishing harness. The tight-lipped rancher didn't pay much for that kind of work, but for once the boy didn't mind. After so many long days of stumbling along the furrows behind a plow horse he was ready for a rest. It wouldn't be much of a rest, because there was a bunch of fresh-caught mustangs being driven in the next day, and now that he'd shown the "makins," McMaster had invited him to join in the fun of introducing them to saddle leather.

He was working on the saddle that he himself would use, replacing a broken stirrup, when she came into the tack room.

"Oh, it's you," she said, sounding very surprised, and this puzzled him a little because he'd seen her watching him from a window in the house as he walked around from the entrance of the barn to the tack room.

"Good morning, Miss McMaster." It was the first time he'd ever spoken to her.

"I was looking for . . ." She started to explain but didn't finish, and he wondered what or whom she was looking for, cherishing for an instant and then quickly dismissing the thought that it might be himself. Instead of telling him what or whom, she asked suddenly, "Why were you looking at me that way during the meeting last week?"

"I . . ." he began, feeling his face warm red with embarrassment as he tried to think of something besides the play of the breezes on the back of her pretty neck, ". . . don't know. Guess maybe I didn't feel like looking up at Brother Mitchell," he said lamely.

She smiled at that and with three long strides came over to stand directly in front of where he was sitting on a bench working. The saddle was resting between them on a sawhorse, and she rested one hand on the pommel. It was a beautiful hand, though a little large for a woman, strong-looking, with long tapering fingers, not at all like the small delicate hands of his mother and sisters or even his own, which were, in spite of years of heavy farm work, relatively small and slender. The boy looked at it but did not raise his eyes from the saddle, though he was fully conscious of her ample bosom beneath the silver embroidered Mexican riding jacket she was wearing and the gracious curving of her hips beneath the leather riding skirt.

"You aren't afraid of much, are you?" It wasn't a question so much as a statement of fact.

"Why . . . why do you say that?" he replied, puzzled.

"On account of what I see. The way you nearly got yourself killed by that bronc when Daddy prodded you. But mainly . . ."

She paused for a moment, as though she were a little unsure of how to say what she wanted to say, and he raised his eyes to look at her directly. Again he met that look of wondering, the look of a wild thing watching a man for the first time.

". . . on account of how you looked at me," she said finally. "A man in town looked at me that way once and said something," she went on quickly. "Daddy horse-whipped him in the middle of the street. He might have done the same to you if it hadn't been the middle of a meeting."

Not believing a word of it, he said, "If that's true, then how come he didn't try to horsewhip me when I came over here to work today?"

" 'Cause I told him you were just a kid who didn't know what he was doing."

At this John Ringgold felt the beginnings of anger along with the other feelings she was managing to stir inside him. He stood up and confronted her across the saddle, reassured that he could look down on her even though she was tall for a woman and had on riding boots.

"I didn't want him to hurt you," she said.

"Why should you care, Miss McMaster?" he asked, unable to keep the anger from coming through in his voice. "You've never said a word to me until this minute."

She didn't answer his question. Instead she asked, "How old are you?"

"Eighteen," he snapped, giving himself a couple of years, to be a little closer to her own age, which he'd heard was around twenty. She smiled a little, and he knew that she probably didn't believe him, but it didn't matter then. He disliked her thoroughly, resented her concern for his welfare as something that went along with contempt, the pitying contempt of almighty rich and powerful ranchers for lowly dirt-farming folk. Feeling the anger grow, he added, "Old enough to take care of anybody who thinks he can horsewhip me."

"Surely. I know you are," she said, trying to mollify him but angering him a little more instead because he saw that she didn't mean what she said.

"Look," she said suddenly, before he could make another angry reply, "we can't talk here. Daddy could walk in here any moment. Will you meet me this afternoon over at the big pool?"

Utterly bewildered, he did not reply, and she asked again, "Will you?"

He nodded dumbly, and she said, "I'll wait till you've finished working here. Then I'll follow you."

Still bewildered, he watched her turn and walk out of the tack room. After she left, he realized that his mouth was hanging open like an idiot's.

"Has there been anything in my life but women? Anything that mattered?" Ringo scrawls these questions at the top of a fresh piece of foolscap. But instead of trying to answer them, he sets his writing board down next to him, tilts his hat forward onto the bridge of his nose to shield his eyes against the late afternoon sun, stretches and crosses his long legs.

A boy can dream, he is thinking, and a man can remember. But neither a young man's dreams nor an older man's rememberings can approximate . . .

"Daddy wants me to marry the right kind of man," he can remember her saying. "Someone he can respect."

"What kind of man is that?" the boy asked, glancing over at her, still not quite able to believe that she was really there right next to him. They were sitting on a big cottonwood log beside the deep hole on Comanche Creek known to all the youngsters in the area as "the big pool." It was everybody's favorite swimming hole during the warmer months, but now that it was early spring and much too cool for swimming, they had the place to themselves. On a nearby rise, Cindy, Lucy's maid, a black girl McMaster had acquired over in Louisiana, was keeping watch.

"I used to think I knew," she replied thoughtfully. "Somebody like him. Strong and good. Able to take care of me. A gentleman. Back in Vicksburg, where he sent me for schooling, I met someone I thought was . . ." She paused for a moment, and he regarded her curiously, noting with mild wonder how one could discern in her delicately molded handsome features the hard predatory visage of her father. She had the same prominent cheekbones, the same bold aquiline nose. Only the mouth was totally different, full and generous, the lips a little parted now, but even when they were together, never like the steel trap set of her father's mouth. ". . . right for me."

"Did your daddy meet him?"

She nodded. "He came out here from Vicksburg to meet Daddy . . ." Again she paused, and he saw her lips purse together, as though she would hold back her words. ". . . and then he went back to Vicksburg. I never heard from him after that."

"Seems your daddy's mighty particular where you're concerned. Can't blame him a whole lot for that, I guess. He's just trying to be a father," he said, not really believing what he was saying but wanting to sound like a man of mature judgment who could understand an older man's way of thinking.

She laughed a little at his words, as though he'd unwittingly made a joke. Judging from the expression in her eyes, as she stared down into the water at her feet, it must have been a bitter joke. But then she turned to look at him, and the bitterness seemed to vanish.

"Tell me about your daddy. What was he like?" Someone had told her that his father was dead. Had someone also, he wondered, told her how he died?

"He was a lawyer, wasn't he?"

"Ye-es, he practiced law in town while we ran the farm." He didn't add that his father had generally been too drunk to "practice" much of anything in town besides faro and poker and had seldom been able to ride home to the farm without falling into the Medina River.

"I've heard," she said, "that he was a fine-looking man and mighty well educated."

"He surely was that," the boy replied, still wondering how much she knew. "He read just about everything you can read in Greek and Latin. Mama wants me and my brother Clayton to be just as well educated. That's why we take lessons from Padre García over at the mission. He's the only one around here who can teach us Greek and Latin."

"Are you going to be a lawyer?"

"Not likely. If I could afford to go back east to a college, I'd go to a medical college. Right now, though, it looks as though my future's going to be peeling broncs and punching cows for your daddy."

Without intending to, he had let out some of his own bitterness. Then he was silent, and for a moment or two he nearly forgot the girl beside him. Leaning forward, he rested his elbows on his knees and held his face in his hands, staring blankly down at the water lapping against his worn boot toes and letting himself remember an evening six years in the past that he usually tried not to remember. It was all this talk about his father that brought it back, brought back everything. Good Lord, why had he done it? The boy himself and a neighbor had been the first to find him lying there on the riverbank. Why had he done it? The neighbor had tried to prevent him from seeing what the bullet had done, but for half an instant he saw, and what he saw would remain with him for the rest of his life, whenever he thought of his father.

Suddenly he felt her hand resting on his arm. He turned to look at her, and he could see in her eyes that she knew. Looking into those great moist violet eyes, he wondered how it was that he could bitterly resent her pity one minute and welcome it the next.

"Let's walk a little," she said.

They stood up and began to walk slowly along the path that ran near the water's edge. With some effort he managed to put away thoughts of his father and turn all of his attention to the girl. The path was wide enough for them to walk side by side, and he wished that he had the courage to put his arm around her waist or even to take her hand. But he was afraid. Living in a house full of women did not give him any confidence whatever that he understood female ways of thinking. She was lonely. That much he understood. She had chosen him to talk to because he didn't matter, what he thought didn't matter. She would talk to him as she would talk to her maid Cindy up there on the hill, knowing he would never betray her confidence, because he, like that slave girl, knew his place.

So his thoughts ran until he felt her strong hand clasping his, forcing him to stop. He turned to her and saw that she was smiling at him in a kindly way, sort of the way his mother and other kind ladies often smiled at him. He bent down to kiss her cheek lightly, thinking that might not offend her. But then she raised her mouth, half closed her eyes and put her arms around his neck. Not quite believing what was happening, he let himself be drawn into the reality of a dream.

Remembering, the man Ringo is even more grateful to her than the boy had been at the time and during all the times that followed that first afternoon by the big pool. He had, he remembers painfully, been such a clumsy big kid, had so little control of himself, that her own pleasure must have been pretty minimal, at first anyway.

"It's all right, Johnny. You're doing real fine," she had whispered, reaching up to touch his face with her fingers, ready to wipe away the hot tears of shame that were welling up in his eyes. It had been all right, as long as he half-believed that she wasn't really there, was part of a dream, even as she lay with him in the tall grass beside the pool, letting him stroke every part of her with his trembling fingers. She was beautiful, so much more wonderfully made than he'd imagined when he'd dreamt of her that he had become terribly frightened, and his flesh, feeling the intimidation of his spirit, had been harder to manage than a fresh-caught mustang. When it failed him altogether at first, he had been ready to weep.

"It's all right," she said again. "Just let me help you a little."

And her strong gentle fingers and tender lips brought him to life again, gave him so much life that he went off like an overcharged musket almost the instant he was . . . Again he had been ready to weep, but she clasped him tightly, stroking his sweat-dampened hair, kissing him softly on the cheek and neck.

"Real fine, Johnny. You're just real fine," she said, and he almost let himself believe her.

In time, he did believe he was able to give back to his gentle, patient teacher some of the pleasure she had given him. In time, he almost came to believe what she told him more than once: "I've never known a man like you, Johnny. There's just nobody like you."

How many others had she known? He often wondered but never had the nerve to ask her. There couldn't have been many, he told himself, what with her mean-eyed daddy keeping watch the way he did. But then again there they were, meeting whenever she could arrange to get away from the house. He wondered and burned with jealousy, but said nothing. Finally, late one afternoon, just before the start of the spring roundup, she told him.

They were walking along the sandy bottom of an arroyo two miles from the ranch house. The walls and rim of the arroyo were covered with dense growths of scrub oak and mesquite that hid them from the view of anyone passing above them. Down at the mouth of the arroyo Cindy was keeping watch with their horses.

There were times when she didn't want to make love with him, times when she just wanted to talk, and this was one of them. About one thing he had been right. She was terribly lonely. Her mother was dead, had been since she was a little girl. There were no young women her own age living on the neighboring ranches, and her daddy had managed to scare off any eligible young fellow who tried to court her. She had no one to talk to but the young farm boy she had taken as her lover. Though he couldn't help desiring her, he refrained from pressing her to make love with him, being happy enough simply to be with her. Sensing that he wouldn't press her, she relaxed altogether and began to talk. What came out first was simply a name:

"Reverend Doctor Ellsworth."

"Who?"

"The Reverend Doctor Ellsworth," she repeated. "He's what they call a rector. He was the rector of the school in Vicksburg where Daddy sent me to finish up becoming a young lady."

"Some kind of teacher?" he asked.

At this she laughed out loud, a little bitterly, and said, "Yes, you might say that he was some kind of teacher." She laughed some more at her own little joke before she went on to explain. "He was the rector, the head man there at the school, the man in charge of all the teachers and . . . all the young ladies there."

"How old were you?" the boy asked, trying to be tactfully attentive without prying.

"How old was I when?"

"When . . ." He felt his face going red with embarrassment.

"It's all right, Johnny," she said, laughing a little at his blushing confusion and laying her head against his shoulder. "I was sixteen. Just like . . ." She might as well have said "you." So she'd known all along. Well, he told himself if it doesn't matter to her, it doesn't matter . . .

"I was sixteen and he was forty-six, the same age as my father. He wasn't like my father, though. Daddy's still not an old man. Dr. Ellsworth was an old man, even then. I felt kind of sorry for him, even when he . . ."

The boy didn't really want to hear any more, but she seemed determined to tell him everything. What could he do but listen?

". . . when he took me up in the choir loft. He told me I had such a beautiful voice. It was the Lord's own gift to me, and I owed it to Him to make it even more beautiful by practicing. So he'd take me up in the choir loft in the middle of the afternoon, while all the other girls and Mrs. Ellsworth were resting. And I did sing for him, all his favorite hymns. All the time he watched me real closely, but I didn't think anything about it 'cause he was telling me things about posture and breathing and all. It seemed right for him to be looking at me that way."

Still listening, seeing with his mind's eye the scene in the choir loft, John Ringgold put his arm around her shoulders and was a little surprised when she stiffened up and seemed about to draw away. But then she relaxed again and put her arm around his waist. She went on:

"When he put his hands on me that first time, I was so surprised I just let him do it. Then when I saw what he was trying to do, I got kind of sick. Then I got mad and told him he ought to be ashamed and that I was going to tell Mrs. Ellsworth. But then he went down on his knees there in front of me. He seemed so old and weak, and he kept begging me to forgive him, and I started feeling sorry for him. That's how it happened that first time . . . right there on the floor of the choir loft."

The boy put his arms around her, and she pressed her head against his chest.

"Then I came home to the ranch, and there was this man who was Daddy's foreman . . ."

"Please, Lucy . . ." he begged her.

"Oh Johnny, you think I'm wicked, don't you?"

"No, no. Course . . ."

"Please don't think I'm wicked. I just want you to know everything. 'Cause you're my friend. You're my best friend. I can tell you anything."

And so he listened, alternately raging with jealousy and overwhelmed with pity. When she had told him everything, she drew back for a moment and looked into his eyes.

"I am wicked, aren't I, Johnny?"

"No, no. Course not." He couldn't think of anything else to say, so he kept on saying "no, no" as he took her in his arms and kissed her hair and forehead. She shut him up by raising her mouth to his, and he found suddenly that all of his feelings of rage and pity were being fired out by something much stronger than either. His desire for her was suddenly much stronger than it had ever been. When they made love there on the sandy floor of the arroyo, he found himself more completely in harmony with her body than ever before. For the first time, he knew that he was able to give her as much pleasure as she gave him, and he marveled at how he was able to feel that she was really his, in spite of Reverend Ellsworth and all the others. When, at the highest point of her passion, she began to cry out, he thought that maybe he ought to cover her mouth, lest the sound draw God only knew who into the arroyo. But instead he cried out himself and that seemed to give her even more pleasure. She began to laugh and weep at the same time, and her fingers, which had been raking his back like cat claws, suddenly relaxed and began to stroke him, like those of a mother with a shuddering child at her breast.

". . . nobody like you, Johnny. Just nobody . . ."

Stirred by the memory of Lucy McMaster's passion and his own, Ringo comes out of the drowsy state into which he has been lulled by the late afternoon sun. He sits up and pushes his hat back from his forehead, now glistening with sweat, which a little breeze from down the canyon quickly cools. Right now, he is thinking, it would take an icy blast whipping right through me to cool off the rest of this too damned solid flesh. Can anything be sweeter than memory? Can anything be crueler? There were other women, so many others, and one he loved far more deeply, but right now the only woman he aches for, aches to touch again, is Lucy McMaster.

He picks up his writing board and begins to write again:

"It was a kind of miracle that Lucy's daddy never found out about us. We thought we were discreet, but I don't guess that lovers ever really are. In spite of the terrible chances we took, though, nobody seemed to know what was going on. Nobody seemed to suspect anything. Nobody, that is, except . . ."

At this point he stops writing and lets his sweet memories of his first love be swept aside by more painful ones.

"John," he hears his mother demanding, "I want you to tell me where, how, you got those scratches."

"Mama . . ." he began, thinking quickly, furious with himself for his carelessness in taking his shirt off in front of her to wash up at the pump. ". . . a branch caught me. I rode under it coming back from McMasters."

"How could it catch you that way, on both sides? And how come your shirt isn't torn?"

"I had it off, Mama. I stopped at the big pool for a swim to cool off after working, and . . ."

It was no good. Those beautiful, fiery gray-green eyes that could look through walls could, it seemed, look through every part of him, too. For the moment, though, she seemed to forget about the scratches as something else came to mind.

"Padre García was wondering where you've been lately. You made your brother lie for you. He told me you were over there with him at the mission when you weren't."

"I was working, Mama, over at McMasters. See all the money I made," he said, desperately producing three painfully earned dollars. "We need it, don't we?"

She shook her head. "Johnny, Johnny, you know how much I care about your education. It's your only chance to be a gentleman, like your daddy, like my father. Your daddy was a lawyer. Mine was a high learned divine, the best preacher, everybody said, in Jackson County, Missouri. He could read the Bible in all its real languages. They didn't have lots of money, like Mr. McMaster, but they were gentlemen just the same. That's what I want you to be, a real educated Christian gentleman."

"Yes, Mama, I'll surely not miss any more lessons," he promised, hoping that she'd forgotten all about the scratches. But she had not.

"John, I asked you how you got those scratches. You'll tell me, won't you?"

"I told you, Mama, some branches . . ." He had never been more miserable. Such a short time before, with Lucy, he had felt like a sure enough man. He'd come of age. Now he was a kid again, utterly intimidated by his mother, unable to endure being told what he knew he'd be told, right down to the chapters and verses, if he told her the truth. So he stuck to his story of being raked along both flanks by branches. Finally, she gave up her questioning, and he hoped it was the end of it.

Later that evening, he found her out on the porch by herself sitting in one of the weathered old chairs with the Bible in her lap, watching the sunset. At first he hesitated to join her, fearing more questions, but then he thought she might be more suspicious if he seemed to be avoiding her. When he sat down next to her, she looked over, smiled and reached out to pat his arm. Then she looked away again toward the sunset.

"You're growing into a fine-looking man, John, just like your daddy. Such a fine-looking man he was," she murmured dreamily, as though to herself. "When we'd go walking along High Street in Independence, all the ladies riding by in their buggies would turn around to look at him. It made me proud, real proud, to think that he could have any woman he wanted and he only wanted me. That was wrong, being proud that way. And the Lord punished me for it."

The boy thought he knew what she meant. He remembered the evenings when she used to wait up for his father, remembered some of the things she said to him when she thought none of the children were up listening. She was right, of course. She was always right. Even a ten-year-old could see that they were getting poorer by the day and hardly able to feed themselves, let alone support vicious ungodly habits. But all the same he felt sorry for his father, having to take what he did from her. She had a mighty sharp tongue and knew how to shame a man.

If only his father had used all those wonderful talents he possessed. He knew everything a lawyer was supposed to know, had read more books than any lawyer needed to read, knew how to prepare any kind of case, and when it came to scrapping it out in the courtroom, convincing a judge or jury that black was white or white was black and anyone who disagreed was a liar, there was no one who could stand up to him. His talents were well known, and it was, folks agreed, a shameful waste that he was rarely sober enough to use them. It was, Judith Ringgold was in the habit of adding, a shameful waste that the Lord would punish.

Yes, the boy reflected, she had had to put up with a lot. Thinking about what she had just said, he guessed that she was seeing all the years of worry and the death of her husband as just punishments for her sins of vanity and concern with the flesh, and he was trying to think of something to say, some way to make her see that this was nonsense, when she startled him by bringing up those damned scratches again.

"I'll believe what you tell me, John, about those marks on your body."

"Mama, you've just got to believe—"

She cut him off. "Surely. There's not much a woman can do sometimes but believe." Then she looked away toward the sunset, and he could hear her murmuring something to herself, something he couldn't quite make out: "That which is joined . . . one flesh," it sounded like. Maybe it was the Scripture she was reading before the sun went down. Did he also hear another word? "Har . . . harlot." Maybe not. Maybe it was just his own memory of a Scripture playing tricks on him. And the guilt he was feeling for having lied to her.

For a moment or two she was silent, then she murmured something he could make out: "Such a fine-looking man. All the ladies . . ." So she was still thinking about his father. Why, then, had she brought up those scratches again? A woman's mind worked mysteriously, the boy was discovering, worked so much differently than a man's. And no woman's mind seemed to work more mysteriously than his mother's. Maybe it was because he had known her for so long. The more you were around a woman, it seemed, the more mysterious she became, as he was discovering with Lucy McMaster. Glancing over at his mother, seeing the dark outline of her finely chiseled features against the last yellow glow of the sunset, he was struck by feelings akin to awe. What was in that beautiful head besides all those bits of Scripture? Surely a great deal she would never reveal to her children. And it was not just her mystery that gave him these feelings. It was as well his sense of her strength. He sensed that this small, delicately made, pretty woman had more inner toughness and strength than any man he would ever meet. If he was asked to name a weakness he had noticed in her character, he would have a difficult time naming even one. And if his father's character had been lacking, surely she had enough left over for both of them. Which was surely part of the trouble.

That evening, the boy did not work out the rest of his thoughts about why his parents had been so unhappy with each other. Saying that he had to catch up on his Latin for Padre García, he excused himself and left his mother to her musings and her memories. He was still puzzled about why she had questioned him so closely about the scratches, and the thought that it had something to do with his father did occur to him, but, as with other reflections on his father, he put it away quickly. Whenever he thought about his father, it seemed, he wound up thinking about the way he looked that evening on the riverbank. Unlike his mother, he could not remember a "fine-looking man," only what was left of him.

As he had promised her, the boy did not miss any more lessons with Padre García. Three times a week, when their chores were done, he and his brother Clayton climbed on one of their old horses together and rode over to the mission. Remembering his old mentor, Ringo writes:

"As I read over what I've written about my good Christian upbringing, I see that I've neglected to mention my exposure to what some folks call the True Faith. There was at the old mission near our farm a good old Franciscan padre, Padre García, who was certainly the most learned man in the neighborhood. Like other Catholic priests he had studied Greek and Latin in order to better understand the Good Book, but then he had gone well beyond what he needed merely to analyze Scripture and was what I'd call a real classical scholar. He had it all, by God—Homer, Euripides, Roman poetry—and my mother, who was determined that Clayton and I become sure-enough educated Christian gentlemen, paid him to supplement the meager fare of study at the little country school we had attended as youngsters. She had no money to pay him, but she sent over chickens and eggs and whatnot with us when we went for our lessons."

As they rode into the mission courtyard, he was usually sitting by the fountain, a beautiful piece of pink stone masonry that trickled water into a deep stone tank full of carp. Sometimes he would be feeding the carp with pieces of bread. Other times he would be muttering sleepily to himself over his breviary. Beside him, on the rim of the tank, was whatever text they were studying—Greek grammar and Homer during their first two years with him, Latin and the Roman poets for the two years after that.

"*Salve*, young scholars. It is good to see you." He gave them the same greeting always, but he was sincere, and his round face radiated more loving warmth for humanity than John Ringgold ever saw in the countenance of any other Christian teacher or preacher.

"What have you learned since I saw you last?"

"Just what you told us to learn, Padre." And it was usually true. They were conscientious students because they didn't want to disappoint their mother. They studied hard, often well into the evening by the light of the fireplace, memorizing paradigms while they were becoming acquainted with the grammar and then, later on, struggling to render immortal lines of poetry into the best English they could manage.

"The padre would ask us," Ringo writes, "to take turns reciting or translating, correcting us from time to time, but always in a gentle, kindly way that didn't make us overly anxious about mistakes or discouraged. He was especially helpful with the Greek grammar that nearly drove my brother and me crazy. Much later, when we got to the point where we could begin struggling with Homer, he began to open up for us a world that was unlike anything a Texas farm boy's imagination might conjure up, especially if his reading has been confined pretty much to the Good Book."

"Ah, my sons," Padre García exclaimed one day, with a sigh that came from the depths of his ample, brown-robed belly, "these Greeks lived in a harsh world."

"What do you mean, Padre?" Clayton asked.

"I mean they had no one but themselves to rely upon. Their gods were either unconcerned about them or hostile, like the forces of nature they represent. Look at this poor fellow Odysseus. He has nothing really to rely upon but his own wits. As I told you, Pallas Athene may simply represent his own human wit and wisdom, and she is his only friend among the gods. The other gods, if they care at all, are vengeful and unforgiving, like Poseidon. We Christians are so much more fortunate." It was seldom that the good old man brought up religion with them. Their mother had probably made it clear to him that she had taken care of their religious training. But John was curious nonetheless about where the padre stood on some of the matters that were vexing him, so he asked:

"What's the difference between his gods and the God we read about in the Old Testament? This first part of the *Odyssey*, up on Mount Olympus, doesn't seem all that different to me from the first part of the Book of Job, where you see God and Satan up in heaven placing bets on Job and then sitting back to see how much he can take in the way of suffering."

"Juanito, Juanito," he replied, shaking his wise old

head slowly in its thick jowled cushion and smiling sadly, "you must believe that our Christian God is always concerned and loving. He *is* love. He and Jehovah are the same, and He and His divine son are one. He can be vengeful, but His mercy is infinite."

"But, Padre, there are some He doesn't forgive," the boy objected, bringing up again what he'd given up trying to discuss with his mother. "The ones He chooses to harden in the heart are about as bad off as Odysseus up against Poseidon."

"Yeah, Padre," Clayton chimed in, picking up on a few things his brother had pointed out to him, "what about Pharaoh?"

"Even those whose hearts have been hardened by a lifetime of sinning may be forgiven, my sons," he replied, raising his hand over them in what appeared to be a blessing. "They need only ask while a breath of life remains within them. It is never too late. Remember, He is love."

"We talked about all of this on various other occasions," Ringo remembers, "and I've never forgotten the things he told me. When I was seventeen and about to leave for college in Missouri, he gave me a copy of the Bible in St. Jerome's Latin, the Vulgate. I guess he hoped that someday it might convince me that there's always hope for a sinner. God knows, I'd love to be convinced, but I've just never been able to see it. Though I hate to admit it, I'm more prone to agree with the hellfire thinking of people like Asa Mitchell. I look around me at my fellow creatures, and from time to time I get up the courage to look inside myself, and it seems to me fairly clear that the world is made up of a few straight-living righteous individuals you might call the Saved or Elect and a great many more poor devils like myself given over to a reprobate will. The Elect may be fooling themselves about a heavenly destination in the hereafter. I don't know. For the rest of us, what they call salvation can't even be a possibility. That much I do know."

He looks again at the questions he's scrawled at the top of his page. Still unanswered. Instead of trying to answer them, he sets his writing board down beside the boulder and stands up to ease the stiffness that has set in.

Then he walks over to his tent to draw out a quart bottle of whiskey.

Off to the west the sun is dropping behind a big conical peak, setting its apparently unscalable granite shoulders afire. The evening sky is streaked with crimson, like, Ringo thinks suddenly, the blood of a dying god. As he lifts his eyes to the bleeding heavens he seems to hear from a great distance, from somewhere down near the mouth of the canyon, a despairing cry: "One drop . . . just one drop . . . would save . . ." His imagination plays tricks with his memory of something he's read, something in an old play. As darkness settles over the stronghold of Cochise, the imaginary cry is drowned out by the real sound of yelps and howls, the sound of a wolf pack hunting. Time to build up the fire, he is thinking. But first, I'll stoke up what's inside. He raises the bottle to his lips and lets the fiery stream course down his throat, receiving it gratefully. One drop for sure . . .

THREE

MISSOURI COUSINS

With trembling hands, he raises the steaming cup to his lips, thinking how the coffee smells strong enough to take the varnish off the top of the bar in the Oriental Saloon. A sip confirms that it is at least that strong. In a little while, maybe he will force down some food—a slice or two of bacon, some hoecakes baked on the hot stones of his fire. A clear head is what he needs, a whole lot clearer than it usually is before noon, if he is to make the kind of progress he intends.

The nature of his task is becoming clearer to him now that he has spent a day setting down recollections of his youth in Texas. As he reads over what he has written, he begins to see that it isn't going to be, as he thought, just a matter of recording the progress of his life and being able to see from that how it is that he has become what he is.

"I could spend all my time here," he begins, "just bringing back the sweeter memories of my life to help console me with the thought that it hasn't all been a total waste that the Lord, if He exists, will punish. I might even be able to comfort myself by thinking I could be forgiven a little for loving much. Consoling myself that way, though, won't help at all to make it clear to me why I am what I am. I didn't become a killer and a thief by the name of Johnny Ringo because women were good to me and showed me the sweetness of their loving.

"A man is what he is because he's made some choices. If he made them differently, he'd be a different man altogether. And because he's made those choices, others just naturally follow. A man crosses you and you choose to fight him. A woman invites you and you choose to follow wherever she wants to lead you. If your name is Johnny Ringo, those aren't even real choices. They just naturally follow because of choices you made a long time ago that made you what you are.

"What I'm doing now, I see, is trying to figure out what my real choices were and why I made them. It may not be an easy thing to do. It may be a little like going inside that cave yesterday with those red devils looking for Cochise. At least they had some light and that crazy old medicine man to lead them. There's no one to lead me into the big dark cavern inside me. The only 'medicine man' who might be able to is that good old man who tried to teach me something about his religion along with Greek and Latin.

" 'You must look into your heart, Juanito.' I remember him saying that, when he was telling me about what Catholics call 'confession.' How old he is, I remember thinking, seeing how the fringe of hair circling his crown was silvering out and the way he had trouble hearing me sometimes. He was sitting there beside that old rock fountain, feeding his carp with pieces of bread, trying to make it all clear to me.

"You had to 'look into your heart' and tell Him, the Lord God Himself, what you'd done, even though presumably He already knew, because, as it says, He's set a watch over you. Still, you had to tell Him through His priest what you'd done and why. If you did this and were truly sorry for all your wrongdoing, the Lord would forgive you.

"Well, for all I know that good old padre might have been right about the whole business and about the fact that it's never too late while you have any life left at all and can turn to God and repent 'with your whole heart.' And maybe if I could bring myself to believe in his all-loving God, I might even believe I could be forgiven.

"But that's not my concern right now. Like I said, I'm not here to seek consolation. My only concern right now is how I'm going to find my way back down a long dark twisting tunnel of memory into God only knows what. Somewhere in there, if I can follow it far enough, maybe I can find out why I made some of my choices and why I am what I am. 'Look into your heart, Juanito.' Seems at times I can actually hear the old man telling me that again, speaking to me from an almighty great distance, all the way from that little graveyard inside the mission where he's been these last twenty years. And I even catch myself answering him, muttering, 'Surely, Padre, I mean to try.'

"In a way I envy my cousin Cole, if he really believes what he used to tell folks, that he was the way he was, an outlaw, on account of the war. He and his brothers, so he said, went along with Frank and Jesse because they were still fighting the war, robbing banks and trains that belonged to the rich Yankee sonsofbitches who'd taken over their country. The damned Pinkertons, so they said, just wouldn't let them stop.

"Well, maybe Cole wasn't stretching things all that much. Maybe he and his brothers did become what they were on account of the war. All I know is that I can't use the same excuse, even though I fought in the same war with them. The war surely had its effects on me, changed my way of seeing a lot of things, but I can't say that it made me an outlaw. I fought for the South in Missouri and Kansas, was a Confederate soldier for sure, even though the Yanks didn't choose to regard guerrillas as such and hung any of us they captured like we were criminals. But it wasn't till I came back to Texas that I truly did become a criminal and killed without any patriotic excuses.

"I can honestly say, though, that when I left Texas at the age of seventeen, being a killer of any kind was just about the furthest thing from my mind. What I wanted and actually thought I was going to be, I damn near laugh to remember."

He remembers how, as a way of paying for his lessons, he helped in the infirmary at the mission, where the very poor, mostly Mexicans and Indians, were treated by the padre and another Franciscan, Padre Dominguez. Back in Mexico, the two priests had been given some rudimentary medical training to assist them in caring for the temporal needs of their flock. John assisted them as they set broken limbs, patched wounds, and even once when Padre García had to deliver a child before the midwives could be summoned. Watching the old man, seeing what he could do with his very limited training, the boy discovered that he wanted to become a healer himself.

"It is a wonderful calling, Juanito," the padre said. "And you have the hands of a surgeon—strong, steady, gentle hands. But there is so much to learn that I cannot teach you. Greek and Latin will help you, but there is so much more to learn."

Ringo remembers the padre's words and an afternoon as distant in the past as hope itself.

It was mid-July, the hottest hour of the day, and he and his brother were resting in the shade beneath a wagon they had borrowed from a neighbor for haying. Clayton was asleep, and John was fighting to stay awake as he leafed through an ancient textbook on anatomy that Padre García had loaned him. It was in German, and he couldn't understand a word, but he could see from the illustrations and diagrams that there was a whole lot a doctor needed to know, so much he wished he could learn, if only he had a little money for schooling. As it was, he would be lucky if McMaster kept his promise and put him on the payroll as a regular hand. Then again, considering what his relationship with Lucy had become, he might be better off if her daddy didn't keep his promise.

Not that they hadn't been almighty careful about when and where they met, and always having Cindy posted as their lookout. They took few chances deliberately, but the chance that they might be caught still remained as long as they kept on meeting. And as dangerous as those times were, they were in some ways less dangerous than other times when they were together.

"It's your eyes, Johnny, they just give away everything. . . . You've got to . . . someone's going to notice. . . . Please. . . ."

She was right, he knew. Sooner or later, someone *was* going to notice, not just the way he looked at her but the way she looked back. What happened after that, when someone passed his suspicions on to McMaster, he could only guess. Men like McMaster did pretty much as they pleased in that country, and men like Asa Mitchell were there to help them in the name of Christian Decency and Morality. He remembered Old Man Franks, whose alleged crimes of murder had apparently been aggravated by the fact that he was McMaster's rival in the horse-trading business and had snared an army contract McMaster wanted. A Godless man who died swearing on the end of a rope, Franks had been a lesson to all potential offenders against the Law of God and, it was said more privately, the interests of Jake McMaster. As for young John Ringgold, the lesson was clear. If McMaster's suspicions were aroused before the summer passed, he probably wouldn't live to see his seventeenth birthday. He should have worried a little more, at least enough to try to conceal his feelings, quit looking like a sad-eyed pup around Lucy, but the bitterness and frustration he was feeling about things in general didn't leave much room for fear.

"Life just didn't seem to offer much then," Ringo remembers. "I didn't have a chance in hell of becoming a doctor or anything else I wanted to be. A dirt farmer, maybe, spending my life behind a mule's ass, wondering if what I'd planted would come up as and when it should, at the mercy of the goddamn weather and the merchants in town, who gave you just enough credit to stay alive if you could call that living. You could see what it did to a man, that kind of living, when you went into town for supplies and met your neighbors—slow-moving, heavy-footed men with stooped shoulders and tired eyes. Their women generally looked even tireder, faces dried up and pinched if they weren't overfleshed and puffed out like biscuits, and their worn-out bodies sagging through their calico. How Mama maintained her beauty was a mystery to me, working as hard as she did. But then she hadn't always been a widow on a dirt farm. Once upon a time she'd been able to live like a lady. God, why had he done this to us? Dammit. You had to feel sorry for a man who suffered that much to do what he did, I told myself, but I still couldn't help the anger I felt.

"Being a cowpuncher seemed to be about the only alternative. Some alternative. Spending the rest of my life eating dust for fifteen dollars a month, routing longhorns out of the goddamn chaparral, peeling broncs till my insides gave out, lying awake nights in McMaster's bunkhouse remembering his daughter, trying to believe it had really happened. My relationship with Lucy, I figured, could never be anything more than it was, and it was just a matter of time till either we were caught or she got tired of me and found somebody else. Rather than live to see either of those things happen, I'd honestly have preferred getting rolled on by one of McMaster's killer broncs or having one kick my fool head off."

There was another alternative, one that came to young
John Ringgold from time to time during these black
moments. He would remember the day, just two years
past, when he and Clayton and some other boys rode
into San Antonio to watch the Rangers lead out Gabe
Tyler, the notorious renegade they had just captured
over on the Llano Estacado. The Rangers had lodged
Tyler for the night in the San Antonio jail and word of
his presence spread rapidly. Tyler the renegade, said to
be the most dangerous man in west Texas, who led the
Comanches in raids from the Canadian River to the Rio
Grande and down into Mexico. He was led out of the jail
manacled hand and foot, but he held himself as proudly
erect as a Comanche chief. Clad in a tunic he had appropriated from a Mexican officer, wearing leather leggings
fringed with human hair, and with his own long blond
hair braided Indian-fashion, he surveyed the jeering mob
in front of the jail with fearless contempt. When someone yelled, "Dirty murdering renegade!" his bright blue
eyes showed no anger, only disdainful amusement. Afterward, when John and the other boys talked about the
renegade, one of them passed on what his father had said
about how Tyler started out as a Comanchero trading
with the Indians and had taken himself a chief's daughter
for his woman, and then started riding with the braves.
Now he was a chief himself, a sure-enough Comanche with
a red devil's heart inside his white skin. "Wish I could go
over to Austin to see him swing," one of the boys said.
"They oughta kill him slow, the way the Comanches do,"
said another.

John Ringgold was silent, keeping to himself the admiration, the envy he felt for the handsome renegade who
looked with such disdain, the great-spirited godlike disdain of one of Homer's heroes, upon his enemies. Tyler
hadn't lived long, but he had lived a sure-enough man's
life, strong and free, the kind of life that stirred a boy's
imagination. Lying there beneath the wagon, turning the
pages of the anatomy book and looking at the illustrations without really seeing them, John saw himself riding
at full gallop across the Llano Estacado at the head of a
band of savages. Lucy McMaster was behind him, clinging to his waist and telling him how grateful she was that
he had rescued her from her father. She even forgave

him for killing McMaster, since it couldn't be helped. His wild followers had rounded up McMaster's prime stock and were driving them toward the secret cañón in the llano where his lodge was waiting, where Indian women were preparing a wedding feast and scenting the buffalo robes and blankets of their bed with aromatic sage. Their lovemaking would be unhurried, prolonged, savored—that night and always.

As he closed the anatomy book and stretched out to catch a few minutes of shuteye, he was startled out of his half-waking dream by a shout that came from across the field. Looking out from behind a wagon wheel, he saw his mother running toward him across the heaving stubble-covered rows, stumbling every few yards over the long faded dress she tried to hold up with one hand. In her other hand she was carrying something that flashed white in the sun. Her head was uncovered and her burnished-copper hair was starting to come undone and stream out behind her. He crawled out from under the wagon and stood up to meet her.

"Mama, you've no business running yourself that way. . . ."

"Praise the Lord, Johnny!" she gasped as she reached the wagon. "Praise the Lord!" For a couple of moments she was too out of breath to say anything more, and her son, still in his bleak, bitter mood, just barely managed to restrain himself from asking, "Why should I?"

"Here." She handed him the piece of paper she had been carrying. He saw that it was a letter very neatly penned in a hand he didn't recognize, though it resembled his father's a little.

"It's from a lawyer in Liberty, Missouri," his mother was explaining, too excited to let him read it for himself. "He says that your daddy's cousin Jennifer has left some money to help educate his children. It's not a whole lot, but it's enough to send you away for some schooling. Jennifer always was real fond of your daddy and wanting to do things for him. It was hard for me to write and tell her about what happened to him, but I had to since she cared so much about him. I hardly knew her, but she must have been a fine lady—"

Her son interrupted her. "Why me, Mama? Why not Clayton? Or the girls?"

She didn't answer right away, and by this time his brother had awakened and crawled out from beneath the wagon to stand up next to him. As Judith Ringgold looked from one to the other of her tall sons, her eyes shone with love, but she seemed worried about something and her face, already flushed with the exertion of running, became even redder.

Clayton answered for her. "I'll tell you why, John. It's 'cause of what Padre García told her the other day."

"Clayton . . ." she began, now looking clearly upset.

"It's all right, Mama. Just as well I overheard." Clayton was nearly a year younger than his brother, but already an inch taller, a big, slow-moving youngster who already had more than an ordinary man's strength in his arms but a disposition so gentle that he could never be prodded into using it against any man. "I overheard her and the padre talking about you, big brother." He rested a big hand on his brother's shoulder. "Seems you've just got too many brains for your own good. He told Mama he'd done just about all he could with me and said I probably had all the learning I'd need to see me through life, but he said it would be downright sinful if you didn't get a lot more schooling. You've got the brains to be a doctor or whatever you want to be. He only wished that the good Lord who gave you all those brains would provide some way to help you learn to use 'em."

"And He has, Johnny, He has. Don't you see?" his mother exclaimed. Then she turned to her younger son, obviously still worried about what he might be feeling. "Oh, Clayton. . . ." She hugged him tightly.

"It's all right, like I said, Mama. This farm ain't big enough for both of us, and John here ain't much of a farmer. He'd rather be peelin' b—" He caught himself seeing his brother wince. ". . . books. Yeah, books is for him." He winked at his brother, who was so full of gratitude and affection toward him then that he could hardly speak.

"And so the Lord had provided, so it seemed," Ringo writes. "The lawyer said in his letter that the money was waiting in a bank in Liberty. He went on to mention that there was a good Christian college there called William Jewell that had been founded ten years before. As an alumnus himself, he could recommend it. I was so damned excited I could hardly wait for the rest of the summer to pass. The rest of that afternoon I pitched bundles of hay like a madman, too happy to feel the tiredness. That evening, though, I started to think about what, who, I'd be leaving behind. . . ."

In a way, she made it easy for him. Riding toward one of their favorite meeting places, a tiny cottonwood-shaded spring near the mouth of a canyon less than a mile from the Ringgold farm, he tried to imagine how she would react and tried at the same time to think of things to say that would make her see how much he really cared about her. For one thing, he'd ask her to wait for him. When he came back from the East a full-fledged medical doctor, even her daddy would have to let him court her properly. Then he'd take her with him back to the East, maybe New Orleans or Baltimore. He had utterly forgotten the lesson she had been the first to teach him: When you are dealing with a woman's feelings, expect the unexpected, then expect to be surprised.

"That's just real fine, Johnny. I'm happy for you," she said, and he believed she was sincere. But he sensed that she had suddenly withdrawn from him, withdrawn all the warmth and passion she had put into the kiss with which she had just greeted him. They were sitting together on a flat-topped boulder next to the pool created by the welling spring, and he put his arm around her shoulders. She didn't shake it off, but he sensed that she wanted to, and after a moment he withdrew it. Glancing sideways at her, he saw that she was gazing ahead vacantly across the gray empty flats beyond the canyon mouth.

"Will you wait for me, Lucy?" he asked.

"Wait for you?" she answered, as though she couldn't understand what he was asking.

"Till I become a doctor. Then I can come back here and take you away with me."

She looked at him then, and one corner of her mouth started to work into a smile, but there was no smiling in her eyes.

"No, Johnny, I won't," she said with a finality that seemed clearly to discourage any attempt on his part to argue.

"Why won't you?" he persisted nevertheless.

"I won't because I . . . won't."

"Why . . . ?"

"Don't ask me that, Johnny. Don't . . . ask . . . me . . . anything."

"But—"

She cut him off. "And I guess we might as well say good-bye right now. Easier that way," she added as she stood up and began to straighten out her riding skirt.

"Lucy . . ." She started to turn away and walk over to where her horse was tied, and he leaped up to grasp her by the shoulders. What happened then amazed him more than anything she had ever done. At his touch, she whirled and slapped him hard across the face. The blow, as hard as any a man might have delivered, snapped his head sideways. Stunned, he reached his hand up to his cheek and stared at her in wordless confusion.

"Don't touch me! Fool kid!" she nearly screamed at him, as her father might have done. He had never seen her angry, but now it occurred to him fleetingly that she had probably inherited her father's capacity for rage, which he had seen on more than one occasion. The only difference was he had never seen her father shed a tear in his rages, while her eyes at this moment were streaming. "Damn you, leave me alone!"

Deeply hurt and too confused to think of anything to say, he nodded and turned away from her. He hadn't gone but a few steps, however, when she called him.

"Johnny."

As he turned back, she ran to him and threw her arms around his neck. Clasping him tightly, she wept against his chest in great heaving sobs. Finally, when she was able to speak, she said, "Please forgive me, Johnny. It's not your fault, not your fault at all."

"What isn't?"

At this she began to sob again, and he sensed that he'd better not ask any more questions. Whatever she wanted to tell him, she'd tell him. He couldn't help wondering, though, what it was that had turned her so fiercely against him just a moment before. Was it because he was going away? Surely she must see that he had to go away if he was going to make anything of himself. Surely she must see . . . But plainly she was in no state to see anything.

After a little while she was calm again, and she said to

him: "Johnny, I mean what I say. I won't be waiting for you, and we've got to say good-bye right now."

"But why?" he couldn't help asking again.

"It'll be best, believe me. It'll be best." She was still speaking calmly, but he could tell that it was an effort for her. "Please don't come back to the ranch. You can find work somewhere else."

"I guess I can, but I still don't understand. . . ."

"You will, Johnny. Someday you will." Then her voice broke again. "Oh my God, Johnny. Oh my God. . . ." She clung to him fiercely, digging her nails into his back the way she did when they made love.

And when they made love again that afternoon, there alongside the still, green pool, she kept on murmuring things that seemed to mean it was the last time for them. About how she wouldn't forget him, not ever, and how he mustn't forget her either. He heard her but he couldn't believe her. Not when she was loving him the way she did that afternoon, making him wonder at times if he wouldn't lose consciousness altogether, faint dead away beyond her power to revive him. But then there seemed to be nothing beyond her womanpower. She could always bring him back, breathe into him the life spark that made him a man.

"Just nobody like you, Johnny. God's truth," she murmured dreamily, momentarily at rest from her passion. And looking down at that serene beautiful face pillowed against his own warm flesh, stroking her soft damp hair with his fingers, he just could not believe that it would be their last time.

As she made him promise her, he stayed away from the McMaster Ranch. And from prayer meetings, in spite of his mother's pleas and accusations of being ungrateful to the Lord, who had provided. He told himself that it was just some peculiar mood of Lucy's that she'd get over, that soon she'd be getting word to him, would send her girl Cindy over to the farm on some pretext or other to let him know when and where.

But then it came to be the end of July without any messages. By then he was aching to see her again, was feeling a kind of anguished longing he could never have anticipated, having never, in his innocence, let himself be bound that way to anybody before. Whatever he was doing, he thought of her, to the point of nearly getting his brains kicked out once while he was helping the blacksmith who hired him when he quit McMaster. He could hardly even think about the bright future that the letter from Liberty, Missouri, seemed to promise, though his mother seemed unable to talk about anything else. Not that he didn't still want that future, being a medical doctor with the power of life in his hands, if only he could have Lucy McMaster as well.

It was his fourteen-year-old sister Mary who told him why he hadn't been hearing from Lucy, and wouldn't be. She told him one Sunday afternoon just after the family had returned from the prayer meeting, without him as usual, partly because he couldn't bear any more of Asa Mitchell's sermons and partly because he feared he might give himself away if he met Lucy there. Unable to contain himself he drew his sister aside and asked if she had seen the girl and her father.

"Lucy McMaster? She was there with her new husband."

"With who . . . ?" he gasped.

"Name's Conover. Chase or Mace or . . ."

"Pace Conover?"

"That's the one. Mama says he owns the bank. Not the kind of man I'd ever want to marry, but I guess he's rich, just about as rich as her daddy."

"And just about as old. Why did she . . . ?" It was like being struck in the face by Lucy. He thought of Conover, a jowly, spread-bottomed toad of a man, and he remembered what she'd told him once, about how the banker had tried to court her. He seemed to be the only suitor her father would accept, and she loathed him, had actually shuddered when she told her farmboy lover, "I'd never let a man like that put his hands on me." Why, then, had she . . . ?

"What's the matter, big brother? You weren't sweet on her yourself were you?"

Amazed, horrified, barely believing what he'd just heard, he almost forgot about his sister. Then he saw her regarding him shrewdly with that penetrating gray-green gaze she had inherited from their mother.

"Were you? Are you?"

He just shook his head, not really intending to deny the truth of what she was saying but too stunned to reply in words. Seeing the misery in his eyes, which never could conceal anything, she put up her small hand and stroked his cheek.

"I'm sorry, Johnny," she said, and he knew that he didn't need to explain anything to her.

That evening he saddled their old plow horse Frank and rode off in the direction of the town, explaining vaguely that he had left something at the blacksmith's. He rode as swiftly as he dared without winding the old horse, leaning forward into the wind whipping in from the west.

Near the edge of town, Pace Conover had made his home in a sprawling fortresslike hacienda that had once been part of the largest Mexican cattle ranch in the area, a grant from the king of Spain. A banker, not a cattleman, but also a man who regarded himself as a gentleman of the Old South, Conover had sold away most of the grazing land but kept a few hundred acres planted with cotton and sorghums, which were worked for him by four or five slaves under an overseer.

On a low rise overlooking the hacienda, John sat his horse and let his fancy out to run like a dog set free after being tied too long. Though tied to the promise contained in the letter from Missouri, it had strained hard during the weeks of painful longing that had passed since he last saw Lucy McMaster. Sometimes it even managed to break loose, riding like a devil, like a Comanche, westward toward the llano, across the endless sweeps of barren tableland, along the nameless twisting cañóns, stopping occasionally to drink from secret springs, then on again, leggings fringed with human hair, his own hair flowing out in the wind like an Indian's.

She would go with him, he never doubted that. After he helped himself to McMaster's best animals, the two Andalusians just brought up from Mexico, he would go to her and say that it was time for them to go. Conover would come out of his hacienda, blustering with his toadlike jowls all puffed out and say, "See here, young man, what do you think you're doing?" and he'd say, "I've come for my woman." And she wouldn't say anything, except maybe, "Try to understand, Pace," as she came forward and took the reins he held out to her, looking him directly in the eyes and smiling her pleasure, her relief that he had come for her at last. And when Pace Conover reached for her bridle, her high-spirited Andalusian would save John the trouble of shooting him by rearing up and smashing down with his hooves. And they would be gone.

As full darkness settled over the Conover hacienda and the lights came on inside, John Ringgold watched and brooded bitterly. Finally he turned away, feeling the western breezes at his back as he rode for home.

"It was my little sister Mary who wrote to me the following spring about Lucy's baby. She and Pace Conover had had a son. The baby was premature, so the doctor gave out, but he lived, and according to my sister he's grown up to be a fine young man. Just a few months ago she wrote to me about how she'd met him while she was back visiting our sister Beth. He'd come home to visit from the East, from Harvard College, where he was attending divinity school. A mighty fine-looking young man, she said, and she guessed he'd be some preacher. Must have his mother's looks. She's a widow now, the wealthiest woman in Bexar County and still as beautiful as ever, so Mary tells me."

Ringo closes his eyes tightly for a few moments and tries to clear his head of an aching that has just set in. Then he gets up, stretches, and pours himself a drink for breakfast. He was grateful to his sister for what she had written to him, even though it filled him with a hopeless longing to see young Reverend-Doctor-to-be-Conover and his mother. It was a very long time after that last afternoon at the spring before he saw Mrs. Conover again, and now he knows there won't be another time.

2

Six weeks later, in mid-September, he took the stage east to Missouri. He wondered where his mother found the money to pay for his fare, but she refused to tell him, and it wasn't until much later that he found out she had borrowed it from Asa Mitchell.

"And so I went to Missouri in the fall of 'sixty," Ringo

writes. "On the advice of that lawyer. I enrolled at William Jewell College." Leaning back against the rock with his pencil poised, he tries to recall the big farm boy from Bexar County, Texas, tries to remember how he felt when he first arrived in Missouri—gawky as hell but trying not to stare at people and things, imagining hay sticking out from under his hat brim and hogshit still clinging to his boots. His mother had told him to look up some cousins, the Youngers, and some even more distant cousins, the Jameses, who lived near Liberty, but this he had no intention of doing.

"I was a little reluctant to look up either set of relations, to take advantage of the accident of a thin blood tie and impose upon them."

Also scared, painfully shy, afraid, in fact, to meet anyone, he began attending lectures at William Jewell, having enrolled in a course of study designed to prepare him for a medical college—chemistry, physiology, Latin and plane geometry. It was his first exposure ever to the physical sciences, and his mathematical background was pretty limited, having been picked up mostly in the shade of haystacks while he was resting between sessions of pitching bundles or in the evening by the light of the fireplace. He wondered if he would survive.

Luckily, he already had enough Latin from Padre García to make that an easy course. He would rather have kept up his Greek, which, in spite of or maybe because of, its head-twisting irregularities was more satisfying to him than the tidy systems of Latin, but one of the professors, a wizened little classicist by the name of Grimestone, who was in the habit of beginning each of his lectures with a sentence out of Seneca or Cicero and was fond of holding forth on heroic Roman virtue, convinced him that Latin would be more useful to him as a medical student:

"And it will be good for your soul, Mr. Ringgold," he went on to say, nodding sideways at a bust of Augustus, as though it expressed all the goodness of soul one could hope to attain by learning one's Latin. "Remember, *'Vita non est vivere sed valere.'* Life is not just to live but to live well."

Which didn't mean a whole lot then to the boy from Texas, though he'd understood the *sententia* clearly enough without a translation. He couldn't really grasp what "living well" meant to a man like Professor Grimestone. Presumably it was a secret he shared with that eyeless marble head next to him, something to do with preserving *virtus* and scorning *fortuna*, the boy gathered subsequently from other of the professor's favorite *sententiae*. The boy from Texas gathered further that he personally would probably never live well, by the professor's standards. Certainly he knew that by his own very different, more tangible standards, he was not then living well.

When he wasn't attending lectures and classes at William Jewell, he was holed up in a wretched little boardinghouse that was mostly for those who could barely afford something better than the street—broken-down laborers of various kinds, drummers passing through and the like. It was all he could afford, and he knew that he would have to find some part-time work soon, as a blacksmith's helper or bronc peeler for one of the horse raisers in the area, even to stay there.

"I don't know how I'd have survived, if Colonel Henry W. Younger, Harry, who was my mother's first cousin, hadn't practically adopted me. My mother had written to him ahead of me, and I hadn't been in Liberty but about a month when I had a visitor at the boardinghouse where I was staying."

The visitor was a good-sized fellow, better than six feet tall, with a full square set of shoulders and a pleasantly rounded handsome face, well dressed in a gray jacket, vest and trousers that were, unlike the clothes the boy from Texas wore, well cut and fitted to his big frame. He looked to be about the same age as John Ringgold, seventeen then, which, as it turned out, he was.

"Mr. Ringgold? Mr. John Ringgold?"

"Yes."

"I'm your cousin, Cole Younger." He stuck out a big square hand and warmly grasped his cousin's smaller hand.

"My daddy wants to meet you. We'd like to have you over to our place for a visit. If you can come now, we'll take you with us."

"I . . . I'd be pleased," he stammered, miserably conscious of how pathetically his little room was furnished— the tiny cot with straw sticking out of the mattress, the

dresser made of old crating, upon which Cole Younger
had set his hat, next to the cracked pitcher and washbasin. Cole's warm blue eyes and smile tried to reassure
him.

"Being homesick as hell," Ringo writes, "I was delighted
to accept their invitation. He told me they'd like to have
me stay a few days."

While Cole waited for him, he rolled a few things
inside a clean shirt and stashed the bundle inside the
ancient carpetbag in which he'd brought all he had to
bring from home. As they left the room, he worried a
little about the books he had left there but figured hope-
fully that his fellow boarders wouldn't find them worth
stealing.

When Cole had said "we," John assumed that he meant
his father and himself. But as they came out of the
boardinghouse, Cole steered him toward a buggy in which
he could see a woman seated. She was wearing a light
brown riding habit, and although her head was hidden by
a wide-brimmed hat with a yellow silk ribbon tied around
the crown, her slim straight back suggested that she might
be young. As they came alongside the buggy, he felt
Cole's big hand clapped on his shoulder.

"Well, here he is, Margaret, this is our Texas cousin,
Mr. John Ringgold. John, this is my sister Margaret."

"She wasn't what you'd call a pretty girl," Ringo recalls, trying in vain to remember objectively someone
who was to become and would remain ever after the
most important presence in his life. ". . . didn't have
what you might call picture-book beauty, all snowy white
and fragile like a goddamn china doll you want to put up
on a mantel someplace. What she had was a subtler kind
of beauty. . . ."

He thinks that he will try to describe Margaret's subtler kind of beauty, but he finds that he can't even begin.
None of the words that come to him are right, but even
more distressing than his inability to find the words is his
sudden awareness that he can't even remember exactly
how she looked. Must be the damn whiskey. . . .

"Margaret, Margaret," he whispers closing his eyes tightly
and leaning his head back against the rock. As though in
answer, her first words to him come back:

"Hello, Cousin Johnny. Welcome to Missouri."

And with this remembered greeting come some fragmentary recollections of how she looked. Aside from her fair, deep bronze hair, she didn't look much like her brother, looked in fact as though she came from very different stock. The warm dark eyes she fixed on him, almond-shaped above almost excessively prominent cheekbones, were like those of ladies he'd seen frequently coming and going from the mission back home, ladies with mantillas and lace fans. Her skin was like theirs too, olive-gold with just a hint of something darker, the blood of the conquered mingling with that of the cross-carrying, sword-swinging conquerors. Her mouth, however, was a little wider and fuller than was usual among them, a generous mouth that smiled and laughed easily.

"I . . . I'm pleased to meet you," he said.

"We're pleased to meet you. We've been looking forward to it, ever since Papa got your mama's letter."

He can almost remember the way she looked at him that first time, appraising him in an amused, quizzical sort of way, but also, like her brother, trying to reassure him with the warmth of her smile.

"I . . ." He stood there, a big clumsy Texas farm boy clutching his hat in front of him with both hands, trying to think of a reply, besides the unutterable truth that he'd had no intention of calling on them.

"Climb on," Cole ordered, having stashed the old carpetbag beneath the seat and taken his own place in the middle of the seat. John Ringgold obeyed, scrambling next to him with all the grace of an overgrown bear cub or a longhorn bull calf.

Cole slapped the reins along the glossy backs of the team of matched black thoroughbreds and they moved swiftly up the main street of Liberty. Still unable to think of an appropriate reply to Margaret's warm greeting John said, "Liberty's a fine town."

"Not half so fine as Independence or Kansas City," she replied, and he felt a little foolish for having revealed his ignorance about what was and was not a fine town in Missouri. He wished fleetingly that he knew some fine big cities he could mention having seen.

"We'll show you around Independence," she was saying. "We live right near it."

He remembered then that Independence was where his

mother and father had been married and where his grandfather had acquired such a reputation as a preacher. He was going to mention these things to her, but he thought better of it and said nothing. When he didn't reply, she said, "Tell us about Texas. Is it really as wild out there as they say it is?"

This irritated him a little, though she obviously did not intend to offend him, was only trying to draw him out.

"Don't know what folks have told you," he said. "It's not so wild, really. San Antonio's a pretty civilized place," he added, with a good deal more conviction than he felt.

"Are there still wild Indians?" she asked.

"Oh surely. Especially up north and out to the west. Comanches, Kiowas, a few Cheyenne. Some others, too. No wild savages around here, I suppose."

"Wild Indians, no," Cole answered. "Savages, yes, mostly from over in Kansas. They're white, and they're called Jayhawkers."

"What are Jayhawkers?" John asked his cousin innocently.

Cole Younger glanced at him and chuckled a little before replying:

"Well, John, if I had to describe them in as few words as possible, I'd say they're bandits with abolitionist leanings. If I had to say much more, I'd be forced to use language it wouldn't be proper for my sister to hear."

At this Margaret patted her brother's arm and looked across him to smile at her cousin in a playful sort of way, rolling her dark eyes sideways at her brother, as if to say, "Is there anything sillier than a big brother trying to sound like a daddy?" His own little sister Mary did the same sort of thing with her eyes whenever he started taking himself seriously around her. He smiled back at Margaret, liking her already, even though, he guessed, she probably regarded him as some kind of clodhopping wild man from the Texas plains.

"What do these Jayhawkers do?" he asked Cole. He really wasn't much interested, but it seemed only polite to feign an interest in something his cousin obviously felt strongly about.

Again Cole glanced over at him, apparently finding it hard to believe that anyone could be unaware of who the

Jayhawkers were or what they did, but then he went on to explain:

"Well, like I said, they lean toward being abolitionists. They ride in here from Kansas, using the excuse that they want to free our Negroes, but mainly they use the opportunity to pick up whatever they can in the way of plunder from good honest Missouri folks who may or may not have any slaves."

"Does anybody do anything about it?" John asked.

"Oh, we try to protect ourselves, and sometimes those abolitionists over in Kansas get a little of their own medicine, when the Border Ruffians drop in on them. They're not much better, though, I must admit, than the Jayhawkers. Near as I can tell, a Border Ruffian is just a bandit who believes in slavery."

John remembered then overhearing some conversations about the border troubles. On Sundays, after the meeting, the men would gather and talk politics. The last time he'd gone to a meeting, the talk had been mostly about secession, about what Texas had to gain or lose by going with the other slave states, and someone—Asa Mitchell himself maybe—had remarked that the war had already begun over along the Kansas-Missouri border. It had all started back in '54 with something called the Kansas-Nebraska Act, which made it so the abolitionists and the pro-slavery folks had to fight it out for the control of Kansas.

"A lot of poor folks on both sides of the border," Cole was saying, "just trying to scratch out a living get caught in the middle."

"I don't imagine," Ringo recalls, "that Cole intended to include his own family among these 'poor folks.' 'Poor' they were destined to become, in every way, among the innumerable victims of the border wars, but at the time I first met them they were far from poor in any material sense. As I was to find out, Cole's daddy, Harry Younger, was then one of the wealthiest men in that part of Missouri. He owned two large and very productive farms, the one toward which we were headed, which took up about six hundred acres in Jackson County, ten miles south of Independence, and another, which included a lot of prime acreage on the outskirts of Harrisonville, in Cass County. His stables housed some of the finest horseflesh in west Missouri, including the fine team of matched blacks Cole was then driving. He was also, I learned, involved in merchandising in Harrisonville."

As they followed the road to Independence through the low rolling hills, which were mostly covered with hardwoods if they hadn't been cleared and plowed for crops, he continued to marvel, as he had been ever since his arrival in Missouri, at the lush greenness of the country. Compared with southwest Texas, the only other country he knew, it looked like a piece of Eden. Everywhere he looked there were patches of woods and bodies of water large and small. By many of the farms there were big green ponds, and they crossed stream after stream, including the Missouri itself, by ferry.

Finally, near sunset, they reached the Youngers' farm. It had been a good long ride but a pleasant one. John was beginning to feel more at ease with his Missouri cousins, as though he'd known them for years, and it was just a matter of becoming reacquainted. Having always been one who made friends slowly, he was a little surprised at how much he already liked both of them. Cole reminded him a little of his brother Clayton, not quite a man yet but already showing that open, easy generous manner of a big man who knows his own strength and has enough confidence in himself to need little in the way of reassuring. At the same time, he sensed in Cole an element that hadn't showed itself yet in his brother, maybe never would, a kind of high-spiritedness not unlike what a horse raiser looks for in a good breeding stallion. Having no small amount of that same volatile element in himself, he could sense it in others, had seen it even in some of the other bronc peelers at McMaster's, men who would, unlike the animals they rode, never be tamed. It wasn't just a male thing either, as Lucy McMaster had showed him.

"Looking back over twenty years to that afternoon," Ringo writes, "I fancy I could sense right off what there was in Cole that would make him what he became during the war and would also make it so the war wouldn't ever end for him. You want to call it fearlessness, but that's not quite what you mean. Because fearlessness, or more exactly the hankering for a kind of joy and excitement that only comes when you have a good chance of getting your back broken or a piece of metal through your mid-riff or the like, is only a part of it. There's also the feeling that you're not quite of the ordinary run of men, not a common mortal so to speak, even though you know, in the abstract anyway, that you're probably going to die sooner than most mortals.

"It may be that I sensed these qualities in Cole right off. Or it may be that I'm having trouble separating my memories of a well-bred, high-spirited southern young-ster from my memories of a war-hardened guerrilla leader and leader-to-be of the James-Younger gang. I do re-member distinctly not being altogether astonished by some-thing Cole's older brother Richard told me during my first visit with the Youngers, about how Cole had proved his manhood earlier that year. Seems they were bear hunting down by Table Rock Lake, close to Arkansas, and their dogs raised an uncommonly large animal. When the hounds had it cornered, Cole called them off and waded in with a Bowie knife to finish it off. It was surely what a man was supposed to do, Richard told me, but he admitted to me that he'd never done it himself, nor was he likely to. I must admit I was some impressed, and a few years later on it gave me an occasion to tease Cole a little. When we were leaving Lawrence with Quantrill and he had his horse shot out from under him and I turned back to see him standing in the middle of the road fanning shots at a big Kansas cavalryman waving a saber and about to ride him down, I dusted the Yank and pulled Cole up behind me, then told him, 'Now I know why you hunt bear with a knife. It's 'cause you can't shoot worth a damn.' And it was true. He had less talent with a Colt's than anyone I ever knew with a comparable reputation, but God knows he had the heart of a lion to make up for it.

"As for his sister Margaret . . ." Here Ringo pauses and sets his writing board aside. He is starting to feel a little dizzy and is aware that he is wandering off into recollections that aren't likely to make it any clearer to him why a relatively innocent Bible-bred youngster who wanted to be a doctor turned into Johnny Ringo. Which is why he is here, after all; why he's retreated into a place from which no one will coax him out into the world in which he's made the name Johnny Ringo, using that

good brain and those fine strong hands that might have
made him Dr. John Ringgold, upstanding if not God-
fearing giver of life. . . .

Then the dizziness passes, but not the feelings that
come to him as he picks up his writing board and stares
at the name he has scrawled.

"Margaret, Margaret," he whispers again, half hoping
she will answer him again out of that time when they
were both in a state of innocence, untouched by the war
and everything that came with it. If only he could bring
back that time, the feeling of that time. . . .

Knowing that the dizziness will return if he doesn't get
something into his belly, he stands up, slowly, pressing
the ache out of his back with both hands. Then he goes
over to where he has suspended a side of bacon in a
canvas sack from an oak branch, out of the reach of night
prowlers. Directly beneath the branch, the tracks of a
frustrated grizzly show him that this has been a prudent
measure. But then he remembers, dimly, how his horse
and pack mule made a commotion in the night, and he
sees that both animals are now gone from the meadow.
Hobbles and all, they've managed to get away, or else
the bear has gotten them, or maybe those Apache hunters on their way back to San Carlos have appropriated
them. Whatever has happened to them, he is now in that
state in which no white man should ever find himself in a
place like the Dragoons—afoot. He should be alarmed,
he guesses, or at least annoyed that, if he wants to leave,
he is going to have to foot it fifteen or twenty miles to the
nearest ranch and help himself to whatever he can find
there. But, strangely, he is quite indifferent to the potentially alarming facts of his situation.

His attitude of amused indifference toward his situation, his casual acceptance of the fact that he might not
be able to leave these mountains alive, is due in part, he
realizes, to simple light-headedness and a kind of apa-
thetic, weary acceptance, not unlike that which comes to
a shipwreck victim who has left a floating wreckage in a
hopeless attempt to reach a shore beyond reaching, or to
a man struggling aimlessly through a blizzard.

"Professor Grimestone would be damn proud of me,"
he reflects aloud, chuckling a little to himself. "Misfor-

tune can't touch me. Guess I'm finally becoming a philosopher, learning to live well at last, he might even say."

Still chuckling, he lets down the sack and cuts himself a few slices of bacon with the knife he carries at his hip, a Bowie honed to hair-splitting sharpness, though nicked a little as a result of the recent altercation in a Janos cantina. Then, resisting the temptation to pour himself another drink, he puts the bacon in a frying pan and sets to work rebuilding his fire.

"I guess she intimidated me a little at first," he begins again, having finished his meager breakfast. "She seemed so much older than sixteen. I'd known clever women before—the women in my family and Lucy McMaster—and God knows I wouldn't think of diminishing them by any comparisons. The fact is, though, Margaret had something I've found to be a whole lot more uncommon than cleverness. She had, you could tell right off, a rare gift for seeing through people and things. Sensing this, and imagining that she'd probably seen right off just about all there was to see in me, I was indeed a little intimidated. But then, by the time we arrived at their farm, I could also sense that there was nothing scornful or critical in her attitude toward me. She'd seen me clearly and accepted me, as presumably she saw and accepted people and things generally, with a remarkable womanly wisdom I would soon come to appreciate, along with her other uncommon qualities.

"What drew me to her especially that first afternoon was her warm, mischievous good humor. She could be serious and was when the moment demanded it, but her gift for seeing things enabled her to see as well how most people will take themselves more seriously than they should."

"My goodness," he remembers her exclaiming in mock amazement when Cole finished holding forth on the Jayhawker problem, "you're going to make our cousin wish he'd stayed back in Texas amongst the wild savages, where it's safe. The fact is, Cousin Johnny, there's nobody you're liable to meet here in Missouri that's much wilder than the Younger brothers, especially when they're racing horses or, as you'll see tomorrow night, on a dance floor. Compared to a Younger, when he's in a state of high excitement, any Jayhawker's bound to seem pretty tame."

Cole had no choice but to chuckle a little and come back in kind: "And wait'll you see what she's like on that dance floor, the way she handles all those poor young devils who've come from miles around for the sheer pleasure and privilege of dancing with her. That's what I call cruelty, downright savage cruelty."

"I remember this delighted her, and they kept up their good-natured teasing for quite a while, with Margaret staying always just a little ahead of her brother. He wasn't slow by any means, but I saw that keeping up with her was probably beyond the wit of most young fellows, myself surely included. It didn't take much imagination to guess what Cole probably meant about her 'cruelty' to her young admirers. I was glad that there were barriers between us. One, of course, was the fact of our being related. An even more effective barrier, though, was that I hadn't gotten over Lucy and couldn't imagine I ever would.

"Just at dusk we arrived at the house itself, approaching it along a wide, tree-lined driveway. Seeing it that first time, I know I must have gaped like an idiot. I wondered how many farmhouses in Missouri could look like this. Compared to it, the houses of the wealthy I'd seen in Texas looked like Mexican shanties. It was nothing less than a mansion, not unlike some I would see a few years later down in Arkansas and Louisiana, ones the Federals chose to leave standing."

Along with his amazement, John had a feeling he couldn't at first explain, that he'd seen such a structure somewhere before. The very high white portico and the fluted columns were strangely familiar. He remembered then the illustrations in one of Padre García's books about ancient Greece. He wondered if these white columns were stone, like those of the ancient temples. The next day he saw that they were not, that they were wooden, but it didn't diminish his awe or appreciation of the mansion's grandeur.

On the porch a tall, broad figure was illuminated by the light from the enormous double-doored entrance.

"We found him, Papa," Margaret called, whereupon her father, accompanied by a black servant with a lan-

tern, came down the porch steps to greet them. He came
over to John Ringgold and shook hands, gripping with
the same strength the boy had noticed in his son's handshake.

"Welcome to our house, John," he said. The boy felt
the warmth of his welcome in the hand and the smile,
which was also like the son's. At the same time he was
made a little uneasy by bright, steel-gray eyes that seemed
in the lantern light to go right through him. Resisting the
impulse to look away, he returned Harry Younger's firm
grip.

Ringo has little trouble remembering how his cousin
looked when they first met:

". . . well over fifty he was then, but he looked fit for
a campaign—slim in the waist and wide through the
shoulders, holding himself perfectly erect in that way
he'd learned at West Point. You could see at a glance,
feel it in the way he fixed you with those bright gray
eyes, that his title of 'colonel' wasn't any meaningless
assumed honorific of the kind southern men who may or
may not have seen a little service will appropriate. Just
meeting him, you knew he'd commanded men."

Standing next to Harry Younger, a lean, stoop-shouldered
man who could have been anywhere from forty-five to
sixty scrutinized John Ringgold with the same bright gray
gaze but without the air of command.

The Colonel introduced him. "This is my brother, Frank
Marion Younger."

"Pleased to meet you, sir," the boy said, taking the
older man's bony hand.

Frank Marion Younger shook hands wordlessly.

"First impressions can be mighty misleading," Ringo
muses. "My cousin Frank impressed me that evening as
the quiet sort, and I guess he was most of the time. Give
him a little whiskey, though, and you could find out
anything you wanted to know and a lot more about the
Youngers. It was from him that I learned about how
Harry Younger had distinguished himself as a commander
of men—beginning in 'thirty-four with his service as a
young lieutenant with Colonel Dodge's hard-luck expedition into the Comanche country, resuming in 'forty-seven
down in Mexico, where he led a company of Missouri

volunteers and was in on the storming of Chapultepec at the head of some marines who'd lost their officers. . . ."

"Supper is just being laid on. Let's go inside," Harry Younger said, touching the boy's elbow lightly to guide him up the steps toward the imposing entrance. John was about to offer to assist Cole with the horses, but two Negroes suddenly appeared, materializing almost magically out of the darkness, and took charge of the rig. Another one, in the livery of a house servant, came down the steps and took John's old carpetbag from Cole's hand. John had seen slaves in Texas, but mostly from a distance working out in the fields of the more well-to-do. His own feelings about slavery had been influenced to a large extent by the dimly remembered arguments of his Georgia-bred father, to the effect that it was a monstrous injustice and a blight that would destroy the South, arguments which, uttered eloquently and publicly, had nearly gotten him killed in a couple of saloon fights in San Antonio. His mother had been less strongly opposed to it, allowing that there was some justification for it in Scripture if Negroes really were the descendants of Ham. John himself had already decided that he personally would never own slaves no matter how wealthy he might become, but this would not, he realized even that first evening, in any way affect his feelings toward his slave-owning Missouri cousins. Even then he sensed that it would be difficult, if not downright impossible, for him ever to condemn or criticize anything about them.

The house servant showed him to his room upstairs, where he could wash up for supper. They climbed the first spiral staircase he had ever seen, and he could not resist running his hand along its polished banister and gawking at two huge oil paintings on the walls above him. One of them was of, he guessed, the mother of Cole and Margaret, a handsome woman with eyes that were dark like Margaret's but not quite the same. The other was of a young officer in military dress of the last century. As John was to learn, this was Harry Younger's father, as he looked while serving with Francis Marion, the "Swamp Fox," who had harried the British in the Carolinas during the War of Independence and after whom Frank Marion Younger had been named.

When he came back downstairs, most of the family was

assembled before the entrance to the dining room. He
had not asked Cole and Margaret how many brothers
and sisters they had. In fact, there were three girls and
six boys, and all but two of them were there in the
hallway. Still burdened with his natural shyness, in spite
of the afternoon with Cole and Margaret, he was more
than a little uncomfortable surrounded by all these cousins, even though they were all obviously eager to make
him feel welcome. Cole introduced him to each of them
and to his mother, Busheba Younger, an extraordinary
lady who, though her hair was silver like her husband's,
seemed to have changed little since her portrait was
painted nearly twenty years before. It was she who, with
the help of Frank Younger, had seen to the management
of both farms and the store in Harrisonville while Harry
Younger was away serving in Mexico. She had also seen
to the raising of children who were, John Ringgold thought,
as handsome as any that mortals might be expected to
produce, even with a little help from the gods.

"It's been more than twenty years since I've seen most
of those cousins," Ringo writes, "and my recollections of
how some of them looked are a little vague. Fine-looking,
well-bred youngsters, I do remember that. If Tiresias
himself had come up out of the Underworld that evening
and prophesied their futures accurately, I would have
scoffed at him. No seer could have convinced me that
ten-year-old John Younger, for instance, would, long
before he started shaving regularly, become a seasoned
gunhand. As I recall, he was sort of an angelic-looking
towhead with wide wondering eyes in which you could
see a capacity for healthy mischief but nothing to suggest
a future killer. How could I have believed that within five
years of that very evening, at the age of fifteen, he would
be tried for murder? He was acquitted, had killed his
man in self-defense, but it was the beginning of something, and nine years after that, in 'seventy-four, the end
came when the Pinkertons shot him dead down in St.
Clair County. Cole wrote and told me how he took two
of the bastards along with him even while his life was
pouring out of the wound in his throat. The youngest of
the boys, Bobby, was only eight at the time of my first
visit, a frisky towhead like his brother, and again I could
never have believed an accurate prophecy of his future,

which will end God only knows when in that Yank prison up in Minnesota. Unlike his older brothers, including even young John, he didn't leave home to fight in the war, but that surely didn't prevent the war from coming to him."

It is, Ringo reflects, so much less painful not to let one's recollections drift beyond a certain point, and he deliberately tries to restrain them by remembering as vividly and clearly as he can how it was to be with his cousins while their happy golden world was still intact. He turns his thoughts again back to that first evening and remembers meeting Richard Younger, the eldest son, who was even taller than Cole and who held himself as rigidly erect as his father.

"Hope you'll be staying for the festivities tomorrow night, John," he said.

Margaret answered for her cousin. "Of course he is. We're not letting him go till we've shown him a good time." She was just coming into the hallway, having changed from her riding habit into a long flowing crinoline dress that was just the shade of green to set off the rich golden beauty of her olive skin. She had also unbound her masses of soft bronze hair so that it tumbled about her shoulders.

"Well, look at our little sister," Richard said with a bow that expressed genuine admiration but also a hint of the affectionate teasing of an older brother. "We should have visiting cousins more often."

Margaret flushed a little but smiled at him with obvious delight. Then she came over to join her cousin as Harry Younger and his lady led them into the dining room. John had the honor of being placed at Harry Younger's right hand. Busheba Younger sat at the opposite end of the table from her husband, while Frank Marion and the children took their places on either side. Margaret took the place across from her cousin, next to her father. It was apparently where she usually sat, and he gathered, during the course of this and subsequent visits, that while the Colonel was a loving father to all of his children, she was his favorite. If he could see this, then it must have been pretty obvious to her brothers and sisters, but while such favoritism is usually cause for resentment, he came to see that in this case the affection they all had for her was such that there was apparently none at all.

"And how is your mama?" Mrs. Younger was asking from the other end of the table.

"Oh, she's managing, ma'am," he replied. "My brother and sisters are old enough to handle most of what needs to be done on the farm."

"It's been a good many years since I've seen your mother, John," Harry Younger remarked. "I met your father at the time they were married. He was going out to Texas to practice law, wasn't he?"

"Yes, sir, he was." He looked at Harry Younger, and something in the older man's expression told him that he knew all about what had happened to his father.

"I can't say that I knew him," Harry Younger went on, "having met him just that once, but I knew his cousin Jennifer over in Liberty. She told me he was a wonderfully gifted man. The loss of a man like that is a real tragedy. It must have been terribly hard on your mother, not to mention the rest of you."

"Like I said, sir, she's managing, and so are the rest of us." Looking across the table, he could see Margaret's dark eyes warmly moist with sympathy, and he could feel the beginning of tears in his own, though why he couldn't say, for he had thought himself incapable of shedding any more tears over his father's death.

"Do you think you might be going into law yourself?" Harry Younger was asking. It was a question he had been asked so many times by those who knew of his father's talents.

"Not likely, sir," he replied without hesitation. "I mean to go on into medicine, once I have the sciences I'll be needing to study at a good medical college."

"That's a fine ambition, John, wanting to heal people." It was Margaret speaking, and her approval pleased him so much that he felt himself flushing red and hoped that his deeply sunbrowned face, paler now after a month as a student, wouldn't show it.

"It certainly is," her father agreed. "I only hope that nothing prevents you from achieving it."

This puzzled him a little, but again he replied with as much self-assurance and conviction as he could muster:

"Nothing will, sir. I mean to be a doctor."

"Don't misunderstand me, son." Harry Younger laid his hand very gently on the young man's arm. "I'm not doubting your ambition or determination. I'm only saying that certain events could alter the future for all of us."

Again John was puzzled, though he guessed that Harry Younger was referring to the possibility of war. Before he could reply, the older man asked:

"Tell me, what are they saying in Texas about secession? Are many people in favor of it?"

John hesitated a moment while he tried to recall the conversations he'd heard in San Antonio after prayer meetings and when he went in for supplies.

"Well, sir, as near as I can tell, yes, a good many people are in favor of it."

At that the older man shook his head sadly. Then he asked:

"How do you feel about it, John?"

John was at a disadvantage because he hadn't really thought or talked much about it, but he was afraid to appear an ignoramus, especially in front of Margaret, so he said:

"Folks say the abolitionists want to change our way of life. I don't see as how they can do that just by freeing the Negroes. Where I come from there aren't even many slaves. I guess I'm against secession if it's going to mean a war." He was influenced not a little by his perception that the Colonel himself was against it.

"Good, I'm glad to hear that. Would that more people in the South would see how little they have to gain by it. I happen to be a firm believer in slavery. I believe that it's natural and right for some of God's creatures to serve others and to be cared for by them . . ."

John listened attentively and, as far as he was able, sympathetically to his cousin, though he was troubled by a nagging memory of something his father had said on more than one occasion, about how slavery permitted supposedly God-fearing pious Christians to use their fellow human beings in ways they wouldn't dare use their other domestic livestock. What his father had said conjured images that still remained with him, stored away in memory but ready to be brought forward whenever the subject of slavery came up, images that never failed to arouse disgust. He couldn't, however, or maybe wouldn't connect these images with the handsome patriarch at the head of the table, who went on to say,

". . . but if it comes right down to it, to a choice I mean, I'm willing to see slavery abolished and give up my own Negroes rather than see the country I fought for torn apart by a war."

Cole entered the conversation. "But, sir, those folks in Texas may be right. Folks around here say the same thing. Freeing our slaves is only just a part of what the abolitionists want to do. They want to change our whole way of life—either make us like Yankees or kill us all trying."

Suddenly Margaret spoke up:

"You don't really believe that, Cole, do you?"

"Well, maybe not," her brother admitted grudgingly, "but all I know is what I see around here. The only Yankees anybody sees around here are Jayhawkers."

"But you've said yourself they're just a bunch of bandits who use slavery as an excuse." She was the only woman present to get involved in the discussion, and John listened with pleasure and some surprise as she argued with her brother.

"You see," Ringo is remembering, "I had never heard a woman enter into this kind of conversation. Like any well-bred southern youngster, whether he's been raised on a little farm in Texas or in a fine great city like New Orleans, I had been brought up to revere womankind, but along with this reverence and bound up with it, I see now, was a belief that woman is somehow removed from the problems of the man's world around her. A man, a southerner especially, just doesn't expect her to be able to talk about such things as politics and the causes of war."

"So I did, little sister, so I did," Cole was saying, "but they're just some of the Yankees who hate us."

"I'm afraid Cole's right there, Margaret," Harry Younger said. "We have some powerful enemies in the North who will see to it that we are crushed if we give them the excuse. Keeping slavery out of Kansas wasn't enough for them. They want to free every slave in the South." He paused for a moment and again shook his head as he reflected. "I love the South, and we're part of it here in Missouri. I love the life we have here, and secession will mean the end of it. We must try to reason with our people, persuade them that secession is not the way. And we must try to reason with our enemies and persuade them that certain changes take time."

"Brother," Frank Marion protested, "I don't see why we have to change anything atall for them. I mean, what right do they have to tell us we can't have Nigra slaves?"

Harry Younger smiled sadly at his brother and reflected a moment before replying:

"As we see it, Frank, they have no right. As we see it, even the Good Book makes it acceptable, and as far as that goes, the people I saw working in mills and factories in the North while I was attending West Point were worse off than any of the Negroes on my father's plantation. They surely had as little in the way of freedom, were owned body and soul by the masters who owned the mills and factories. If our Negroes were freed now, they'd wind up, most of them, in the same kind of servitude, only without anyone to care for them. But that isn't the point. The point is that you can't convince an abolitionist to see it that way. You can't convince an abolitionist that Negroes are better off now. . . ."

All this while they were being served by two of those cared-for creatures of God under discussion. John wondered fleetingly what their opinion in the matter might be. He was not naïve enough to imagine that it would ever be asked but he couldn't help wondering all the same what kinds of thoughts were passing behind those impassive black faces.

He also wondered what was in his cousin Margaret's mind as he shifted his glance from Harry Younger back to Cole—whose eagerness to make a spirited, albeit respectful, reply to his father's remarks could be virtually felt in the air—and found her regarding him thoughtfully. Could she sense that he was not one with them in their view of slavery? If so, could she see, he wondered, that he didn't condemn them for owning slaves, would never let the disgust his father had bequeathed him affect his attitude toward them? She must, he told himself, judging from the gracious smile she gave him as she caught his eye.

Cole was unable to make his reply, for his father, seeing that the servants had completed the task of filling all the wineglasses, suddenly halted his own discourse on slavery and raised his glass.

"To our cousins in Texas," he said. "And to John's future in medicine."

Being toasted was a novel experience for John Ringgold, and when Mrs. Younger, Frank Marion, and the older children raised their glasses with the Colonel, he raised his own. Just for an instant, as he raised his glass, he looked over the deep red glowing stuff at his lovely cousin, and for just that instant he saw the flush her own glass imparted to her features. Meeting his glance, she smiled again, and the warmth of that smile ran down inside him with the sweet warmth of the wine.

The taste of wine was as novel as being toasted. Largely because of the example his father had provided, he had had little to do with any kind of drink. On a couple of occasions he and Clayton had joined some other boys to sample the product of one of the stills operating on practically every farm in Bexar County but theirs, but neither of them had much taste for it. This wine, though, was an altogether different experience.

"It wasn't a sweet wine, actually," Ringo recalls. "Actually, it was a dry red scuppernong from North Carolina, but yet it was like tasting freshly gathered honey or the sweet golden warmth of autumn sunshine. I noted carefully, out of the corner of my eye, how the Colonel sipped his, not tossing it down like whiskey but savoring it appreciatively, and I tried to do likewise."

After supper, the ladies and the younger children excused themselves, and the Colonel, with a simple nod to one of the servants, had port wine and brandy brought out. The servant went to the sideboard and fetched a little silver cart, upon which were set two crystal decanters. Then, as he wheeled the little cart around and poured their drinks, another servant brought out a silver box and went to each of them offering cigars.

"At that time, my smoking experience was as limited as my drinking had been—a few not too enjoyable experimental sessions as a small boy with corn silk out behind the barn and later on an occasional pipe shared with Clayton or a friend when a little tobacco could be found to mix with some red willow shavings—but I took a cigar anyway and tried to ape my cousins as they deftly cut off the ends and had the servant light them up."

"These are imported, John," Harry Younger said, letting out a pungently aromatic cloud, "just like the port and the brandy. Probably came into Mobile from Cuba. When you stop to think about it, what folks in the South like to call their gracious way of living depends pretty much upon what they can bring in from other countries and from the North itself. Here in Missouri we're even more dependent and vulnerable than the rest of the South. People who think we ought to secede just haven't given that fact a lot of thought."

"But, sir," Cole protested, "I just don't see that we need the North for anything. What we need the South can bring in from other countries. Don't we raise enough on our farms and plantations to trade for what we need?"

"If," Harry Younger replied, "the North chooses to let us."

"How can they stop us? If they try, we can raise an army they can't stop. You said yourself that most of the Yankees you saw were just about like slaves. How can men like that prevent us from doing anything? We're free men, sir, and there isn't a white man I know around here who can't ride or shoot."

Harry Younger shook his head sadly and let out another aromatic cloud.

"There's a whole lot more to fighting a war than riding and shooting, Cole. When I was in Mexico in 'forty-seven and 'forty-eight we had a supply line from Mexico City to Vera Cruz. That's a fairly long supply line, I'll tell you, over mountains higher than you can imagine, and the Mexicans, guerrillas actually, made it awfully hard for us to maintain. We were mighty glad to pull out of that country when the treaty was signed."

"I don't see, sir—"

"Course you don't. You and all the other young fire-eaters around here just don't stop to think what the North could do to us by cutting off our commerce with the rest of the world. It wouldn't be just a matter of giving up our cigars and brandy, I'll tell you."

And so the argument went, the same argument that could be heard elsewhere over glasses of brandy and scuppernong, across country store counters and elegant dining tables, after prayer meetings and slave auctions, wherever southern men gathered to discuss what was foremost on their minds in that autumn of 'sixty. John Ringgold listened with an interest he hadn't had before, hearing the same arguments in Texas, where in spite of the fact that there was slavery and widespread concern over what abolitionism might bring besides the end of it, he'd felt largely removed from the problems of the South. The problems of day-to-day survival on a prairie farm were absorbing enough, and what was left of his consciousness he'd spent dreaming of how he might escape. Now, however, he began to feel as though he could become part of the world of his Missouri cousins, could even share their view of themselves as being part of the South, in spite of how he felt about slavery. Because the Youngers had welcomed him as a member of the family, their family. Their acceptance meant a great deal to him, he realized even that first evening, almost as much maybe as fulfilling the ambitions that had brought him to Missouri.

"Another thing, Cole," Harry Younger went on. "There are plenty of folks here in Missouri who don't even share our opinion that we're part of the South. Over around St. Louis especially, but around here, too. You can't just pretend that those folks don't exist. They surely won't let Missouri secede without a fight."

Grudgingly, reluctantly, Cole conceded all of the points his father made. John gathered that they'd had this argument frequently and Cole wasn't really as committed to his viewpoint as he let on at the outset. He was actually making things clearer to himself by arguing with his father. John had often wondered what kind of relationship he might have had with his own father if he'd lived, and couldn't help envying Cole a little.

3

"The next day Cole showed me around the farm, and my initial impressions of the Youngers' wealth were amply confirmed. First we went through the stable, and as we passed between the stalls I saw animal after animal that made Jake McMaster's prime stock look like what the Comanches used to haul their squaws and baggage."

"He's what they call a hunter," Cole said, nodding toward a big slab-sided bay that was being groomed by a tall handsome mulatto with shoulders as wide as a gate. "Daddy had him shipped over from England last summer. I guarantee he'll clear any fence in this county." He addressed the mulatto: "Ain't that right, Cyrus?"

"Yes sir, Mister Cole, you're sho'ly right about that," the man replied with a little smile that seemed less in response to Cole's question than to the thoughts of his own that Cole had interrupted. His deep negroid voice was unlike that of the other slaves John had heard at the Younger farm, had none of their tone of anxious subservience.

"Yeah, you take good care of ol' Wellington. Hear now?" Cole went on, stopping to stroke the gleaming, well-groomed neck. The mulatto did not reply to what was clearly a superfluous injunction, and John Ringgold's gaze shifted from the magnificent animal to the man's own impressive physique. Standing next to each other, the mulatto slave and Cole Younger could be seen to be of a size, though the slave was even broader through the shoulders as a result, John gathered, of having engaged in kinds of work that the likes of Cole Younger would always be spared. Regarding them together, John Ringgold had a thought that he quickly dismissed: If Cyrus's nose hadn't been broken, his features would have been as fine as Cole's.

"We plan to make a little money out of that animal, John," Cole was saying as they moved on between the stalls, "just as soon as breeders around here catch on to what they are."

"That man Cyrus take care of all your horses?" John asked, still curious but not about to ask any questions that might offend his cousin.

"Yeah," Cole replied, "he's in charge of the stables. We've made a little money out of him, too," he added with a laugh. "Ain't a nigger inside three counties can stand toe-to-toe with him."

"That how his nose got broken?"

"Yeah, only it's usually him that does the damage to the other buck. Richard and I wanted to take him down to Fort Smith and fight him there, but Daddy wouldn't have it. He's sort of special, I guess you might say." He started to say something more but then checked himself.

"How'd he get the name Cyrus?"

Cole laughed again. "Oh, that's one of Daddy's customs, naming our bucks for great conquering heroes he's read about. In Cyrus's case it fits." Cole added, "Cyrus was born on this place a year or two after Daddy and my uncle Frank moved here from Carolina."

They said no more about the slave Cyrus as they moved along between the stalls.

Halting before a stall in which there was a magnificent deep-chested sorrel with a blaze on its forehead, Cole said, "This one's strictly for breeding. Won't let anybody ride him. Will you, Blaze?"

As he reached out to stroke the animal, it tossed its head and rolled a fearful eye at him. Cole chuckled a little and dropped his hand to his side.

"I'll have Cyrus saddle us a couple of mounts. Then I'll show you the rest of the place."

"Mind if I try this one?" John asked, wondering even as he did, what was in his own mind.

Cole laughed considerately, as though his cousin had attempted a joke and hadn't quite succeeded.

"I'm serious, Cole, if you wouldn't mind. I won't hurt him."

At that Cole laughed as though the joke had succeeded.

"I surely believe that, John. You won't hurt this old horse. What he might do to you, though, would make my daddy and all the rest of us pretty unhappy. We didn't bring you all the way down here from Liberty to get your neck broke."

"My neck."

"John, nobody has *ever* stayed on that horse. Maybe you know what you're doing. . . ."

"I do."

Cole quit smiling then and shrugged, letting out his breath and shaking his head in a way that said he was still far from reassured but he wouldn't argue the matter further with this wild cousin from Texas.

"All right, I'll have Cyrus saddle him for you," he said.

"Do that myself, if you don't mind."

He always saddled his own broncs. You could get acquainted with an animal and sometimes even gentle it some.

There was no gentling this animal, however. When John slipped a lead rope around the sorrel's neck, it reacted with the apparent intention of kicking the stall into splinters. Getting the saddle on out in front of the stall required the help of both Cole and Cyrus.

"Lord almighty, John, you sure you want to do this?"

Hanging on to the big stud's reins with all his strength as it tried to throw off the saddle, he wasn't sure, but he answered without hesitation:

"I want to."

John's doubts increased after the sorrel threw him the first time. A month as a student had softened him, diminishing his extraordinary strength of legs and hands, which was, along with a reckless spirit, his principal asset as a bronc peeler. When he was bucked off again, however, he cursed himself, regarding it as an avoidable result of carelessness, a failure to anticipate that the horse would turn again suddenly in just the way it had been turning whenever it came near a fence. Climbing on again, he knew that he could stay aboard if he avoided mistakes. Just for an instant, before the stallion began again, he saw Harry Younger and Margaret running toward the stable from the house, heard them shouting. Then it was all fragmentary blurred glimpses of bright blue Missouri sky, the gleam of sunlight on shiny green leaves, the white-painted front of the stable and the thick reddish brown dust out of which the sorrel erupted tirelessly again and again. Then, abruptly, the animal stopped, stood perfectly still, though he trembled a little, and John heel-tapped him into a slow walk around the dusty space in front of the stable.

While the sorrel was bucking he'd heard shouts from Harry Younger and his daughter but couldn't make out anything. Now he could hear Harry and Margaret raging at Cole:

". . . could have gotten him killed," Margaret was almost screaming.

"A mighty low trick, I'd say. Why didn't you tell him . . . ?"

"I told him, sir," Cole protested. "He insisted."

"That's the truth, sir," Cyrus corroborated. John gathered that most slaves would not have spoken up at such a moment, but then he'd also gathered that Cyrus was, as Cole had said, "sort of special." For the moment, he didn't say anything to his cousins, directing all of his attention to the trembling, gasping stallion, who now seemed, if not content, at least able to bear the burden of a rider.

"Easy, Blaze, easy fella. You're all right," he muttered softly, trying to share his relief with the animal now that their first and, he devoutly hoped, last contest of this kind was over. Then he dismounted and led Blaze over to where his cousins were standing. Like the sorrel, he was trembling now. He saw Harry Younger's face aflame with a rage that had been directed at his son but was now, he feared, directed at himself. Margaret's naturally dark olive countenance had faded to a sickly pallor.

"Son, I don't know what I'd have told your mother if you'd been hurt," Harry Younger said, shaking his head.

"You're all right, aren't you, Johnny?" Margaret was asking anxiously. Suddenly he was terribly ashamed. This wasn't Texas, and these weren't the McMasters. It had been a damn fool show-off thing to do.

"I'm fine," he answered Margaret. "Where I come from, this is how a man starts the day." He tried to smile, wanted desperately to see the color return to her face, but his sudden shame wouldn't let him. "Sorry, sir," he said to Harry Younger. "Cole warned me."

Harry Younger came over and clapped a hand on his shoulder.

"That was quite a ride, son. Guess you knew what you were doing. You gave us a fright, though."

"Sorry, sir," he said again.

"That's all right, son," his cousin said with a laugh. "If you can ride that horse, you're welcome to ride him back to Liberty. He's not a bad animal, actually, just afraid of men. Fellow I bought him from treated him pretty badly."

"I'll bet you learned to ride that way from the Comanches," Margaret said. The color had returned to her face now, and she came over to stand directly in front of him, gazing up at him so intently that he felt himself reddening and had to look away.

"Naturally," he answered, with a little forced laugh. "They taught me everything I know."

"Even how to dance, I'll bet."

"Oh surely . . ." He remembered then the "festivities" Richard had mentioned, which made him suddenly almost as anxious as he'd been about mounting Blaze.

"We can't wait to see what they taught you," she said, laughing mischievously, as though she knew for certain that dancing with young ladies in splendid mansions was in fact just as remote from his experience as dancing with Comanches around a fire somewhere in the Staked Plains. The painful embarrassment he was destined to feel would, he reflected, amply make up for the fright he'd given her and her father.

But as it turned out, the evening was far from painful. Cole provided him with a suit that one of the servants managed to alter to fit John's leaner, lankier build, and he even persuaded his cousin to keep it, assuring him that he, Cole, was putting on so much heft that it could never be made to fit him again. Running his hands over the fine, nearly new, gray broadcloth and seeing in the mirror how it fit him, John began to feel a tiny bit of confidence in himself, though he still dreaded the arrival of evening, when he would have to own up to his ignorance of what was obviously an important social grace in the world of the Youngers.

That evening, as he entered the enormous sitting room, from which most of the furniture and the carpet had been removed, his ears were filled with the sounds of a country ball—the plucking and strumming of guitars and banjos, the sawing of fiddles, the clang of an iron triangle, the thudding of boots upon the polished floor, the swishing of crinoline, and the roar of several dozen conversations trying to make themselves heard above the music and made still louder as the evening wore on by champagne and scuppernong.

He made his way to the punch table and tried champagne for the first time, unaware that it had anything in it that a man might feel. Meeting Richard there, he was introduced to several young fellows from neighboring farms—two brothers by the name of Walker, a slightly older man named Ol Shepherd, who had lost an eye, and

a smaller blond youngster who introduced himself as
Arch Clement.

"Mighty pleased to meet you, John," Ol Shepherd
said, and John did not feel any absence of sincerity in the
greeting, or in the greetings of the others. Clearly, to be
introduced in this part of Missouri as a cousin of the
Youngers was to be readily and warmly accepted.

The conversation, which John was welcome to enter,
was about crops, whether sorghums or tobacco or rye
and oats seemed most promising for next season's planting. He listened with polite attention, contributed a remark to the effect that a farmer's problems and planting
options here were surely a whole lot different from those
of farmers in southwest Texas and helped himself to
more champagne.

While he found the conversation less than absorbing, it
was a safe place to be—chatting with these young fellows, holding a glass in his hand, watching the dancers.
As the couples whirled and stamped before him, parting
and meeting in time with the sawing, strumming and
clanging, he tried to get the hang of how it was done,
mainly how a man could move around a girl that way
without crushing her little feet under his big heavy boots.
He watched Cole in particular and was amazed by the
easy way he managed his big body. Along with his good
looks and warm, easy manner, his competence as a dancer
made him obviously a great favorite with the pretty young
girls in their bright crinoline and taffeta ball dresses. He
looked for Margaret, but she had not come in yet, had
apparently been delayed where he'd seen her earlier,
helping her mother supervise the preparation of the most
astonishing variety of foodstuffs he had ever beheld.

" . . . a good year for cattle feed, I'd say."

He turned back to the punch table and exchanged his
empty glass for a full one. By now he realized that this
sharply edged, deliciously refreshing stuff had something
in it, and he was delighted with the way it enhanced the
pleasure he felt watching the dancers ride the currents of
the music—muscular, red-faced farm youths in well-tailored
suits and shining-eyed girls with gleaming locks tumbling
about their shoulders. He wished that he had the courage
to plunge in and ride the currents with them, but he

knew that no amount of champagne would give him that kind of courage.

"Why ain't you aht there, young fella?"

The voice was familiar-sounding, a little like Harry Younger's, but such were the effects of the champagne and the noise that he didn't recognize Frank Marion Younger until he turned to face him.

"Not ready yet, I guess, sir," he answered, grinning sheepishly and feeling himself redden with embarrassment.

"Wal, don't you worry, they'll get you aht there sooner or later." The old man laughed and patted him on the arm. John Ringgold caught a strong, rankly sweetish whiff that reminded him of the stills he'd sampled back in Bexar County, though he couldn't imagine a Younger drinking such a homely product. He noticed that Frank's already ruddy complexion was deeply flushed, almost plum-colored.

"You'd never guess, would you?" Frank Marion went on, as though he and the boy from Texas had been conversing about something else.

"Sir?"

"This place, I mean. All of it. The whole damn place. Every acre."

"Sir?"

"I won it fur him, I did. One horse race an' he had his start."

By now John Ringgold was half convinced that the champagne had affected his hearing. But then, for a second or two, the older man's whiskey haze seemed to lift a little, and he was able to see from the boy's puzzled expression that he needed to do some explaining.

"You don't know what I'm talkin' about, do you, son?"

"No, sir, I'm afraid I don't."

"I'm talkin' about how my brother got his start here in Missouri. Guess you wouldn't know 'bout that."

"No, sir, I wouldn't."

"Wal now, seein' as how you're our cousin, I'll tell you all about it."

John had the feeling that relationship didn't have much to do with it, that he was about to hear something that anyone within earshot of Frank Marion might hear once the older man had downed a little whiskey, but he maintained a respectfully attentive attitude nonetheless.

"When we come aht here back in 'thirty-six," Frank Marion began, "aht from Carolina, waren't a lot o' white folks livin' here. Just Indins mostly—Otos, Iowas, Missouris, livin' under the pertection o' the Pawnees. They was signin' away their land to the white man fast as they could, startin' with the treaty of Prairie du Chien in 'thirty-six, but when we come here they still owned most o' west Missouri. There was this one old chief, an Oto by the name of Shaumonekusse, had his lodge set up right about where this house is standin'." Frank Marion paused to sip out of a cup of what a careless observer might have taken to be cider. Then he continued.

"Mean-tempered old cuss, but one o' his wives was sho'ly a beauty. Young enough to be his daughter. Name was Hayne Hudjihini, meanin' the Eagle of Delight. You look at Margaret you kin tell—" Abruptly the old man stopped himself.

"What about Margaret?"

"Nothin'," the old man snapped. "Nothin' atall. Anyway, gettin' back to what I was sayin', we interduced ourselves to this old chief, with the help of a half-breed interpreter, an' my brother didn't lose no time gettin' the conversation around to horses an' wagerin'. The old chief tried to put up one o' his wives, any one or all except the Eagle of Delight, but my brother wouldn't take nothin' less'n a piece of land big enough to pasture two dozen horses. Shaumonekusse finally went along, figurin' I guess that the land wouldn't be his much longer anyhow, way it was bein' signed over to the Great Father. We'd brung out a wagonload o' trade goods to put up, but some o' his braves wanted in on the bettin' an' pretty quick my brother found he'd staked damn near all he owned, 'cludin' his sidearms an' striped cavalry britches, everythin' but our niggers, even though the old chief would've doubled the land if he'd throwed them in too."

Another pause to sip from the cup, followed by a cough, and the old man looked at John Ringgold with reddened eyes as he wiped his mouth with the back of his hand.

"Course we run was about sixteen furlongs right acrost the pasture land we was bettin' fur. We'd already decided that I'd do the ridin'. I ain't no West Point-educated fella, but I do know horses, 'sides bein' a whole lot lighter'n my brother. Our daddy had left us two thoroughbreds, a stud an' a mare. Them an' the niggers was all he didn't leave to our older brother back in Carolina. The mare was a little faster over a shorter stretch, but I figured we'd be better off with the stud over that distance. I was right too, by God. The Oto brave I was ridin' against couldn't've weighed much more'n the feathers he was wearin'. Good little rider, too, forkin' a filly that could move like a damn prairie fire. I didn't ketch him till the last furlong, an' it was only the people standin' right by the finish could see I'd won."

Recollecting the triumph, Frank Marion grinned a little and shook his head. Then he upended his cup.

"So there you've got it, young fella," Harry Younger's brother said with a chuckle that didn't quite go with the grin, carrying as it did just a suggestion of bitterness. "That's how we done it. I won us enough Indin goods, furs an' the like, to make a trip over to St. Louis worthwhile an' brung back enough trade goods to start us a little store over where Harrisonville is now. My brother's one o' the richest men in west Missouri now, thanks to me an' that stud."

"That's a mighty interesting story, sir," the boy said, sincerely, because everything about the Youngers was enormously interesting to him.

"Ain't it," the old man replied, and the bitterness in his tone was more clearly audible. For a moment or two he looked down into his empty cup, apparently forgetting that John was listening to him. Then he looked up, saw the boy and grinned good-naturedly. "Don't listen to an old man," he said. "You'll never meet a better man than my brother Harry. If you'll excuse me now. . . ." He patted John Ringgold on the shoulder and turned away. Watching him make his way through the crowd toward the door, beyond which, perhaps somewhere in a nearby moonlit thicket, there were jugs filling, the boy tried to imagine the two old men as penniless young adventurers in the wilderness.

As he finished his third glass, Margaret came into the room, and the effect on a substantial number of young, and even not so young, men there was virtually instantaneous. They crossed over from every corner of the room, and some who were engaged in conversations with other young ladies seemed to wish that they could disengage themselves. Some, he found out later, had come from as far away as Independence. Watching them surround her, seeing her greet a well-made curly-headed fellow whose looks as a man seemed comparable to her feminine beauty, John Ringgold tried to pick out what it was that drew them. Her ball gown of pale yellow silk was less flattering, he thought, than the green dress she had worn the night before. The dark golden womanflesh it molded was the same, however, as were the brilliantly flashing almond eyes and the handsome, high-boned features beneath the artfully piled masses of bronze hair. Watching her manage her admirers, thinking of what Cole had said, he was again thankful for the barriers between them. He turned away from the dance floor, helped himself to another glass of champagne and rejoined the young men, whose conversation had shifted from the merits of sorghums to secession and the possibility of war.

" . . . could whip those nigger-loving sonsofbitches inside of six weeks, I'd say."

"Now they've got Kansas you'd think they'd leave us alone."

" . . . I'd like to see 'em all hang with Old Brown."

Inevitably, he was asked what people in Texas were saying about secession, and he told them what he had told Harry Younger. He was suddenly, however, unable to feel that he had or could have much in common with these young men, and he began to feel depressed, for he couldn't altogether resist an awareness that their world was also the world of the Youngers. It drove him back to the punch table, and he was reaching for still another glass of champagne when he heard a woman's voice, sharp and reproachful, uttering his name:

"Johnny. Cousin Johnny."

Guiltily, though he couldn't understand why he should be feeling guilty, he turned to face the owner of the voice, guessing who it was but not really believing it could be.

"Are you just going to ignore me all night?"

"Oh . . . Margaret," he exclaimed in genuine surprise,

for he'd been certain that her circle of admirers would
never let her out.

"Are you?" she asked again, obviously irritated and
maybe even a little hurt.

"Course not. Looked to me, though, like you were
pretty well occupied."

"You haven't even asked me to dance."

"Well, that's because . . ."

"It's the Virginia reel, Johnny. Come on." And she
grabbed his arm to drag him out onto the floor.

"Margaret, please, I can't . . ." he pleaded, but she
either couldn't or wouldn't hear him above the sawing of
the fiddles as they struck up the reel.

It was as well that she gave him no chance to think
about what she was dragging him into. The several glasses
of champagne helped as well, shielding him with a numbness from the sharp thrust of fear that would have gone
right through him if he'd had time to wonder what he was
going to do on that floor.

She must have known. Surely she must have known
even before she got him out there, before he showed how
little he knew. The laughing mischief in her dark eyes
said as much. Suddenly he laughed out loud. Partly it was
the champagne working, but also it was his sudden awareness that he was going to look silly as hell and it just
didn't matter. Why not, he asked himself, since he was
going to look ridiculous anyway, see if he could imitate
the movements of the fellows who seemed to know what
they were doing? Nearby was the handsome curly-headed
fellow who had been Margaret's first partner of the evening. Now he was paired with a dark-haired, Irish-looking
beauty. John and Margaret were paired as a couple with
them in the reel, which, as near as he could figure,
involved moving through something like a figure eight.

Moving through the first two figure eights, he was so
far out of step that he laughed out loud again, and
Margaret couldn't restrain her own laughter. But then
she helped him, prompting in a low voice that reached
him somehow through the squealing of fiddles:

". . . left, stop, turn to me. Fine, Johnny, you're doing
just fine."

By the time they finished the Virginia reel, John could
almost believe that he had the hang of it. At least he
hadn't stepped on Margaret's feet, and he found that he

didn't have to be so completely conscious of his every movement, could trust himself a little to the music.

"We did it, Johnny!" she panted, squeezing his hands and beaming with the pleasure of her achievement in having gotten her shy, stumbling Texas cousin onto the floor. Sharing her pleasure, he couldn't help feeling a little pleased with himself. Still, he felt compelled to confess the obvious and, in an incongruously solemn tone, began:

"Margaret, this is the first time I've ever—"

She cut him off. "Really? I never would have guessed. Those Comanches taught you something, didn't they?" Then he saw the mischievous light again in her eyes and how she was trying to restrain a giggle but couldn't. And he found himself giggling with her, unable to stop, partly because of the champagne he'd drunk but mainly because her own infectious laughter wouldn't let him.

They were interrupted in their giggling fit by a red-headed fellow who reminded Margaret that the next dance had been promised to him.

"Oh, Tyce, I'm sorry," she said, just managing to bring her laughter under control. "I'm a little tired now. Would you ask me later?" The redhead nodded and forced a rather sour smile, which, as she turned away from him and he shifted his gaze to John Ringgold, became a resentful scowl. The boy from Texas gathered that he'd probably made an enemy, but this didn't trouble him even a little. Having survived the Virginia reel, he couldn't be threatened by anything.

"I'd like some champagne, Johnny," Margaret said and started toward the punch table. John followed her, noting as he did that a couple of her attentive admirers from across the room were moving in their direction with the apparent intention of asking her to dance. Apparently Margaret saw them too, and when he had filled their glasses she said, "Kind of hot in here, isn't it? Let's give ourselves a little air."

She led the way out through some glass double doors onto a porch that ran the length of the house and was illuminated from within through the windows. The crisp October evening air cooled his face, and he filled his lungs with it, noticing dimly how it seemed to increase the pleasurable numbness he'd been feeling.

There were couches and chairs set against the wall and a hammock upon which another couple was seated. He thought that Margaret, having excused herself out of weariness from dancing with her redheaded admirer, would want to sit, but she did not. Instead she walked over to the railing and leaned out over it. He moved alongside her and put his hand next to hers. Because of the light from the windows behind they couldn't see anything in the darkness before them, and the noise inside drowned out the sounds of the night, but they could smell the pungent odor of burning hickory wood coming up from fires in the slave cabins down behind the stable.

"Can't see the stars," she said, sounding a little surprised and disappointed.

"They're out there, though, sho'ly," he answered.

"Sho'ly," she said, shuddering a little and leaning against him for a moment. He wanted to put his arm around her shoulders to warm her but thought better of it. Glancing sideways he saw how her masses of bronze hair and the bright pin curls on the back of her neck shone in the light.

Then she moved a little away from him and raised her face to look up once again toward the stars she couldn't see, gazing intently with wide dark eyes and parted lips. He turned to watch the play of light and shadow upon the fine bones beneath the golden skin.

"Listen, Johnny," she commanded suddenly, mysteriously. "Listen."

He listened intently, trying to hear something besides the sounds of the ball, the laughter and loud talk contending with the music and nearly drowning it out, but he heard nothing.

"I can't—" he started to say, but once again she interrupted him, began to murmur words that were barely audible above the noise at their backs.

> "I cannot see what flowers are at my feet,
>   Nor what soft incense hangs upon the boughs,
> But, in embalmed darkness, guess each sweet
>   Wherewith the seasonable month endows
> The grass, the thicket, and the fruit-tree wild . . ."

Then she stopped and glanced over at him, a little self-conscious half-smile forming on her lips.

"That's poetry," he said, remembering the effort of rendering Greek and Roman lyrics into something like poetic English under the patient guidance of Padre García. "You're a poet." He wasn't really amazed, as he'd been amazed the night before when she entered into the argument between her father and brother, but it gave him a strange feeling of wonder.

She chuckled a little and looked down into the darkness below the railing.

"Not really, Johnny. I write poems, but I didn't write that. A real poet wrote that. In a book I have. . . ."

"I'd surely like to hear something you wrote," he said.

She smiled at him then, a little shyly it seemed, and placed her hand over his on the railing.

"Sometime, Johnny. Sometime."

Sometime was not long in coming, the man remembers. She shared her poetry with him, shared the poem she was, and the verses were still flowing through him, along with the verses of Keats. It was, in fact, impossible for him to separate his lifelong fondness for the poetry of Keats, begun that evening, from his feelings for the girl who had murmured his lines into the darkness.

"Darkling I listen . . ." Ringo murmurs aloud. But no nightingale responds, only the first coyote of the Dragoon mountain evening. He stands up and stretches, amazed that the day has passed so quickly. It is time to build up the fire for supper. Tonight, he promises himself, he will have something for supper, something besides whiskey. He makes the promise even as he fills his cup, a beaker full of the warm South, raises it in salute to the evening star, and begins to recite:

> "She dwells with Beauty—Beauty that must die;
> And Joy, whose hand is ever at his lips . . .

"And because that's how it is," he goes on to mutter, "there's many a time I've been half in love with easeful Death."

Striding over to where he left one of his panniers near the spring, he pauses to glance westward at the high naked peak glowing crimson once again with the approach of evening.

"Tell me, ol' Purgatory," he demands of the mountain

in a loud, near-shouting voice, "do I wake or sleep? Was she just a dream? Tell me, goddammit."

Then he waits for an answer. Finally, after nearly a minute has passed, he utters a loud, scoffing laugh and turns away from the mountain.

FOUR

CAPTAIN WALLEY

He rode back to Liberty on the sorrel Blaze, a loan—
actually a gift—from his cousin Harry Younger. The
warmth of his feelings for the Youngers mingled with the
golden warmth of autumn was reflected in the patches of
goldenrod lining the roads, the yellow butterflies in the
air and the bright yellow hickory leaves carpeting the
hillsides. He took his time getting back to Liberty, frequently leaving the roads to follow trails that wound
through clumps of scarlet sumach and wahoo, bright orange sassafras and copper-leaved hardwoods. Rounding a
turn on one of these trails that led nowhere, he startled a
deer. She regarded him for a moment with an anxious
eye, then she bounded in among the flame-colored bushes
and was gone.

In the pocket of his coat, gift of Cole Younger, he
carried a letter from Harry Younger to be presented to
one Mr. Hockensmith, owner of a livery stable in Liberty. Mr. Hockensmith, so he'd told Colonel Younger,
was looking for someone to tutor his son. He would
make it well worth the while of anyone who could teach
the boy to read and do figures. The idea of recommend-
ing John Ringgold as a tutor had come to Harry Younger
when his young cousin had asked if he knew of any horse
raisers in the area in need of a bronc peeler.

"Son, you'll kill yourself making a living that way,"
he'd said, circling the boy's shoulders with a kindly arm.
"Not that you aren't some horseman. But even the best
rider's luck can run out. You know that. And think about
what you're doing to your body in the meantime."

He had to agree, remembering the "stove-up" condition of some of the older riders at McMaster's, but there
had seemed to be no alternative. Now maybe there was.
At least he'd see what Mr. Hockensmith was offering.

112

Mr. Hockensmith, as it turned out, was indeed a generous man. He even promised a bonus if the boy could be taught to read by Christmas. The boy, a sullen-faced fifteen-year-old by the name of Andy, was unwilling at first to cooperate in the learning process, until he managed to persuade his tutor to drink with him during and after at least some of his lessons.

"Makes learnin' a mite easier for me," the boy said.

"I'll bet," John Ringgold answered skeptically, but he agreed to share a jug with the youngster from time to time. He soon won the trust of his pupil, and after two weeks had passed, the boy began trying to press some of his own spending money on his tutor.

"Take it, John. Plenty where that came from. Stingy old fox. Bet he don't pay you nothin'."

"Doesn't pay you anything." He felt compelled out of duty to catch slips he frequently fell into himself. "As a matter of fact, your daddy pays me very well."

"Aw hell, I don't believe it. You're a good ol' boy. You take it."

And sometimes, later on, when he had doubts about whether or not he would be able to make expenses, he took it.

Sometimes after a lesson, as a condition of future cooperation and scholarly effort, the boy would coax his tutor into a ride in the country. They wouldn't ride far, usually no further than one of the smaller farms near the town. Andy would take a long pull at the jug, then approach the house boldly. Sometimes, when the owner or tenant of the farm answered the door and heard his proposition, the boy wound up on the seat of his pants in the front yard. But, knowing the farms and the brown women whose owners or overseers would make them available for a price, the boy would more often succeed in getting what he wanted. Having paid for Doreen or Prissy or whomever, he could flash John Ringgold a grin and head for the nearest clump of trees to wait.

Then the tutor would settle himself under a tree and try to get on with his premedical studies, would try to concentrate on plane geometry or whatever, in spite of what he was feeling.

"That's how I began my career in education. Sort of like old Quantrill himself, who was in fact a schoolteacher long before he was a guerrilla raider. In my case, though, the question of who was educating whom wasn't all that clear. One thing I learned in a hurry from my over-experienced pupil was that my Georgia-bred father hadn't been stretching things when he talked about slavery. The idea of women, brown or white, being used that way against their will, rented out to a kid with pockets full of money, like animals from his daddy's livery stable, made me pretty sick at first. I told myself that not all slave owners were like those greedy farmers, that there were men like Harry Younger who treated their slaves like human beings, but it didn't change the fact of the relationship between slaves and owners, the nature of which I was being made to see. It seemed to pleasure Andy to make me see it, and he did his damnedest to talk me into partaking of his pleasures."

He remembers one conversation in particular, which nearly led to the end of his tutoring. In fact, it very nearly led to the end of Andy Hockensmith. The boy had just enjoyed himself with a young woman who walked past John Ringgold with downcast eyes on her way back to the cornfield whence she had been summoned by her overseer. She was not out of earshot when the boy said sneering—

"It don't make them no nevermind, John. Ain't like they's anythin' but goddamn animals. Feed 'em an' breed 'em, we say."

The boy was grinning and on the point of guffawing in his usual manner when his tutor's lean, strong hand shot out and grasped him by the shirtfront. The shirt was twisted hard against his throat and he was pulled up onto his toes. Gagging, he found himself raised nearly to John Ringgold's eye level, and what he saw in his tutor's eyes made Andy afraid. Not a very intelligent youngster, with the sensitivity of a rooting razorback, but cunning enough to recognize mortal danger, Andy Hockensmith was frightened.

"If they're nothing but animals, what does that make you?" John snarled in reply. He could see the boy's fear, feel it with the hand that held him while the other hand cocked itself into a fist ready to smash the now grinless gap-toothed mouth into a shapeless pulp.

The fist remained where it was, cocked and ready,

albeit trembling to strike, because John knew that one blow wouldn't be enough to satisfy his yearning to inflict pain on Andy Hockensmith. If he began, he wouldn't finish until all the rage within him was spent, and by that time his pupil might not be living.

"Please . . ." the boy gasped, still hateful and deserving of punishment but now pathetic in his fear and helplessness, and John let him go.

Released, Andy retreated quickly out of reach, coughing and then forcing a weak grin as he began to breathe easily again.

"That waren't real nice, teacher," he said. And then, when he had retreated a little further out of reach and his grin became broader, he said, "I bet you ain't never had any yourself. Ain't I right?"

John Ringgold did not answer, being so strongly possessed by a sudden resurgence of the fury just past that permitting himself any action, even the uttering of a word, would have been enough to launch him upon the youngster again.

"How 'bout me fixing it up for you?" Andy sniggered. "I know a little darkie belongs to Jed Carpenter over on the Little Blue. High yella, she is, with a pair on her you cain't hardly get your hands over. Do you good, teacher. . . ."

As John came for him, the boy scampered like a rabbit for his horse and made it just in time. Watching him ride away, hearing his triumphant, mocking guffaw, John swore that he was finished with Andy Hockensmith. But even as he swore it to himself he knew that the money he had left in the bank wouldn't carry him even to the end of the school year, that he was trapped if he wanted to continue his schooling. He cursed the youngster, knowing that he was bound to him by his own ambition to succeed in the world and become someone who couldn't be bound to anyone by a need for money.

For all his determination, however, there were times when the pressure of his rigorous courses at William Jewell and a depressing awareness that he was being somehow corrupted, if only vicariously, by his young pupil almost caused him to put the little money he had left into a stage ticket back to Texas. What kept him in Missouri, enabled him to survive, was the knowledge that he was always welcome at the Youngers'. Hardly a month passed that he didn't make the long ride up to their farm for a visit. His second visit was only two weeks after the first. The excuse he gave himself was that they could surely use another hand with the corn harvest.

"You're family, John. You don't ever need any excuses for coming here," Harry Younger said, reading him easily.

But they let him help out, gave him a long well-honed knife to join in the work of cutting down the dry stalks and putting the corn up in shocks. He worked alongside his cousins and their slaves. There weren't enough slaves to complete the work of harvesting the huge fields in time, and Harry Younger was his own overseer.

After all the weeks of being a student, John found the work genuinely pleasurable. His lean muscular body, inured to much harder farm work in Texas, craved activity. It was still the golden season and warm during much of the day. He enjoyed the feel of the sun on his back and the smell of the freshly turned earth from the adjacent fields that had already been harvested. Mainly, though, he enjoyed the company. After two weeks of communicating with no one but his professors, the other denizens of the boardinghouse and Andy Hockensmith, he savored the company of Harry Younger and his sons. There was also, as he worked beside them, the pleasure of anticipating Margaret's arrival. Each day, around noontime, she and one of her sisters came out from the house with baskets full of food, and all the men and boys, including the slaves, would fall to.

Before they began eating, however, there was usually an interval of sport. John soon found out that next to horse racing, cock fighting, and other games of chance, the Younger brothers enjoyed nothing more than foot racing and wrestling. Inevitably, he was challenged.

"I know there's nobody around here can match you riding wild horses, John," Cole began, "but tell me, do they ever get off their horses in Texas and run a little?" They had just watched a race between young Bob and Richard Younger.

John grinned at Cole and began pulling off his boots. Cole packed so much weight that it would be no contest between them. But it turned out that what Cole had in

mind was a race between his Texas cousin and his brother
Jim, a lean, slightly built sixteen-year-old who was said to
be one of the fastest sprinters over two furlongs in the
county.

"I'll bet you half a dollar you can't stay close to Jim.
How about it?" Always, it seemed, there had to be a bet.

"Sure," John answered without hesitating, though, as
usual, he didn't have half a dollar.

"You'll win, Johnny," Margaret said. "I just know you
will."

"Sure," he said again, though he was anything but
sure. Back in Texas he was used to traveling long miles
afoot over the prairie when a horse was unavailable, and
he generally found it less tiring to take off his boots and
run than walk. But he'd been a student for six weeks.
Aside from an occasional barefoot evening run along one
of the roads outside Liberty that he'd take after an afternoon of tutoring and being disgusted with the antics of
his pupil, when he'd try to run out what he was feeling
about himself as well as Andy, he hadn't given his legs
much exercise. He didn't really think that he could stay
close to Jim Younger.

Harry Younger himself started them off. The course was
a stretch of road alongside the big cornfield in which they
were working. Run both ways it was nearly three furlongs.
Everyone, including the slaves, gathered around them as
the Colonel drew out his old service pistol and raised it.

" . . . marks. Get set . . ."

Jim was a very fast starter. As the gun went off he
sprang out nearly two yards ahead of his Texas cousin.
And before they reached the turnaround he'd added
another yard to the distance between them. After the
turnaround, however, John Ringgold felt himself getting
into his stride. His long powerful legs still had their
spring, and even though his breathing came in great
tearing sobs, he knew that his lungs would bear it.

Margaret's screaming encouragement could be heard
above the shouting of everyone else. "Come on, Johnny!"

With every few strides he moved a little closer, and
twenty yards from the finish he moved past his astonished cousin, finally finishing about a yard ahead. Gasping and wheezing, he nearly collapsed, and Cole's big
hand pounding him on the back nearly sent him sprawling.

"Some runnin'," Cole was saying as he drew out a half-dollar. "Next Fourth of July we're going to make a bundle, aren't we, Daddy? Won't nobody suspect he can run like that being as big as he is."

"Here, Johnny." Margaret was handing him a glass of lemonade. Shining-eyed, she seemed on the point of bursting with delight.

Even Jim Younger seemed to be delighted, though he made John promise to race him again the next day.

The next day, however, it was not running but wrestling, with the challenge extended in the same affable Younger manner.

"Tell me, John," Cole began, "do they wrestle much down in Texas?"

"Oh surely," he answered with a grin, knowing full well what was coming next.

"Well, I was wondering if you'd mind . . ."

As he stripped off his shirt, John Ringgold thought, hoped, that he might acquit himself reasonably well, in spite of Cole's much greater heft. Having wrestled for hours with his brother Clayton, he was used to grappling with a heavier, stronger opponent. He and Clayton had come to be about evenly matched, in spite of Clayton's enormous strength, because he was quick enough to avoid or slip out of holds in which he had to match his brother strength for strength.

Seeing the broad, bulky-muscled physique Cole revealed as he stripped to the waist, John hoped that quickness might save him again, but he wasn't overly optimistic. As they circled each other, he guessed that Cole would be expecting him to be evasive and slippery. Accordingly, he went in at once with a leg dive and managed, amidst much cheering from the watching Youngers, to upend Cole, who, wearing an amazed expression, went down on his back on a soft ridge between two plowed furrows. He recovered quickly, however, and when John tried to hold him down, he twisted over onto his belly, rose up on his knees and, with disconcerting ease, peeled off the headlock John had clamped onto him. The two of them then scrambled to their feet and began circling again. Cole was grinning with unfeigned confidence.

"Nice takedown, John. That's one for you," he said.

"You can beat him, Johnny. I know you can," Margaret encouraged him.

John wished that he had a little of her confidence in himself. Having felt Cole's strength, he guessed that he was about to lose the half-dollar he'd won foot racing unless he handled himself prudently. Still, instead of being cautious, he went in recklessly for a hip throw, which failed, and he found himself being lifted off his feet, circled round the waist by Cole's bearlike grip. Cole then drove him shoulder-first into the ground and fell on him. The fall and Cole's weight on him nearly knocked out his breath.

"Take it easy with him, Cole," Harry Younger admonished sharply.

"Get up, Johnny!" Margaret was urging with unshakable confidence. "Throw him off!"

Barely able to breathe, he tried to twist himself under Cole but found himself held rigidly with one of Cole's massive arms circling his head and the other gripping his left leg so that he was unable either to raise or turn himself. With Cole's huge chest covering his own, he was helpless.

"Throw him off, Johnny!" Margaret pleaded. "You can do it!"

He heard her, and if he hadn't been nearly suffocating with his face pressed into Cole's huge sweating shoulder, he might have laughed out loud with what little remained of his power to breathe.

"Let him up, Cole," Harry Younger ordered.

When Cole released him, the Colonel gave him a hand, and somewhat shakily he rose to his feet.

"Don't feel badly, John," he said, resting a hand on his shoulder. "You gave him a good fight."

"Yeah, John," Richard was saying. "What you ought to know is nobody around here can beat him. He took all comers this year at the fair. Didn't you, little brother?" He pounded a playful fist into Cole's shoulder.

Cole said nothing in reply. He was grinning a little sheepishly as he said to his cousin, "You surely made me sweat, John. Guess they know something about wrestling in Texas."

John didn't have a chance to reply, for Margaret was suddenly reproaching her brother.

"Oh, Cole, look what you did!" She had come over to her cousin and noticed a long gash in his shoulder made by a small sharp stone as Cole was driving him along the ground. "Oh, and look!" She stepped around him and found more lacerations on his back.

"Just some scratches, Margaret," her cousin said, a little embarrassed by her concern.

"Pretty nasty," Harry Younger remarked and frowned at Cole.

"I'm surely sorry about that, John," Cole said, and John could tell that he was sincere. But it wasn't enough for his sister.

"You're a beast, Cole," she said, flashing an angry look at him.

At that, the two wrestlers grinned at each other and chuckled. She was beautiful in her rage, John was thinking, thankful he wasn't on the receiving end of it.

"Come with me, Johnny," she commanded him. As she grasped him by the wrist and started to lead him away, he looked back at his other cousins and shrugged. They looked at him and then at each other and were obviously suppressing amusement at their sister's outburst, as well as at his apparent helplessness in her grasp.

She led him about two hundred yards to where a little creek flowed slowly between grassy willow-shaded banks. Then she made him sit down on the bank, knelt beside him, and with one of the towels that had been covering a food basket began washing off his scratches.

"Awful, downright awful what he did to you!" she exclaimed, still incensed. "I'll never forgive him for this."

"Oh surely you will," he said, grinning but also wincing a little at the touch of the cold wet towel on his raw marks. Vowing she'd "never forgive" was one of his little sister's favorite ways of expressing her rage about one thing or another. " 'Cause Cole and I were just having a little fun. . . ." He started to go on but had to wince again. "He didn't hurt—"

"Sorry." Her touch became more gentle. "I mean it, Johnny. I'll never forgive anyone who hurts you."

He turned to look at her, and she dropped her eyes to the grass in front of her knees, biting down on her lower lip as she did. She seemed to be blushing, but he guessed it was the midday sun heightening the natural glow of her olive-gold skin.

"You don't hardly know me," he said.

At this she raised her eyes and regarded him thoughtfully.

"Yes I do," she replied. Then apparently something occurred to her, for suddenly she got up.

"Come on. You've worked enough for today. My brothers are using you like one of their Negroes."

"Honest, Margaret, I don't mind. I came here to help with the harvest."

But she wasn't listening. They went back to where the men and boys were either still eating or sprawled out in the shade of trees and bushes, letting their midday meal settle. She had no trouble obtaining her father's permission for the two of them to leave the harvest for a couple of hours. He gathered that there was precious little her father would ever refuse her.

They set out across a freshly plowed field, stepping awkwardly among the black, shiny clods and occasionally disturbing large black crows engaged in their own harvest of earthworms. Beyond the field was a peach orchard, its leaves bright orange and about to fall and the ground beneath it carpeted with small white aster blossoms. Just before they entered the orchard Margaret paused to look around her. Closing her eyes and drawing in her breath she again commanded him, as she had the night of the ball:

"Listen."

Half expecting her to recite more poetry, he listened. From across the field he could hear the sounds of the corn harvest, and high overhead a V of ducks calling to each other as they headed south. Margaret said nothing. After a moment of listening, she grasped his hand and led him through the orchard. Beyond the orchard was a hardwood forest, which they entered by way of a path that seemed not to be much used. Copper and russet oak leaves crunched beneath their feet. Beside the path were clumps of bittersweet hung with bright red berries and various flowers he couldn't name, and she did. She seemed to know them all.

"That's Indian pipe," she said, pointing to one plant. "Some folks call it ghost plant. Those blue ones over there are lobelia."

He noticed how she moved along the path—not with mincing ladylike steps but with a long easy springing stride. Clearly she was at home in these woods as much as in her father's mansion.

After maybe three-quarters of a mile they came to a wide shallow pond, its shallowness concealed by the bright blue October sky it mirrored. Except for one marshy spot, it was surrounded on every side by crimson-and-yellow-leaved hardwoods.

"Look," she said, stopping him suddenly.

He looked but saw nothing at first. Then, as she pointed toward the marshy area, he made out the delicately majestic form of a blue heron fishing among the reeds.

"I was hoping we'd see him. I usually do when I come here."

"You come here often?"

"Yes."

"Alone?"

"Yes." Then she added, "I come here to be alone."

"Why did you bring me here, then?" he wanted to know. Back home in Texas he'd had a few secret retreats that he shared with no one, not even Lucy McMaster.

She looked at him and smiled, a little shyly, but didn't answer. Then she grasped his hand and led him toward the pond. There was a patch of dry matted grass beneath a sycamore and they seated themselves on it. He leaned back, propping himself on an elbow and stretching his long legs toward the water, and helped himself to a stem of the fragrant dry grass. She sat upright next to him with her legs tucked beneath her long skirts.

"Do you miss Texas a lot, Johnny?" she asked.

"Not all that much," he answered truthfully. "Missouri has a lot to offer."

"Bet you miss your family, though, your mama and sisters and your brother."

"Well, I surely did when I first came here. Thought I was near dying of homesickness. Getting to know you folks has made a lot of difference, though. You've treated me like family."

"You are family, Johnny. The Youngers are your blood kin, even if I'm not."

Startled, he looked up at her. Knowing she'd startled him, she grinned and said, "God's truth Johnny. I'm not

your kin. Papa and Mama gave me their name, but I'm
not really their daughter."

"How . . . ?"

"They made me their daughter near twelve years ago,
after Mama had a little girl stillborn. She wanted another
girl mighty badly, and Papa brought me to her."

"How . . . ?"

"He found me with Preacher Herbert and his family
over at Blue Springs. There used to be a trading post just
outside of town before all the Indians got moved out to
the Nations. My real daddy was a trader there. His name
was Villon. He was a Frenchman who came down from
Canada. My real mama was the daughter of a princess.
They called her—my grandmama—Hayne Hudjihini,
which means the Eagle of Delight. Her husband was
chief of the Oto people, but he died, and my grandmama
married a white man by the name of Steiner. Mama
called herself Villon till my father left her, then she took
her own name back."

"Well," John Ringgold replied carefully, "that's mighty
interesting. What happened to your real mama?"

"She died two years after I was born. Of the smallpox.
The man who was my father went out to the Nations with
the Indians and left us both with my granddaddy. I can't
remember my father at all, but I do remember my granddaddy. He had a big dark bushy beard with some silver in
it and the bluest eyes I've ever seen. He used to hold me
in front of him on his horse and sing songs in a deep
rumbly voice that made me laugh, even though I couldn't
understand a word because he sang in a language I didn't
know. The Herberts told me he was Jewish, and when he
was very young he came from Germany. He was a student at a university and left Germany on account of some
trouble, something to do with politics. I was four when
he died, and the Herberts took care of me till the Youngers adopted me."

John was noticing now how very different from the
Youngers she looked, and he remembered how Frank
Marion had nearly blurted out half drunkenly that one
could see the beauty of the Eagle of Delight in Margaret.
Except for the fair hair that came, he guessed, from her
German-Jewish ancestors, she looked like an Indian prin-

cess. Her French-Canadian father had, likely, passed on
a little more Indian blood of his own.

He was deeply moved by what she had told him and by
her trust in revealing to him what the family tried to
conceal in order to protect her, he guessed, from the
prejudices of the fearful and ignorant. Missouri was tame
now, but they were still close enough to the frontier for
the effects of old fears and hatreds to manifest themselves. Wanting to share something with her, perhaps to
replace the now vanished tie of blood kinship, he said:

"I've got German blood in me, too. My daddy told me
that his people came from Germany, from up around the
North Sea somewhere. They changed their name to
Ringgold when they moved down into Georgia from Penn-
sylvania. Their real name sounded kind of like Ringgold
in German, Rinegold or something. He told me there
was a story behind the name, a legend sort of, about
maidens guarding a treasure."

"Really, Johnny? I know that story. It's in a book I
have that's all full of beautiful pictures of warriors in
armor and gods. Maybe they should have named you
Siegfried," she suggested brightly, looking him up and
down as though measuring him for a suit of armor.

"John'll do just fine, thanks," he answered, chuckling
a little.

"If they'd called you Siegfried," she went on excitedly,
"then maybe I would have been Brunhild, and you would
have released me from my enchantment with your magic.
Only . . ."

"Only what?" he wondered, trying to remember the
legend as his father had related it.

"Only I wouldn't want to marry the king of Burgundy."

"Why not?" he replied, still trying to piece out the
story from memory. "Wouldn't that make you a queen?"

"But I'd still need the magic of Siegfried," she said,
looking down at him in a way that reminded him of Lucy
McMaster the first time they met by the big pool. Maybe
it was because it was the same kind of place, a still pond
and a soft grassy bank that seemed to be part of an
enclosed little world within the sheltering woods. And
again the woman seemed to invite him with warm, trusting eyes. Only now he wasn't quite so innocent. The
frustrated hopeless yearning of a boy had been replaced

by the hunger of a man to taste again what he had known. Still, in spite of the throbbing and the familiar delicious aching that worked its way down from his loins into his legs and began to turn his bones to jelly, he drew away from Margaret.

"Guess we'd better be getting back," he said, starting to rise.

But she held him still, grasping his sleeve with her delicate fingers and holding him down as firmly as Cole's brawny arms had held him earlier.

"They'll be wondering, your daddy and brothers . . ." he said weakly, uttering words without feeling, as though from a head unconnected to his body. And as she shut his mouth with hers, putting her arms around his neck, the unuttered words remained in his mind: . . . trust me. They trust . . .

The sense of betrayal did not leave him, and it grew as he became aware of Margaret's innocence. Beyond the first kiss, which she had initiated, he was the initiator. He could tell that what he did with his mouth, what Lucy had taught him, was unfamiliar to her. But she learned quickly, responding with her own mouth. When he brushed her collarbone lightly with his lips and softly kissed the side of her neck, she tilted her head back, exposing the long golden curve of her throat.

"Johnny . . ." she whispered.

And as his palm touched her breast, moving lightly in a circular motion, she whispered his name again, almost sobbing it in a way that made him still more aware that he was the initiator, the betrayer. A spasm of guilt caused him to stop the movement of his hand, and he started to draw back from her, but then she clasped his hand tightly to her breast and covered his mouth with her lips. And now the sense of guilt and betrayal that had inhibited him began to fuel his overpowering desire. He began to fumble with the buttons on the back of her dress and she was helping him, when they were both suddenly frozen by a terrifying sound. From somewhere across the pond, from a ridgetop close to a mile away but sounding much closer rolling across the water, came the sound of a rifle shot.

She drew back from him then, and they looked at each other fearfully.

"A hunter," he said and glanced in the direction of the sound. "I don't think he sees us."

"We'd better go," she said.

He nodded and shut his eyes for an instant against the agony of frustrated desire. Then he stood up and gave her his hand. As he helped her refasten the buttons of her dress, he found the sight and touch of her golden back excruciating. When the last button was secured, she turned and clung to him, nestling her head against his chest. But when he tried to kiss her, she shook her head and pulled away. Wordlessly they walked back through the woods. He was feeling utterly wretched, his frustration mingling with guilt and a terrible fear that he might have ruined a precious friendship. At the edge of the woods, he stopped her, blurting out:

"Margaret, I'm sorry."

She looked sideways at him then, and he wished that he could read her expression. She was regarding him with that same quizzical appraising smile she had when they met in Liberty. Her eyes were warm and sympathetic, but there was also curiosity in them.

"Don't be, Johnny," she said, kissing him lightly on the lips.

Remembering the boy's feelings, the man Ringo smiles to himself.

"It was a good thing," he writes, "that her daddy had already planned to send her back that very week to the finishing school in St. Louis. He never lived to see us become lovers, and I seriously doubt that it would have been something he could have accepted. For some reason, the fact that she was about to leave didn't come up until that evening at supper, and I was hard put to conceal my unhappiness. Whenever I looked at Margaret, I caught her watching me, but then she'd look away, and I remembered what Lucy said about how poorly I hid my feelings.

"The next day, as I was about to ride back to Liberty, she followed me out to the stable and watched from just outside the stall as I saddled Blaze. He was, I recall, unusually accommodating as I smoothed out the saddle blanket on his back and got ready to heave on the saddle."

"I'll write to you from St. Louis," she said.

John didn't answer right away, having most of his

attention absorbed then by the big restive animal, who seldom accepted anything on his back without at least some token resistance.

"Will you answer my letters?" she asked, sounding a little anxious.

Still absorbed in the business of getting the saddle right, he did not reply. When the cinch had been tightened, he finally answered, in an unintentionally offhand way:

"Oh, sho'ly."

"Well, don't bother if it's going to be any trouble for you," she said, sounding irritated and a little hurt. When he turned to her, he was amazed to see her dark eyes luminous with the beginnings of tears. He quickly let himself out of the stall and took her in his arms.

"Course I'll answer your letters," he said soothingly. "Only I don't suppose you'll have much time to write me once all those fellows in St. Louis find out about you."

This prompted a scornful little laugh from Margaret.

"Don't worry about that, Johnny. This school is run by Catholic sisters who do whatever they can to make us girls live their way of life. About the end of last May I thought I was a sister. All I needed was a black habit and some beads."

He laughed at the thought of Margaret in such a costume and also with a degree of relief that her finishing school was apparently very different from that of Lucy McMaster in Vicksburg.

"I'll be back here for Christmas. You'll be here then, won't you?"

"If your daddy invites me," he said.

"Of course he will, Johnny. You're already like one of his sons."

It warmed him to hear her say this, but it also revived his sense of guilt and betrayal, so that when she raised her lips to him, he resisted the impulse to show her the passion he had shown the day before. He touched her lips as softly as he would have embracing one of his sisters. But Margaret was not his sister, nor would she accept the mild warmth of brotherly affection. Her ardent response to the touch of his lips instantly reawakened everything he had felt the day before.

"That's so you won't forget about me while I'm off in St. Louis," she said.

"Not likely I'll do that," he whispered, holding her gently and brushing her hair with his lips. Just for an instant, he wondered how it was that he could find himself involved again so soon with a woman who was forbidden and who dared not reveal what she felt for him. It had occurred to him that whatever Lucy McMaster felt for him was intensified, or even made possible, by the danger of discovery. Maybe it was the same with Margaret.

Margaret's departure for St. Louis did not make his visits to the Younger farm less frequent. Whenever his studies and the tutoring of Andy Hockensmith permitted, he would spend a few days with his cousins. There were more foot races and wrestling matches, as well as several hunting excursions. Cole had a passion for hunting, and John, who had learned to hunt on the prairie out of the necessity of supplementing what a small dirt farm produced, was happily initiated into the rite of hunting in the game-rich Missouri woods and fields. At first, he lacked the shotgun skills of his cousins, for it had not been possible at home to waste ammunition practicing. But having to get close to his quarry—antelope, sage grouse, or rabbit—over ground that offered little cover had forced him to acquire more than one of the hunter's arts. The abundant cover of these green woods enabled him to virtually disappear. Occasionally, when he and Cole would separate to drive deer toward each other, he would be unable to resist playing the prank of moving up to within arm's reach of his cousin before the latter had even an inkling of his presence.

"Dammit, John!" Cole shouted, whirling with his gun ready, the first time he was surprised in this way. "You move like a damn ghost. Sure you ain't part catamount?"

"Could be," he said, laughing at Cole's amazed expression. "Where I come from, mere humans don't survive."

That autumn and winter Ringo remembers as the happiest seasons of his life, in spite of Margaret's absence. She wrote to him frequently, long entertaining letters about St. Louis and about conditions in her "prison house."

"It's like all there is to being a lady is doing what you're told, like a good little soldier," she complained in one letter. "If I wanted to be a soldier, I'd disguise myself as a man and enlist in the army. I don't want to be

a soldier, and I surely don't want to be a nun. I want to
be walking through the woods to my secret place with
you, my dear friend. These sisters won't even let me read
Keats' poems. Two of them came into my room and
found my book open to where Porphyro and Madelaine
escape from dwarfish Hildebrand and the others. Maybe
that's what they didn't like. Or maybe it was what he said
about the old Beadsman telling off his thousand aves till
he slept among his ashes cold. Anyway they took it away,
my book, but they can't take those poems out of my head
or my heart, and I can still share them with you, my
dearest friend—

> "And there shall be for thee all soft delight
>   That shadowy thought can win,
> A bright torch, and a casement ope at night,
>   To let the warm Love in!"

John Ringgold cherished these letters, reread each one
so many times that it was committed to memory, so that
later, even after they fell into the hands of a Yankee
interrogator who was trying to torture information out of
him, he still had them in his heart. His own letters to her
were, he thought, dull and uninteresting by comparison,
but if he delayed in responding to her letters, she became
bitterly reproachful:

"You can't stop writing to me, Johnny. You just can't.
I need your letters. I'll go mad in this place if I don't hear
from you!"

At Christmastime she came home, and he was sustained during the ordeal of his examinations by the knowledge that he would be seeing her again. As soon as his
last examination was finished, he set out for Independence, risking disaster on the mud- and ice-slicked roads
as he gave Blaze his head. In an almost unrecognizable,
mud-spattered condition, he arrived at the Younger farm
two days before Christmas.

"You're here! What took you so long? I thought you
weren't coming. I thought maybe you'd decided to go
back to Texas," she said in her delightfully exasperating
way, hugging him in spite of his filthy condition.

"I'll never be a doctor if I don't take a few examinations," he tried to explain.

"I know, Johnny, I know," she said. "It's just that . . . God I've missed you!"

As he peeled off the mud in a steaming hot bath poured by one of the house servants, he savored the happiness of being with her again, if only for a few days. It was, he thought, just as well that it was too cold to be walking much outside, for they would have to be discreet. Just as well that the pond where they had begotten a memory that tormented him ceaselessly must be frozen over now. He would, he told himself, be satisfied with the sweet harmless pleasure of her company, surrounded by all the other Youngers.

At supper that evening there was another visiting relative, a cousin of Mrs. Younger's by the name of Jack Fenton, who had come down from Jackson County on his way to Osceola in St. Clair County. Over brandy and cigars, after the women had excused themselves, Fenton related news of some recent Jayhawker activity in Jackson County. He told them how Morgan Walker, a very wealthy farmer whom the Youngers knew, had managed to foil an attempt to jayhawk his slaves.

"If't waren't for that fella Quantrill, he'd o' lost more'n his niggers. They was fixin' to take all his horses, too, an' mules, an' money, an' then maybe kill him besides."

"Who is this Quantrill?" Harry Younger wanted to know.

"Well, as a matter o' fact," Fenton began, coughing a little on his cigar smoke, "I met Mr. Quantrill at Thorndike's general store in Blue Springs. Pleasant sort. You'd never take him for a killer. He had a most interestin' story to tell about why he led those niggerlovers into a trap. Seems he's originally from Maryland an' came to Kansas by way of Ohio with his older brother. They was goin' out to California, but one night while they was camped along the Cottonwood River, a gang o' Jayhawkers jumped 'em, killed the brother an' left Quantrill wounded to die there. An Indin found him an' took care o' him. When he recovered, he swore he'd hunt down every one o' those jayhawkin' devils. He said the three who went with him to jayhawk Walker's niggers was part o' the same gang."

"Funny they didn't recognize him," Frank Marion remarked skeptically.

"Guess it was too dark to see that night in Kansas," Fenton replied. "Anyway, he talked these three into walkin' in from Kansas with him, said they'd find all the mounts they could steal at Walker's farm. Then, while they was waitin' in the woods for it to get dark, Quantrill went in to scout the place alone. He found Morgan's boy Andy an' told him all about what was goin' to happen. When he come back later leadin' the Jayhawkers, the Walkers was ready for 'em. Andy had rounded up some neighbors to help with the ambush. Quantrill stayed in the house to cover Morgan, he said. When the other three come out to help themselves to the niggers an' horses, the neighbors was ready with their shotguns. John Tatum killed one of 'em on the spot. The other two ran through somethin' like a wall o' buckshot that wounded one of 'em. Next day a nigger belongin' to George Rider come upon those two out in the woods an' told Rider. Serves them damn abolitionists right, I say. That nigger knew what was good for him."

"What happened then? Where was this man Quantrill?" Harry Younger wanted to know.

"He was stayin' with the Walkers. Morgan was so grateful for what he done, you know he give Quantrill fifty dollars, a saddle an' a mighty fine black horse—pure Kentucky stock."

"What happened to the Jayhawkers?" Cole prompted.

"Oh, them," Fenton replied, emptying his brandy glass and nodding to a black servant to refill it. "Well now, when that nigger told Rider, Rider told the Walkers. Quantrill went with the Walkers to where they was hidin' in the woods. Morgan hisself got one of 'em with his shotgun when he went for his pistol, an' Quantrill finished off the wounded one."

"Sounds like a damned sorry business," Harry Younger remarked with disgust. "I don't think I'd trust this Quantrill."

"What do you mean, Daddy?" Cole responded. "Sounds to me like he did us all a real favor. That's three less Jayhawkers we have to worry about."

"He had the trust of those men he led into that trap. Somehow he had their trust or they wouldn't have taken the risk of walking in there from Kansas."

"You're too suspicious, big brother," Frank Marion said, nodding at his glass for more brandy.

"No, Frank, let's just say that I know men, and I know what it takes to get them to do things. Those three abolitionists had to have reason to believe that Quantrill was one of them."

Fenton reentered the conversation. "Well now, colonel, I might as well tell you that some other folks thought the same way at the time. The county sheriff brought Quantrill into Independence for questionin' an' made no charges against him, but some o' the folks there wanted to string him up anyway, just on account o' his havin' come in from Kansas with a bunch of abolitionists. There was a big mob outside the hotel where he was stayin', an' Andy Walker stood 'em off, said that if they lynched Quantrill it'd be over his dead body."

John Ringgold listened with mixed feelings to this account of betrayal and bloodshed. On the one hand, he tried to see it the way Cole did, tried to feel some satisfaction over the demise of enemies from Kansas bent on theft and possibly murder. On the other hand, he was persuaded by the words of Harry Younger that the Jayhawkers were probably the victims of treachery.

The Jayhawker troubles were all but forgotten in the ensuing days of festivity. There was another ball at the Youngers' between Christmas and New Year's and what seemed to be an endless stream of visitors, including some more cousins from up near Liberty, the Jameses. For the first time, John met Frank James, a soft-spoken young man about his own age who liked to talk about the Bible. He also met Frank's kid brother, Jesse, a bright-eyed youngster just turned thirteen. With all these visitors, John had even less time with Margaret than he had anticipated. He tried to conceal his disappointment, but she voiced it for both of them.

"I wish we could get away from here for a little while, Johnny. I love my family, but I need to be alone with you."

They finally did manage to escape one afternoon when Margaret persuaded her family to let him drive her in a buggy over to a neighbor's for a visit. There was snow on the ground and the streams were half iced over. Both of them were warmly dressed and they shared a Hudson's Bay blanket across their knees, as well as a buffalo robe over their shoulders. In the sunlit thickets the frost-crystaled trees and bushes shone brilliantly, and occasionally they could hear the piteous chirp of a bird enduring the cold. From time to time, John pointed out the tracks of deer and other animals as he noticed them in the snow, but otherwise they said little, and they had not gone more than two miles from the Youngers' farm when Margaret asked him to stop the buggy.

"Let's walk a little," she said.

He helped her down into the snow and secured the team to a bare sapling. Then she watched as he rolled up the blanket and robe and slipped them over his arm.

"Might want to sit someplace," he said, hearing a nervousness in his voice.

She smiled at him in an unusual, shy sort of way and said nothing. As he gave her his arm, she leaned against his shoulder. Walking in the snow was easier than in the muddy patches, for they both had fur-lined overshoes, his having been borrowed from Cole.

Next to a brook that ran gurgling between banks of ice, he spread out the buffalo robe and the blanket. As he put his arms around her, she drew his head down and kissed him hungrily. Then, as they sank to their knees and he began to help her out of her coat, she said:

"You'll be gentle with me, Johnny, I know you will."

"Of course I will," he murmured gently as he clumsily undid catches with fingers that seemed to have grown to the size of fence posts.

"It's the first time for me."

"Me too," he lied. He regretted having to lie to her, but he was grateful to Lucy for the gentleness she had taught him. Gently, unhurriedly, he prepared Margaret to become one with him. Gently he entered, whereupon she gasped a little and began to moan. Her moaning became a great sobbing cry that alarmed him at first when he saw tears streaming down her cheeks, but then her sobbing gave way to laughter, and he began to laugh with her, even until the moment when he died within her. Feeling the moment, she stroked his damp hair and kissed him.

The flesh of both of them shone with sweat in spite of

the temperature, and he carefully covered her nakedness and his own with the buffalo robe. Beneath them was the Hudson's Bay blanket, and beneath it was the snow. They dared not remain there long for fear of pneumonia, but John wondered for a moment or two if he had the strength to get up.

"I knew it would be you, Johnny, ever since that day by the pond," she said. "But I never guessed it would be like this. And in the snow!" She laughed. "It could've been a driving rain and I wouldn't have known it. I don't think I'd have felt a drop."

"Let's try it sometime," he said, laughing. "In the rain, I mean."

That put the both of them into a giggling fit, not unlike the one they got into the night John was initiated into the Virginia reel. When her giggling subsided, Margaret nestled her head beneath his chin. He stroked the gleaming bronze head tenderly with his fingertips. In a minute or two they would be vulnerable to a chill, and he was about to suggest that they get on some clothes, but Margaret spoke first.

"Johnny, that was more wonderful than I can tell you. I was wondering if . . ." She seemed strangely embarrassed, wouldn't raise her head to look at him. "I mean, can you . . . ?"

Understanding fully, he bent and softly kissed every feature of her beautiful face. Then he began to love her again, using devices Lucy had taught him that he hadn't used the first time for fear of repelling her. Once again she wept and laughed, and the threat of a chill vanished as they let the warm love in.

What puzzled him a little that evening, though he didn't give it much thought, was the total absence of any feeling resembling guilt. Their lovemaking had a rightness about it that wouldn't permit guilt or even any worry that discovery would mean the end of his relationship with this family he had come to love as his own.

It was a good thing, Ringo reflects, that Margaret was packed off again to St. Louis after the holidays, though at the time he was wrenched by a terrible longing and fear that he would never see her again.

"I'll be home in May, Johnny. Be here, please," she

begged him as she was about to be driven by her father to the stage in Independence.

He tried to assure her, feeling his own eyes well up in response to her tears. "Nothing'll stop me. You know that. I'll be here in May if I have to walk from Liberty."

When he returned to Liberty and she was once again in the care of her "jailers," they maintained an even more frequent correspondence than before. Her letters were still entertaining, amusing accounts of her struggles with elocution, French, and black-habited tyranny, but now they contained utterances that could transport him with joy even as they filled him with a hopeless yearning to be with her.

"You are the first man I've ever had, Johnny, and I truly believe you'll be the last. I've relived that afternoon a hundred thousand times, and I'll always be yours, my sweet darling."

Reading this in a letter he received near the end of March, he nearly climbed on Blaze and rode to St. Louis. Only a long, difficult inner struggle, during which he reminded himself that he was as yet nothing but a poor farm boy who had become a penniless student and who wouldn't, if he didn't master his chemistry, biology and the rest, ever be anything else, prevented him from riding to visit the woman he loved.

"The only woman I ever really loved," Ringo murmurs, still aching twenty-one years later.

He consoled himself that time with a weekend visit to the Younger farm, where he was warmly welcomed as always. Within minutes of his arrival, however, he discovered that things were not as they had been, that the prosperous, peaceful world of the Youngers had been invaded.

"Jayhawkers!" Cole practically spat the word out. "Rode right in here yesterday and took some of our best stock, 'long with one of our niggers."

"How many were there?"

"Six maybe. Daddy and Uncle Frank and Cyrus held 'em off till Richard and Jim heard the shooting and came in from the hemp field. I was over in Harrisonville, dammit!" he said, shaking his head. "I thought we'd be spared those devils, but I guess I was wrong. We're just too close to Kansas."

That evening there was a dance in Independence. Because the Jayhawkers might still be in the neighborhood, Cole decided not to attend it, as he had planned. Two of his little sisters, Becky and Ida Mae, who had expected him to drive them there in the buggy, were very disappointed.

"You go on ahead, Cole," John urged him. "I'll stand guard here with Jim and Richard." Any opportunity to do something for the Youngers he jumped at eagerly.

"Sure you wouldn't mind, John? Sure you don't want to go yourself?"

"I'm sure. Truth is I'm not much for dancing."

"Maybe that'll change when Margaret comes back," Cole said with a grin that made his cousin wonder if maybe the Youngers weren't a little wiser than he had thought.

After Cole and the girls drove off that evening, John took the shotgun Richard gave him and went to the stable to join Cyrus guarding the horses. The handsome mulatto was reading by lantern light with a shotgun across his knees, and he looked up as John Ringgold walked into the stables.

"Evening, Cyrus."

"Evening, Mr. Ringgold," he replied, regarding John with an enigmatic half-smile that John had come to see was his habitual expression. Next to his left eye was some plaster over a bit of swelling. John remembered having overheard Cole and Richard talking about when Cyrus would be "ready again." They had been speaking quietly, just out of earshot of their father, and apparently they had been exploiting the mulatto's fighting talent somewhere in the neighborhood. When John moved into the lantern light he saw that Cyrus was reading a Bible, and he remembered that literacy among slaves was rare.

"How do you feel about Jayhawkers, Cyrus?" he asked and was not certain why he asked. He guessed, knew from what he had seen of the mulatto's proud manner, that Cyrus wouldn't bother to answer him in any sort of ingratiating darky way.

"They're enemies of my people, Mr. Ringgold. If they come back here, I'll use this again, just like I did yesterday." And he patted the breach of the shotgun across his knees.

"But they'd make you free, wouldn't they?"

"I'm free," Cyrus answered shortly and then repeated, "they're enemies of my people."

"Who are your people?" John couldn't help asking.

The mulatto didn't answer right away. His half-smile tightened and his long dark eyes narrowed a little as he regarded the cousin from Texas. Then he said:

"The Youngers are my people."

Driven by an overpowering curiosity, John was about to probe a little more, but at that moment a woman, a female slave, came into the stable. Her head was covered slave-fashion, but as her face was revealed in the lamplight, John found himself momentarily bereft of the power of speech. She was quite simply the most beautiful human creature he had ever seen. Her exquisitely sculptured face reminded him of a picture he'd seen on a wall of the college library, the portrait bust of an ancient Egyptian queen, consort of the king who had tried to impose worship of the sun-god. Her narrow, delicate high-bridged nose and her sensitive mouth were queenly, as were the large, fine-lidded dark eyes that flashed defiantly, almost disdainfully at him in the lamplight. She must have been close to six feet tall, and she held herself as proudly erect as a queen, even though at the moment she was about the business of a servant. In her hands was a covered tray upon which she bore Cyrus's supper. She knelt beside him on the straw and uncovered it. As she handed him a steaming plate, Cyrus closed his Bible and set it aside, along with the shotgun. She regarded him intently as he began to eat, and he paused to look at her with an expression John had never seen on his face. The proud, almost derisive half-smile had softened, and there was unmistakable tenderness in the way he looked at her. He seemed to have utterly forgotten John's presence, and the boy from Texas remained rooted where he stood, full of wonder and perhaps a little dazed by the spectacle of their beauty together.

"Guess I'll take a look around," he heard himself say, as he moved in an almost trancelike state toward the stable door. Cyrus nodded wordlessly in reply but did not take his eyes from the woman's face.

The cool evening air quickly resharpened John's senses, and he catfooted from point to point around the Younger farm, shotgun at the ready and eyes flicking from side to side. The slave cabins were set back along a creek nearly two hundred yards from the house. Between the house and the cabins was a fringe of hardwoods, the most likely cover for an attacking party, and John went through it carefully. At the edge of these woods, well removed from both the house and the slave cabins, was a house he had never noticed before. Half again as large as any of the slave buildings, it was, unlike the typical slave cabin, firmly set upon a stone foundation. The light inside shone through brightly colored window curtains, and there were chairs and a hammock on the covered porch. From inside he could hear the sound of an infant crying. The crying went on for a minute or two until suddenly he heard, from the direction of the stable, the sound of running feet. A dark figure ran up onto the porch and flung open the door, and just for an instant, in the frame of the lighted doorway, he saw the woman he had seen in the stable. The child's crying quickly subsided into a relieved and contented gurgling.

Finishing his rounds, John stopped at the house, encountering Richard on the darkened porch. The barrels of Richard's shotgun gleamed in the light of the rising moon.

"See anything?"

"Not a thing."

Richard walked to the edge of the porch and spat over the railing.

"I reckon they're back in Kansas by now, damn their souls, devils!"

John said, "I didn't know Cyrus had a wife."

"Ain't she some!" Richard responded with a low whistle. "Daddy bought her for him at an auction in Charleston two years ago when he and Uncle Frank went back home for a visit. You know, she's straight from Africa, but she came from a different part, not from the west where they round up most of the darkies. Cyrus told us she's the daughter of a chief of one of those lion-hunting tribes in the interior. Some Arabs captured her and brought her out to the coast to sell."

"Cyrus told me he was free," John said, still nagged by curiosity.

"He told you right, John. He's had his papers since I

can remember. He could walk out of here tomorrow, only he'd rather stay."

"What about his wife?"

"Well, like I just told you, Daddy bought her for him. She belongs to him. But I don't guess she'd ever want to leave him anyhow. They sort of belong together, if you see what I mean."

"I surely do. They have a child, don't they?"

"Yeah," Richard answered shortly, and John sensed that his cousin had said all he wanted to say about Cyrus and his wife. The mulatto had called the Youngers his "people." The nature of the connection John could only imagine. It was obviously something not discussed openly, even with a cousin.

John was about to excuse himself to make another patrol, but suddenly the sound of pounding footsteps in the darkness caused them both to whirl with shotguns ready. A huge dark running figure with coattails flapping and no hat came up the driveway and bounded onto the porch.

"Who the hell . . . ?" Richard began, cocking the hammers of his shotgun.

"Don't shoot me, dammit!" the runner gasped.

John spoke up, recognizing the voice in spite of the exhausted gasping. "It's Cole, isn't it?"

"Yeah, it's me," Cole answered. He flung open one of the huge double doors and let himself be revealed in the light of the entranceway. Having, not two hours before, seen Cole so neatly attired and groomed in a fine suit tailored to his big frame, driving his little sisters off in the Youngers' best buggy, John was amazed at his condition. His cravat and collar had been discarded and his shirt was dark with sweat. There was a rip in one trouser leg and bloodstains around it. As they soon found out, Cole had been running through the woods, hadn't dared show himself on the roads.

They followed him into the hallway and were met by Harry Younger and his brother. The older men had been sitting in the parlor while the Colonel's sons stood guard, but Harry Younger had his old pistol beside him, and now he emerged with it in one hand and a volume of Prescott's *Conquest of Mexico* in the other. Frank Marion had a cup in his hand.

"Cole! My God, what happened?"

"I can't stay, Daddy. They'll be here soon looking for me."

"Who will? What's going on? What happened to your leg?"

"My leg's fine. Just a scratch. I don't have time to explain. Somebody's got to fetch Becky and Ida Mae. They're still at Harper's where the dance was."

"I'll do that," John volunteered.

"Thanks, John," Cole said, patting him gratefully on the arm as he went to the gun cabinet standing near the entranceway and pulled open one of the drawers beneath the glass-doored rifle and shotgun racks. In it he found a cap-and-ball pistol, which he took out and began to load.

"Cole, you've got to tell me what this is about," his father demanded.

Cole looked at his father and nodded, accepting the necessity of an explanation.

"There's a militia officer. His name's Walley. A captain, I think. He's trying to kill me."

"Why for the love of God?"

"I cut in on him at the dance."

"What the hell!" Frank Marion exclaimed. "Since when did somebody try to kill somebody over somethin' like that?" He raised his cup and drained it.

"All I know," Cole replied, "is he tried to shoot me, creased me right here." And he pointed at the rip in his trouser leg. Cole went on to tell them in as few words as possible how, after he had cut in on Walley, the captain had called him aside.

" 'I'll make no trouble in here, farmer boy,' he said to me, 'but I'll be waitin' for you outside.' Dick Harper overheard what he said to me, and he told me to watch out. He said Walley's downright vicious and not afraid of blood. Sure enough, when I came out of the dance he and another man jumped me. I whipped 'em both, but then Walley pulled out his pistol and took a shot at me. I couldn't get to the shotgun I had in the buggy, so I just took off running. I heard Walley yell to his friend, 'Go round up the men. We'll run him down.' So I stayed off the roads and got here fast as I could through the woods."

"Where are you going, Cole?" his father wanted to know. "You don't have to run from this man. We can stop him."

"No, sir, it's just better I disappear for a while. If I'm gone, the militia will leave you alone. I'll be back when things cool off a little."

"But where are you going?"

"Maybe it's better you don't know, Daddy."

"You'd better tell me right now," Harry Younger demanded, laying his hand on the pistol Cole was loading.

Cole gave in. "All right. You remember that man Quantrill? The one who led those Jayhawkers into that trap at Morgan Walker's?"

"Yes, I do. I said then that I wouldn't trust him."

"Well, from what I've been hearing he may be all right. He and Andy Walker've been leading a bunch of fellows who try to stop Jayhawkers from raiding Jackson County. They've been doing some pretty good work, so I hear."

Harry Younger was amazed. "You're going to join them?"

"Yes, sir. I can't live with having us be raided by Jayhawkers. If we don't strike back, they'll hit us again."

"So you're going to be a Border Ruffian, is that it?" his father asked, and there was disgust in his voice.

"No, sir, that's not it at all. If Quantrill's anything like that, I won't ride with him. Please, sir, I've got to leave now."

"All right, Cole," his father replied wearily. "You go on. Take Wellington. Chances are you're going to be going over a few fences. We'll take care of this man Walley, and we'll try to get your mother not to worry." Busheba Younger was then in Harrisonville caring for an ailing cousin.

Awkwardly, self-consciously, Cole Younger embraced his father, and there were tears in his eyes as he shook hands with his brother, his uncle and his Texas cousin.

"Take care of Margaret when she gets back, John," were Cole's parting words as he rode the hunter Wellington out of the stable. John called after him that he surely would look after her and the rest of the family as well.

"And God knows I sho'ly tried," Ringo murmurs, remembering. He writes:

"We met Walley that night not twenty minutes after Cole rode out. I was saddling Blaze to go and fetch the girls when I heard the sound of a large party of horsemen arriving. I called to Cyrus and he grabbed his shotgun. He handed me a pistol which I didn't know how to fire, having never handled one before, and the two of us ran out and took cover behind a picket fence near the porch. My cousin Harry was standing unarmed out on the top step of the porch with the lighted doorway behind him. I hesitate to say it was a damn fool thing to do, making such a target of himself while he could hardly see the men he was facing. I guess maybe he figured that somebody who needed a whole detachment of soldiers to settle his quarrel with another man must be a coward who'd back down if he was confronted."

Ringo remembers the confrontation as though it were happening at that moment. He and Cyrus were less than fifteen feet away from the mounted militiamen.

"We've come for Cole Younger," a stocky, round-faced officer shouted at the tall, erect figure on the porch.

"What do you want with him?" Harry Younger replied coolly.

"We've come to arrest him for attacking two officers of the Fifth Missouri Federal Militia."

"Are you one of those officers? Are you Captain Walley?"

"Matter of fact, I am. Who are you?"

"Colonel Henry Younger. I'm Cole's father. He tells me you're the ones who did the attacking."

"Well now, 'colonel,'" the stocky officer replied with a sneer, "if he told you that he's a—"

What prevented Walley from completing his sentence was the ominous clicking sound of four shotguns being cocked nearby in the darkness. One of them was next to John in the hands of Cyrus.

Richard Younger spoke up from behind a tree not ten feet away. "You're covered, captain. Best watch what you say about my brother."

The militiamen, eight of them, looked around nervously. Their pistols were holstered, and their carbines were still in their saddle scabbards. They'd been expecting to run down an unarmed man, and the prospect of facing buckshot out of the darkness clearly had little appeal.

"You'd best get on back to your post, captain," Harry Younger said.

Walley glanced around him, saw that his men were waiting for orders and wondering how he would handle this delicate, dangerous situation. He tried to save face with a little bluster.

"You haven't seen the last of us, 'colonel.' Your boy's going to be punished for what he did."

"We'll see who's going to be punished, captain," Harry Younger retorted. "I intend to report you to your commanding officer."

Walley didn't answer. He jerked his head at his men by way of ordering a retreat, and they wheeled about in the driveway. After they rode off into the night, Harry Younger's sons and his brother left their cover to join him on the porch. Frank Marion spoke first.

"That's a bad man, big brother. You're lucky he didn't have you blowed off this porch 'fore he knew we had him covered."

"He's a coward, Frank."

"Don't make no nevermind. It don't take a brave cottonmouth to bite a man."

Harry Younger sighed and nodded his agreement.

"You're right. We'd better get word to Cole to stay away until I've had a chance to straighten things out with Walley's superiors."

Later that evening, when he arrived in Independence to drive Becky and Ida Mae Younger home in the buggy, John Ringgold received another account of the evening's events and the character of Captain Walley.

"You tell Colonel Younger to watch out," Dick Harper cautioned. "Walley's a bad one, and Cole whipped hell out of him."

"How'd it happen?"

"Well now, there ain't no way we can keep the Federal Militia out of our dances, and most of 'em behave themselves, but I knew as soon as Walley came in that we were likely to have trouble. He'd had a little whiskey and you could tell he's one of those sawed-off runty kind of fellas that holds it against any fella that has a few inches on him. He asked Beth Tyree to dance. You know, she's kind of sweet on Cole, but she said yes anyhow 'cause everybody was dancing with everybody else. Came the

end of the dance, though, and Walley wouldn't let her
go. Made her dance the next one with him and the one
after that. She kept looking over at Cole in a pleadin'
sort of way, and finally he came over and cut in. That's
when Walley threatened him."

"What happened then?"

"When I heard what Walley said to him I took Cole
aside and told him he'd better leave. He agreed and I let
him out the back door. Then I brought out his sisters and
helped them into the buggy. But Walley and another
officer, a fellow as big as Cole, were hiding beside the
house. When Cole started to climb into his buggy, the big
one grabbed him from behind and held his arms while
Walley started in hitting him and kicking him where it
hurts. I was about to lend Cole a hand, but he took care
of those two all by himself. Getting kicked that way
must've made him mad. He peeled the big one off his
back and slammed his head into a porch post. Then he
grabbed Walley and started slapping him like you would
a kid who'd smart-mouthed you. When he got through
slappin' Walley, he picked him up and dropped him in
the horse trough. Then he started to get into his buggy
again, but Walley climbed out of the trough and ran over
to his horse. He pulled a gun out of his saddlebag and
took a shot at Cole. I guess you know the rest."

"Yeah, I'm just wondering if Walley's much of a threat
to Cole's family."

"I wouldn't be surprised, John. Ed Kincaid was just
telling me about him. Said he's one of the Federal officers folks suspected of helping out the Jayhawkers when
they come through this county. It seems funny how those
Kansas Jayhawkers know just which places to hit over
here, where they'll find the most to steal. Ed told me that
Walley killed a man where he was stationed before down
near Arkansas. He was cleared, but Ed heard that he'd
really done it. That's why I tried to get Cole out of here.
Yeah, if I was you, I'd tell all the Youngers to watch out."

John Ringgold did just that, and he wanted to stay and
help the Youngers watch out for their enemies, but his
cousin wouldn't hear of it.

"It's your future, John. You still want to be a doctor,
don't you? You go back to William Jewell and study.
We're warned and we can look out for ourselves."

So he rode back to Liberty and poured his energies into his studies. Tutoring Andy Hockensmith was becoming an ever more loathsome chore, but he consoled himself with the thought that he could find other work once the school year was over. In the meantime he was sustained by Margaret's letters. She told him how St. Louis was full of soldiers now, Germans in the home guard who didn't even speak English, and how everyone, even the sisters, was talking about the likelihood of war. He heard the same talk at William Jewell, where students and professors, mirroring the rest of Missouri's population, were divided into Unionists, conditional Unionists, and pro-secessionists. He didn't tell her about Cole's trouble, and he gathered from her letters that her family had decided not to tell her about that or the Jayhawker attack, probably for fear of her leaving St. Louis and coming home to help.

On the morning of April 13, John left the boarding-house early, as he usually did, and walked to William Jewell to attend his first class, which was Latin. He noticed groups of people on various corners in what appeared to be animated conversation, but he didn't stop to ask anyone about the reason for the excitement. As he entered the classroom and took his place, Professor Grimestone was writing on the blackboard: *Caesare duce, nihil timebimus.*

"Will you translate, please, Mr. Ringgold."

John studied the words a moment, then he said, "With Caesar the commander, we shall fear nothing."

"Very good, Mr. Ringgold. Perfectly correct. Though you could also say, *'Since* Caesar is the commander' or *'When* Caesar is the commander' or even *'If* Caesar is the commander,' we shall fear nothing.' This construction is called the 'ablative absolute,' and it is used—"

Professor Grimestone was interrupted at that moment by a student entering the classroom to hand him a note. The professor scowled at the interruption but thanked the student for the note. Then, as he read it, the little man paled visibly. The beads of sweat that always broke out on his hairless crown when he lectured became profuse, and he sat down behind his desk at the front of the classroom.

"God help us," he said, in a genuinely prayerful voice,

and rested his bald head in his hands. Then, aroused by the murmuring of the students in front of him, he took up the note and read it to them: "Yesterday morning at four-thirty, Fort Sumter in Charleston harbor was fired upon by batteries of the Confederacy. The bombardment is continuing."

"It's war, then," a student next to John blurted out.

The professor nodded sadly. "It's war all right. Civil war, God help us."

"Wasn't it Horace who said, *'Dulce et decorum est pro patria mori'?*" piped up a blond, freckled youngster who had frequently let the class know that he was pro-secession. Professor Grimestone looked at the boy and shook his head before answering.

"When Horace wrote that, Mr. Tyler, he wasn't thinking about civil war. He was in a civil war himself and he knew that there was nothing sweet or decorous about killing or dying at the hands of one's own countrymen."

"The South's my country," the boy retorted. "I'm ready to die for it."

Seeing the futility of any answer, the professor looked around at the room full of young faces, wondering perhaps how many of them would live to question Horace. It was, John was thinking, one of those moments for the professor to utter one of his favorite *sententiae*, but he did not. Instead, he simply rose to his feet and said, "Class dismissed."

Not all of Professor Grimestone's colleagues reacted as he did to the news that the war had begun. Mr. McGillivray, John's mathematics instructor, appeared the following week before his class in the uniform of a Confederate officer and demonstrated happily how some of the principles of geometry they had been learning could be applied on the battlefield, especially in the erection of defenses. John's biology teacher, on the other hand, announced that he was joining the Missouri Federal Militia at the end of the term, and he urged his students to do likewise.

John himself was completely undecided about what he would do if he was forced to choose sides. He would rather stay out of the war altogether, but if he had to choose, he would probably, influenced by Harry Younger's arguments against secession and his own private feelings about slavery, join the Federal army. He wondered how the Younger brothers would choose, wondered if they would remain under their father's influence now that the war had broken out. He also wondered how they were coping with the Jayhawkers and Captain Walley.

With these things on his mind and in his eagerness to see Margaret, who had already returned from St. Louis, it was all he could do to finish the term. At the end of the first week in June, he wrote his examinations and with no small relief gave Andy Hockensmith his last lesson.

"So long, teacher," the boy said handing him a jug. "You done a right fine job with me. Hope you and me don't wind up on different sides o' this war."

"You're a little young to be thinking about that, aren't you?" John replied, declining the jug.

"Not so young I can't kill me a few niggerlovin' abolitionists," the boy answered with a scornful laugh.

John's feeling that he would probably choose the Union side became considerably stronger then. He imagined Andy Hockensmith in a gray uniform, like that of his mathematics professor, charging across a field with others like him—wild-eyed, howling like wolves—in pursuit of a hapless Negro they were bent on lynching.

When he had finished his last examination, he cleared out his few belongings from the wretched boardinghouse, discarding what he couldn't fit into his saddlebags, and set out for Independence. He planned to spend a few days with the Youngers, then, with maybe a little help from his cousin Harry, find some summer work with one of the horse raisers in the area. But as he rode south toward Independence, he was repeatedly made aware that things were not as they had been, that a young man's options might soon be affected by what had taken place in April in Charleston harbor. Near Independence, he passed a company of young fellows marching along the road behind a man in a blue uniform with gold sergeant's stripes. Not long after that, he encountered another company, mounted, led by a bushy-bearded man in a gray tunic with gilt insignia on the collar.

The officer greeted him. "Hello, young fella."

"Hello, sir," John responded warily, noticing that the officer and most of the men with him were heavily armed.

"You look like a true son of Missouri," the officer began in the friendly fashion of one who wants something.

"Fact is, I'm from Texas," John replied shortly, wondering why he bothered to volunteer the information.

"Well, that's even better," the officer said, laughing expansively. "You're already in the Confederacy. How 'bout joining up with us? I'm Colonel Hayes, up here from Arkansas to recruit men from Missouri for the Confederacy."

John thought quickly. He said, "I plan to join the army back in Texas."

The officer looked a little skeptical, but he replied, "All right, young fella. See that you do that. This is no time for neutrality. Good luck to you."

After that encounter, John was even more eager to reach his destination, mainly because Margaret was waiting but also because he desperately needed the guidance of Harry Younger. What *was* he going to do? That rebel officer might well be right in saying that this was no time for neutrality. But was he ready to join the Union army? Harry Younger would help him to see the matter clearly, even as he helped Cole and his brothers straighten out their thinking.

He didn't arrive at Harry Younger's baronial farmhouse until well after dark, after a hard day's ride. Approaching the house, he was overjoyed to see Margaret out on the porch. At first he imagined that she was anticipating his arrival, but he soon found out that other concerns were foremost on her mind.

"Johnny. Oh my God, I'm glad to see you!"

"Came just as soon as I could," he said, hugging her tightly and then releasing her as her mother came out of the house.

"You didn't see my husband on the road, did you, John?"

"No, ma'am," he answered, sensing that the women were much alarmed by something.

"Now, Mama, I just know there's nothing to worry about," Margaret said, but she wasn't very convincing.

When they went into the house, the women told him how the Colonel, accompanied by his man Cyrus, had gone to see the Union commander at Harrisonville. The Youngers' troubles with Captain Walley had not ended with the departure of Cole, nor had their troubles with the Jayhawkers. Moreover, the two problems were apparently related.

"Jayhawkers took Papa's best team. You know, Johnny, those matched blacks?" Margaret said, and he nodded that he remembered the team.

"Well, right after they took them," she went on excitedly, "Cyrus told Papa that he saw a militia officer driving the team down the main street of Harrisonville big as life. Cyrus knows our horses better than anybody, and he swore it was them."

Busheba Younger spoke up angrily. "It was that Captain Walley, the one who came after Cole. It's because of him that my boy can't come home."

"Is Cole still with that fellow Quantrill?" John asked.

"As far as we know, he is," Margaret replied. "As soon as the war started, a lot of the boys around here joined Quantrill. They're going to fight for the South."

"How does Colonel Younger feel about that?" John wondered aloud.

"Papa's real upset about it, about Cole being a guerrilla. He says it would be bad enough if Cole were in the rebel army, but being a guerrilla with that man Quantrill makes it worse."

"John," said Mrs. Younger anxiously, "will you do us a favor and ride along the road to Harrisonville? I'm so worried I can't tell you. Harry said he'd be back before supper. Now it's close to ten o'clock."

John left immediately. The road to Harrisonville was illuminated by a full moon. He rode at a fast walk and after nearly an hour was at a point roughly midway between Harrisonville and the Younger farm. Suddenly, as he started to round a sharp turn between a pair of giant oaks, Blaze shied away from something in the road. John felt a shiver run across his shoulder blades as he saw that what was lying in the road was a pair of human figures. Full of dread, guessing what he might find, he dismounted and stood over the two forms.

Harry Younger was lying on his back in the middle of the road. His face was set in an expression of amazed outrage. In the middle of his white satin vest was a dark stain the size of a man's hand. Beneath the vest could be seen the butt of the old service pistol still stuck in his waistband. Next to Harry Younger, the mulatto Cyrus was lying facedown. His powerful arms were stretched out before him and his huge hands were clenched into fists. Nearly the entire back of his shirt was covered with bloodstains.

John felt himself choking with rage and horror. He sank to his knees beside his cousin's body and began to sob uncontrollably, weeping as he had not wept since the afternoon he found his father lying on the riverbank with a pistol in his hand.

After an indeterminable number of minutes passed, he was able to hear something besides his own choked sobbing. He heard a voice whispering to him from some bushes next to the road.

"Mistah Ringgold. That you, Mistah Ringgold?"

"Who is it?" he managed to reply.

"It's me, Jackie."

When Jackie emerged from the bushes, John recognized one of the Youngers' slaves. Jackie was about eighteen, around John's age, and the two of them had worked together during the corn harvest. Now he looked around him with wide frightened eyes, as though expecting to be attacked. Seeing nothing, he knelt beside John Ringgold and said:

"I seen it all, Mistah Ringgold. I seen it all."

"What did you see, Jackie? Who did this?" he asked, responding in the same low hushed tone.

"It was dat Cap'n Walley. He the one shot Colonel Younger."

"How do you know it was him?"

" 'Cause dat's what dem others, dem Jayhawkers called him."

Jackie told him how Colonel Younger, accompanied by Cyrus and himself had driven a buggy into Harrisonville. There he sought out Colonel Tipton, Walley's regimental commander, and demanded the return of his horses. Colonel Tipton then summoned the captain, who produced a bill of sale for the horses, which he allegedly acquired in Olathe, Kansas. Colonel Tipton had already reprimanded Walley for his conduct the night of the dance at Harper's, but now, perhaps because it was known that Cole Younger was with Quantrill, he chose to back up his subordinate. Harry Younger responded by telling the two officers that he would be visiting the district commander in Kansas City, who happened to be an old comrade with whom he'd fought in Mexico.

"Colonel Younger was plenty mad when he come out from talkin' to dat Colonel Tipton. He tol' Cyrus all about it, an' I hear 'cause I was sittin' right behind 'em on de back end o' de buggy. So we started out for home an' we got just dis far when dat Walley an' a bunch o' other men on horses come outta de woods from both sides."

"How many were there?"

"Eight of 'em. Dey was six Jayhawkers an' de cap'n an' another soldier wid yella stripes here." Jackie patted his own shoulder. "Dey all have guns out, an' Walley say to de Colonel, 'Ol' man, you ain't goin' to Kansas City. You ain't goin' nowhere.' An' den he shot him, just like dat. Den he say to Cyrus an' me, 'Nigger boys, you're free. Dese fellas gonna take you back to Kansas wid 'em.' But Cyrus, soon as he see de Colonel dead, he come outta dat buggy like a wil' man. He pullt Walley off his horse an' started whuppin' him t'death wid his fists. Dat when de other soldier wid de stripes shot him in de back, musta been four, five times. 'Bout den I got off de back o' dat buggy an' started runnin'. Dey come aftuh me too, but I jump down a real steep bank where dere's a little creek goes along 'tween big high rocks an' you can't get no horse in dere. I hid in dem rocks till it was dark, den I come back here an' wait for somebody to come along. Dere wahn't nothin' I could do, Mistah Ringgold," he concluded, and his voice was breaking.

"You did just fine, Jackie," he said, resting a hand on the Negro's shoulder. "If they'd killed you, we might never have known for sure who did it."

But now he knew, and he meant to act on what he knew, just as soon as he brought Harry Younger home to his family. With tears streaming down his cheeks, he reached out and closed the old man's eyes.

The funeral of Colonel Harry Younger was attended by grieving friends and relatives from every county in west Missouri. Jim Younger had managed to locate Cole with Quantrill's band, and the two of them rode all night dodging Federal patrols and roadblocks to arrive just as the funeral procession was moving to the graveyard from a little country church Harry Younger had attended. The words of the Baptist preacher who conducted the service were in John's mind as he walked behind Mrs. Younger and her daughters and the coffin borne by her sons. Having spoken of the high regard in which all who knew him held the Colonel and of his distinguished Mexican War record, the preacher said:

"I'd like to tell you, brothers and sisters, that everything we suffer is for the best, that every sorrow is a blessing, if only we could see it that way. But the fact is, some things we suffer are the work of the evil one. The Good Lord, in his infinite wisdom, permits the evil one to walk the earth amongst us and use evil men to carry out his fiendish work. Why this is so we may not understand until that day when we are raised up and permitted to see things clearly and no longer in a glass darkly."

As Busheba Younger and her children wept beside the open grave, John grieved with them, but in his heart, as there must have been in Cole's and in the hearts of all of Harry Younger's sons, was a raging passion for vengeance. He saw the agony of inconsolable sorrow in Margaret's face, and he vowed silently that he would never rest while Walley lived. But as he looked around him at Cole and the other fellows with pistols stuck in their belts, he realized that he was as yet ill-equipped for the business of vengeance. He carried a shotgun in the funeral procession as a sign of his readiness to join in avenging the murder, but he felt miserably inadequate for the task of seeking out a Federal officer surrounded by his men and his Jayhawker allies. There was only one way he could prepare himself and as soon as the ceremony in the graveyard ended he went up to Cole and said quietly:

"When you go back to join Quantrill, I'm going with you."

Cole looked at him with reddened eyes, forced a little smile and nodded.

Margaret was standing nearby with an arm about her mother. Somehow she heard his words, and she left her mother to come over to him.

"I heard, Johnny. I heard what you said. You mustn't, you just mustn't. Papa didn't want Cole going off with Quantrill, and he wouldn't want you to either."

"Don't you want them to pay, Margaret? Don't you want the men who did this to pay?"

"Yes, I do. But more than anything I want you to live.

Johnny, I've lost too many people I've loved. I can't lose you, too."

"Margaret, I have to go."

She didn't argue any more after that. Shutting her eyes tightly, she nodded, and he forced himself to turn away from her. But as he started to walk to where Cole was waiting for him, she called out his name and ran over to him. Indifferent to what her brothers and sisters might be thinking, she threw her arms around his neck and kissed him as a lover.

"Please come back, Johnny. I won't live if anything happens to you."

"I'll be back," he promised, the touch of her lips almost diverting him momentarily from his thoughts of revenge. "Look for me in the fall."

As he and Cole walked back to the church, where their horses were tied, they passed near another graveyard, where Cyrus was being buried among the people of his race. All the Youngers' slaves were there, along with others from neighboring farms, and John could see and hear the tall, regally beautiful widow of Cyrus kneeling by the grave with her arms raised to heaven and blood streaming down them from self-inflicted wounds, keening in the manner of the women of her tribe when a warrior-husband has fallen. It was a sound that moved John profoundly, and it would remain with him, along with the image of Margaret's sorrowing countenance, for the rest of his life.

FIVE

FIRST BLOOD

On the fifth day he rises early, as the first rays of the sun are striking the bare conical peak to the west of his camp. In a little while its warmth will bring the sweat out, but for now the air is chilly enough to make him shiver into an old gray jacket that looks as though it might be, like its owner, a much-patched survivor of the war.

He gathers some dead branches of scrub oak and starts a fire, warming his hands over the flames before he goes to the spring to fill the coffee pot. For a moment or two, as he warms them, he studies his hands closely, as though looking for some alteration or defect, other than their barely perceptible whiskey-begotten tremor. They are beautiful hands, or so he has been told, usually by a woman who has offered him her flesh to be stroked and is gratified and maybe a little surprised at his gentleness, and notices his hands, how slender and strangely delicate they are, how out of harmony with the rest of his big body. Delicate but strong enough for other work, they might be the hands of a painter or a pianist or, he reflects wistfully, a surgeon. They are in fact the hands of a killer, delicate but strong enough to handle the instruments of death he has been carrying for over twenty years, the heavy pistols and the Bowie knife at his hip, the hideout knife on its lanyard suspended down his back.

When did they become the hands of a killer? During the war, surely, but when? Was it during the Lawrence raid? He remembers clearly his state of mind during that raid and realizes that his transformation had already taken place long before it. The nineteen-year-old guerrilla who rode into Lawrence with Quantrill thirsting for the blood of Red Legs was already Johnny Ringo. When, then? Was it the night he discovered Harry Younger in the road where Walley had left him, staring up into the night sky? The horror of that moment and the all-enveloping rage he felt had changed him surely, had filled him with a deadly resolution. But even then, for all his resolution, he had not become what he would become. He had not yet discovered within himself that readiness to confront another man and whatever that other man might be bent on using to destroy him. He hadn't yet discovered that strange, cruel, some would say inhuman, satisfaction that accompanies the fatal thrust or shot, in the moment when the enemy knows he has been killed and the murderous rage in his eyes is suddenly replaced by amazement, bewilderment and then, as he begins to grasp the incomprehensible fact of death, terror.

There was a time, he can still remember it clearly, when the very thought of inflicting pain, let alone injury, on another human creature was enough to sicken him. From the mother and sisters who stroked and spoiled him, from the other women who gave him their love, he had learned gentleness. And there was still a part of him that would always seek the loving tenderness of woman, valuing it above everything. But there was something else within him, caged there like some exotic man-eater from a distant land, which padded and pawed restlessly, yearning to be released.

He tries to remember when exactly during the war this beast, his killing nature, was first caged inside him. Perhaps it had always been there, from the moment of his conception, an inheritance passed through the centuries from large-limbed, red-haired ancestors who had raided and raped their way down into Europe from subarctic wastes. But even so, he might not have discovered its presence if it were not for the war, and not knowing it was there would have been a kind of innocence.

But the war had come to him, or rather, he had gone to the war, determined to avenge Harry Younger, filled with bloody visions of himself returning to Margaret with Walley's scalp, or maybe his whole head, to throw at her feet. He would prove his love for her, prove that he was her true knight. Full of rage and resolution, but still innocent, he rode from the graveyard with Cole to join Quantrill's guerrillas.

Quantrill had moved his camp twice since Cole left it

to attend his father's funeral, but they finally located it several miles up the Little Blue from Pleasant Hill in a clearing near Job Crabtree's farmhouse. As they approached the clearing they were challenged by a sentry, who stepped out suddenly from behind a fat-bellied oak and confronted them. He was young, barely sixteen, with a pathetic growth of downy whiskers that didn't half cover the pustules on his cheeks, but the double-barreled shotgun he leveled on them had to be taken seriously.

"Halt, damn you. Password?"

"Password?" Cole repeated. "Hell, I don't know any damn password. I'm Cole Younger."

"Yeah, I know, but it don't make me no nevermind. Nobody gets by me 'thout the password. I got orders."

"Now look—" Cole began, starting to heat up, but John cut him off, having suddenly recognized the sentry. "Andy?"

"Yeah? Who . . . ?" He came forward a step and pushed back his floppy hat for a better look. "Well, goddamned if it ain't my old teacher. What're you doing here?"

"I'm here to join Quantrill. How about letting us by?"

"Sorry, teacher, I got orders. Tell you what I'll do, though. I'll take you in there myself. Wait here."

He stepped off the path into a nearby thicket and reappeared in less than a minute mounted on a splendid bay horse. Then he motioned them to ride ahead of him.

"Quite a fine animal you're riding, Andy," John remarked, making conversation.

"Yeah, he was the best in my daddy's stable."

"How is your father?" John still had a warm spot for Mr. Hockensmith, who had given him a hopeless task in educating this young demon but had paid him generously anyway for the effort.

"All right, I s'pose. Last time I saw him he was where I left him. We had some differences about the war an' about whether or not I ought to join Cap'n Quantrill. I didn't hit him real hard."

At this Cole turned and looked sharply at the boy.

"You hit your father?" he gasped in disbelief.

"Had to. Just like I'll have to blow you out of that saddle, Mr. Cole Younger, you don't behave yourself an' learn the password."

Glancing sideways, John could see that Cole was ready

to bend Andy's shotgun around his head, and he hoped that Cole could see what he saw, had seen even at times while he was trying to teach the boy his numbers or whatever, that Andy Hockensmith was missing something, something that should have been inside his head or his heart or some other place it's located in most people and prevents them from striking their fathers or blowing the lights out of someone else with a shotgun.

"Easy, Cole," he said softly. To Andy he said: "I'll bet being a guerrilla cuts into your funning a little, Andy."

At that Andy Hockensmith guffawed in a way that reminded John of many an afternoon when he'd wondered who was the teacher and who the pupil.

"I still take what I want, teacher. Bein' with Cap'n Quantrill you can take whatever this country has to offer, an' like I used to tell you, a man's a fool not to take what he can."

Emerging from the trees they entered the guerrilla encampment itself. There were about sixty men there, many of them hunkered down over little fires in front of lean-to shelters, cooking their evening messes. Here and there among the lean-tos were captured Federal tents with *U.S.A.* stenciled on them. It was John's first look at an "irregular" fighting unit.

"Truth is," Ringo recalls, "they looked a whole lot more like Curly Bill's gang resting up after some serious rustling than a company of soldiers. As we rode through the camp, I could make out here and there the glint of brass buttons on military tunics. A few of them had served in the regular Confederate army before joining Quantrill, and they still wore proudly whatever they had left of their old uniforms. Others had appropriated the uniforms of dead or captured Federals which they proceeded to alter in various ways so they wouldn't be mistaken for Yanks. Somehow, if anything, these assorted bits of uniform made them look even less military than they would have looked without them. They wore them the way a bunch of wild Apaches or Cheyenne would wear what they'd stripped off the bodies of dead troopers after an ambush. No two uniforms were alike. The only item they all seemed to have in common was a black plume or feather, usually stuck in the hatband, an ornament the color of the flag they rode under.

"At the time I joined Quantrill I was wearing a gray jacket and trousers, which a kind lady down in Arkansas later transformed into my own eccentric version of a Confederate uniform by stitching red flannel stripes down the trouser legs and sewing onto the coat some brass buttons I'd ripped off the tunic of a dead Yank."

"A pretty hairy-looking bunch," he remarked to Cole as they approached the farmhouse.

"They are that," Cole replied, with a grim little chuckle, the closest thing to a laugh John had heard since the death of Harry Younger. "Some of them have sworn they won't either shave or cut their hair till they've won the war."

They rode up to Job Crabtree's farmhouse and dismounted just as two men in uniform came out onto the porch. These men, unlike those squatted around their supper fires in the clearing, were fully uniformed, and though their uniforms were not the same, they had in common that attention to military correctness that was so notably lacking in the others. At first glance, one of the men, wearing a dark blue tunic with gold bars on the shoulders, might have been taken for a Federal cavalry officer. But he was also wearing red-striped Confederate dragoon breeches, and there was a long black plume in his hatband. The other man was unmistakably a Confederate officer. His fine-quality gray wool tunic, adorned at cuffs and collars with swirling gilt-braided insignia, was immaculately pressed and brushed, as were the matching yellow-striped trousers. Around his waist was a gold-fringed yellow sash. The only thing missing was a saber. In its place was a belt with two Colt's Navy revolvers.

Andy Hockensmith addressed one of the officers. "Cap'n Quantrill, sir. I stopped these two and brung 'em in here. Happens as I know 'em both, but you said not to let nobody by 'thout they give the password."

"That's right, Andy," the officer in immaculate gray answered, "you did just right. Now go on back to your post."

The boy "yessired" and departed with respectful alacrity, and John Ringo would remember how Quantrill, a former schoolteacher, always knew how to maintain, like any good schoolteacher, complete control over every big or little savage in his command, how to keep them all

docile and respectful before him, no matter that a lot of
them were, like Andy Hockensmith, missing something
that generates respect in and toward most of humanity.

The two officers came down the steps, and the one
who'd revealed himself to be Quantrill came over to
Cole.

"Mr. Younger, it's good to see you back. I want you to
know how very sorry I was to hear of your loss. The loss
of a man like Colonel Younger is a real blow to the
southern cause."

Quantrill had never met Harry Younger, surely, might
not have been able to tell him from Abe Lincoln, and
what he'd just said revealed his total ignorance of Harry
Younger's outspoken views on secession, but it was well-
intentioned nonetheless, the sort of thing one ought to
say to a grieving member of a prominent west Missouri
family, and Cole was visibly moved.

"Thank you, sir. This is my cousin John Ringgold,
from Texas. He's come to join us."

As they shook hands, Ringo guessed that Quantrill was
close to thirty. "But I found out later," Ringo writes,
"that he wasn't near that, was in fact about twenty-four.
He seemed to be quite a bit shorter than either Cole or
me, but that was because he tended to slouch a little.
Actually he stood about five-foot-eleven and must have
weighed around one hundred and seventy. He had blond
hair and dark skin, the kind of sallow flesh that sun and
wind will tan deeply. His rather lean face was what I
believe most would call handsome. It reminded me of a
sketch I'd seen in a Latin grammar of a bust of one of the
Caesars, with the same thin, high-bridged nose and the
same thin-lipped mouth turned down at the corners in a
way that suggested either cruelty or determination or a
mixture of both. You'll see Indian bucks with those same
bird-of-prey facial lines and suspect that they've made
their mark with plenty of coups. What I remember especially, though, were his eyes. They had heavy lids that
tended to droop in a sleepy sort of way, but when they
focused on you, they became as hard and sharp as bits of
blue-gray glass. He was smiling at me in a pleasant,
quizzical sort of way, but I felt those eyes probing right
into me like cold sharp blades."

"From Texas, eh?" Quantrill asked.

"Yes, sir," John answered. "San Antonio."

Cole broke in. "Captain, he can outride any Comanche in Texas. Moves through the woods like a ghost. I've hunted with him."

"Might have the makings of a scout," Quantrill reflected. "We'll assign him to John McCorkle. Can you shoot, Mr. Ringgold?"

"Oh, surely, sir," he replied without hesitation, being reasonably competent with a shotgun and not realizing that Quantrill meant pistols.

"Do you have a Colt's?"

"No, sir. I'm afraid I didn't bring a weapon with me." His mother kept a loaded pistol, an old Paterson Colt's, in a kitchen drawer, ready for raiding Comanches or any other unwelcome guests who might happen by, but he had never fired it, never wanted to.

"That's all right," Quantrill said in a warm reassuring tone that didn't quite go along with his coldly penetrating gaze. "We'll see that you're armed. Lieutenant Todd here will take care of you." He nodded at the man in the dark tunic, who came over and offered his hand.

"I'm George Todd. Real pleased to meet you." Todd's handshake was more prolonged than Quantrill's, and he had a grip like a vise. John wasn't surprised to find out a little later that he'd been a stonemason before the war. He was, like Quantrill, a good-looking blond fellow, but much more powerfully built, and looked to be not much older than John and Cole. The warm dark blue eyes with which he appraised John Ringgold seemed to radiate good humor and a capacity for funning.

"Pleased to meet you, lieutenant," John said, trying his best to return the warmth of that grip.

"Call me George."

John liked Todd instinctively, responding to his apparent easygoing good nature, even as he recoiled a little from Quantrill's apparent coldness. It wasn't until much later, after he'd lost most of his innocence and met such jovial killers as Arch Clement and "Bloody Bill" Anderson and had come to know George Todd himself, that he came to react just as instinctively to good-ol'-boy grins with suspicion, wondering what capacities lay coiled or poised in an S shape behind them.

He followed Todd down into Job Crabtree's root cellar, which was one of the guerrillas' many arsenals in the neighborhood. There Todd issued him a revolver and ammunition. As John took the weapon, he felt a little tightening of his insides, the same sensation he felt every time he pulled open the drawer in his mother's kitchen and saw the old Paterson Colt's.

"You can start with this, John. It's a Navy Colt's, .36-caliber. Sorry I don't have a six-shot for you, but we'll be picking up some more pretty soon. You'll want to have more than one. Some of the men carry five or six pieces. That's too many . . ."

Something about a pistol, and he guessed he knew what it was. It was remembering a hand clutching one on a riverbank and remembering what the pistol had done. How could he bring himself to carry one and learn to shoot it? He didn't think he could. But then how could he ride with Quantrill, avenge Harry Younger, if he didn't?

" . . . if you ask me, but I guess it gives 'em some firepower."

"This'll do fine," John said. It really was a beautiful piece, if a man had an eye for such beauty. The bluing was hardly worn, even along the barrel. The trigger guard and part of the frame were of polished brass, which shone against the varnished black walnut grip and the blued steel. On the five-shot cylinder was engraved a naval battle, which gave this particular type of Colt's its name.

"Do you have a knife?" Todd asked.

"Oh, surely," he answered, producing a three-inch jackknife from his pocket. Todd chuckled a little when he saw it.

"I mean a knife, John. Like this."

He drew a Bowie knife out of a sheath stitched inside his boot. Tossing it lightly in the air and catching it deftly by the blade, he handed it over haft-first for John to examine.

It wasn't the first time he'd seen a Bowie knife. Plenty of them could be seen sheathed on the hips of men around San Antonio, where, after all, Bowie himself, with one in his hand, had been bayoneted in bed by Mexican soldiers. But John had never had any occasion to examine one closely. Now he hefted the famous killer and started to test the edge with his thumb.

"Don't, John. It'll go right down to the bone, you even touch it lightly."

So he kept his fingers away from the blade, which was no less than ten inches in length and heavy enough to split kindling. Along the bottom edge, from the brass guard to the curving tip, it was sharpened, and from the tip almost three inches back along the concave upper edge.

"Tryin' to think who might have an extra one for you."

"Maybe I can do without," he said, wondering if he would ever be able to handle such a weapon without losing a finger.

"Naw, you got to have one of these, if not a couple. The Yanks carry sabers. This is what we carry. Let me see now. . . ."

It turned out that a guerrilla by the name of Jim Lilly, a huge man with a beard and hair down to his waist, had one more Bowie knife than he thought he needed. It, along with other weapons, had been bequeathed him by the late Perry Hoy, a guerrilla who had managed to transmit a last will and testament out of Fort Leavenworth shortly before he was hanged there. (In Hoy's memory, Quantrill had executed a captured Federal lieutenant and two other prisoners and then led a raid into Kansas to kill ten more men.)

So now John Ringgold was armed. The fact that he knew nothing about pistols and would tense up inside every time he handled his new Navy Colt's was a matter of concern. It became more so the day after he joined the guerrillas, when he saw what some of them could do with their pistols.

That day, shortly after supper, he and Cole and some others were drawn by the sound of firing to a gulley behind the Crabtree barn. Seeing the others stroll over in a relaxed manner, they could figure that it wasn't an attack and followed after.

In the gulley they found two dozen men mostly squatted down watching a shooting performance. The performer was a man called Hi George, a medium-tall, stoop-shouldered fellow with a pistol in either hand. Some twenty-five yards in front of him another man was tossing bottles in the air. One after another the shooter exploded them in midair. Then one of the watchers called out:

"Ten dollars says you cain't hit three at oncet."

Holstering one of his pistols, Hi George drew a gold piece out of a trousers pocket and tossed it to one of the watchers. Then he reloaded and holstered both pistols as two men got up to assist with the bottle throwing.

Since no one else got in on the betting, John inferred that hitting three in the air was not an unusual feat for Hi George. What amazed him, though, was the speed the marksman exhibited. Two of the bottles were still ascending when he shattered them, and the third had just reached the top of its arc before it became a shower of glass.

There were a few low appreciative whistles and Hi George collected his gold piece with another to match it. Then, as he moved back to reload his pistols, another man stepped forward. Instantly, John knew that he'd seen this man before, but it took him a while to remember where. The man was maybe half an inch over six feet in height, with wide sloping shoulders and a waist as slim as a girl's. He had handsome angular features, clean-shaven except for a neat moustache, but what was most readily noticeable was the black eyepatch he wore.

"Let's see some shootin', Ol," one of the men called.

Hearing the man's name, John remembered meeting him, even before Cole muttered, "That's Ol Shepherd. Best shot in the camp. Fastest, too."

Shepherd performed the same feats with flying bottles that Hi George had managed. Watching him, John could believe that he was even faster than Hi George. Both men drew and fired with a speed beyond the eye's power to follow, but Shepherd gave a watcher the illusion that his guns never had been holstered in the first place, that he simply raised his hands and they sprouted iron.

"He kin cut a quarter-inch rope at twenty paces," Jim Lilly rumbled to Ned Vaughan, a newcomer like John Ringgold.

"Hell he can," Vaughan answered skeptically.

"Bet you ten he can," someone else spoke up.

Bets were quickly placed and Shepherd was informed. His only response was a thin dark stream of tobacco juice spat sideways. Then he drew out a twenty-dollar gold piece and tossed it to George Todd, who was holding the bets. While he reloaded, someone went to fetch a length of rope.

The rope was attached to a tree branch, and Todd paced off the distance. Shepherd walked over to where he was expected to stand, moving with that deceptive slowness big, fast men will often affect when there's no immediate need for quickness. The man who attached the rope informed him that it was moving a little in the evening breeze.

"Don't matter," Shepherd replied, facing his target with an utterly relaxed stance. He spat another stream of tobacco juice and contemplated the target for several seconds. John watched his right hand, waited for the draw, knowing it would be just a blur of electrified flesh, like a snake striking. Even so, he was astonished when the shot came. Shepherd fired just as the barrel cleared his holster, and the rope was instantly severed.

There were more low whistles of appreciation as the men came over to collect their winnings from Todd. John stood for a moment or two, mouth ajar like an idiot's. Then as Ol Shepherd started back toward the camp, he followed him. Falling in beside the one-eyed gunman, he introduced himself.

"Don't know as you'd remember me . . ." he began.

"Don't know as I do . . ." Shepherd replied. Then, having scrutinized John Ringgold carefully with his single bright blue eye, he said, "Oh, yeah, now I do remember. At the Youngers'. You're their Texas cousin."

"That's right," he said. "I've just joined up with Quantrill. I was wondering if I might ask you a favor."

"Well, surely," Shepherd replied expansively. "Not much I wouldn't do for a cousin of the Youngers."

"Would you teach me how to shoot a revolver?"

At this Ol Shepherd laughed out loud, as though he'd just heard something pretty funny.

"You mean to tell me you're from Texas and you don't know how to shoot? How come you ain't been skelpt by some wild Indin yet?" He laughed loudly again. Then, seeing that John didn't seem to appreciate the joke, he reached out and clapped him on the shoulder. "Sure, I'll be glad to he'p you. Meet me out here at noon tomorrow."

Shepherd was a good teacher, patient and encouraging, and John made rapid progress as a marksman. Within less than a week his nervousness about handling a pistol had totally disappeared. The feel of the Colt's in his hand was completely natural, and he wondered how it had ever been otherwise.

"You got real fast hands, John, real fast," Ol told him. "But you got to slow down and learn to place your shots. Plenty of time to work on your speed later on. Don't do you no good to get off a fast shot you don't hit anything with."

He listened to Shepherd and learned to place his shots. It would be a good long while before he could cut a rope with a bullet, but after a week he was beginning to hit some of the tin plates and bottles Shepherd tossed for him, and his confidence began to grow. He was, however, far from being the shot he wanted to be when he had his first test under fire. It was a test he would remember well twenty-one years later.

"After a week we moved from Crabtree's to another farm about six miles west of Pleasant Hill and made camp in a meadow. Cole and I didn't have a tent then, but it was still June and the nights were warm. Putting together a lean-to seemed like a lot of trouble, especially when it was so pleasant to lie out under the stars. But then one night the stars were covered over, and pretty soon we were being drenched by one of those prolonged Missouri summer evening showers. Cole and I wrapped up together in our blankets under a tree and tried to keep warm in spite of the puddle that spread out around us. I couldn't have slept more than an hour or two that whole night."

"John," he remembers Cole muttering, "I'd mightily appreciate it if you'd just transform yourself into something nice and warm and womanly."

"Hell," he muttered back, "you don't start bathing yourself a little more often, I'm liable to be the best you'll get."

Cole replied with a chuckle, and in a few minutes his snores were adding to the misery of the night, one of many John would spend as a guerrilla, when it seemed that God was deliberately withholding the relief of dawn until the endurance of His wretched creatures had been tested to the limit and beyond. One can learn at such

times the stoicism of the Indian, the ability to detach
one's mind from the sufferings of the poor dumb brute
one calls a body. Or if one is young enough, still innocent, one can dream, imagine the sympathetic concern of
a woman for whom one is willing to undergo such trials.
Lying there in the rain huddled against her brother, who
wasn't really her brother, John dreamt of Margaret
Younger—tawny, doe-eyed German-Jewish-Indian maid
of the woods.

Still unable to sleep, he tried to recall those lines of
poetry she had spoken that night out on the porch over
the noise of the ball, those strange beautiful lines by that
poet whose name he couldn't remember at the moment,
though Margaret had loaned him a volume of his poems
along with some others, to take back to Liberty. Keats?
Yes, Keats. Lines about an embalmed darkness and soft
incense on the boughs. About being half in love with
easeful death and not knowing whether he was awake or
asleep. On such a night as this, they made a different
kind of sense. But had he known what the next day
would bring, he would not have yearned for this night to
end.

With the belated coming of dawn he rose wet and
shivering, drew out his new Bowie knife and began to
whittle some sticks and logs down to dry wood for a fire,
while Cole spread their blankets out to dry in the morning sun. He was just about to touch off the shavings he'd
whittled when they heard sentries firing.

Having been surprised by Federals three times in less
than a month, Quantrill had finally learned the wisdom
of posting a mile-wide ring of sentries even on a rainy
night. Now the guerrilla chief scrambled out of his tent
and sprinted—hatless, coatless, and half shaven, with a
razor in one hand and a pistol in the other—past John
and Cole across the meadow. The two young men grabbed
their own pistols and ran after him, and by the time they
reached the fringe of woods beyond the meadow, they'd
been joined by a dozen others, including George Todd,
Bill Gregg and Ol Shepherd. Halting just inside the trees
they beheld, less than half a mile away, a dark blue,
fast-moving mass approaching along the muddy road from
Pleasant Hill. Here and there within the mass one could
make out the flash of sunlight on brightly polished metal.

"About sixty, wouldn't you say, Bill?" Quantrill addressed Gregg.

"Yeah, I guess, cap'n," the lieutenant answered doubtfully. When it came to sizing up an enemy force or a situation, Quantrill was always way ahead of any of his men.

"We can handle 'em," he asserted with the brisk confidence of a leader encountering a familiar situation with men whose ability to carry out his orders he has no reason to doubt, when in fact, none of them, not even Quantrill himself, had yet faced anything like what was now coming toward them. Still, his mood of confidence was infectious, and no one questioned the orders he flung at them.

"Bill, go back and get the rest of the men out here. Deploy them among these trees and tell them to stay out of sight. George, you round up the horses and drive them into that ravine over west of the clearing. The rest of you wait here."

Having stashed the razor in his pocket and wiped at the dried film of shaving soap on one cheek, Quantrill checked his pistol. Then he crouched low and left the cover of the trees. Running in a crouch he made for a fence that intersected the road. Reaching the fence he knelt behind it and beckoned for the others to follow. One after another, each man imitated his leader's crouch as he crossed the open space to the fence, and John Ringgold was the last. By now the Federal column was less than three hundred yards away, and as John peeped through the weeds that rose to the top rail of the fence, he could make out drawn sabers flashing brightly in the morning sunlight.

"As a matter of fact," he remembers, "there is no weapon quite so useless as a cavalry saber. During the war I saw more men killed and wounded than I care to remember, but not one did I see mortally wounded by a saber. On the other hand, a charging column of cavalry with drawn sabers can be a mighty impressive and threatening sight, especially when you're not even eighteen and untested."

In fact, he was so scared that he wanted to scurry back into the trees, only he doubted his ability to move. It was like the first time he climbed on a bronc. His bowels were filling up with something that felt cold, and he began to wonder if he could control them. Must be, he thought, what a crouching rabbit feels like watching a hunter's feet tramping toward him.

"Steady, men," Quantrill said in a low calm voice. "Don't fire till I say."

John drew his pistol, checked the cylinder, and wondered if he would be able to use it. He had learned a great deal from Ol Shepherd, was able to break bottles on fence posts consistently and even sometimes in the air. But firing at a man? As though he had heard the younger man's thoughts, Ol rested a hand on his shoulder and whispered to him:

"You'll do fine, John."

John nodded and grinned weakly in reply.

Quantrill didn't give the order to fire until the column had almost reached the gate across the road and was less than thirty yards from their hiding place. As the young captain slowed his column to a halt, ordering a sergeant to go ahead and open the gate, Quantrill rose to his feet.

"Cut 'em down, men! Blue-bellied sonsofbitches!" he snarled, and his own first shot doubled the captain over in his saddle.

John rose with the others, brought up his Colt's just as Shepherd had taught him, but couldn't bring himself to pull the trigger. On one side of him Cole began emptying his pistol rapidly without any apparent effect, sort of whimpering to himself as he did, "I'll get one for you, Daddy, get one, dammit, get one. . . ." On the other side of him, Shepherd was firing more deliberately and every shot seemed to connect, leaving men slumped over in their saddles if not unloaded in the road. Still, John Ringgold held his fire. Above the ear-splitting blasts of gunfire the guerrillas could hear the screams of wounded men and horses, the rending infernal sounds of bestial and human pain so mixed that they became almost undistinguishable from each other. Mingled with the screams were curses and the sounds of confusion.

"Let's get out of here, goddammit!"

"Where's the captain? Lieutenant?"

Apparently the guerrillas' first volley had claimed the officers, for they could see that a sergeant was now taking command.

"Fall back, men, fall back," he bellowed. Ol Shepherd took careful aim and fired, whereupon the sergeant grasped his shoulder. Shepherd aimed and fired again, but the hammer fell harmlessly on a spent cartridge.

"Shit!" the one-eyed marksman hissed and spat tobacco juice onto the fence rail. "Thought I had 'em counted."

The Federals didn't hesitate to obey the sergeant's order, all but a few who were sensible enough either to resheathe or get rid of their useless sabers and draw out their carbines. These men, apparently seasoned and not needing orders, took it upon themselves to cover the retreat of the others.

As the guerrillas traded shots with the rear guard, John felt a little tug at his shoulder and, looking down, saw a rip in his coat. He touched it, and his fingertips came away bloody. Still he did not fire his pistol. Ol Shepherd turned away to reload, and the man next to him, Ned Vaughan, suddenly dropped his weapon and clutched at his breast with both hands. For a moment or two he stayed on his feet, swaying, leaning forward against the fence rail, unwilling to go down in a fall from which he knew he'd never rise. Then another Federal slug took him lower down, well below the midriff and he pitched forward over the rail onto his face, rolled over onto his back in a slow, oddly graceful somersault and lay motionless, staring up at John Ringgold with wide, surprised eyes.

Strangely, John was no longer frightened. A numbness and a feeling that the skirmish wasn't really happening, was actually part of a feverish dream, had set in, and not even the blood on his fingertips or the burning in his shoulder or Ned Vaughan's unseeing eyes could wholly convince him otherwise. He had yet to fire his pistol.

Which turned out to be a good thing after all, for the guerrillas were suddenly threatened by something they could never have imagined.

At first it didn't look like much of a threat. Just one lone cavalryman breaking away from the rest of the retreating column and charging directly toward them at a full gallop across the field all by himself yelling something they couldn't make out at first and waving a saber over his head. As he drew nearer, the words "filthy fucking secesh bastards" came to them, shrieked out in the hysterical pitch of one on the verge of tears. The guerrillas who weren't in the process of reloading directed all of their fire at the man, but their shots either missed altogether or failed to connect vitally. On he came, bent low in the saddle, still whirling his saber and shrieking, " . . . Filthy secesh!"

"Stop him, somebody!" Quantrill barked, frantically reloading his Colt's. Incredibly, at that moment no one had a loaded gun. No one, that is, but John Ringgold.

As though he were in a trance, John raised his pistol, bracing his right wrist with his left hand the way Ol had showed him for when he had time to aim. Now he could see the face of the horseman clearly—a young face, reddened with rage, bright blue mad eyes, straw-colored hair sticking out from under the blue cap.

"Take him, Ringgold!" he heard Quantrill bark again.

"Aim low, John," Ol Shepherd cautioned.

Now the young horseman was so close that John could see tears streaming from the bright mad eyes, and in that instant the memory of Margaret's dark streaming eyes came to him.

"Shoot, dammit!" somebody was yelling. "For Chrissake . . . !"

John jerked the trigger instead of squeezing it the way Ol had showed him, so that the muzzle of the Colt's came up a little and his shot took the man higher in the chest than he'd aimed. The young horseman screamed and sat upright, letting the reins go to clutch at his chest but still gripping his saber in the other hand. Just short of the fence the unreined horse turned abruptly, unloading his rider. The man landed on his back in the tall grass and rolled over twice. Then he lay still less than two yards from the feet of John Ringgold.

"Christ!" someone gasped.

"Nice shooting, Ringgold," Quantrill said and clapped him on the shoulder. "Come on, men. Fall back to the trees."

John heard the order but ignored it. He vaulted the fence and knelt down beside his victim.

The man was still alive, still clutching his saber, which he tried in vain to raise. The bright streaming eyes shone with rage and hatred as they focused on his killer. How young he is, John thought, noticing the unrazored downy growth on his cheeks, which matched the soft blond curls above his forehead. *Younger than I am, surely. Why did the damned Federals let him join their army?*

"I'm sorry," he said to the boy. "I—" He couldn't say any more because he didn't know what to say, and anyway the boy cut him off gasping:

"Damn your black soul to hell, reb. Damn you . . ." Then he began to cough, and bright red bubbles appeared on his lower lip.

"Damn . . ." he whispered. His eyes left John's face and became fixed on some point in the Missouri sky. The rage and hatred were still there, but the mad brightness was fading.

John had never felt so wretched or so helpless in his life. The pistol was still in his hand, and he barely restrained an impulse to fling it away in the tall grass. Holstering it instead, he reached out to touch his victim's hand that still gripped the saber. At his touch, the youngster managed to flash one last furious glance at him, and his lips moved silently in what could only have been another curse. Then he began to cough again, and his eyes shut tight against the pain. When they opened again he was dead.

"Hey, Ringgold, get back here!" Quantrill was shouting from the woods.

"Hurry, John, for Godsake!" Cole shouted along with him.

John heard the voices and rose up slowly, still in a trancelike state, as he had been when he raised his pistol, but now made almost unbearably dreary by a sense of having assumed an enormous burden that he would never shrug off as long as he lived. For a moment he stared down at the boy in the Federal uniform, still grasping his sword and staring up into the Missouri heavens.

Then he turned toward the fence rail, reaching out to grasp it and vault over. As he did so, a large chip flew off the rail next to his hand and puffs of dust rose from the ground just beyond the fence. Glancing back, he saw a line of figures advancing toward him on foot. The ambushed cavalrymen had dismounted and become a skirmish line. Some of them were pausing to drop down on one knee and shoot while the others moved on ahead.

Then, when the kneeling skirmishers had reloaded, got up and moved ahead, the others dropped down to shoot. From the woods the guerrillas answered the skirmishers' fire and continued calling out to their comrade, who seemed so strangely unaware that he was the skirmishers' main target.

"Ringgold, get back here now, goddammit!"

"Run or you're dead, John!"

Belatedly, he vaulted back over the fence and ran for the trees. More dust puffs rose ahead of him and on either side, and as he reached the trees, a bullet probably intended for him caught a man named Donahue in the throat. Donahue went down on his knees grasping his throat as though he would strangle himself. John stopped to help him, and another man left his cover to help drag the wounded man behind a tree. Having dragged him to cover, they could only watch helplessly while he coughed and gagged to death on his own blood.

Quantrill ran over and knelt down to examine Donahue. Seeing that he could do nothing, he stood up and shouted at the boy from Texas:

"Damn you, Ringgold, when I give you an order, you listen! Hear?"

John looked at Quantrill but didn't answer. It occurred to him fleetingly that he would rather have the guerrilla chief's blood on his hands than that of the nameless boy soldier he'd just killed.

"You all right, John?" Cole was asking anxiously.

"Yeah, I'm all right," he answered somewhat dreamily, as though Cole had just brought him out of his trance.

Quantrill took a step toward him, was about to say or do something more, but he was stopped by Ol Shepherd, who laid a hand on his shoulder.

"Best leave him alone, cap'n. I'll talk to him."

Quantrill might have shrugged off the hand, but the groan of a man nearby who'd just caught a Federal bullet and a shower of bullet-cut twigs falling on his head reminded him that there were more urgent matters at hand than the disciplining of a man who'd been tardy in obeying an order.

The skirmishers halted their advance just out of pistol range. From there they maintained a steady fire into the woods with their carbines, and it wasn't long before still another guerrilla was wounded. The guerrillas, armed only with pistols, were now at a disadvantage, but what convinced Quantrill to retreat from the woods was the sudden appearance of a sizable body of Federal reinforcements. Whether or not it had been planned that way, the skirmishers had succeeded in keeping them pinned down until a much larger column arrived.

"How many you think they are, cap'n?" Gregg was asking.

"Hard to say, Bill. Two hundred anyway. We'd best fall back." There was no longer any excitement in his voice. Having shifted his attention from John Ringgold's insubordination back to the problem of meeting the Federal attackers, he was completely calm. Like the men who followed him, Quantrill was still learning. Never again would they make such a stand without reconnoitering an area to see just how large an enemy force they were encountering.

"Follow Gregg" was the order passed through the woods. Quantrill ordered his lieutenant to lead most of the guerrillas back to the ravine where Todd had driven the horses, while he, with six picked men, remained behind to slow down the Federal pursuit.

As he joined the retreat from the woods, John saw a man, a boy actually, limping after Gregg and the others and falling behind on account of the bullet in his leg. John knew him slightly, having talked with him one evening. His name was Zack Hayes, and he had just turned fifteen, a skinny awkward kid whose mother had brought him to join Quantrill six months before, after Jayhawkers raided their farm and forced her to set fire to her own house.

"Come on, Zack," he urged, "let me help you."

"Don't need no he'p," the youngster muttered, grimacing against the pain in his leg. "I'll make it."

"You've got to move faster. Here . . ." He wrapped one of Zack's skinny arms around his neck and grasped the boy around the waist, half lifting, half dragging him along.

"Let me go, John. They'll get us both."

Which was likely, but John knew that there was no way he'd leave Zack behind. The Federals would surely

hang him just as fast as they would a grown man. John
hardly knew him, had been drawn to him mainly because
he didn't seem to belong in the guerrilla band. He'd
noticed the boy sitting alone at the edge of the camp with
an open Bible in his lap, and they'd talked a little about
the passages he was reading from Second Samuel, about
the wars of David.

"Do you think He's on our side, John?" the boy had
asked him.

"Who?" he answered, though he knew perfectly well
whom the boy meant, and the boy knew he knew. And
he would have laughed out loud and said, "Oh, surely"
or made some smart remark, but the boy was obviously
sincere in his concern over the matter. If there was anyone more innocent than John himself in that camp, it was
Zack. He had to be looked after.

Suddenly the burden of Zack was lightened, and John
looked over to see that Cole was helping him.

"Let's get movin', John," he panted. "Those fellows
can't hold 'em for long."

Between them they mostly carried the boy at a near
run across the meadow to the mouth of the ravine. Inside
the ravine Todd and five other men were holding the
horses. Some of the animals were undisturbed by the
sound of gunfire from across the meadow but others,
including his own big stud Blaze, were fighting to break
loose. Foreseeing the likelihood that they would be needed,
Todd had ordered the horses saddled, but as soon as the
skirmish began, Blaze and some of the others had become unmanageable. Someone had put a bridle on him,
but no one could saddle him. Having helped Zack to
prop himself against a sycamore trunk, John went to
calm his horse and secure him to the same tree.

"Where's the captain?" he heard Todd demanding of
Gregg, who was still gasping for breath after his run.

"Over in them woods," Gregg answered between gasps.
"Too goddamned many Fedruls . . ."

He didn't have time to explain any more, for suddenly
Quantrill himself appeared at the mouth of the ravine
accompanied by Ol Shepherd and four other members of
the rear guard. Later, Ol would tell John how they'd
killed two more cavalrymen but paid for it with one of
their own.

Remarkably, Quantrill was now attired in his full Confederate uniform, having pulled it out of his tent on the run across the meadow. The magnificent gilt-braided tunic hung loosely from his shoulders, unbuttoned, and he had the yellow sash in his hand.

"Deploy the men on both sides of this ravine," he told his lieutenants, as he buttoned his tunic. "They'll try to surround us." Pausing for a moment to whip the sash around his waist, he added, "You might as well know they have enough men to do that."

Todd and Gregg nodded grimly, then ran to carry out his orders. The wounded who couldn't fight were placed in the bottom of the ravine near the horses. Four men, including Cole and John, were ordered to guard the horses.

For maybe a minute or two, it was quiet. The men scrambled up the sides of the ravine and positioned themselves, pistols ready. Quantrill sprinted the length of the ravine, stopping a couple of times to reposition some of them. As he passed the horses, one of the men called down to him from the rim above.

"Hey, cap'n, we's a little short of ammunition up here."

"I know, Ab," the guerrilla chief answered calmly but a little wearily. "You'll just have to make what you have count. Let 'em get close enough to hit."

Whereupon the shooting began again, and one of the first ones hit was the guerrilla called Ab. Shot through the forehead, he tumbled down the side of the ravine and came to rest near the horses. Quantrill ran over and knelt beside him. Then, shaking his head and cursing to himself, he rose and scrambled up to take the position Ab had vacated. Watching him, John wondered if Quantrill had any regrets about what he'd led his men into.

Maddened by the smell of blood and the firing, the horses fought to break loose from the tie rope that held them. A few of them succeeded, and before John or any of the other horse tenders could grab their reins, they had galloped off toward the entrance of the ravine.

"Dammit," he heard himself shouting, "let's not lose any more!"

The loss of the horses meant the loss of their only apparent means of escape. Even with his inexperienced eye, John Ringgold could see that the guerrillas could not hold their position. An extended line of cavalrymen armed with Sharps carbines were advancing rapidly on foot, firing as they came. The guerrillas returned fire, but their ammunition was running out, and when Quantrill saw that the Federal line's advance was not even slowed by their fire, he shouted an order that no one hesitated to follow:

"Fall back and mount up, boys! We're getting out of here!"

Instantly everyone was scrambling down the sides of the ravine, but no sooner had most of the retreating guerrillas reached the bottom of the ravine than the blue-uniformed attackers appeared on the rim above them. Deploying themselves along the rim, they rained carbine fire on the men below. When a bullet plowed through the rump of one of the horses, it went mad with pain and tore itself loose from the tie rope. As the animal next to it pulled loose to follow, John grabbed its reins. A guerrilla who may or may not have been the animal's owner ran over, snatched the reins from him and started to climb into the saddle, but a bullet from above caught him between the shoulder blades. As the man fell dead at his feet, John seized the animal's reins again, pulled out his Colt's and aimed it up at the rim. By now the dust raised by the horses and the wreaths of gunsmoke floating in the still, stove-warm air of the ravine were making it nearly impossible to see as far up as the rim. He could barely make out the dark figures crouched there firing down on them. No longer hesitant, he started shooting. His first shot may have connected, but his second went wild as the horse he was holding nearly jerked him off his feet.

For several long minutes the only sounds in that smoky, dust-choked hole were blasts of carbine and pistol fire and the screams of wounded men and animals. But then the guerrillas heard something rising above these sounds, something inhuman, like a strong wind coming up in the desert, or a rockslide starting in a mountain canyon, an inhuman sound of mindless destruction, made all the more terrifying by the fact that its source was human. It came, becoming a sound of mindless animal rage, from the dark crouching figures on the rim above who were suddenly no longer crouching but on their feet plunging down the side of the ravine.

The guerrillas who still had loaded pistols picked their targets from among the charging figures, while those who didn't drew their knives. No orders were passed. None were needed. John fired at one of the dark figures rushing toward him, a figure that the smoke and dust made faceless, that threw up its hands and sprawled headlong ten feet in front of him. Then another dark figure leaped over the body of the first, a huge figure swinging a carbine like a club. John fired again but either missed or connected with something more demonic than human, something that could maybe laugh at bullets. Then his Colt's was empty, and the thing was upon him, casting its carbine club aside and dragging him to the ground.

The enemy was a man, not a demon, but he must have outweighed John Ringgold by close to seventy pounds, a red-faced goliath with a neck as big around as a keg and small dark eyes that radiated more concentrated malevolence than anything John had seen since the last time he smashed the head of a Texas diamondback. Straddled by that enormous bulk, John could barely move. He tried to reach for his Bowie knife, but the big cavalryman caught his wrist in a grip that might have cracked the bones if he'd put his mind to it. With his other hand the giant reached for and found a rock half the size of a bread loaf.

"Gonna brain you, reb," he snarled, raising the rock high above his own head.

John's free hand reached up automatically to catch the hand with the rock, but he knew full well that there was no stopping the blow, and there was a part of him, maybe lodged somewhere inside the brain the giant was about to smash, that felt sorry for the body that was about to be killed this way, like some kind of snake or scorpion. Strangely, he felt very little fear, only a kind of weary regret during the split second he waited for the rock to descend on him. Still reaching in a vain attempt to block the huge rock-filled hand, he shut his eyes.

But the rock never fell. Instead he felt a lessening of the enormous weight on him. Opening his eyes he saw a gray-sleeved arm encircling the thick neck, and there was a flash of bright metal as a hand appeared driving a blade into the giant's chest. Bull-bellowing with rage and pain,

the giant rose to his knees and reached back to grasp his
attacker. In spite of the knife in his chest, he managed to
throw the attacker over his head onto John Ringgold.
Then he started to grasp the haft protruding from his
chest but fell sideways and sprawled on his back alongside his intended victim.

"You all right, John?" Cole was asking.

"Fine, Cole, real fine. Alive, thanks to you."

Cole helped him to his feet and nodded toward their
antagonist, who now lay still, his small dark eyes fixed
and shining in that same attitude of concentrated malevolence.

"Ain't he a big one?" Cole said as he jerked his Bowie
knife out of the man's chest. "Tougher'n a damn bear,
too," he added with a nervous little laugh, thinking maybe
of how there were damned few eighteen-year-old masters
of the Bowie knife who could base such a remark on
experience. He couldn't hit a thing with a Colt's, but that
didn't mean he wasn't a good man to have with you in a
fight.

All around them in the dim infernal smoke-wreathed
light of the ravine, men were grappling hand to hand.
Hardly any shots were heard, for the Federal cavalry,
like the guerrillas, had used up most of their ammunition, and their wild spontaneous charge down the side of
the ravine had come when they realized that their sabers
and empty carbines were all they had to finish the guerrillas. Against the clubbed carbines and sabers the guerrillas wielded pistol butts, knives, broken-off tree branches,
and rocks. Along with the heavy panting of the fighters
could be heard inarticulate snarls and groans, not unlike
what their troglodyte ancestors must have uttered encountering each other upon a disputed piece of hunting ground.
They panted and snarled like wolves, and the madness of
their rage was intensified by the terrible heat within the
ravine. Above them the sun, like the great red eye of an
all-devouring sky god, looked down through the smoky
haze.

John drew his Bowie knife and started to follow Cole
toward where four guerrillas were trying to prevent six
cavalrymen from getting to the few horses still attached
to the tie rope. He felt a hand on his arm and swung

about in a ready crouch, nearly slashing the hand that had touched him.

"Easy, Ringgold, for Chrissake!"

He recognized the lank, bushy-bearded figure of Bill Gregg.

"Sorry. . . ."

"You got a horse, Ringgold?"

"I don't know." In fact, the haze was so thick that he couldn't even see the tree where he'd tied Blaze and left Zack Hayes.

"Wal, find out. If you got one, meet me up t'other end o' this gulley. Cap'n wants us to cut our way out."

Gregg ran on over to where Cole and the others were fighting to keep the remaining horses. John paused a moment to get his bearings, then he ran through the haze past shadowy dust-covered figures locked in combat like fiends fighting for the privilege of tormenting the damned.

Doubting that he would ever find Blaze where he left him, he was overjoyed to see the big stud still secured to the tree. His elation quickly disappeared as he made out the dark figure of a soldier with a carbine standing over Zack Hayes. The soldier, a square-shouldered, powerfully made fellow, had his legs braced apart and was about to drive the steel-plated butt of his carbine into Zack's face. The boy had one skinny arm up to ward off the blow.

"Don't!" he heard himself shouting as he ran toward the tree.

The man didn't hear him, wouldn't have paid any attention if he had, being totally preoccupied with smashing the boy's head as though it belonged to a venomous reptile or insect. But as the soldier drove the rifle butt downward, the boy twisted out of the way, avoiding the blow, and this gave John the seconds he needed to reach the man. Still intent upon smashing the reptile or bug thing between his feet, the soldier did not hear the running feet behind him, was raising his carbine again, and was amazed when a lean muscular arm went around his throat. Before he could even attempt to struggle, his whole chest cavity from the lower ribs on up was filled with a searing, tearing presence that completely paralyzed him. Dying, he sprawled on his face next to the boy he had tried to kill.

"Good work, Ringgold! You'll make a soldier yet, providing you learn to follow orders."

John whirled toward the voice, bloody blade ready for more work, and found himself face-to-face with Quantrill and about two dozen guerrillas. Quantrill chuckled a little as he looked down and saw the blade not six inches from his midriff. Wounded in the thigh, his immaculate uniform half covered with his own blood and that of his enemies, he was not intimidated by the wild-eyed young guerrilla from Texas who seemed so ready to disembowel him then and there.

The boy himself had a fleeting desire to repay with a knife thrust the man who had led him into this bloody baptism, but he was restrained by a curious sense that the effort would have been futile.

"I guess maybe I sensed that Quantrill couldn't be killed then, not by me or any man. It might be that every one of those men with him would be killed that very day by the Federals, but he wouldn't be. I knew that somehow. He was as invulnerable as a holy martyr in boiling oil whose hour hasn't come or a holy prophet being charioted off to heaven before his hour can come. Not that there was anything holy about Quantrill. He was, at times like this especially, more like a demon than a man. What he might have had in common with the holy ones was a mission, a purpose he had to fulfill before he could be killed. Once that was done, then presumably all it would take would be some nameless enemy raising his weapon 'at a venture' to smite him where it counted. Until then he was safe, and the fact that he took as many chances as he did that day tells me that he knew he couldn't be killed. At that moment, standing there facing him with that knife in my hand and both of us looking as though we'd been slaughtering hogs, I think maybe I wanted to kill him for what I felt myself becoming, what I sensed I'd be if I lived through that day. But I knew I couldn't, and he knew it too. That's why he smiled at me the way he did, looking right through me with those gun-metal eyes."

"That your horse, Ringgold?" the demon was asking.

"Yeah, he's mine."

" 'Yes, sir,' don't you mean?" Only Quantrill would have insisted on such a formality at such a moment.

"Yes, sir, captain," John answered wearily, all the rage and hatred of the moment before gone out of him.

"Well, climb on him and catch up with Gregg up there at the other end. We're surrounded. These boys and I are going to fight our way out on foot from this end. Get a move-on if you want to live."

"Yessir," he mumbled and resheathed his bloody knife. Then he turned to help Zack Hayes onto his feet.

"Come on, men," he heard Quantrill say, and as the men followed their demon chief into the smoky haze, John thought he was alone with Zack. The boy was very pale from losing blood and from the fright he'd just experienced. John didn't know how he'd get him onto Blaze's unsaddled back. Then he heard the reassuring, familiar voice of Ol Shepherd:

"Get yourself mounted, John. I'll boost him up."

"Much obliged, Ol," he said, wishing he could express the enormous gratitude he felt. But there was no time to think about that. As he looked about him through the haze, he saw groups of blue-uniformed figures everywhere and no guerrillas except for a few still figures stretched out here and there on the ground. Grabbing the reins and a handful of Blaze's red mane, he swung himself onto the big stud's back. Without a saddle, he might have been thrown, for all his experience as a bronc peeler, if the animal had put its mind to it. But after a few restive jumps Blaze settled down. Ol Shepherd helped Zack over to where John held the animal nervously prancing and lifted him like a child up behind the rider.

"Hang on, boy," he said, and the boy responded by wrapping his skinny arms tightly around John's waist. Obviously frightened nearly to death, he hadn't said a word since John rescued him from the skull-crushing cavalryman.

"Gregg 'n' them're up that way," Ol said, pointing up the ravine, which was now so hazy that one could have easily become confused about which way to go.

"Watch yourself Ol. There're Yanks all over here."

The one-eyed gunman laughed a little before replying:

"Don't worry, John. This chile weren't born to be Yankee meat. You just get on out of here yourself." And he gave Blaze's rump a slap that echoed like a pistol shot.

The big stud responded like a well-trained cow pony with a calf in front of him, nearly leaving his two riders in the dirt, and as John guided him up the ravine, drumming his heels into the surging flanks, Blaze put on a show of speed that made the newly baptized guerrilla profoundly grateful to the man he was avenging, Harry Younger, whose gift he was. Ahead of him and on either side were blue figures with clubbed carbines and sabers ready. It was a deadly gauntlet, through which Gregg and the others had already passed, made ready for stragglers by their passage.

John bent himself so low that his face was brushed by the flying mane, and the wounded boy clung tightly to his waist. As he passed through the first knot of Federals, most of them jumped to one side or the other, but one managed to connect his hard-swung carbine butt with John's already wounded shoulder, and he nearly lost his knee grip on Blaze. Recovering just as Blaze carried them into and through another bunch of soldiers, he saw a brief flash of metal as an officer hacked at him with a saber. At the time he felt nothing, but later he discovered that his right trouser leg was soaked with blood from a long shallow flesh wound.

Reaching the head of the ravine, he encountered the largest cluster of Federals, some of whom still had ammunition. Warned by the sounds of his flight, they were ready. John saw puffs of smoke in front of him, heard shots on either side and from behind as he passed through the gauntlet. He also thought that he heard Zack cry out but was unable to focus any of his attention away from the obstacles ahead, which included three soldiers who chose to stand their ground. At the last second, two of these men leaped aside, but the third went down cursing under Blaze's hooves.

Then they were clear. The big stud never slowed his gallop coming out of the ravine, and John headed him across a mile-wide meadow toward a hardwood forest in the opposite direction from Pleasant Hill, guessing that was where most of the guerrillas had gone. In fact, the guerrillas, both those mounted and those on foot, had scattered in every direction. Those on foot, led by Quantrill, were slowed by the wounded, none of whom were left behind, where they would have been easy prey for the pursuers. But the Federal cavalry were in no condition to pursue. Exhausted by the fight in the ravine under the stupefying sun and burdened with their own wounded, they rested and waited for fresh troops to finish what they'd begun.

"We made it, Zack, by God!" John yelled as they flew across the meadow on the big tireless animal, who seemed to have sprouted wings. "Sure as hell we did!"

Never had he felt so exhilarated. He had been ready to die, had looked death in the face again and again that day, but now he was alive to fight again. All the weariness he'd been feeling, running and fighting for his life under the pitiless sun after a night without sleep, was now gone. It was an excitement unlike anything he'd felt since the best lovemaking he'd yet enjoyed, when every vital drop of his young manhood had been drawn out and spent, only to be restored miraculously by a shared passion. To come so close to death, even to go down into an underworld full of raging fiends, and yet to come out of it alive—was there anything like it?

As they were about to enter the hardwood forest, he looked back to see if they were being followed. Seeing no pursuers, he slowed Blaze to a walk.

"Sure as hell we did!" he said again to Zack. But Zack didn't answer. And suddenly the skinny arms that had been gripping his waist so tightly let go. Without uttering a word or any sound at all the boy fell off the horse into some tall grass next to the deer trail they were following.

John slid off the horse and ran to where the boy was lying on his back, perfectly still and nearly invisible in the tall grass. He knelt beside Zack, whose eyes were shut tight and who did not reveal any sign of life whatever.

"Zack?"

Slowly the boy's eyes opened. He looked up at John and started to smile, but the smile turned to a grimace of pain. His already pale face had become nearly as gray as the Confederate drummer boy's jacket he wore.

"I'm mighty grateful, John," he said in a voice that wasn't much more than a whisper.

"Is it your leg, Zack?" he asked, ignoring the boy's thanks.

"No, John, they got me again. Comin' through that last bunch that was shootin' at us."

It was then that John noticed the dark stain beginning to spread along the boy's side from underneath.

"My God!" he cried out, horrified and furious at the nameless marksman. He started to lift Zack by the shoulders for a better look.

"Don't, John, don't move me," the boy pleaded in a whisper.

John released him then and rocked back on his knees, letting his useless hands hang down at his sides. All of his weariness had suddenly returned.

"God, Zack, I'm sorry," he said in a voice that nearly broke.

"Waren't your fault. You did real good to get us outta there. Saved my life, you did." His whisper was now very faint.

"You saved mine. That slug'd be in my back if you hadn't been behind me. And by God I'm not going to let you die on me. I'm going to find you a doctor, get you patched up and back to your mama. . . ." He caught himself babbling senselessly this way, knowing full well there was nothing he could do but watch the boy die, as he had watched that other boy die. It was so easy, so goddamned easy, he was thinking, for a man to kill another man. Only God could keep a man's life inside him. He wished that he could pray now, that he'd let Padre García teach him how, along with the Greek and Latin, and that Asa Mitchell's frog eyes up to heaven didn't come to mind whenever he thought of praying.

"Oh my God . . ." was as far as he could go, however, in the direction of a prayer. He saw the boy's lips moving in an inaudible whisper and put his ear down close to hear. So faintly that he couldn't be sure he wasn't imagining them, the words came through:

"We're . . . in . . . His . . . hands."

"Course we are, Zack," he said warmly, as though he really believed it. But Zack didn't hear him. John hesitated a moment before listening to the boy's chest, knowing that he was already gone. Then he raised up onto his knees and began to weep, and in place of the prayers that wouldn't come there came curses:

"Dammit! Damn you . . . damn . . . !"

He didn't even know whom or what he was cursing. Tears streamed down through the black grime of battle covering his face and dropped onto his filthy blood-stained jacket.

Finally he rose to his feet and walked slowly over to where Blaze was cropping the lush summer grass in a clearing that was nearly white with daisy blossoms. Unaware of the nearness of death, unconscious of human suffering, as magnificently indifferent to human fear and agony as a god, the big stallion filled his belly, and his powerful haunches gleamed like burnished copper in the sun. John picked up the reins and grasped the thick red mane but paused a moment before mounting to look back to where the boy lay in the tall grass. Except for the places where his own boots had trampled down the grass, which might have been made by an animal, there was no sign of any living human presence.

SIX

FURLOUGH

The summer passed quickly after that bloody day of initiation, and by the time autumn began to arrive, tingeing the hardwoods with reds and yellows to match the all-devouring flames of hatred that licked across west Missouri and Kansas, John Ringgold was a guerrilla of guerrillas. Under Ol Shepherd's patient tutelage he acquired a mastery of the Colt's exceeded only by that of Ol himself. Perhaps because of this, but not this alone, he also acquired a degree of respect from Quantrill.

"I want you to know that I've been following your progress, Ringgold," the guerrilla chief said one day early in October. "You're turning into a first-rate soldier, one we can count on."

"Thank you, sir," he answered, though he actually took little pleasure in Quantrill's praise. For reasons he couldn't altogether pin down, he still disliked Quantrill and always would. He had to respect him as a leader. After the lesson of the battle in the ravine, Quantrill no longer put his command in jeopardy, and nearly all of the men who survived that fight, especially those on foot, credited his cool, courageous leadership with having saved their lives. ("A right mean-fowt fight. But our cap'n, he seen us through't.") But there was, in spite of his proven courage and competence as a leader, an element of falseness that manifested itself in various ways. For one thing, his splendid uniform, which he had gone all the way to Richmond to obtain, now mended and restored to its condition before the battle in the ravine, was revealed by one of the new recruits, who had just deserted from the regular Confederate army, to be that of a full colonel. Upon being told that his men were aware of this, Quantrill said that he had been given a battlefield promotion to colonel by General Hughes. Since General Hughes had

186

just been killed during a recruiting mission through west Missouri, no one could argue. The general had also reportedly promoted George Todd to captain.

"I have another mission for you, Ringgold, if you feel up to it."

John was now one of Quantrill's scouts. He and John McCorkle were the guerrilla chief's "eyes," roaming alone on missions through the Federal-infested countryside and bringing Quantrill information about troop concentrations and movements. It was lonely, dangerous work, but John preferred it to remaining in the main guerrilla encampment, where he had to take orders not only from Quantrill, but from Todd, Bill Gregg and the other elected guerrilla officers.

"Whatever needs to be done, sir," he answered coolly.

"Cole Younger tells me that you're well acquainted with the areas around Independence and Harrisonville."

"That's right, sir." Though he gave no sign of any excitement, his heart was pounding. He had had no communication with Margaret since July, when Jim Younger, who was coming to join Quantrill, had brought a letter from her.

"I'd like you to scout that area for me. Find out which Federal units are operating there, how many men there are, what kinds of weapons they have, and the names of the commanding officers, if you can find them out. We'll look for you on the upper Sniabar in ten days."

As soon as he left Quantrill's tent, John sought out Cole and Jim.

"If you have any messages for your mama and sisters, I'll be at your place in a few days."

Cole and Jim looked at each other, trying to think of what to tell him. The message would have to be oral, for it would be dangerous to the women if any written communication from the brothers fell into the Federals' hands. Some of the Federal units in Missouri, such as the Seventh Kansas Cavalry, or "Independent Mounted Kansas Jayhawkers," and Jim Lane's "Kansas Brigade," would be quite capable of having the women set fire to their own house if there was an excuse. Lately it had happened more than once in west Missouri.

"Tell them we're both well," was all that either brother could come up with finally. "Tell them Captain, I mean Colonel, Quantrill is taking good care of us," Cole added.

John then went to the lean-to he shared with John McCorkle. McCorkle, a big, rawboned Missourian, was stretched out digesting his midday meal. He propped himself up on an elbow and watched as his fellow scout gathered his saddle gear.

"Goin' for a little ride, John?"

"Yep, over around Harrisonville and Independence. Our leader wants to know how many blue uniforms there are."

"You'd do well to wear one of them yourself." Guerrillas frequently wore Yankee uniforms, and there were several available in the cellar of the farm by which they were then camped.

"Don't have my size," John fabricated. The truth was he couldn't bear to put on a Federal uniform, even to disguise himself.

"Just as well, I guess," McCorkle replied. "Not too many Yank soldiers got hair as long as your'n. You'd look more suspicious wearin' a uniform."

John's hair, uncut since he became a guerrilla, now reached his shoulders. Unlike other guerrillas, however, he did shave, and his face was deeply bronzed by the sun and wind of the Kansas prairies.

"Guess I'll just have to pass for a farmer," he said to McCorkle.

"I'm bound to tell you, John, you don't look much like a farmer, either," McCorkle answered with a grim chuckle. "You'd just best not fall into their hands if you can help it."

"I'll surely try not to." He had to admit that McCorkle was right. The faded buttonless red flannel shirt he wore had the sleeves hacked off at the shoulder to facilitate quiet movement through the brush. His gray trousers were not yet adorned with red stripes, but they were thrust into Federal cavalry boots he had appropriated when they plundered a supply wagon near Fort Leavenworth. He took the precaution of removing the black feather from his hat, but still he didn't look much like a farmer.

"Harrisonville, huh?" McCorkle said. "Last time I was over that way the Fedruls had patrols guardin' all the bridges an' fords. I'd watch myself at crossin's if I was you."

"I'll do that. See you in ten days."

Keeping McCorkle's words of caution in his mind, he managed to restrain himself and Blaze as they entered the more familiar parts of Jackson County and approached Independence. The big sorrel seemed to know that they were headed for the Younger farm, or maybe it was John's own eagerness communicating itself to the high-spirited animal that made it so hard to keep him reined in to a walk. John felt as though he were on a furlough, and he remembered hearing how men were deserting the Confederate army to go home and harvest crops, claiming that they were "on furlough." If anybody questioned one of these deserters, the man would usually point to the pistol in his belt and say, "That's my furlough." The difference was, of course, that John's furlough had been in effect authorized by his commanding officer. Moreover, it wouldn't begin until he completed his mission.

From farmers in the area, most of whom were ardently pro-secessionist, hoping and praying that Sterling Price's army would follow up its August victory at Wilson's Creek and lead Missouri into the Confederacy, he found out a great deal about recent Federal troop movements. In mid-September, Jim Lane, United States senator and Republican political boss of Kansas, had led his "Kansas Brigade" into Missouri. Near West Line, John spoke to a farmer who had been burned out by these Kansans.

"Jim Lane hisself was here," he said. "I heard him tell his men, 'Everything disloyal, from a Durham cow to a Shanghai chicken, must be cleaned out!' Then they took everything I owned, piled it in my own wagon and set fire to my place. Hell, I wasn't even secesh! I am now, by God!"

Closer to Independence, he met another farmer and his family driving south in a wagon piled high with furniture. From them he learned that the Seventh Kansas Cavalry, the "Independent Mounted Kansas Jayhawkers," under Jennison and Anthony, had been raiding Parkville, Missouri, in steamboats.

"I knowed some of them fellas," the farmer said. "They used to live by us. But they was Unionist, an' we had to run 'em out. I reckon they went to Kansas. Now I guess they're back here to get even with us. There's some real wild abolitionists with that bunch. I seen Ol' Brown's son, John Jr., leadin' a company o' them Jayhawkers. He's even crazier'n his ol' man, looks like."

He gathered all the information he could from people who were willing to talk, and beyond this he scouted several Federal encampments, spending hours lying in the underbrush while insects preyed on his face and naked arms, counting men and noticing how they were armed. He was happy to note that few men, only officers in fact, possessed revolvers, while most cavalry troopers had only single-shot carbines, and the infantry still carried muskets. It didn't look as though the number of troops in the area was being increased much, if at all, which would please Quantrill should he be planning a raid in the area. By chance, though, he encountered another guerrilla scout, one of Ben Parker's men, who informed him that Jennison's Jayhawkers, the Seventh Kansas, would soon be in the area assigned to protect Federal supply trains from guerrilla attacks.

Five days had passed since he left Quantrill's encampment on the Kansas border, and in five days he had to rejoin the band on the upper Sniabar. It would not be as long a furlough as he had hoped for, but he had carried out his mission faithfully and the few days that remained were his own.

In his eagerness to see Margaret again, he nearly ran into a Federal patrol less than a mile from the Younger farm. Reluctantly, he decided to wait for nightfall before approaching the house, and he knew that he dared not approach it openly. Federal scouts would almost certainly be watching it. Putting his patience to its severest test, he spent an afternoon hidden in the thick brush less than a mile from the Younger house. From time to time, women could be seen walking between the house and the chicken coop or the vegetable plot. He thought he recognized Margaret, but he couldn't be sure. The only male figure he could see was the boy Bobby Younger. Richard Younger, as he was to find out shortly, had enlisted in the regular Confederate army, and Frank Marion Younger had been incapacitated by a stroke shortly after his brother's assassination.

As darkness fell, he cat-footed out of the brush and followed a fringe of woods to the slave cabins beside the creek. He noticed that all of the slave cabins appeared to be empty, and it wasn't difficult to guess that the Jay-hawkers had completed their work of liberation. This presented him with a problem, for he had planned to get one of the slaves to carry a message to the house. But then he remembered that there was another slave cabin nearby, whose occupant might have chosen to remain with the Youngers.

As he approached the cabin in which Cyrus once lived, he was delighted to see light shining through the brightly colored curtains in the windows. He ran and crouched beneath one of the open windows. As he rose up and looked into the house, he saw the woman sitting in a corner reading a book that appeared to be the same Bible he had seen Cyrus reading the night of Walley's visit. Beside her was a cradle, which she rocked from time to time. Just above the covers a tiny brown head could be discerned.

Not wanting to startle the woman but seeing no other way, he tapped the window glass above the opening. Then he stepped back and waited. Suddenly the light in the room went out. The woman had put out the lamp to get a better look at who was outside. In a few seconds, she was at the window.

"Who are you? What do you want?" she demanded in that same unservile tone he had remarked in her husband's voice. He was about to reply, but his tongue froze as he found himself confronting the twin black barrels of a shotgun. Before replying, he raised his hands slowly.

"I'm John Ringgold," he said. Then, for no reason he could understand, he went on to say, "One of the Young-ers' people." Maybe it was because he remembered Cyrus saying, "The Youngers are my people."

"Didn't recognize you, Mr. Ringgold. With that hair an' all, you look like a wil' man."

She put her shotgun aside, let him into the cabin and listened as he asked her to bring Margaret to him from the house. A little reluctantly she agreed, but then she asked him to look after her child while she was gone. After she left, he sat by the cradle, afraid that his wild appearance would cause the child to scream, but it did not. The bright round black eyes regarded him inquisi-tively, and a pudgy little brown hand reached up at him, trying perhaps to reach the long red hair that fell about his shoulders. He smiled shyly down at the child of Cyrus and gave it his finger to grasp.

"Johnny."

The sound of her voice uttering his name was one of the things he had sought to preserve through the three long months he had ridden with Quantrill. Often drowned out by the crash of gunfire and the screams of dying men, it came back to him sometimes as he drowsed in the saddle on long dusty marches or lay out under the stars at night. Now he heard it again, heard Margaret's voice, and as he rose from the chair beside the cradle, she rushed across the room and threw herself into his arms.

"You're back! You're back! Don't ever leave me again, please don't ever leave me," she pleaded as she clung to his neck, and he felt her tears on his naked chest.

"I won't. I won't," he answered, and at that moment he meant it. Quantrill, Walley and the war could be damned for all he cared. He would see that this furlough never came to an end.

For the next three days, perhaps the most blissful of John's entire life, they spent most of their time at Margaret's secret place, the pond where she had taken him from the harvest just a year ago. They also walked through the woods and along the ridgetops surrounding the pond, seeking out what Margaret called "elfin grots."

"I'm your Belle Dame sans Merci, Johnny. I will have thee in thrall," she murmured as she wound her golden limbs about him and kissed him hungrily.

"Thou hast me already, milady," he responded in the archaic love language they shared only with each other. "This is one knight at arms who's all through with war."

"Do you mean it, Johnny? Do you really mean it?"

He did. Two days with her had completely convinced him of what he had guessed that first night he held her again, that he could not leave her. Quantrill and the Confederacy would have to win the war without him. He had already begun thinking about where they could go to escape the war.

"Oregon," he said. "That's where we'll go. They say it's all green out there, just like Missouri, only things grow better. Crops come up all ready to harvest almost overnight."

"I've heard California has a lot to offer," she said.

"Maybe we'll go there, if it's far enough from this damned war."

"What about your ambition, Johnny? Don't you want to be a doctor?"

He laughed a little bitterly as he answered her.

"That just doesn't seem to be in the cards for me. Right now, I'm about as close to being a doctor as I was on the farm back in Texas. My future, if I've got one, looks to be farming. It's not a bad life, really, making things grow." For some reason, he thought of the tiny brown baby in its cradle, being rocked by Cyrus's widow. "If you'll share it with me, I'll be the happiest man on earth."

"Oh, Johnny, I will," she said and went on to show her delight by loving him as no woman ever had or ever would. He marveled at how the mere touch of her, any part of her, could inflame him. He was so filled with the joy of loving her that he couldn't imagine any other feeling in its place. How, he wondered, had these hands with which he stroked her naked flesh shed the blood of enemies in battle?

And so they planned their escape from the war. The evening of the third day, however, they met near the slave cabins, and John could see from her expression that something was terribly wrong. He had been away for part of the afternoon trying to find a good horse for her, since all of the Youngers' prime stock had been driven off either by Jayhawkers or the Federal cavalry.

"Soldiers, Johnny. There were Yankee soldiers here. They threatened us."

"How many?"

"Lots. Close to a hundred anyway. And Bobby said there's a bunch more camped between here and Pleasant Hill."

"What did they say to you?"

"Their leader did all the talking. He was a real mean-looking little man with a moustache and pointy chin whiskers that made him look like pictures you see of the devil. He called himself Colonel Jennison."

"What did he say to you?"

"He said that they were the Seventh Kansas Cavalry and they were 'here to string up reb guerrillas.' Somebody'd told him that all our menfolk were with Quantrill, and he told us we'd better not try to help them. He told Mama that he'd personally make her set fire to her own house if he had reason to suspect her of helping her sons or 'any other damned rebels.' The last thing he said was, 'Playing war is played out.' Johnny, I've never heard anybody talk that way to a woman. And Mama, too. Can you imagine?"

From what he'd heard of Jennison, he could readily imagine. He said, "I had a little trouble finding you a horse. Maybe I can liberate one from that Jayhawker cavalry outfit. God knows they've helped themselves to enough of your stock."

"Johnny," she replied, putting her hands on his chest and looking him directly in the eyes, "I'm not going."

"What do you mean? You said . . ."

"I know what I said, but I can't go now. Mama needs me. Poor Uncle Frank can't even walk. Bobby's a child. He can't do the man's work that needs to be done. My sisters and I have got to do what we can."

"But you knew this before, Margaret. You were still going to go with me. What changed your mind?" His miserable disappointment would not let him sympathize with her reasons for staying.

"It was those Yankees, Johnny, especially that man Jennison. He frightened Mama to death." She put her arms up around his neck and kissed him, trying to make him understand. "It's my family," she said.

Finally he let himself understand. He put his arms around her and held her to him very gently.

"You're right," he said. "You wouldn't be able to live with yourself if you didn't look after your family."

"You go, Johnny," she urged him. "You go out to Oregon or California or wherever. Send for me when the war's over. I'll come to you wherever you are."

She really meant it, he knew, and he hugged her as he said, "No, Margaret. We'll go together when the war's over."

Sensing perhaps that her decision to stay with her family had reawakened his own sense of duty, she asked him anxiously, "You're not going back to Quantrill, are you?"

"I've got to. I'm a Confederate soldier. Quantrill needs the information I have for him. He needs to know about Jennison."

"Don't go yet," she begged him. "Please stay a few more days."

"I can't."

"Just a day."

"I've already stayed too long. They're expecting me day after tomorrow."

She closed her eyes then and nodded, as she had the day of her father's funeral.

"Just be careful, Johnny. Please don't let those Yankees get you," she pleaded, shuddering a little, as though she intuited that they might.

"Don't worry about me, milady," he said, forcing a laugh. Then he mimicked Ol Shepherd, trying to make her laugh: "This chile waren't born to be Yankee meat."

But she didn't laugh.

Twenty-four hours later, John Ringgold found himself tightly bound to a fence post in front of a barn somewhere in western Jackson County. He was naked to the waist, and not twenty feet away, among the dancing flames of a fire made with the parts of a gate, a strip of iron from a wagon wheel was being heated bright red. A Federal sergeant and two troopers were hunkered around the blaze watching the iron's progress. Across the fire from them a stocky Federal officer was examining the contents of John Ringgold's shirt and coat. Finding a packet of Margaret's letters, he pulled one out and studied the envelope by the light of the fire.

"So your name's Ringgold, is it?" the officer said to him.

"That's what I told you," John replied, feeling more wretched than at any moment in his life, whether because of the sight of the letters in the officer's hands or what he anticipated with the hot iron or both.

"Funny sort of name. I've heard it before, though. When I was passing through Georgia. It goes with a nigger-lynching reb, I guess."

"What makes you think I'm a reb? I'm just a farmer," John insisted, trying to save himself with a skill he had never acquired and never would—lying.

"Oh, you're a reb, all right. If you wasn't a reb, you wouldn't've tried to swim that river 'stead o' crossin' the bridge we had guarded. It happens that a couple o' my men used to be with Major Gower's outfit. They figure they saw you with that bunch o' rebs Gower trapped back in June. You're with that devil Quantrill, ain't you?"

John said nothing.

"An' lookee here. Looks like you got a sweetheart by the name o' Younger. Ain't that somethin'! Wouldn't be surprised if she was related to Cole Younger."

At that moment, another trooper came into the fire-light and saluted.

"Cap'n Walley, sir."

"Yeah, what is it?"

"Sir, Lieutenant Wilson wants to know if you want him to take this reb back to Kansas City or if you mean to hang him here."

Walley paused for a moment and regarded the prisoner thoughtfully before he replied. "Tell the lieutenant to go on back to Kansas City. We'll join him there as soon as we've finished our . . . uh . . . interrogation of the prisoner."

"Yessir." The trooper saluted and ran off toward the farmhouse, where the rest of the captain's company was being served supper by the women of Morgan Walker's household.

"That iron about ready, sergeant?"

"Yessir, it's just about right." John Ringgold saw the sparks rising as the sergeant, who had on a pair of black-smith's gloves, turned the iron in the flames.

"Bring it over, will you," Walley said, as he hooked his thumbs in the waistband of his breeches and approached the prisoner. "Now, Mr. Ringgold, I'm going to give you the opportunity to avoid something painful. All you got to do is tell me what you know about Quantrill."

"Who's Quantrill?" he tried lamely. "I'm no guerrilla. I'm just a farmer."

"How'd you know Quantrill was a guerrilla?" Walley snapped, pouncing quickly and laughing with pleasure at his own quickness. When the prisoner did not answer, he shrugged and said, "All right, farmer boy, have it your way." Then he nodded to the sergeant.

John felt the heat of the iron as it moved toward his bare flesh, and he resolved not to cry out. But as it was laid across his midriff he found that he was powerless to control a scream that rose with all the strength of his lungs. And he was equally powerless to control his lower organs. When the iron was removed, having been applied for an instant that felt like a lifetime, and the unspeakable agony of his flesh reached its peak and then began to subside, he became aware of a wetness running down the backs of his legs and a stench that rose to mingle with the smell of burning flesh.

"Phew!" Walley snorted. "That's damn disgusting, I'd say."

John ground his teeth together and fought back tears. A yearning simply to be freed of his pain had all but replaced the rage and hatred he had been feeling toward Walley. "It ain't like I'm enjoying this, farmer boy. Just tell me about Quantrill an' we'll stop."

"Quantrill who?" he gasped, knowing that if he didn't pass out soon, the burning iron would cause him to reveal everything he knew.

Walley nodded to the sergeant, who now brandished the iron in John's face, either to fill him with anticipation of more of the same burning agony or to indicate that his face was the next area to be burnt. Abruptly, though, he was stopped by the captain.

"Just a minute, sergeant." Abruptly the captain's tone of voice changed as he said, "Evening, Miss Walker. What can I do for you?"

John's attention suddenly shifted from the still-glowing iron in the sergeant's hands to the woman addressed.

"Evening, captain," she said. "I've brought you your supper." She was darkly attractive, with masses of soft brown hair framing her handsome features and tumbling loosely over her shoulders. A white, lace-fringed collar surmounted a long, snugly fitting black dress that revealed in the firelight a rather voluptuous figure. Walley looked uncomfortable as he tried to shift his role from that of torturing interrogator to gentleman.

Smiling nervously, he said, "I'm grateful, Miss Walker, but this ain't hardly a place for a lady. We've caught ourselves a dangerous rebel, one of Quantrill's guerrillas, and we're questioning him."

Having handed Walley his supper and a clay jug of whiskey, she walked around the fire and came up to the prisoner.

"He doesn't look that dangerous to me, captain. But I guess you never know with these dirty secesh traitors." As she looked him directly in the eyes, John thought he saw something that didn't go with her harsh words, but he quickly dismissed this impression and sought to compose himself, accepting the utter hopelessness of his situation. The sergeant had gone back to the fire to reheat the iron.

"What are you going to do with him?" the woman was asking.

"Wal, seein' as how he don't seem willin' to tell us anything about his friend Quantrill, I guess we'll have to hang him."

John knew that a rope was waiting no matter what he did or did not say. It was just a matter of how long he wanted to endure having his flesh branded and his bowels rendered out of control. But for a few seconds he gazed intently into the woman's eyes, savoring for the last time a vision of beauty. Her eyes were dark and liquid, like Margaret's, and he was profoundly thankful that Margaret couldn't see him now. He hoped that she would never find out what happened to him.

"Tell you what, Miss Walker," Walley was saying. "I just can't appreciate your good supper sittin' here lookin' at that dirty reb. If you don't mind, me an' the men'll go on up to your house an' eat. After supper we'll finish our business with this secesh scum."

While Walley and the others returned to the house with Miss Walker, one man was left to guard the prisoner. It was a chilly fall evening and the trooper huddled close to the fire, which made him drowsy, and after not many minutes passed he began to nod. Soon his head dropped onto his chest.

Across the fire from him, the prisoner, who had been sweating profusely during his ordeal, was suffering from a chill. As an hour passed slowly, his teeth chattered and he writhed against his bonds trying to gain some warmth. In his miserable condition he half believed he was hallucinating when he heard a woman's voice whispering just behind him.

"Be quiet. Don't say a word." As he started to turn his head for a look at her she said, "No, don't move until I've cut you free."

Still not quite believing his ears, John obeyed and felt the passage of steel across his wrists and finally the haft of a knife being shoved into his right hand.

"There, now you've got to help yourself."

"Who are you?" he couldn't help asking.

"Be quiet," she hissed. "I told you to be quiet. I'm Andy Walker's sister, Anna. Tell him when you see him that we're all right, but the Federals are all over this place. He'd best not try to visit us."

Andy Walker's sister! So that's who she is. He remembered then hearing about how Quantrill had been involved for a time with Morgan Walker's daughter after he arranged the Jayhawker ambush. Until that moment John had no idea that the Federals had brought him to the Walker farm.

He started to turn and whisper his thanks to Anna Walker, but before he could utter a word he heard her steps as she ran off into the darkness. And now the guard, aroused perhaps by a mysterious warning dream, suddenly raised his head and stared across the fire at the prisoner. John kept his arms behind him, clasping the wrist of the hand that held the knife with his other hand, so that his arms would still appear bound. He said:

"I'd surely appreciate it if you'd loosen my tie ropes a little."

"Not likely, guerrilla," the man said with a short, sneering laugh.

"Well, could you at least look and see if my hands are changing color? Feels like gangrene setting in."

More curious than sympathetic, the guard stood up and came around the fire. As he started to move around John Ringgold to examine his bonds, the prisoner's left hand shot out and grabbed the front of his tunic. He pulled the guard off balance and with his right hand drove the knife hilt deep into the man's belly. As the man started to scream, he released the tunic and clapped his hand over his mouth. Then he drove the knife in again, and again, whereupon the man slumped quietly to the ground at his feet.

"I should have picked up his carbine," Ringo remembers. "It would have made things a whole lot easier for me a few minutes later. But by then I was so used to relying on pistols and knives that I didn't even think about using a carbine. I just stuck the knife in my belt and started to run for the barn where I'd seen them take Blaze."

He was halfway across the open space between the fence and the barn when he heard a familiar, hated voice.

"Hey, farmer boy, you plannin' to go for a ride?"

John turned and saw Walley on horseback at the edge of the circle of light thrown by the fire. Even in the semidarkness, he could see that the stocky officer was laughing. Still laughing, Walley drew his saber from its metal scabbard.

"Now I'm gonna reap you, farmer boy," he said.

As Walley spurred his horse toward him, John Ringgold went into a crouch. When the rider was almost upon him, John threw himself to the ground and rolled out of the way, but he could feel the wind of the saber missing him by inches. Walley's horse nearly carried him into the fence, turning at the last instant and almost spilling him. The rider recovered quickly, however, wheeled his mount about and began another pass at the half-naked figure attempting to dodge him.

As Walley passed him a second time, coming so close with his saber that he scratched him on one arm, John threw himself down beside a haystack near the fence, a stack from which hay had been forked into a trough on the other side of the fence. He rolled into the hay, and his fingers encountered a long wooden handle. Desperate for a weapon, unable to use the knife in his belt against the horseman, he drew the handle out of the straw and found it to be a pitchfork.

"Ol' Walley's gonna reap you, farmer boy, reap you like you was wheat," the rider shouted, and his laughter became the kind of high-pitched giggle John had heard Quantrill emit during moments of high killing excitement. At the edge of the firelight, Walley wheeled about again and spurred his horse toward the vulnerable man, who was now down on his knees beside the haystack. Grasping the pommel of his saddle, he leaned out with his saber ready to decapitate the kneeling figure. But suddenly the man rose, and Walley saw the pitchfork tines shining in the firelight. He tried to raise himself upright in the saddle, but the whiskey he'd been drinking with his supper, poured generously for him by Anna Walker, slowed his reflexes. Slashing wildly, trying to ward off the pitchfork, he was carried onto the tines by his running horse and dragged off the animal onto the ground like a speared fish.

John was himself knocked to the ground by the impact of Walley's charge, but he scrambled quickly onto his feet and stood over his enemy, who was now writhing with the tines through his midriff. Groaning and gurgling, Walley tried to pull the tines out of his body, and for a moment or two John Ringgold considered leaving him in this condition. But it occurred to him that Walley might somehow recover. His troopers might manage to get him into Kansas City for medical treatment. Considering this possibility and unmoved by any feeling other than a desire to increase the agony of Walley's last moments, he picked up the handle and drew the tines out of the captain's thick middle.

As the steel was drawn out of his body, Walley cried out. Then he began to whimper, holding his wounded belly with both hands. John Ringgold stood over him, poising the fork, demonically animated by the unspeakable joy of vengeance. Instead of finishing Walley at once, he drove the tines again into his belly.

"That's for Harry Younger, you bastard!" he snarled. Walley cried out again, so loudly that the troopers up at the farmhouse must have heard him, whereupon John drew out the fork and drove it into his chest.

"And that's for me!"

Walley's eyes bulged like a frog's as he looked up at his killer, and he grasped feebly at the tines with bloody fingers. Finally, after a prolonged shudder that went through his whole body, he lay still.

With considerable effort, John Ringgold restrained himself from plunging the fork again into his enemy's body. Remembering Walley's stubby fingers flipping through the packet of Margaret's letters, he reached into the breast pocket of the dead officer's tunic. The letters were there, but when he drew the packet out, he saw that it was covered with Walley's blood. Shaking his head in disgust, he went to the fire and dropped the packet onto the coals.

By now, the troopers up at the farmhouse could be

heard shouting at each other, wondering what was going on down at the barn and where the captain was. Because of the generosity of Anna Walker and the other women of the household with their whiskey, the men were in no hurry to investigate the sounds, each man being willing to let his comrades attend to the matter, some assuming that Walley was again engaged in torturing the captured guerrilla. By the time one of them, the sergeant, wandered down toward the barn in search of his captain, John Ringgold had Blaze's saddle on and was about to mount him. Seeing the sergeant approach, he pulled Walley's pistol out of his waistband and checked the cylinder. Then he swung onto Blaze and walked him to the doorway of the barn.

At the edge of the shadowy circle of firelight, the sergeant nearly stumbled over Walley's body. Instantly sobered by the discovery, he drew his pistol and looked around him in alarm. Suddenly he became aware of a rider bearing down on him, and he heard the chilling, savage sound of a Missouri rebel yell. The sergeant raised his pistol toward the rider and squeezed off a wild shot, but his shot was quickly followed by the crash of another, and he was doubled over by the impact of a slug in his lower belly. Rolling on the ground in his agony, the sergeant was but dimly aware of the sound of hoofbeats fading into the night.

The rider bent low over the stallion's neck and let him maintain his own pace, but after nearly two miles, he slowed him to a walk and began to look about warily. He had been captured the previous evening by a night patrol, crossing the Blackwater River at a ford below the bridge guarded by Federal militia. The Federals were not altogether foolish, whatever else you wanted to say about them. The patrol had been watching the ford precisely in anticipation of the likes of John Ringgold, Confederate guerrilla scout. And now John Ringgold made a fervent vow that he would never be taken again, at least not alive.

Moving slowly, warily, but never stopping, he reached the guerrilla encampment on the upper Sniabar in twelve hours. There he was challenged by a sentry who turned out to be none other than Andy Walker.

"Password?"

"Abe Lincoln's underwear."

"Ringgold? John Ringgold, izzat you?"

"Yeah, Andy, it's me. Thanks to your sister."

He dismounted, and Andy led him to Quantrill's tent. As they walked toward the tent, he delivered Anna Walker's message and told him how she'd saved his life. Then Cole suddenly appeared, running out to throw a great bearlike arm around his shoulders, now covered by a Federal army blanket, and he told Cole how he had visited the Younger farm and how it, like the Walker place, was constantly visited and watched by the Federals. He told himself that if he had any energy left after reporting to Quantrill, he would tell Cole how his father had been avenged.

"It's the women we got to worry about," Andy Walker said.

"You're right there," John replied. "If those bastards can't get us, they're liable to take it out on our women."

"I can't believe that even Yankees would do that," Cole said.

John paused at the entrance to Quantrill's tent to turn and look at Cole.

"Believe it," he said.

SEVEN

CAESARE DUCE

As the sun climbs toward its zenith above the Dragoons, the tall man rises from his place beside the spring and walks toward the meadow in front of his camp. The warmth of the late morning sun on his shoulders and the back of his neck is a pleasing sensation, not like the oppressive heat that will come with the afternoon. He stretches his arms above his head, then swings them about in a kind of swimming motion to loosen his cramped muscles. Pausing at the edge of the meadow, he hunkers down to study some tracks in an ungrassed sandy spot. He shakes his head as he recognizes the huge prints of the grizzly that had visited his camp. Glancing across the meadow, he looks again for his horse and pack mule but is not surprised when they are not to be seen. Looking up, he sees an eagle crossing the cloudless blue heavens on its way to a craggy perch somewhere up on the unscalable shoulders of the tall conical peak at the west end of the little mountain valley.

"If he feels like it, he might just wing himself on down to Sonora," the man says aloud, smiling a little enviously to himself. "That's where I'd like to be if not a lot further south, down in the Yucatán where the *rurales* don't know me."

Turning back to the spring, he is not a little depressed by the awareness of how he must again wing his thoughts back twenty years into the infernos of bleeding Kansas and Missouri. Memory can, he reflects, be a source of so much pleasure, endlessly reviving those moments one would trade for years of one's ordinary existence, but if a man would have the pleasure of these moments, he must endure the revival of others. The sweet memory of the love he knew in the war is inextricably bound up with the almost unbearable recollection of how it ended.

"A history of that war," he begins, "should rightly include a chapter on how it was fought in Missouri and Kansas. It should at least give us guerrillas—Quantrill's men and those of Bloody Bill Anderson, Dick Yeager, Parker and the rest—credit for tying up thousands of Yankees who would otherwise have been available to fight the Confederate armies over in Virginia and Georgia. Throughout 'sixty-two and 'sixty-three especially, we kept the bluebellies busy. In 'sixty-two alone we raided into Kansas three times, hitting Aubrey, Olathe and Shawneetown. We also attacked the Federal garrison at Lamar, Missouri, and would have taken the place if those damned Confederate cavalry regulars under Colonel Lewis had done their part. After that, during the winter of 'sixty-two—'sixty-three, we served with Joe Shelby's regiment of Missouri regulars down in Arkansas at the battles of Cane Hill, Fayetteville and Prairie Grove, where a Yank musket ball nearly finished me. At Fayetteville, we even saved Shelby himself from some Arkansas Mountain Federals who'd captured him. Later on, all by ourselves, we whipped General Blunt and a hundred regulars at Baxter Springs and damn nearly captured the general in the process.

"But I'm terribly afraid that when our chapter is written, there won't be much in it about Prairie Grove or Fayetteville or Baxter Springs. We'll be damned lucky if those actions are mentioned at all. The sand and spirit our boys showed and the mentions in dispatches to General Price will probably be forgotten. What won't be forgotten, I'm afraid, will be our visit to Lawrence, Kansas, in August of 'sixty-three.

"Shortly after our Lawrence raid, I read a newspaper account that called it 'the worst atrocity of the war.' That newspaper was the *Leavenworth Daily Conservative,* which tended to exaggerate the evil of our actions generally, but in this case they might have been right. I haven't heard of anything comparable to the Lawrence raid being carried out by anyone, Union or Confederate. What I wish more folks were aware of, however, were some of the reasons why we did what we did.

"General Thomas Ewing, Jr., had something to do with it. He was the Union commander of the District of the Border at Kansas City. I had the pleasure of being part of the guerrilla welcoming party that, so to speak, greeted the general the day he took command. A bunch of us long-haired partisans under George Todd bush-whacked a 150-man detachment of the Ninth Kansas Cavalry just outside Westport and killed about twenty of them. They ran like rabbits, and we chased them damn near into Westport. I remember Will McGuire sticking a note into the mouth of a dead bluebelly officer. The note said, 'Remember the dying words of Jim Vaughn.' Jim had been hung publicly at Fort Leavenworth back in May by General Blunt as a way of showing Kansas that he was doing something about the guerrilla problem, and just before he died, Jim told the folks who were there to watch the show that some of them would suffer for his death.

"Anyway, getting back to General Ewing, he seems to have come to the conclusion that he would never get rid of us by purely military means. Because, for one thing, most of the folks living in west Missouri had relatives fighting with one guerrilla band or another. These folks kept us supplied with food, clothing and good Missouri horseflesh. What we needed in the way of guns and ammunition we could always appropriate from the Yan-kees themselves. When the Federals came after us, we faded into the woods and hills, and there was no catching us. Sometimes they were lucky, as when Jim Vaughn walked into that barbershop in Wyandotte and let him-self get caught by a squad of bluebellies or when I got caught crossing the Blackwater, but generally they couldn't lay a hand on us. We didn't lose a single man in that Westport ambush.

"General Ewing came up with the idea of shipping several hundred families of known guerrillas out of the state, down into Arkansas. I guess he figured that the guerrillas would follow their families, who would then no longer be able to provide supplies. So along about the middle of August, in accord with General Ewing's or-ders, the Federals started arresting men and women sus-pected of helping us. They were taken to the provost marshal in Kansas City and told to get out of Missouri immediately with whatever livestock or property they might manage to take along with them. After our Law-rence raid, the general drastically extended his order, enforcing the removal of people who couldn't establish their loyalty. I remember seeing the roads near Kansas City crowded with poor folks, old men and kids driving milk cows and oxen, harmless gentle women with babies in their arms walking along barefoot and shivering or maybe bareback on some piece of crowbait horseflesh. It was a damned sorry spectacle, and I for one regretted being partly responsible for the way they were suffering the general's wrath.

"As for 'the worst atrocity of the war,' as it's come to be called, I came to regret my part in that too, but not for some time after the event. At the time, I was so full of rage and hatred for Ewing and the others responsible for murdering our women that I regretted nothing.

"What Andy Walker and I and some others feared finally came to pass. Even before General Ewing came up with his plan to depopulate west Missouri of Confederate sympathizers, the Yankees had begun rounding up our women and putting them in jail. At the time Jim Vaughn was hung, his sisters were confined in Fort Leavenworth, and not long after that we got word that a number of our women had been imprisoned in Kansas City. We didn't know who they were at first, and so we sent our Negro spy John Noland in to find out. The Yankees never paid Noland any mind, couldn't imagine a black man spying for Confederate guerrillas, and he was always able to get us all the information we needed. What we found out in Kansas City that time put us all in a state of frustrated rage, but it was as nothing to what came later.

" 'My God!' exclaimed John McCorkle. 'They've got both my sister and sister-in-law!'

" 'Wait'll Anderson finds out about this,' Todd said, shaking his head after Noland revealed that three of Bill Anderson's sisters were among the prisoners. Anderson and his band had just ridden down from Clay County to join Quantrill for a raid into Kansas. When he gave out the names of two others, Susan Vandiver and Armenia Gilvey, Cole stood up swearing. 'They're my cousins,' he said. But he hadn't heard the worst. Noland completed his recital of the prisoners' names:

" 'Becky Younger and her sister Margaret.'

"Cole and I both immediately went over to Noland

and demanded to know if he was absolutely certain of those last two names.

" 'I'm certain,' he said, regarding us with wide sympathetic eyes.

"It took us both a few minutes to collect ourselves and start thinking clearly about how we were going to free them. Noland told us that the women were confined on the second floor of a three-story brick building on Grand Avenue. It was a rotten old building that anybody could see was on the point of collapse. A Federal lieutenant we captured later told us how a Federal army surgeon went in to visit the prisoners and then went right to General Ewing to suggest that they be moved to a safer place. The sonofabitch paid him no mind.

"I hadn't seen Margaret since the early part of June, when she and Anna Walker rode up together into the Sniabar camp to visit George Todd and me. That was the first time I'd seen her since my 'furlough.' Again, it was a sweet, blissful time during which I tried my damnedest to convince her to go to Oregon with me, but again she wouldn't desert her family. We both thanked Anna Walker endlessly for saving my neck. Anna was then Todd's lady, being no longer involved with Quantrill. I was pleased to tell Margaret how I had avenged her father but was a little disappointed when the news didn't give her more pleasure. 'I'm just glad you're safe, Johnny,' was all she said when I told her about killing Walley. Then she begged me to be more careful and not let myself fall into the hands of the Yankees again. 'Anna told me that they were going to hang you. You mustn't let them catch you again.'

"Now she was the one who was caught. How to free her and the others was all that Cole, McCorkle and I could think about. Finally, after everyone had had a chance to present his bright idea, I came up with my own plan, and I didn't give a damn if anyone else approved of it.

" 'I'm going in there tonight,' I said.

" 'You're what?' McCorkle snapped angrily, being apparently at that point where nothing irritates so much as a dumb remedy or solution to a problem.

" 'You heard me,' I replied in kind, being at that point

where nothing irritates so much as being questioned by someone who has no plan of his own to offer.

" 'I seem to recall that you was captured by Missouri volunteers, Ringgold,' McCorkle reminded me. 'I don't guess you recollect that the garrison in Kansas City is made up of them same Missouri Fedruls, just waitin' to string up secesh guerrillas.'

" 'I didn't take your advice before, John. Now I will.' I then explained to my mystified fellow scout how I planned to fit myself out as a Federal officer in one of our captured uniforms. 'And I'll produce an authorization to remove our women from that house to Fort Leavenworth.'

" 'Where will you get that?' he asked.

" 'From our own colonel. You know he could authorize Jennison to cut Jim Lane's throat and Jim wouldn't question it. Our colonel can make something like that read like it came from Abe Lincoln.'

"They were skeptical but seemed to become more hopeful when Quantrill himself agreed to forge the order.

" 'It's crazy as hell, Ringgold,' Quantrill said, but then he chuckled grimly and added, 'just crazy enough to work. It just happens that I have a good supply of official stationery for the District of the Border. I also have a dispatch which some of our men picked from a Federal rider containing a fine sample of General Ewing's handwriting and his signature. While you make yourself a little more presentable as a Federal officer, I'll get to work on the authorization.'

"Obediently, I went to work with a razor and gave Cole a scissors to snip off all the long red hair hanging down my back. Luckily, a Federal captain's uniform fit, more or less, and McCorkle was handy enough with a needle and thread to patch the bullet holes in the tunic. We also found a Federal sergeant's uniform that fit Noland perfectly. Passing ourselves off as a white officer and his aide from one of the Kansas Negro regiments seemed to be a good plan.

"We weren't ready to leave for Kansas City until after midnight, and it was well after daybreak before we reached the outskirts of the town. Noland was driving the wagon we had brought along to carry the women. I had wanted to bring horses, but Cole pointed out that prisoners were generally moved by wagon.

"As we drove through the town, we passed soldiers in nearly every street, and I had to remember to return the salutes they threw me. Aside from saluting, nobody bothered to look twice at us, and I had to quell the excitement I was starting to feel that my plan might really work after all. The forged authorization I carried in my breast pocket looked official enough to fool General Ewing himself.

" 'There it is, Mr. Ringgold,' Noland said.

" 'Captain to you, sergeant,' I replied, grinning to reassure him that I meant no rebuke. Right then my gratitude to him knew no bounds for the risks he'd taken gathering information and coming with me. Then I looked where he was pointing and shuddered.

" 'I believe that I could actually see that dilapidated old structure swaying on its crumbling foundations, and it wasn't hard to imagine its termite-riddled timbers and rotten brick tumbling into rubble. There was a sentry in front of the place, an infantryman with a grounded musket who saluted with his hand across his chest. I waved him a salute and we tramped inside the front door, which was open and through which we could see particles of plaster dust dancing in the air of the dark entranceway. My insides began to knot up with a sense of urgency.

" 'What can I do for you, captain?' By the dim light of an oil lamp in what had once been a parlor, I made out the well-tallowed figure of a sergeant standing more or less at attention behind a table bearing the lamp and some coffee cups.

" 'I'm here for the prisoners, sergeant,' I said, thrusting the forged authorization at him. 'Orders from General Ewing.' With the maddening slowness of the self-important who will not be hurried, the fat sergeant took the authorization and scrutinized it.

" 'You're with Colonel Jennison's Seventh Kansas Cavalry, sir?'

" 'Yes we are, sergeant, and we're in a hurry.'

" 'Didn't know there was any coloreds in the Seventh,' he said, regarding Noland suspiciously.

" 'Well there are now,' I snapped, wishing that Quantrill had assigned us to one of the colored regiments in his forgery, as I had asked him to. 'We're the Independent Mounted Kansas Jayhawkers. Sergeant Noland was freed by us from his bondage in Missouri and he has joined us to assist in the freeing of his brethren from their chains. Now we'd appreciate your assistance in helping us to transport the secessionist women you're holding to the security of Fort Leavenworth.'

"This seemed to convince him. He 'yessired' politely and told us to wait while he and the guards upstairs brought down the women. With that same maddening slowness of a fat gila monster moving uphill, he turned and climbed the stairs, and the creaking of the stairs under his weight joined the ominous sounds of the walls around us. It seemed that the swirling of dust particles had thickened a bit.

"After a few minutes that dragged endlessly, we heard female voices on the landing above. Margaret and another woman, who was, I believe, McCorkle's sister, Mrs. Charity Kerr, were the first to be led down. Their dresses were ripped and soiled and their hands were bound in front of them. Margaret's eyes widened with amazement when she saw me, but she caught my quick headshake and said nothing.

" 'Here's two of 'em, captain. We'll go fetch the others.'

"As soon as he and the guard went back up the stairs, I took Margaret in my arms and held her.

" 'You're all right now,' I whispered. 'I'm taking you out of here.' How little I knew. How little I expected the disaster that was almost upon us, though I might have guessed when I kissed Margaret's hair and found it covered with powder and particles from the crumbling ceilings and when I felt through my own boot soles a tremor running through the old house.

" 'Johnny, I can't believe it,' she said in the breaking voice of one holding back a sob. 'You're here!' She burrowed her head against my chest, and I wanted desperately to cut the rope bindings around her wrists, but I didn't dare for fear of arousing the fat sergeant's suspicions.

"Then suddenly a large piece of plaster fell from the ceiling almost at our feet, and we heard shouting and screams from upstairs. More plaster fell around us and the whole house began to shake as though in the grip of an earthquake. A guard with a musket appeared in the doorway to the staircase shouting, 'Run for your lives! It's all coming down!' He was closely followed by the fat sergeant, who had suddenly acquired the fleetness of an Indian runner. From upstairs could be heard the screams of the women: 'Help us! Please help us!' But the two bluebellies gave no sign of hearing. They ran on past us out the front door.

" 'Let me go, Johnny!' Margaret cried out then, freeing herself from my arms.

" 'You can't help them, Margaret!' I shouted over the cracking and rumbling of the collapsing house. But she wouldn't listen.

" 'Becky!' she called out to her sister as she ran toward the stairs. Mrs. Kerr followed her across the room, and by the time I reached the stairs the two of them had climbed back up into that vomiting hellmouth of dust and crumbling debris. I lunged up the stairs, taking them three at a time, and as I reached the second landing I saw Margaret just ahead of me. I called to her; she stopped for an instant and looked back, pleading, 'Help me, Johnny.' Then she ran on down the hall toward the screaming that rose above the cracking of rotten timbers and the crash of falling beams. I started to follow, but something, a beam probably, came down like a club and left me senseless.

"I hesitate to say that I was unconscious, for while I was no longer capable of moving like a conscious man, doing what needed to be done, I was strangely conscious of what was happening around me. I saw a figure, a woman silhouetted in the dim light of the hallway, trying to drag another figure toward me. There was a shower of debris and heavy objects, beams and pieces of the roof, and the woman was beaten to the floor, where she lay still for several moments. Then she raised herself to her knees beside the still figure she had been dragging, bent over it and her shoulders trembled with her sobbing. Her face was concealed by her long hair, but as she raised herself in an attitude of supplication, lifting hands that were bound together at the wrists, I saw who she was, and when I heard her cry out my name again it was like the touch of that iron Walley's sergeant laid across my belly. I tried to reach out to her, and when I couldn't, I began to scream with the pain I was feeling.

" 'Easy, Mr. Ringgold, take it easy.' The voice came from someone very close by me, close enough to speak softly and be heard above the sounds of the falling house. 'We gonna make it.' I was conscious then of Noland lifting and dragging me down the stairs, and I wanted to make him leave me, tried to speak, but nothing came out except a moaning like some speechless idiot's cry. Then I blacked out again.

"Maybe two or three hours later, as I lay in the bed of the wagon we had brought for the women, rain spattering down on me revived the capacity to feel pain in my head and other parts of my body that had been struck by falling debris, but this was nothing compared to what I felt remembering what had happened. The same falling debris striking me had struck Margaret, buried her in that house. I already knew, even before Noland told me, that I had lost her.

" 'Dead. They's all dead.' He gripped my wrist when he said it, having stopped the wagon and climbed back to check on me when he saw that I had come to.

" 'Why didn't you leave me, dammit?' I said, barely able to control my voice.

" 'Your lady wouldn't want that, Mr. Ringgold. I seen her go back tryin' to save them others. She want you to live.'

"We hardly knew each other, but somehow he knew what to say to me, was able to say something that checked my first impulse to follow Margaret as quickly as I could put a gun to my head. I turned away from him and wept like a goddamn baby. He patted me very gently on the arm, then he climbed back onto the seat and started the team. After a while I climbed up beside him, and we drove slowly through the hub-deep mud and sloshing rain back to Quantrill's camp without exchanging another word.

"Cole, McCorkle and a couple of Anderson's men were waiting for us at the edge of the camp. 'Well?' McCorkle demanded. I just shook my head and looked over at Noland. He understood that I was in no condition to describe what had happened, so he began. He told them how the building had taken the building next to it down as well and how rescuers were at work digging the women out of the rubble but that there was no hope that any of them would be found alive. He himself had seen

three of the victims uncovered while I was lying unconscious in the wagon. As we soon found out, there was
one survivor, Mary Anderson, but she was left a cripple
for life.

"I'm told that when Anderson was informed of his
sisters' murder he literally went crazy and started foam-
ing at the mouth. Whether this is true or not, I have no
doubt that the blood lust we all saw him display that
earned him the name 'Bloody Bill' was ignited at that
moment, even as my own living coal of rage and hatred
was fanned to life by Noland's account of what I had only
partly seen. He hadn't told me about seeing the victims
dug out, and though he refused to say one way or the
other, I could guess that one of them was Margaret.

"When Noland had finished, I climbed down off the
wagon and started toward my lean-to. The rain had
stopped, but a cold chilling breeze began to whip through
the camp. My teeth chattered and my head was throbbing like a drum, but I was determined. McCorkle and
Cole were weeping openly for their sisters, but I didn't
join them. The time for mourning has passed, I told
myself. Dizzy and swaying but nonetheless determined, I
stumbled on toward my lean-to. Inside it was my saddle,
along with the three pistols I carried when I wasn't trying
to pass myself off as a Yank officer. I wanted to tear off
the uniform I was still wearing, but then I decided it was
just what I needed for the piece of work I had in mind.
Wouldn't those bastards in Kansas City be surprised to
be cut down by one of their own officers!

" 'Where are you going, Ringgold?' George Todd called
to me as I slung my saddle up on my shoulder and started
toward the pasture where our horses were grazing. I
didn't answer him, and he started following me, along
with Cole, who must have told him what had happened,
and some other fellows. As I slipped Blaze's bridle on
and put the blanket on his back, Todd gripped my shoulder with one of his big powerful stonemason's hands and
asked me again, 'Where *are* you going?'

"Without any thought whatever, I whirled around and
drove my fist into his jaw, and he went down flat on his
back in the grass. I guess I really didn't know what I was
doing because, having just struck the most dangerous
man in Quantrill's band in the face, I turned back to the

business of saddling my horse as though nothing had happened. But now Cole grabbed me from behind and with the help of Will McGuire wrestled me down onto the ground. Then Cole held my arms while Todd sat on me and kept me pinned to the ground with his weight.

" 'You damn fool!' Todd snarled down at me. There was a trickle of blood coming out of the corner of his mouth where I'd hit him, and I fully expected him to even things up now that I was helpless under him. 'Bet you was goin' to climb on your horse an' ride into Kansas City to kill yourself a few Yankees. Wasn't that it?' he demanded.

" 'You guessed it, and you aren't stopping me,' I snarled back at him, hating him as much at that instant as I hated any of our enemies.

" 'Well, first you listen to me, Mr. Yank killer. You want to hurt the Yanks? You really want to hurt 'em?'

"I didn't reply, and Todd went on.

" 'Colonel Quantrill's plannin' somethin' big, and he needs every man he's got. If you're man enough, he can use you.'

"Cole was speaking to me. 'John, she was my sister. Believe me, I want to make 'em pay, too.'

"I let go of my rage then, and they let me up. Todd was wiping the blood off his chin with a bandanna.

" 'I'm mighty sorry about that, George,' I said to him.

" 'That's all right,' he replied magnanimously. 'You wasn't yourself.' Then he chuckled and rubbed his jaw. 'Damn, you hit hard!'

"Cole said to me: 'We're going to make 'em pay, John. Believe me, we are.'

"After they left me, assured that I wouldn't be making a one-man attack on Kansas City, I finished saddling Blaze and rode out toward the Missouri River. Noland's words were still pounding in my head—'Dead. They's all dead'—but I couldn't really accept at first that this meant Margaret too. By the time I reached the river, though, I had come to accept it. Dismounting beside that big muddy monster I looked down into its greenish-brown swirling depths and found myself strongly impelled by a yearning to throw myself into them. It must have been how my father felt the night he chose to die, and it even occurred to me that his way might be the best. I drew out my right-hand Navy Colt's and checked the cylinder. Why not? I asked myself. Killing Walley hadn't brought back Harry Younger. Killing all the bluebellies in Kansas wouldn't bring Margaret back to me.

"I really might have done it then, but I seemed to hear a voice coming right up from those dark river currents and calling me by name. I remembered then something Margaret said to me the last time we were together: 'Johnny, I know we'll always be near each other, no matter what happens. If you ever think you've lost me, remember that I'm always near you. Just listen for me.' It was, I thought at the time, a strange thing to say, but it moved me deeply, and I wanted to believe it. She had always been telling me to listen, to poetry out of the night, to the sounds of autumn, and now she was telling me to listen for her voice, even when I thought it was beyond hearing. When she told me that, a kind of shudder went through me, along with those deep warm feelings and the yearning to believe her. A part of me sensed that I was going to lose her. She must have known herself that something was going to happen to her.

" 'Ringgold, what're you doin'?' It was John McCorkle.

" 'Just visiting the river, John,' I answered.

" 'Wal, I've been looking all over for you. Quantrill wants to talk to both of us. I think we're going to get a chance to pay back those murdering bastards.'

" 'Where do you think we're going?' I asked McCorkle as we rode back to camp.

" 'I figure a raid on Kansas City,' he said. This suited me just fine, and I was grateful to Todd and Cole for preventing me from riding in there all by myself. Hearing, or thinking I'd heard Margaret's voice had the effect of expelling some of my suicidal thoughts, and McCorkle's conjecture that we were going to 'pay back those murdering bastards' diminished my sense of the futility of revenge. Admittedly, revenge would not bring back those women we loved, but it wasn't right that we should leave that crime unavenged.

"Quantrill knew all about the murders, and he knew that both McCorkle and I were close to some of the victims. As always, he knew what to say:

" 'Gentlemen,' he began, 'I want you to know that I sympathize deeply with you in your grief. It's bad enough that they are driving our people out of Missouri and hanging our men like criminals when they capture them. Now they are murdering our women. It shows you how the abolitionists think. They do not respect the codes of honor and chivalry. They respect nothing but fire and the sword!'

"Also present in Quantrill's tent were Todd, Bill Anderson, Andy Blunt, Dick Yeager, Bill Gregg and Ol Shepherd. Our arrival had apparently interrupted a meeting of Quantrill and his lieutenants, but having expressed his sympathy, he went on to include us because of our role as scouts.

" 'As I was just telling these other gentlemen, it's time we quit letting the damned abolitionists have their way, time we quit letting the Red Legs come over here and attack our people with impunity. I say, let's go to Lawrence!'

"At that, the lieutenants looked around at each other, and some of them shook their heads. Lawrence, as Gregg and others began to point out, was a long way from home, almost forty miles inside Kansas, and no small village either. Not that they wouldn't enjoy putting the torch to Lawrence. Lawrence was, we all knew, the home of Jim Lane and the headquarters of the Red Legs, whom I guess you would have to call our northern counterparts, though I'd like to think we never sank quite to their level. Even General Ewing despised the Red Legs and denounced them in a speech in Olathe for stealing themselves rich in the name of liberty. We regarded them as less than human, and while I never joined my comrades in scalping dead Federal soldiers, I did occasionally adorn Blaze's bridle with Red Leg hair. Lawrence was their town, but cleaning it out of those animals was not enough of an inducement by itself. Quantrill knew this, so he went on:

" 'Lawrence is the great hotbed of abolitionism in Kansas. All the plunder, or the bulk of it, stolen from Missouri in the name of liberty, will be found stored in Lawrence. We can get more money there, and . . .' He paused to look around at McCorkle and me and then over at Bill Anderson. '. . . more revenge than anywhere else.'

"Again Gregg and the others began to argue that a

raid on Lawrence was too dangerous. Quantrill proceeded to answer each of their arguments. It turned out that he and two of his men had just recently scouted most of the country between the state line and Lawrence. There were a few Federal outposts, but they were spread out a long way from each other and not strongly garrisoned. Not many people lived in that country. There would be few to raise the alarm. Todd, Anderson and Andy Blunt were quickly won over, but Gregg and Ol Shepherd were not. Lawrence had its own home guards, who would fortify themselves inside the town's brick buildings, and even if we managed to take the town there was the matter of getting back to Missouri. Quantrill answered that they could be in and out of Lawrence before the home guards could get into action and certainly before any kind of pursuit could be organized. His most persuasive arguments that this was possible were there in the flesh before their very eyes—Dick Yeager and Bill Anderson. Back in May, Yeager had led two dozen of his Jackson County boys 130 miles into Kansas following the Santa Fe Trail all the way to Council Grove. On the way back he lost about half of his men killed or captured, but the rest of them managed easily to evade the posses and troops sent out to intercept them. Anderson, who used to live near Council Grove until he was forced to flee to Missouri by his Unionist neighbors, had gone along with Yeager's bunch to pay his former neighbors a visit. They raised a fair amount of hell by all accounts, and there was so much criticism of General Blunt by the Kansas folks that he felt compelled to hang Jim Vaughn publicly as an example to the rest of us partisans.

"Listening to them argue, I could see why Gregg and Shepherd feared being caught forty miles inside Kansas, but right from the start I was with Quantrill. It was his talk of revenge mainly, and the risks meant nothing because I have never been so ready to die. Having Margaret taken from me, crushed in the ruins of a deathtrap because she tried to save her sister, had left me without any reason to live other than revenge. Dying in the Red Leg capital after I had taken along a few for company would suit me just fine.

"Quantrill's arguments were in fact persuasive. If Yeager and his bunch could make it all the way to Council Grove and back o Missouri, why couldn't we make it into and out of Lawrence? It was, after all, less than a third the distance. Finally, Quantrill had them all won over. He had an amazing gift for winning trust and confidence, and he could persuade men to put themselves in danger. That Latin line Professor Grimestone called on me to translate came back: *Caesare duce, nihil timebimus.* With Caesar in command, we shall fear nothing.

"Four days later we all rode out of Blue Springs and headed south to a farm near Lee's Summit. On the way there, Todd ordered me and five other men to follow him. We left the main column and rode to the house of a man named Wallace. He called Wallace outside and proceeded to scare hell out of him.

" 'You Yank-lovin' sonofabitch!' he snarled. 'We know you're giving information to the Federals.' Then he drew out one of his pistols.

"Wallace went down on his knees and pleaded for mercy, and George showed him what was perhaps the closest thing to mercy he could manage. He leaned down and pistol-whipped the man, saying:

" 'If we hear any more about you talking to the Federals, we'll come back here and kill you.'

"Then George really amazed us. He got off his horse and went inside the house. There was an organ in the parlor, and George actually sat down and played it for about ten minutes, played a couple of hymns I recognized. A man of many talents, our Captain Todd.

"As we rejoined the main band, riding into the camp at Lee's Summit, we could hear Bill Anderson shouting at Quantrill, 'Jest ten years old! Won't never walk again! God damn 'em to hell!' The news had just arrived that Mary Anderson was now the only survivor of the disaster in Kansas City, and Quantrill had just tactfully expressed his sympathy to her brother. Anderson was a powerfully built fellow in his early twenties, just under six feet tall, with long dark hair and beard, and gray eyes, which were generally expressionless yet filled during moments of high excitement with a kind of demonic light. Quantrill listened to his curse, and a little smile started to play about the corners of his hard, thin-lipped mouth. My guess is that he was privately congratulating himself on the timing of his Lawrence raid. At no other time could he have found Anderson and the rest of us in such a ready, determined state.

"As Anderson walked over to rejoin his men, I noticed one of them who looked familiar, a tall, lanky, sandy-haired fellow. He noticed me at the same time.

" 'You a cousin of the Youngers?' he asked me.

" 'Yes, that's right. I'm John Ringgold, from Texas.'

" 'Well, I guess we're related, too. I'm Frank James. As I recall, we met at Christmastime a couple of years ago.'

"We shook hands and I asked him, 'You had a brother, didn't you?'

" 'Still do. Jesse. He's back home at our place near Liberty, just itchin' to join up with us. He's only sixteen, though, so we told him he'd have to wait a little while. After the damned Unionist militia tortured our stepdaddy, I joined up with Anderson. It's a good outfit. How long you been with Quantrill?'

" 'Two years now.'

" 'I've been with Anderson about a year. I hope he and Quantrill can work together.' As we were talking, a short, blond youngster sidled up, and Frank James introduced us.

" 'This here's Arch Clement.'

"As we shook hands, I remarked to myself upon the almost cherubic appearance of innocence the young fellow had. He couldn't have been over twenty and looked younger. There was little in that rosy-cheeked, blue-eyed countenance to suggest that he was a born killer who would make as bloody a mark as his leader. You would have never imagined 'Little Archie,' as we came to call him, scalping dead Yank soldiers. You would never imagine it, that is, until you saw him do it.

"Thinking about what followed, how I came to be one in spirit with 'Bloody Bill' and 'Little Archie,' I wonder again about how deep in hell, if there is a hell outside this infernal earth, I'll be planted. Not that I really care that much. My revenge for Margaret's death was hardly sweet, but at the time I'd have sold my soul for it. Maybe I still would, and if that's what I did, so be it. The devil was the god of that war, and his instrument, his Mephistopheles, if you will, was named William Clarke Quantrill. Here's to you, Quantrill. You were a fiend out

of hell, but you were the leader we wanted. Thinking
about the hell we created with you on August 21 of 1863,
I get mighty thirsty. I haven't written much today, I see,
but I need to fortify myself a bit to go on. At times I've
drunk to forget what happened that day, what we did to
earn our name. But now, having brought back again the
agony of learning that Margaret was dead, I think that I
can bring back that other day as well. I'm drinking now,
not to escape but to make it clearer, so that tomorrow I
can set it down just as it happened.''

"That Quantrill was absolutely right about Lawrence's
vulnerability to attack was confirmed by the two spies he
sent ahead to look the place over, Fletch Taylor and
good old Noland. And so it was that we found ourselves
on the morning of August 21 on the outskirts of Lawrence. We had ridden all night to get there. Along the
way we'd met a Colonel Holt with a hundred new Confederate recruits. When Quantrill asked him if he'd like
his boys 'christened,' Holt thought it was a good idea and
joined us. All together, Quantrill had a force of about
450 men.

"The streets of Lawrence were deserted when we rode
in. It was about five o'clock, and the thick dust of the
main street, Massachusetts Street, I believe it was called,
muffled our hoofbeats. When we reached the center of
town, Quantrill ordered Colonel Holt to take his company of recruits and prevent anyone from escaping from
the east side of town. Then he told Andy Blunt to take a
detachment and cover the west side.

"Our first target was a tent camp over near the Wakarusa
River occupied by some Kansas Federals. There were
only about twenty of them, and they had the look of raw
recruits. We just literally trampled them into the ground
in their tents, and I don't believe more than two or three
could have gotten away. One of our men, a former
Baptist preacher and former Border Ruffian by the name
of Larkin Skaggs, took down their U.S. flag and tied it to
his horse's tail to be dragged in the dust. None of us liked
Skaggs, but his gesture with the flag expressed what we
all felt pretty accurately.

"Next we turned our attention to another camp nearby,
where a bunch of colored soldiers were bivouacked. Some

of our boys had a special hatred for Negro Federal troops. Personally, I didn't give a damn what color a man's skin was inside his uniform. As long as the uniform was blue, I'd try to kill him, and the death of a white Federal gave me fully as much satisfaction as the death of a black one. These darkies were pretty fortunate. They saw what we'd done to their white comrades, and most of them got away.

"Having taken care of these camps, we were ordered by Quantrill to surround the Eldridge House, which was a big four-story hotel in the middle of Lawrence. It was one of those big brick buildings Gregg and Shepherd had worried about, and we were a little apprehensive as we approached it, seeing how easily it could be fortified. When a gong went off inside, we all dismounted and took cover, expecting a fusillade from the windows. But not a shot was fired. A Yank captain by the name of Banks stuck his head out one of the windows waving a white bedsheet.

" 'I want to speak to your commander,' he yelled down at us.

"Quantrill promptly climbed back on his horse and rode up beneath the window.

" 'What are you after here in Lawrence?' the captain asked him.

" 'Plunder,' Quantrill answered frankly.

" 'Well, we are defenseless and at your mercy. We surrender this house, but we demand protection for everyone in it.'

" 'You have it,' Quantrill assured him, 'as long as no one in there resists.'

" 'Hey, captain,' Todd called up to the officer. 'Come on down here.'

"The man complied, and when he came out on the porch, George walked up to him.

" 'We seem to be of a size, captain. I'll give you jest two minutes to surrender that uniform. It jest happens I'm a captain myself and I need a uniform. Ain't that right, colonel?'

"Quantrill just chuckled a little. Then he stood up in his stirrups and addressed the rest of us.

" 'Kill! Kill and you will make no mistake!' he shouted,

and he went on: 'Lawrence should be thoroughly cleansed, and the only way to cleanse it is to kill! Kill!'

"We responded with wild Indian whoops, rebel yells and shouts of joy. This was what we'd wanted to hear. Quantrill raised his arm to quiet us, just long enough to deliver one other command that we didn't mind obeying:

" 'You are not to harm any of the women or children. But kill all the men you see. Any man you see here is liable to be a Red Leg or a Jayhawker. They're all abolitionist Yankee sonsofbitches.'

"I won't pretend that I was any less involved in what followed than any of my comrades. We broke up into small bands and spread out through the town. Quantrill's final words had sunk in, and I found myself shooting at practically every adult male I saw. Some I killed out-right. Others I just wounded, and my comrades generally finished them off. Their women tried to protect them sometimes, and we left quite a few being mourned over by grieving widows. Women were not otherwise harmed by us in Lawrence. None were raped. None were killed. I could not feel much sympathy for the grieving women of Lawrence, as I had for the women in Olathe and Shawneetown. I couldn't feel much of anything besides a strange kind of pleasure I'd never known before. It was the pleasure of complete abandonment. The people I was killing weren't human beings. They were Red Legs, Jay-hawkers, Yankees, Margaret's killers. I didn't feel any-thing but a compulsion to get as many as I could. As I picked off one fellow, who was crouched up behind a balcony railing and who may or may not have been aiming at me, Quantrill rode by.

" 'Nice shooting, Ringgold,' he yelled, and he put one of his own bullets into the corpse that my shot had draped over the railing on the balcony. As he did so, he laughed aloud, a shrill, high-pitched laugh that I'd heard before, the time we wiped out a patrol near Blue Springs, when we were riding them down and he killed one him-self. It was the kind of laugh you might expect from the devil himself as he watched the arrival of some new souls. If I heard it now, it would give me the same kind of chills I felt when that old medicine man was going crazy in Cochise's cave. But then I just laughed right along with him as I reloaded my pistols.

"And I rode along with him when he went to pay his respects to Jim Lane. According to one of our spies, Noland, Lane was not in Lawrence. In fact, he hadn't been, while Noland was there. So Quantrill was in no great hurry to get to Lane's house. What we didn't know was that Lane had returned a day or two before the raid. Hearing us shooting up the town, he scampered out into a cornfield near his house with nothing but his nightshirt on and hid there until we left. Had we caught him, Quantrill would have been able to carry out his original plan, which was to bring Lane back to Missouri to be burned at the stake.

"When we rode up to Lane's house, we were met by his wife, and I must admit I was much impressed by the kind of spirit she showed. Quantrill dismounted and took off his hat with a great flourish, saying, 'I'd be grateful, Mrs. Lane, if you'd inform your distinguished husband, Senator Lane, that Colonel Quantrill desires an audience with him.'

"She was a handsome woman in her middle forties with iron-gray hair and brown, almond-shaped eyes, like Margaret's. Picking up Quantrill's tone of mock gallantry, she replied in kind: 'I regret to inform you, colonel, that my husband is not presently at home to receive visitors. Perhaps he may see you another time.'

" 'Let us hope so, Mrs. Lane,' Quantrill answered dryly. 'Now, if you won't mind, we'll just take a look around the senator's home. Boys.' He gestured for us to go inside the house. Mrs. Lane stood to one side of the doorway, rigidly erect and with a proudly defiant expression on her face. She looked me directly in the eye as I walked by her, and I had to look away. Lane was a real sonofabitch, by all our accounts, but somehow he'd gotten himself quite a woman for a wife.

"When we went inside the parlor, McCorkle exclaimed:

" 'By God, here's the Fristos' piano! And this one belongs to the Bledsoes!'

"According to McCorkle and two of the other fellows with us in the house, it was full of loot from Lane's raid on Osceola back in the fall of 'sixty-one. We went upstairs and one of the fellows went into Mrs. Lane's bedroom. He came out with a load of silk dresses.

" 'I reckon most of these belong to the girls back in

Osceola,' he said. We'd heard that Lane had taken as his personal share of the Osceola spoils a number of silk dresses to distribute among his female friends, but I suspect that these belonged to Mrs. Lane.

"Since Noland had told Quantrill that Lane was out of town, we didn't look for him outside, and he was smart enough to stay where he was in the cornfield.

" 'Okay, boys,' Quantrill said, when we'd finished looting and searching the house, 'I guess there's nothing else to do but touch her off.' Mrs. Lane stood by and watched us set fire to the place, still proudly erect, with her head high, but I could see tears starting in her fine eyes. The house, a splendid, newly built wooden structure, went up very quickly.

"And so did most of the town. As we rode back down Massachusetts Street toward the business district, we had burning houses on either side of us. There were bodies lying everywhere—in the street, on the sidewalks, in the yards and gardens around the burning houses. Among the glowing embers of one house, I saw a skull and some bones sticking up, and a little further on I saw two guerrillas in the process of heaving a man into the flames of a burning house with his hands and feet tied. 'This is for Osceola!' one of the guerrillas yelled as he let go. 'And Jennison!' the other one yelled.

"The screams of the dying and the crackling of the flames filled our ears, and the smell of burning flesh, the most sickening odor I know, filled our nostrils. It had been a bright, clear summer morning, but now the sun was obscured by a thick cloud of smoke and rising ashes. From time to time Quantrill laughed aloud in that strange shrill way he had, and we all laughed along with him.

"Down in the center of town we encountered Bill Anderson and Arch Clement. Anderson had a pistol in either hand, and he, like Quantrill, was laughing, only it came out as a kind of sobbing or whimpering. His eyes were full of that same light I'd noticed earlier, and he didn't seem to even recognize us. 'Little Archie' was tying something to the bridle of his horse. It looked like the skin of a small animal, but then I saw the corpse of a Federal soldier lying nearby with a bloody crown where his scalp had been.

"Then we met Cole and Frank James. They were just coming out of a bank, each carrying sacks of money.

" 'Give us a hand, will you, John?' Frank called to me. 'We're going to see that the people of west Missouri receive some compensation for what these damned Red Legs have done to them.'

" 'Sure,' I said, and went back inside with them to help clean out the vault. As a matter of fact, every bank in Lawrence was robbed that day. The idea of bringing money back from the Red Leg capital to the suffering folks of Missouri had a lot of appeal, probably made some of the raiders feel like Robin Hoods. But I'm afraid this noble scheme never was carried out. It was, as far as I know, the first time Cole and Frank had worked together to empty a bank. Of course, as everyone knows now, it was by no means the last.

"As we finished with the bank and went on to loot some stores, I noticed that most of the men around me had been drinking. What with all I'd seen and done that morning, I needed a drink myself, and when some of Anderson's boys went to work and broke into a saloon, I joined them. When we got inside I went behind the bar and set up the glasses. Then when I'd poured us each a tall whiskey, I raised my glass and said, without really thinking about why I said it:

" 'Here's to the South. And victory.'

"They all raised their glasses, and after that toast we had a few more—to Anderson, to Quantrill, to our ladies back in Missouri, to the good fellowship of comrades in war.

" 'Mount up!' We all heard the order being shouted out in the street, and I recognized the voice as that of Todd. By this time, we were none too sober, but we managed to stumble out into the street and locate our horses. Todd, mounted on his big stud Sam Gaty and resplendent in Captain Banks's uniform, spotted me and rode over.

" 'How do I look, John?'

" 'Mighty fine, George. Shplendid,' I slurred.

" 'Hey, we gotta get outta here fast, John. The lookout reported there's a big bunch of troops comin' in from the east.'

" 'Mount up! Mount up!' It was Quantrill himself this time. Seeing George, he rode over to him and gave his orders for the retreat: 'South end of town, George. Tell Gregg to form them up there in fours. Have somebody hitch up a wagon for the wounded.' We had in fact suffered only three casualties so far. Jim Bledsoe and two of Holt's recruits had been wounded by some soldiers and surveyors stationed across the Kansas River who'd cut loose at us with their rifles. Holt's recruits generally seemed to be having a hard time at their 'christening.' I saw a couple of them retching in the streets, and some others were looking pretty sick. Looking at them, I remembered how I'd been 'christened' that day in the ravine, and I thought to myself, You've come a long way, Ringgold.

"Remarkably, Quantrill and Todd succeeded in getting our men, as well as those of Anderson and Yeager, to leave off their looting, drinking and other activities and to ride down to the south end of Lawrence, where Gregg began forming them up for the retreat.

"Meanwhile, Todd ordered me and six others to help him round up the stragglers. We succeeded in rounding up all save one. Larkin Skaggs, the ex-Reverend Larkin Skaggs, was so drunk and evidently so caught up in the excitement of killing and burning that he didn't even hear us when we shouted at him to go join the others. He and another man were coming out of a hotel where some townsfolk were being held as prisoners.

" 'They've killed the prisoners!' we heard a woman screaming, and this was probably true. Skaggs had a gun in each hand as he staggered over to his horse and climbed on. His companion heard our shouts and rode to join the others, but Skaggs went off in the opposite direction. We heard later that he tried unsuccessfully to set fire to a woman's house and then, when he realized belatedly that we'd all gone, he panicked. Still too drunk to ride in the right direction and frightened out of his wits besides, he was trapped by a mob of angry surviving citizens and killed. Some of the Negro soldiers who had escaped our attack on their camp untied the U.S. flag from his horse's tail and tied Skaggs' body, stripped naked, in its place. Then they dragged it through the streets of Lawrence.

"Skaggs was the only guerrilla killed in Lawrence, and I didn't notice anyone mourning the loss. We only wished that we could have given him some company in whatever part of hell is reserved for murdering preachers by sending down the soul of the Reverend H. D. Fisher, chaplain in Lane's Kansas Brigade. He was high on our list of special victims to be paid off for atrocities in Missouri. But his wife saved him by rolling him up inside a rug, dragging him out into the backyard and piling furniture on top of him, while we set fire to their house and stood around waiting for him to emerge. Another spirited woman, like Mrs. Lane, whom I have to admire. It's a wonder to me how those miserable Jayhawking bastards could have won the devotion of such fine brave women. But then I guess the whole mystery of woman's love is beyond any man's power to grasp. Why women have loved me is certainly more than I can grasp.

"As we started to ride out of Lawrence, Frank James rode up to Quantrill, saying: 'There's about sixty Red Legs come into town. Hadn't some of us boys better go back and take care of 'em?'

"Quantrill shook his head and pointed out across the prairies, off to the east and then off to the north, where you could just make out the dust clouds raised by large bodies of mounted troops. 'You boys,' he told us, 'are going to have all the fighting you want, all the way back to Missouri. And we'll have to stick together if we're going to make it at all.'

"He was dead right about this, as he usually was about anything connected with mounted guerrilla warfare. You can say what you will about Quantrill as a man. He was a ruthless killer who enjoyed his work, and I suspect that he was an opportunist who used the situation on the Kansas-Missouri border to his own advantage and didn't basically care a damn about the South or that part of the South in Missouri he was supposedly championing. But he was a superb cavalry leader, in the same class, I suspect, with Morgan or Stuart or even Forrest, old 'fustest with the mostest.' And he proved it on the Lawrence raid, among others. I'm not talking about the massacre itself. That, admittedly, was no great achievement, just so much necessary, or unnecessary, butchery, more like a mass execution than anything else. But getting to and from Lawrence through eighty miles of largely open territory swarming with Yankees—that was a project that even Jeb Stuart might have hesitated to undertake. And it was in the retreat especially that he showed us what kind of a leader he was.

"Leaving the smoking ruins of Lawrence, we soon picked up the Santa Fe Trail and headed east. When we reached a little place called Brooklyn, we left the trail and picked up a road running south toward another little place called Ottawa. But we hadn't gotten very far south of Brooklyn before we looked back and saw that one of those big pursuing columns was catching up fast. As some of the men looked back and saw the Federals, they began to panic and tried to gallop ahead of each other in the line. Their panic really showed when we rode up on a wide fenced cornfield and found that the only way across it was along a very narrow lane running through the middle of it. The men bunched up in the lane, crowding each other, and when they got to the end of it and reached open prairie again, they began to scatter in every direction.

"Todd and those of us who'd helped him round up the stragglers were back near the rear of the column. George saw at a glance what was happening and what needed to be done in a hurry. As we came through the gate at the end of the field, he swung his big stud about and stopped about twenty of the men behind him.

" 'Hold on a minute, boys. Ain't none of us gettin' back to Missouri if we don't stop them Yankees. Goddammit, Smith, stay where you are!' he yelled at a guerrilla who was edging his mount away toward the retreating column. 'Jarrett,' he addressed another guerrilla, with a gray beard down to his belt, 'you take half these men. Let down those rail fences and go on up through the corn so you can hit 'em in the flank. By God, we're gonna charge 'em!'

"And by God, or the devil, we did. We rode back up the lane until we got to the middle. Then we all dismounted, and five of us, including George, Ol Shepherd, Jim Lilly, Will McGuire and I, stood shoulder to shoulder in front while the fellows behind us held our horses.

The Yankees came right on, having seen from a distance the signs of panic in our ranks and therefore neglecting to exercise enough caution even to have scouts out in front. They were riding four abreast and didn't even see us until they were less than fifty feet away. It was one of those rare times when I used two pistols at once. While I'm a reasonable shot with my left-hand Colt's, I generally keep it in reserve and do most of my work with my faster right hand. But this time I had a Colt's in either hand, as did each of my comrades. Those bluebellies and their horses in the first rank were hit by so many bullets that they just went down in one big cursing, screaming, whinnying heap. And so did the rank behind them. And the ranks behind these first two didn't have time to stop, so they began piling up on top of those in front. Then, as George had promised, we mounted our horses and charged them.

"We had a little difficulty getting around the pile of men and animals that seemed to be rising as high as a house, and George's magnificent horse was shot from under him in the charge, but we went on to stop them cold with another fusillade. One of their officers seemed to be rallying them for a countercharge, but then he went down, apparently hit from the side. Good old Jarrett was attacking their flank.

"With the Yank advance temporarily halted, we turned back down the lane and caught up with Quantrill and the rest. Todd climbed up behind me, and I noticed that he'd discarded his new captain's tunic.

" 'I hated to give up my new coat, but I don't feel like getting shot by one of my own boys,' he explained. Then suddenly he cursed aloud: 'Goddammit, I left four thousand dollars in Yankee greenbacks in that coat!' I had to laugh at this.

" 'Good thing it wasn't Confederate money. You might have lost something,' I said with a chuckle. He tried to force a laugh in spite of his disappointment, for we'd often wondered out loud if Confederate money had as little value in Virginia as it had out west.

"When we caught up with the main column, George took his pick from among the many horses we'd rounded up in Lawrence. These horses were mostly too fat to maintain our pace for any length of time, but we started riding them and leading our good Missouri mounts to let them rest. This was Quantrill's idea and a good one, for it gave us our final edge over the pursuing Federal cavalry. But we had a long way to go, and the Federals, having re-formed, were closing in again on us. Quantrill called George over.

" 'That was damned fine, George. We're all much obliged to you and the rest of the boys in that detachment.'

" 'Think nothing of it, colonel,' Todd replied easily. 'We want to get back to Missouri just like everybody else.'

" 'I'll see that you're rewarded when we do get back, George. But right now I need to rely some more on your skills as a rear-guard commander. If there's any man here who can take charge of securing our rear, it's you. Pick out fifty or sixty of the best men for a rear guard and throw out a skirmish line. I know the country and will take the main body and lead them out. If I run into any Federals in front of me, I'm going to cut right through them.'

"George immediately rounded up the best shots in our outfit, which, thanks to Ol Shepherd's tutelage, included me, and he asked Anderson and Yeager to give him their best as well. He then divided us into two groups, twenty-five men each, and these became two skirmish lines. While one line blazed away at the advancing Federals, the other line, a few hundred yards behind them, was loading up. In this way, we slowed the enemy down considerably and prevented their attempts to concentrate an attack. The liquor I'd drunk that morning had long since worn off, and I found that I was placing my shots with deadly effect, as were my comrades on either side. George was pleased.

" 'Nice shooting, boys, mighty nice. Keep it up,' he said, between his own well-aimed shots. 'Guess I know how to pick a rear guard.'

"And so it went through the long hot August afternoon. The Federals gradually began to wear down, and so did we. By the middle of the afternoon, all the excitement of the raid was gone, and the only thing keeping us going was the fear of capture. I looked around me and saw the prairie strewn with plunder discarded by the main column, everything from furniture and saddle gear to women's hats and dresses. I'd taken no plunder myself besides a few bottles of whiskey, and I was a little resentful then that I was working so much harder than the plunder carriers in the main column. Some of the Federals seemed to be swaying in their saddles and letting their horses just drift across the prairie. I knew how they felt. We'd been in the saddle close to twenty-four hours ourselves. In my weariness, I remembered something Harry Younger had prodded me to read, Thucydides' account of the Athenian retreat from Syracuse in his *History of the Peloponnesian War.* It was the wrong thing to think about then, I guess. The Athenians had all been either wiped out or captured. But then they had a fool for a general. Thank God, or the devil, we had Quantrill and Todd.

" 'Fire at will!' George yelled hoarsely as each line took its turn against the weary Federal advance. Then, when the line behind was ready: 'Fall back!' What got us through, no question, was the big string of spare mounts we'd appropriated in Lawrence. When one of these gave out, its rider would just shoot it and help himself to another. The Federals had no spare mounts, and by the end of the day their horses couldn't be prodded into anything faster than a slow walk.

"About sunset, just as we came in sight of Paola, Quantrill called a halt and pulled out his spyglass to look the town over. The first thing he saw was a line of troops, about one hundred of them, drawn up to defend the town against him. It seems the whole of eastern Kansas had been alerted as to our presence, and troops from all over that part of the state were joining in the attempt to intercept us. Even as we halted there in sight of Paola, the Federals who had been pursuing us all day were joined by a fresh company of Kansas militia, and our rear-guard action just couldn't hold them off. We were driven back onto the main guerrilla body. Quantrill met this crisis with his usual cool competence, by simply turning his entire force about and deploying us in a line of battle to oppose the Kansans. This the Kansans hadn't been expecting, and they promptly drew rein. Then the rest of the Federals caught up with them, and we just sat there for a while facing each other, thoroughly exhausted, each side waiting for the other to make the first move.

"Finally Quantrill ordered us to form back into columns of fours, and we rode northward around Paola. The Federals, I gather, just went on into Paola. They'd ruined most of their horses, and some of the troops themselves had died of sunstroke. We only kept going for about five miles beyond Paola. Then Quantrill halted us for a rest. God, did we need a rest! Especially those of us who'd been with Todd's rear guard. Somehow I knew, though, that I wouldn't be getting much rest.

" 'Ringgold! McCorkle!' John and I groaned as we heard our names being called. There's no rest for a scout. He's the eyes and ears of an army, and when the army sleeps he'd better be awake.

" 'I'd like you boys to keep a lookout,' Quantrill informed us. We just nodded dumbly and turned our horses back the way we'd come. I borrowed some tobacco from McCorkle and rubbed it around my eyes to keep them open. Then I rode my horse, which had been led most of the day, up to a ridgetop from which I could survey the country between us and Paola. Fighting to stay awake in the saddle, I cursed Quantrill, but sure enough, he was right again. Not even an hour passed before I made out the approach of another damned Union column. McCorkle had seen them too, and when we got back to Quantrill, he and Todd and the other officers set about rousting the men, which was no easy task. Some had to be kicked to their feet. When they'd all managed to haul themselves back into the saddle, we moved out and didn't stop again until we reached the Grand River in Missouri at dawn. We'd been in Missouri since about midnight, but didn't want to stop until we were well beyond the state line. As we reached a line of timber along the Grand, Quantrill halted us and rode back along the line shouting joyfully: 'We did it, boys! We did it! Now we're back home again. Not all the troops in Kansas can catch us now.'

"For the first time in the course of that raid, Quantrill was wrong. As he found out with his own spyglass, there was a big bunch of Kansas troops still on our tail, and a farmer informed us that a large force of Missouri state militia was just over the next hill looking for us. Up to this point, we'd suffered few casualties. Two men had been killed outright during the retreat and three more, who had been wounded too badly to move, had been finished off before our eyes by the advancing Federals. We still had Jim Bledsoe and those two wounded recruits of Holt's in a wagon, but now we could no longer be slowed down by any wagons. We asked the farmer to look after them, but no sooner had we gone on than a bunch of Red Legs found them. The two recruits, whose 'christening' was also the end of the war for them, pleaded for mercy, but Bledsoe chose to die like a man. According to the farmer, who was lucky enough to be spared by the Red Legs, he shouted: 'Stop it! We are not entitled to mercy! We spare none and do not expect to be spared!' The Red Legs killed all three of them, and an Indian tracker who was with them scalped the three corpses. We also lost a few more whose horses had given out on them or become sick from drinking too much water. Quantrill's main force drew most of the pursuing Federals, and we hoped that our comrades who had been set afoot and who were hiding out in the timber and brush along the Grand would be overlooked and allowed to escape. But Hoyt's Red Legs scoured the area and caught a number of them. They always killed them on the spot and usually any farmer who'd been sheltering them. Some they hung, stringing them up from branches so high they couldn't be reached, and their bodies just stayed there rotting for months. I knew a couple of men who died that way, and I was glad I never saw them hanging up. It was bad enough just seeing them in my mind's eye, imagining how they looked after a while."

Having relived the Lawrence raid and his own part in it, the hardened outlaw John Ringo actually shudders. Twenty years earlier, in the weeks that followed the raid, the shame and revulsion of young John Ringgold had caused more than a shudder. He had writhed in the grip of nightmares in which he saw himself again as what he had become riding into Lawrence—more a demon than a man, possessed by a spirit of vengeance that admitted no pity. And not the least of his torments was the knowledge that she for whom he had committed himself to this vengeful atrocity would have been horrified by it. If what

she'd promised him was true, then she had in fact been
there with him, watching and weeping for those people,
Red Legs and all. And how she must have wept to see
what her "Johnny" had become. Which would have explained why during some of his most horrifying nightmares, when he saw the faces of some of the victims and
smelled burning flesh in the ruins of Lawrence, he seemed
to hear her voice urging him to leave Quantrill's band
before it was too late.

Finally, in the late summer of 'sixty-four, he did leave
Quantrill. He and Cole left together, but not before
they'd participated in actions that made them both capable of seeing themselves again as soldiers and not just
marauding white savages who used the war as an excuse.
Baxter Springs and Fayette were the most memorable of
these actions. One of them, Baxter Springs, was a great
triumph for Quantrill. Only the capture of General Blunt
himself could have made it a sweeter victory. Fayette,
however, was another matter. Ringo still carries a souvenir of Fayette lodged in his thigh, and there his good
horse Blaze had been shot from under him. There had
been no victory for the guerrillas in that place. The
reckless daring of George Todd, which had been partly
responsible for the victory at Baxter Springs, where he
had ordered a charge without awaiting Quantrill's orders,
had been their undoing at Fayette. The town was heavily
garrisoned, and Todd led a charge against a log blockhouse that cost them thirteen good men killed and thirty
more wounded, including John Ringgold.

The wound, which nearly cost him his leg, made him
listen more attentively to the voice inside warning him to
leave while he was still able. He listened as well, he and
Cole, to Bill Gregg, who, with the encouragement of
Quantrill himself had decided to leave the guerrilla band.

" 'The colonel hisself admitted it. Todd's running things
and he only wants men like him around—thieving sonsofbitches who don't give a damn for the Confederacy. It's
the regular army for me.'

"Cole and I looked at each other, and it was apparent
that we were both thinking that Gregg had spoken for us.
Like him, we went to Quantrill, and he gave us the same
encouragement.

" 'You boys can no longer do anything for the Confederacy with this outfit. You'd best go on to Texas and join General McCulloch,' he told us.

" 'What about you, colonel?' Cole asked him.

" 'I'll do what I can. George and I no longer see eye-to-eye on how to fight this war, but the men are absolutely devoted to him. I can't cross him.' Then he shook hands with both of us. 'You've both been good soldiers, good southern men.'

"It was one of those moments when you could see the man Quantrill and how he aroused the loyalty and affection of his men. You could almost forget the killer who could work you into a blood frenzy. Actually, compared to Todd, Quantrill was almost a civilized officer. George was becoming more and more reckless and vicious, even in his dealings with his own comrades. The main reason Gregg left the band was the antagonism between him and Todd, and right after Gregg left, Todd tried to get Fletch Taylor to kill him. Fletch, who was not known for his reluctance to shed blood, refused. At Fayette, Quantrill had tried to talk George out of leading us in that crazy charge against the blockhouse and George accused him of cowardice. When the Federals shot us to pieces and the charge failed, Todd blamed Quantrill and tried to order some of the men to kill him. They refused, but it was clearly the end for Quantrill as leader of the outfit.

"General McCulloch was glad to have us, and with our experience he gave us both officer's commissions. Cole was a major, and I was a captain. We had a few skirmishes with the Federals, but most of the time we were chasing Comanches and Confederate deserters. We were under the illusion that we knew everything there was to know about guerrilla warfare, but those Indians taught us plenty.

"By now, we realized just how decisive Gettysburg and some of those other big battles in the East had been. We knew that the Confederacy was dying, but General McCulloch was one of those who had a hard time accepting the facts. Toward the end of 'sixty-four he sent Cole and me with a recruiting expedition to New Mexico. We were supposed to recruit a whole regiment for the Confederate army, and we tried our best. But Glorieta Pass in 'sixty-two really was the end of the war for that territory. Most of the men capable of fighting had long since gone east to join one side or the other. We finally gave up and drifted over into Arizona, where, because of the Apache threat, we didn't linger. We went on down into Mexico, where we ran into a lot of other fellows from both the northern and southern armies who were down there hoping to make their fortunes fighting either for or against the occupying French forces. Cole and I didn't figure there was much to be gained fighting for either side, so we took ship at Vera Cruz for San Francisco and when the war ended we were with Cole's uncle, who lived near San Jose.

"After that, we returned to Missouri, and Cole tried to start a farm near Lee's Summit. But most of his neighbors were Unionists who were unwilling to let the war be over. They tried to charge him and his brothers with murder for some of the people killed by Quantrill's Raiders during the war, and they also tried to blame him for various holdups in the area. I knew that he was innocent, but who would believe another ex-guerrilla? We left Missouri and went down into Louisiana, and I was there when Cole and another man shot it out after a horse race at Shreveport. He had so damn much reckless courage, but he just couldn't hit anything with a pistol. He was lucky the other fellow couldn't shoot any straighter.

"The last time I saw Cole was while he was living with Belle Starr down in the Nations. He was starting to get fat and his hair was falling out, but honest ranching seemed to agree with him. I was surprised to hear that he was actually pretty restless.

" 'I just heard from Jesse,' he said. 'You remember our cousin Jesse, who joined up with Anderson and Todd about the time we quit and joined the regulars?'

" 'Yeah, I remember. He was wounded and we took him to his mother's place.'

" 'That's him. Anyway, I just got word from him. He wants me to round up Jim and Bob and join him for what he calls "some work on the railroad." I think I know what he means.'

" 'I think I do too,' I said. 'What does Belle think of this?' Belle was now expecting. A big handsome woman bred on the prairies, used to strong men who took their chances, she seemed to belong with Cole. She overheard my question, and as she filled my coffee cup, she said,

'Cole's got to do what's right for him. The Yankees and the Pinkertons wouldn't leave us alone in Missouri.'

" 'What about you, John?' Cole asked me. 'Why don't you join us? I know Jesse'd be happy to have you. The way we figure it we're still fighting the war. The railroads and banks are all Yankee-owned, and they're making it hard for our people. We're going to strike back.'

" 'Well, I wish you luck,' I answered. 'The war ended for me a long time ago. I've made my peace with the Yankees, whether they want to honor it or not.'

"He understood, probably understood that it had ended for me after Lawrence. Shortly after that, he returned to Missouri to link up with Jesse, and that was the last I saw of him."

EIGHT

WILD JUSTICE

He remembers how in the spring of 'sixty-nine, without really thinking about why, he began to drift south toward Texas. Crossing the Canadian River and then the Red and then the Trinity, he felt himself being drawn further and further south toward the home he had left nine years before. At first he had no intention of riding all the way to San Antonio and seeing his family again. It was as though the experience of the war had set the mark of Cain upon him and he had to wander forever toward the land of Nod.

When he thought about it, he was actually afraid to see his family again, afraid that they would see the mark upon him. He remembered the time of innocence and hope when they had seen him off for Missouri, and little Mary's words as she gave him a final hug: "I'm so proud that you're going to be a doctor, Johnny. We're going to miss you, but we're so happy for you."

It was Mary's words that were drawing him home again, he realized, the words she had written. A letter for him care of Ida Mae Younger had finally caught up with him during his visit with Cole and Belle. He still carries it, can remember it almost word for word. "Dearest Brother," it began, "we have never stopped hoping you would come home to us. Ida Mae wrote to us about how you and her brothers went off to fight the Yankees after their father was killed. She said that you were wounded twice but that you are all right now. We thank God for it. Clayton went off to the war too, he and a lot of boys from around here went east with General Hood. Most of them didn't come back, and I must tell you that Clayton lost one of his arms at a place called Antietam. He's so brave. He could have left the army then, but he didn't, and after he came back here he learned to take care of the farm again just as if he had two good arms. He's married now to a wonderful girl whose husband was in his regiment and was killed in Tennessee. She had a son, and now she and Clayton have a daughter. You have a beautiful little niece, Johnny. You must come and see her. She's the image of Mama.

"Johnny, I must also tell you that when you come, Mama won't be here. We lost her two years ago. She was crossing the Medina in a buggy with Brother Mitchell, and some water splashed on her. She caught a chill and it turned into lung fever. I'm sorry to have to be the one to tell you this. I just wish that you could have come home after the war was over. It would have meant ever so much to Mama to see you again. Don't misunderstand me, Johnny. I'm not blaming you for anything. I know that you must have had your reasons for not coming home, but we've all missed you so much. Please come now if you can. Always your loving sister, Mary."

Finally, one afternoon in early April he topped out on a low ridge that overlooked the Ringgold farm. A man was plowing in the lower field by the creek. Even at a distance he could tell that the man was well above average stature. There was something curious about the way he was plowing, and after a minute or so John made out that he had only one arm. He had himself strapped to the plow in such a way that he could manage it with his single arm, but obviously it was a feat beyond the strength of an ordinary man. Only someone like Clayton, who had more strength in one arm than most men had in two, could keep a straight furrow with that handicap. Remembering Mary's letter and deeply moved by the sight of Clayton struggling with the soil and his handicap, John dismounted and watched him for nearly half an hour. After a while, he saw a woman come out into the field carrying a pitcher. With her was a tiny figure in a dress matching her own. Slowly the woman crossed the plowed field, leading the little girl by the hand. Clayton embraced the woman with his one arm and then stooped to lift his daughter.

After the woman and her daughter returned to the house, John noticed a young boy walking along the deep muddy ruts of the road from town. Over his shoulder he bore a satchel, and since he entered the farmhouse it wasn't hard to guess that he was Clayton's stepson home from school.

The farm had never looked so lovely to him. House and barn were both freshly painted, and beneath the windows of the house, with their bright blue shutters, were flower boxes. The surrounding fields, watered by abundant spring rains, were bright green, as green as Missouri, and there were swatches of wild flowers—poppies, lupines, daisies, paintbrush. Along the creek, the cottonwoods, pecans and hickory trees were leafed out fully. He supposed that it had always been this lovely in the spring, but as a youngster longing to escape confinement here, he had seen none of its beauty.

He finally swung onto his horse and rode down to where Clayton was plowing. The fear of being "discovered" was still with him, but as he felt his brother crushing him in a one-armed embrace, his yearning to be with his family again overcame every other feeling.

"My God, big brother, where have you been?"

"More places than I care to remember, Clayton," he said, nearly choking.

"Mary said you'd be back, but we didn't believe her. You never wrote us."

"I know, Clayton. During the war I couldn't, and after that I just didn't. But I won't stop writing again, believe me."

"It don't matter, big brother. You're here now, and you ain't leavin' us again if I have anything to say about it."

Clayton unharnessed himself from the plow and led his brother across the plowed field to the house. On the porch they were met by a small pretty woman with eyes as blue as the cloudless sky above them and a piled-up mass of hair as bright gold as a halo. Clinging to her skirts was a little girl of four or five who, with her combed-out burnished auburn locks and big inquisitive green eyes, was a miniature of Judith Ringgold. Mary hadn't exaggerated the resemblance.

"You're Johnny," the girl's mother said, before Clayton, slow-spoken as always, even had a chance to introduce them. "Clayton and your sisters have never stopped talking about you. Welcome home." She gave him her hand and smiled warmly. "I'm Linda." She addressed the little girl beside her. "Judith, this is your Uncle Johnny."

As he dropped to his heels on the porch step, so that he and she could look at each other eye-to-eye, the little girl stared at him with the stern unsmiling expression of the very young encountering strangers. John Ringgold was filled with an almost unbearable warm sensation and just barely managed to resist the impulse to take the child in his arms. First he would teach her to smile at him, however long it took, then he would take her hand, and if she reached out to him after that, he would lift her in his arms.

It didn't take long for the little girl to warm up to her uncle. During the days that followed, as he worked at various chores to make things easier for his brother—clearing an irrigation ditch from the creek, mending harness, replacing fence posts—she was constantly nearby, watching him, chattering endlessly about the activities of all the creatures on the farm around her, from her pet turtle, Frank, to an expecting mother cat and the milk cows.

"You want one of Melissa's kittens, don't you, Johnny?" She never called him "uncle."

"Of course I do, but I may not be able to take care of it. I'll be leaving here soon. You'll have to take care of it for me."

"Why do you have to leave? Daddy wants you to stay, I know he does, and Mama too."

"I wish I could stay, Judith," he told her truthfully. Just being with his brother's family gave him a happiness he had not known since his long visits with the Youngers before the war. Watching them together, seeing how Linda's son accepted Clayton as a father and how little Judith clung to him, and the loving way Linda had even when she was teasing her husband or was cross with him, John wondered if he would ever have a family of his own. For now, he derived the fullest pleasure out of being an uncle. He built a swing seat for Judith with a back and armrests and suspended it from the oak branch upon which he and Clayton had climbed as boys. When he had to ride into town on an errand for Linda, he would place the little girl on the saddle in front of him. In the evenings, when she was asleep, he worked on a rocking horse, planning to have it ready for her birthday.

His sister Mary was, like him, unmarried. She taught

school in San Antonio, and he visited her frequently during the weeks he lived at the farm. At the end of the third week she told him about someone whom he'd never forgotten.

"I saw Lucy Conover the other day," she announced casually, shifting the conversation. "Someone told her you were back."

"Someone?" he said, grinning wryly at his little sister.

"Not me, Johnny," she answered emphatically, blushing a little as she did.

"How is she?"

"Not very happy, if you want to know the truth. I don't think she ever has been with Pace Conover."

"How do you know?" he asked, trying to read his own responses and sort out some painful memories.

"A woman knows," Mary answered cryptically, and he was hardly surprised, remembering. "She has a son. I wrote you about that. He's nine now. As a matter of fact, he's my best younger pupil."

Brother and sister regarded each other thoughtfully for a moment, and neither spoke. How much Mary knew, how much she guessed, he could only wonder. As one well schooled in suffering, who had come to know the wisdom of avoiding unnecessary pain, John resolved to avoid Mrs. Conover while he was in San Antonio. But this did not prevent him from meeting his sister the following day at the schoolhouse and watching her pupils, who ranged in age from eight to eighteen, run out at the sound of the dismissal bell. It happened that Mary's star pupil emerged last, assisting the teacher with a great pile of books and papers. Seeing her brother there, Mary looked startled at first, but then she smiled at him, and the expression in her all-seeing gray-green eyes was both knowing and sympathetic. She introduced the boy. "This is Johnny Conover. Johnny, this is my brother, Mr. Ringgold."

The boy managed to free his right hand from the pile of books, and John gripped it, looking into the frank, innocent blue eyes and feeling more strangely moved than he had ever felt before. "Pleased to meet you, sir," he said. He was a chunky youngster, but one could see that he was the kind who would stretch out and shoot up to six foot or more when he hit his teens.

"Johnny." Hearing the name they shared, both the man and the nine-year-old boy turned at the sound of another woman's voice.

"Hello, Lucy," he said, removing his hat.

She didn't return his greeting for a moment or two, and he thought that he could see sparks of anger in her violet eyes. She was smiling, but there was little warmth in her smile.

"Hello, Johnny," she said finally. "Are you home to stay or just visiting?"

"Just a visit. I'll be leaving shortly," he said, forcing a smile. That ought to relieve her, he thought. Even though her place in his heart had been taken by Margaret, he couldn't help being stirred by the memory of what he had been led to believe was her love. He couldn't help wishing that she had lost some of her beauty. Regrettably, he could see that she had lost nothing with the passage of nine years.

"You must come and see us before you go," she said, the angry bitter light in her eyes suddenly covered by an assumed veil of cordiality.

"I'll surely do that," he answered, with as little intention of accepting the invitation as she had presumably intended he have.

All the while they were both being watched by Mary, who missed nothing, and Lucy's son, who seemed to miss a good deal less than most youngsters his age. Feeling the eyes of these two on them, the one-time lovers lost no time in bidding each other good-bye.

That evening, as he rode back to the farm, John decided to leave without delay. He could finish Judith's rocking horse if he worked on it all of the following day. She would be terribly disappointed not to have him there for her birthday, but at least the rocking horse would be there. Most of his thoughts were directed toward another child. The sight of Lucy's son and the things Mary had told him about the boy had stirred feelings of pride but also a painful longing for what he knew he could not have. Surely the life of peace, blessed with a wife and children to care for, enjoying their love and the warmth of a home they had built together, was the life for a man. What a fool Cole was to leave Belle and go off with Cousin Jesse. Even Pace Conover was to be envied, in spite of what Mary said about the unhappiness of his wife. At least he had a good woman and a son. Whether or not the boy was his in fact hardly mattered. The important thing was that Conover was able to raise him as a son. He had Conover's name.

Feeling utterly wretched in his envy, wondering if he could ever be anything but a homeless drifter himself, he arrived at his brother's farm. He was surprised to find Linda on the porch waiting for him. She had a piece of paper in her hand.

"Johnny, this is a message for you. That Negress who works for Lucy Conover brought it."

He thanked Linda and slipped the message into a coat pocket without reading it, afraid of what this good woman, his sister-in-law, might read in his face if the message said what he guessed it might say.

"I used to work for Mrs. Conover's father," he said by way of explanation. "She asked me to call on her and her husband." Linda smiled and nodded, accepting the explanation but still looking a little puzzled. After she went back into the house, he led his horse into the barn. Before unsaddling he took out the message. Though he had indeed guessed what its contents might be, he was still not a little surprised: MEET ME AT THE SPRING. TOMORROW NOON.

After a troubled night and an anxious morning, he found himself riding toward the spring, trying to rehearse what he would say, even as he had tried nine years before to prepare himself to tell her he was leaving for Missouri. She had surprised him then, and it was a long time before he figured out, with a little help from sister Mary, the reasons for her strange behavior. Now he was older and harder to surprise. He was also in love with the memory of another woman. He was older, wiser and therefore, he told himself, less vulnerable.

When he arrived at the spring she was waiting, apparently had been for quite some time, though he was not late. She rose from her seat on the rock and came over as he dismounted and tied his horse to a willow. Whether by chance or design, she was dressed as he remembered her from their last meeting here. The brown leather riding skirt and the lace-fronted blouse, even the blue silk neckerchief were the same. Did she remember what she was wearing? Did she want him to remember? Having secured his horse, he greeted her with cool, deliberate cordiality.

"Hello, Lucy." Then he added, unnecessarily, "I got your message."

"Did you, Johnny?" she replied, confronting him and looking up into his face, perhaps searching to see what changes nine years had wrought in him. He reflected fleetingly that she was perhaps the only person whose discovery of the mark upon or within him he did not fear. She was the one who had initiated him into a world of danger and forbidden joy with all its guilt, pain and fleshfast ecstasy. She had, he believed, borne his child. He could share anything with this woman, even as she had shared everything with him.

He started to speak, but she blocked his speaking as she put her arms around his neck and began to kiss him, softly at first but then greedily. His own hunger was more consuming than he knew himself, having been increased rather than satisfied by loveless chance encounters and nights in upstairs rooms. He returned her devouring kisses with an equal voracity, and whereas they had once derived much of their enjoyment of each other from sharing the spectacle of each other's nakedness, they now took each other almost fully clothed, unable to endure a second's delay.

When they had been lovers before, he had become used to her crying out, and now she cried out again. But now he heard feelings he did not remember from before—bitter grief and rage along with the joy of her loving passion, elements at war within her that would not be quieted even after they had reached the summit of their pleasure.

"Hold me, Johnny," she whispered, clinging tightly to his neck and fighting to control a strange terrible choking that wouldn't let her speak. He held her and stroked her very gently, and finally she managed to say:

"I had to, Johnny. You know that, don't you?"

"Had to what?"

"Had to marry him. You were leaving and I couldn't ask you to stay. Don't you understand?"

"Surely, I understand."

"Johnny is your son."

"I know," he said, though hearing her say it added enormous weight to the fact. And made him all the more envious of the man who called himself the boy's father.

"Is Conover a good father?" He had to know.

"Yes, he is. He can give Johnny so much. And Johnny looks up to him, wants to be just like him." As she said this, Lucy reached out to stroke his cheek, as though she knew she was inflicting pain. "He's a good man, really he is," she went on. "I only wish that I could love him. I've tried to be a good wife. This is the first time I've ever . . . Believe me, it is."

"I do," he said, and then again, "I do."

"And it's wonderful. It's so damned wonderful that I'm begging you to leave here as soon as you can, for my sake, and Johnny's."

"I will, Lucy. I promise," he said, grateful for all she had given him but half wishing that he hadn't come back to this place. He foresaw the lonely times to come, sitting beside a fire out on the Staked Plains or wherever, conjuring out of the smoke the remembered shape of her body, trying to remember how . . .

"I mean, it would be so much worse if we were caught now. Pace must suspect, must know that Johnny isn't his, but he's never let on that he does. He trusts me. I can't . . ."

"I'll leave tomorrow."

"Good," she said, smiling gratefully, and then: "Because if you stayed . . ."

Instead of telling him, she showed him. There were no more tears that afternoon. They made love joyfully, guiltlessly, as though the passage of nine years had brought them innocence instead of experience, or that their experience enabled them to see how truly innocent they had been before. Thoughts of Margaret came to him, but he did not feel disloyal. Lucy had been his teacher, and he was returning with her to the time of her gentle tutelage, before he even knew Margaret.

He kept his word to Lucy, though it meant working most of the night on the rocking horse for Judith. He regretted that he was unable to paint it, but he was pleased with its sturdiness and the way it rocked. He finished it by attaching a saddle, bridle and reins cut out of an old pair of chaps.

After that, it took him little time to pack what he owned, and two hours before milking time he was able to cat-foot out of the house without disturbing anyone. He knew that his brother would try to talk him out of leaving, and there was no way he could explain why he had to go. He had already said good-bye to Judith the previous evening, though the child had no way of knowing that was what he meant.

"You were named after a great lady, Judith," he had told her, as the two of them walked along the creek. "You're going to grow up to be just like her, and your old uncle is going to be mighty proud."

"You're my best uncle!" the little girl burst out suddenly.

"I'm your only uncle," he answered, laughing to hide what he felt.

"I mean, you're my best friend," she said.

At that, he dropped to his knees and took her in his arms, too moved to speak. He hadn't promised Lucy that he wouldn't ever come back, he told himself. Someday he would be back here to see his niece. By then, probably, she would have grown into a lady like her grandmother. Until then, he would carry the image of her as she was now.

2

As he rode away from his home into the darkness, he was thinking of all the people he loved who had to be left behind. If only he could justify staying a little longer. But he had given his word to Lucy, and her reasons for wanting him to leave were good ones. She was resolved to be what their son needed her to be, and if he cared for either of them, he would not be hanging around to undermine that resolve. What, after all, did he have to offer besides the kind of ephemeral pleasure they had enjoyed that afternoon? Pace Conover was a man of substance. He could, as Lucy said, give the boy so much. The boy must never know that his real father was a penniless drifter who had been one of Quantrill's raiders in the war.

So he touched the flanks of his horse with his spurs and

put a few miles between himself and home before sunup. He rode north, toward Burnet County, where he'd heard that some big cattle spreads were hiring. When he arrived in Burnet, he took a hotel room. He also paid for a night upstairs with a crib girl at a nearby saloon. The following night, with his money about run out, he got into a poker game down in the saloon. One of the other players was the mayor of Burnet, Charlie McNichols. McNichols was a reading man, and he expressed his pleasure at winning a hand by quoting a line out of Horace, a poem to Fortune.

"When I responded by quoting the next line of the poem—*te semper anteit saeva Necessitas*—he damn near fell out of his chair. It came out that the town needed a schoolteacher. The job didn't pay much and the hours were long, but I was ready for something a little more mind-gratifying than punching cows. So I took the job and taught school for six years, perhaps the quietest but most fulfilling six years of my life. Tutoring Andy Hockensmith hadn't given me a lot of faith in my ability to impart learning, but these youngsters were different— fun-loving, obstreperous but educable."

Ringo smiles to himself, remembering some of his favorite pupils, wondering how they'd made out in the grown-up world. Sammy Fergus, for instance. A gap-toothed, freckled sixteen-year-old with a bright red bush of hair, Sammy was the likeliest pupil in the school. And Lisa Childs, a dark, fragile, pretty girl, also sixteen. While the other youngsters were content to master the basic arithmetic they'd need to keep track of stock or buy supplies, Sammy and Lisa wanted more, and the teacher sent away for algebra and geometry texts to tutor them. Because he took an interest in them, the two shared their aspirations with their teacher.

"A doctor, that's what I want to be. Just like Doc Quinn," Sammy told him.

"You need to go to a medical college, Sammy."

"I know that, Mr. Ringgold. But there's nothing going to stop me."

Nothing except a nearly illiterate rancher-father who was determined to raise the boy in his own image. The teacher rode out to visit Mr. Fergus one afternoon and tried to reason him out of his opposition.

"Why'd you put that idea in his head, teacher?"

"It's not my idea. It's your boy's own ambition. He's got what it takes to make something of himself. Maybe a doctor, maybe something else. Whatever it is, he's going to need more schooling than I can give him."

"I don't agree, teacher," Mr. Fergus replied, planting a gobbet of tobacco juice less than a foot from the teacher's boot toe. "This place is going to be partly his someday, and what he needs to know about running it I'll teach him."

Behind Mr. Fergus in the doorway, his wife listened with interest. She started to invite the teacher in for coffee, but her husband cut her off snapping, "Anything else we can do for you, teacher?"

Shortly after that, Mr. Fergus took his son out of school. Occasionally the boy managed to sneak away from the ranch and visit his old teacher, who, goaded by the memory of his own thwarted ambition, loaned him books and tried to encourage him not to regard his situation as hopeless.

"Mama's working on him, but that won't change his mind," the boy told him bitterly. "I guess I'll just have to light out of here when I get old enough."

"You do that, Sammy, just as soon as you're ready."

"Ready," they both knew, meant when somebody gave the boy enough money to leave home for further schooling. The teacher would have given him the money himself, if he'd had it. Not having it himself, he managed to persuade the mayor, Charlie McNichols, and Doc Quinn to help the boy. Still, Mr. Fergus remained unalterably opposed, but he was suddenly removed as an obstacle one day when his horse was startled by a diamondback and threw him practically on top of the reptile. There's not much even a doctor can do for a rattlesnake bite in the neck. The ownership of the Fergus ranch passed to Widow Fergus and Sammy's older brother, while Sammy went east to Baltimore for schooling.

As for Lisa Childs, Ringo guesses that she probably became a teacher, probably in a little school like the one in which he taught her.

"I want to teach the way you do, Mr. Ringgold," she told him. "You make us all want to learn as much as we can." Which was gratifying to hear even if he guessed that she spoke mainly for herself and Sammy Fergus. It was enough that she spoke for them. She had other aspirations as well, which she shared with him, almost confessionally. "And I'm going to write books. Books of poetry and stories and maybe even novels."

"Don't put off your writing, Lisa. Start now." He encouraged her because she had impressed him with her word handling in the compositions he assigned.

"I already have," she confided, shyly dropping her eyes as she brought out a sheaf of papers she had been concealing behind her back. "These are some poems I wrote and a story. They're not very good, I'm afraid, but I want you to see them because I know you can help me. You will help me, won't you, Mr. Ringgold?"

"Surely," he said with a sympathetic smile. He took her pieces and read them carefully, and though he was no poet himself he had read enough poetry to be able to see that there was some real talent manifesting itself embryonically as it were, in her self-conscious verses with their forced rhymes and overelaborated figures ("like an eager butterfly in its chrysalis enclosed, my heart awaits . . ."). The story was a cleverly contrived romance in an imagined Arthurian setting wherein a young maiden waited for a tall, auburn-haired knight to rescue her from a cruel magician with Saracens and demons at his command. As he read the story with a good deal more pleasure than he'd anticipated, the teacher chuckled over the resemblance of the knight to himself. Sensing an infatuation that could be painful to the girl, he resolved to keep her at a distance, even while he encouraged her with her writing.

He had no way of knowing that the distance between them would soon be reduced by the girl's own mother. Shortly after he began reading the girl's poetry, she brought him an invitation to have supper with them.

Mrs. Childs was a widow in her mid-thirties whose husband had died at Vicksburg fighting for the North. She ran the only dress shop in Burnet, and John Ringgold had noticed her occasionally on Sunday mornings on her way to church escorted by a portly but handsome and prosperous attorney named Wallace. He noticed her partly because of a curious resemblance she bore to his own mother. The resemblance was not a matter of anything

physical they had in common. Indeed they were very
different physical types, though equally striking, Lisa's
mother being very tall and imposing with dark eyes and
gleaming black hair pulled back severely into a bun. But
like his mother, Mrs. Childs bore herself in an erect,
queenly manner that conveyed to the beholder a kind of
self-assured spirituality that could be intimidating. John
was a little apprehensive about meeting her.

As it happened, Mrs. Childs was a most gracious host-
ess, and John soon felt totally at ease with her.

"Mr. McNichols tells me you're a man of learning, Mr.
Ringgold. I think that's a fine thing. We're fortunate to
have you here in Burnet teaching our children."

"Mighty kind of Mr. McNichols to say that," John
replied. "I guess he doesn't run into that many people
out here who read Latin poetry."

"My husband was a man of learning," she went on.
"He attended Harvard College but didn't finish because
of the war." John told her a little about his own interrupted education and admitted that he'd fought for the
South.

"Most men from around here did," she said. "It hardly
seems to matter now, does it?"

"It does to some. What brought you out here?" he
asked, for she was obviously not a native of this region.
He guessed that she was from somewhere in the neighborhood of Harvard College.

"My mother's family is Spanish. They owned property
here from an old land grant. I came out here to sell it and
decided to stay."

"Mr. Ringgold's helping me with my poetry," Lisa
broke in. "And he's going to teach me how to read Latin
and maybe Greek."

Mrs. Childs responded with a nod and a grateful smile
that warmed the teacher but also caused him to flush a
little with embarrassment.

"Lisa's the kind of pupil who makes teaching worthwhile," he said. For some reason, the girl looked upset
and nervous, in spite of the fact that he and her mother
were getting on well. Barely speaking, she served the
supper her mother had prepared, a simple meal but with
a touch of elegance that reminded him of suppers with
the Youngers before the war.

After Lisa cleared the table and excused herself, Mrs. Childs went to the sideboard and brought out a bottle of whiskey.

"One can't purchase good brandy or port out here, I'm afraid." She poured him a generous shot in a cut-glass tumbler but poured herself a cup of tea.

"This is just fine. To you, Mrs. Childs," he said, raising the glass.

"You can call me Grace."

"If you'll call me John."

Lisa came in then to say good-night. She had some papers in her hand, which she held out to him.

"These are the poems you read. I tried to make them better the way you said I should."

John rose to his feet and thanked her, for the poems and the supper she had helped her mother prepare. The girl smiled brightly as she said good-night but seemed to be covering something. After she left the room and was well out of earshot, the mother smiled at him knowingly and said, "She adores you."

"She's a fine girl," he replied, a little stiffly. "Makes it easy to be a teacher when somebody's that willing to learn."

"She's just sixteen. That's a hard age for a girl."

"For anybody," he answered, remembering his own bittersweet initiation by Lucy McMaster.

"Folks say you're the best teacher we've ever had here in Burnet. Did you know that?"

"No, I didn't," he answered, flushing.

"The school board has heard about you. They're going to ask you to be county inspector of schools. That's what Mr. McNichols told me, anyway. I told him that it would be a shame to take you out of the schoolroom, but he said that you could do more good helping other teachers, and besides the job will pay you a lot more."

"The pay doesn't matter that much," he replied honestly. "Nobody teaches school for the money you earn." He didn't mention how he supplemented his meager teacher's income with weekly trips over to Lampasas, where he dealt faro and poker.

"But the laborer is worthy of his hire," she answered him, as his mother might have, with just the right biblical text.

CONFESSIONS OF JOHNNY RINGO

The evening was the beginning of a relationship that might have changed his life altogether if it hadn't been for subsequent events and some choices that might, perhaps, have been made differently.

"Grace," Ringo whispers softly to himself. " 'When once we have forgot our Grace, we would and we would not.' " What might he have done if things had turned out differently? Would he not have married her? She was a little older than he was, attractive, warm, intelligent and good, the perfect wife for the upstanding pillar of the community he was becoming—John Ringgold, Inspector of Schools. When he began to call on her in the evenings, to drive her out in the country for picnics and to escort her to church—in a word, to court her—the girl Lisa reacted by overcoming her infatuation and regarding him as, in her mother's words, "the father she never had."

He cared deeply for both of them. Did he love Grace Childs? Maybe. There were different ways to love a woman. What he felt for Grace was nothing like what he had felt for Margaret or Lucy, but it was a kind of love. He could have done much worse. And did.

"I had made a number of friends around Burnet, including the Beard brothers, Mose and John, with whom I lived for a time. Their mother was a kind lady who looked after me as another son and kept trying to arrange matches for me with various young women in the neighborhood. She didn't abandon that project until I started squiring Grace around and she saw us together in church."

"She's a fine woman, John," Mrs. Beard said. "Just the kind you need. Her friends are mighty glad that she's fancying you instead of that lawyer fellow."

"He'd make her a lot richer," John said with a rueful chuckle.

"But he's not the sure-enough man you are, John. You'll take care of her and make her happy."

Sadly, Ringo remembers Mrs. Beard's kind words and how they had supported him in his resolve to settle down to a peaceful career, married to a good woman. If only Mrs. Beard had been able to exert a comparable pacifying influence on her own sons. . . .

"Along about the end of 'seventy-five Mose and John threw in with a fellow named Scott Cooley, who had assembled a gang over in Loyal Valley for the purpose of avenging the murder of his stepfather, a Mr. Williamson. His stepfather, it seems, had been murdered by one of the German settlers, a man named Pete Bader, over in Mason County with the connivance of a deputy sheriff by the name of Wohrle. Cooley's stepfather had been suspected of rustling, and that killing was typical of the way the Germans in that county were taking the law into their own hands.

"This Cooley was a strange one. His real parents had been massacred by Indians up in Palo Pinto County and he was carried off by them. After he was rescued, the Williamsons adopted him and brought him up. He was short and stocky and so dark that he looked part Indian, but you never met a man who hated Indians the way Cooley did. I remember hearing how he was run out of a saddle shop when he brought in some strips of hide that had a lot of tallow on them which he wanted to be braided into a quirt but which turned out to be stripped from the body of an Indian.

"In those days the best place for a man with an appetite for Indian killing was the Texas Rangers, and Cooley was for a while a ranger. At the time of his stepfather's murder, however, he had settled down farming near Menardville. If it hadn't been for the Beards, I never would have met him, and if Mose hadn't gotten himself killed, I certainly wouldn't have thrown in with the Cooley gang. I'd had enough fighting during the war to last me more than a lifetime. The quiet life of a school inspector was starting to agree with me, and I was just about to ask Grace Childs to be my wife."

He remembers a quiet summer afternoon, one of many, when he and Mrs. Beard were sitting together in her kitchen drinking coffee. He had just told her of his decision to ask for Grace's hand and she had just responded delightedly, "Well, it's about time, I'd say!" when they were interrupted by John Beard, just returned from Mason County.

The news of her son's death nearly killed Mrs. Beard. While two neighbor women looked after her, and Doctor Quinn was sent for, the surviving Beard brother related the particulars of Mose's death to his friend John Ringgold:

"There was near sixty of 'em waitin'. When Mose an' a

fella called Walker started to cross the stream, they was surrounded. I guess Mose said somethin' an' all of a sudden them Germans cut loose. Mose an' Walker was shot to pieces. That's how it was told to us by one of the Germans who was there an' who didn't hold with them sixty-t'-two odds. He also told us the Mason County sheriff an' his deputy was there with them squareheads lookin' on all the while."

So there was no looking to the law for a prosecution. John Ringgold told John Beard that he would be returning to Mason County with him.

"Naw, thanks anyway. We don't need no schoolteacher."

"I wasn't always a schoolteacher," he snapped in reply.

Without elaborating, he told Beard to wait for him. Then he went up to his room and hunted out a pair of saddlebags he hadn't used for over six years. Inside one, carefully wrapped in flannel rags, were two Navy Colts. In the other was a pair of holsters. Buckling them on, he had the sense of one about to take an irretraceable step. He knew full well that a man who buckles on a gun for use in this kind of affair may be choosing never to be without one again. But he could hear the sound of Mrs. Beard's weeping from the other end of the house, and he didn't hesitate.

"We rode on over to Mason County, and during the weeks that followed, we had our share of fights with 'the Dutch,' as we called them. Since most of the Germans had fought for the Union and most of us 'Americans,' as Cooley's gang started calling themselves, had been Confederates, it was like a continuation of the war."

For John himself it was not only a continuation, a return to the war, but a rediscovery of something he had intended, hoped, to leave caged within the bars of his newfound respectability. As a dedicated educator and a family man, one who would be worthy of Grace Childs, he could, so he believed, confine the creature that the war had let out. Remembering, though, remembering the long trail from Mason County to Tombstone, John Ringo, outlaw, sadly doubts that it would have borne confinement long. For now he remembers how, in spite of being confined and well-nigh forgotten during his peaceful years in Burnet, it sprang out of him, indeed became him in his first encounter with the Germans of Mason County.

Elder Creek. That was where they found "the Dutch" late one afternoon in early May. Intending merely to water and rest their horses before returning to Loyal Valley, Cooley and his gang found themselves confronting a nearly equal number of Mason County Germans who had approached the stream from the opposite direction. Instantly guns were out and ready on both sides, but the leader of the Germans, a huge blond-bearded fellow by the name of Faustkampfer, raised his hand to signal a parley. Then he rode into the middle of the creek and sat his horse for a moment, regarding them disdainfully.

"So you fellows would like to water your horses, eh?" he said, his accent barely audible, sounding foreign mainly in the precise way he clipped off his words, so different from the drawling of west Texas natives.

"We aim to, squarehead," Cooley replied, expelling sideways a gobbet of tobacco juice.

The German expressed his own contempt with a snorting laugh.

"Your horses will not drink until you earn the right, until you show us what kind of men you are."

"Suits us just fine, don't it, boys?" There were murmurs of agreement and the hammers of pistols and rifles clicked back in readiness.

"*Nein*, wait a minute." Faustkampfer raised his hand again. "If we start shooting each other, it will prove nothing."

"What do you have in mind?" John Beard called back.

"Let your best man meet me on your side of the creek. We will have no weapons but our hands. Let our fists decide whose horses will drink."

At first no one in the Cooley gang said anything. Then a man named Alf Harper spoke up.

"That squarehead's a prizefighter. Some kinda bare-knuckle champeen back in Sain' Louie, so I hear."

"He's also one of the ones who was in on killing Mose, so I hear," John Beard said and started dismounting to accept the challenge.

"Hold on a minute, John," John Ringgold said. "Let me try him first."

The big German did not hear any of this. Seeing the "Americans" hesitate, he began to taunt them.

"Well now, what do you fellows have between your

legs?" He laughed and turned back to his own men, calling out, *"Sie haben keine Hoden! Nur Scheiden!"* The whole gang of Germans laughed loudly at that. Then their leader turned back to face his enemies. By way of translation, he pointed down at his own crotch and shook his head; the downward set of his mouth added emphasis to his utter scorn.

"He'll whip your ass good, schoolteacher," Cooley sneered as John Ringgold dismounted and began to unbuckle his gun belt.

Though he had only been with Cooley a short time, John had learned to despise him. Only his loyalty to Mrs. Beard and her sons had kept him with the gang.

"This is my fight, John," Beard protested.

"If he whips me, you can have him." And he handed Beard his gun belt and hat.

Seeing him dismount, the big German crossed the stream and did likewise, leaving his gun belt looped around his saddle horn. "You are a brave fellow but a very foolish one," he said as they squared off. He raised his big fists and assumed a classic pugilist's stance.

"That remains to be seen," John replied, dropping into a wrestler's crouch and beginning to circle the German. A good wrestler can always beat a boxer, so Cole Younger had frequently told him. Just a matter of the wrestler's getting his hands on the boxer. What one should add, John was thinking, is: If the wrestler has the heft of a Cole Younger.

The German was about Cole's size, had maybe a thirty-five-pound advantage over John. And it wasn't hard to believe that he'd fought as a professional. John tried to duck and slip aside, but he couldn't avoid jabs that snapped his head back and hooks to the body that nearly knocked the breath out of him. Urged on by cries of *"Zerstör ihn! Töte ihn!"* Faustkampfer moved in to finish off this unworthy opponent, who had yet to land a punch and who seemed barely able to stay on his feet.

Indeed, just for a second, it actually looked to the German as though his opponent were falling backward, but that illusion was instantly dashed away as John Ringgold, using a trick he'd learned from Mick Tyree, the most resourceful brawler in Quantrill's band, left the ground and kicked out with both feet. Totally confident and contemptuous of his opponent, Faustkampfer was hardly ready to parry or dodge the pair of boot heels that landed in his lower abdomen and groin.

He mocked the German as he scrambled to his feet. "You showed me the target." The big man was momentarily helpless, bent over and gasping. John did not hesitate. Grasping the man's powerful shoulders, he brought the German's face down onto his knee. Then he caught Faustkampfer in a headlock and with a tremendous effort threw him over his hip, so that the big German was sprawled in the shallow water of the creek.

He'd won the fight, and Cooley's gang was howling their delight, but John Ringgold was not content with victory. Something had been uncaged by the blows he'd taken from the German. The restless thing within him— burning there like the fire in the taproot of a giant tree struck by lightning, working its secret way up to flame out and devour the tree—suddenly took possession and he sprang into the stream to land on the fallen German. The man was on all fours attempting to rise, but John straddled his back and seized his right wrist, which he then twisted upward along his back in a cruel lock that caused Faustkampfer to bellow like a wounded bull. For a few seconds the German held himself up with one arm, before John's weight drove him face-first down into the slimy mud of the creek bottom.

"Have all the water, you squareheaded sonofabitch!" he snarled, using his free hand to keep the German facedown in the muddy water. The other Germans started across the creek to rescue their leader, but bullets from the Cooley gang dropped two who managed to get near. The big man struggled to rise with his free arm and succeeded in raising his face from the water just long enough to bellow "*Hilf!*" before John thrust him down again.

Finally the rest of the Germans rushed across the creek in a body, and after two of them had belabored John with clubbed rifles until he released his hold, two others dragged their nearly drowned leader to safety.

As John Beard helped John Ringgold to his feet and handed him his pistols, Cooley said, in a tone of sneering admiration, "Well now, teacher, guess you're one of us after all."

"Don't count on it, Cooley," he snapped, but he was strangely reminded of his past, of what he had become in the war. He could tell himself he wasn't one of Cooley's boys, but then why was he here? Loyalty to his friends, surely, but something more as well.

"There was one German in particular that we wanted to get in our sights, Pete Bader, the one who'd started the whole feud by murdering Cooley's stepfather. We'd also heard that he was wearing a ring that had belonged to Mose Beard, and in fact someone had hacked off Mose's ring finger after he was shot.

"John Beard, Cooley and I finally caught up with him. Or more exactly, he caught up with us. We were in a line shack up near the top of Tonkawa Ridge and Bader's gang, about fifteen of them, surrounded it. Luckily I was out before dawn rounding up my strayed horse and happened to be carrying my rifle. Bader's men opened up on the shack just as I was returning. I found a good vantage point up above them and started cutting loose. After I dropped a couple of them, the others ran off and this surprised me until we discovered that one of the men I'd shot was their leader, Bader himself. The other was a half-breed Kiowa named Danton.

" 'Mighty grateful for this, John,' John Beard said, and he held up Bader's hand so that I could see the ring on his finger. He didn't try to slip the ring off but went right to work with his knife performing the same surgery Mose Beard had received.

"Watching Beard at work with his knife seemed to have an effect on Cooley. He went over to the dead half-breed and kicked him, muttering 'red sonofabitch.' Then he kicked the body again so that it rolled over on its back. As he pulled out his knife, I remembered the story about his being run out of the saddle shop, and as he started to cut away Danton's shirt I drew one of my Colts and cocked it.

" 'Get away from him, Cooley,' I yelled. 'Well whaddya know,' Cooley sneered at me, 'our teacher's a redskin lover. He kin shoot 'em, but he don't have no stomach for finishin' the job.'

"Cooley was probably too crazy to see just how close he was to death at that moment. John Beard knew me a little better, and he probably saved Cooley's life when he went over and told him to shut up and put his knife away.

"A little while after that, Cooley and I wound up in jail together, the only time I've ever been locked up. A sheriff by the name of Strickland arrested us for the murder of Bader and took us under a strong guard to Austin. There was a big mob gathered there to meet us, not a hanging crowd but just folks who were curious about all the violent goings-on up in Mason County, and some fellows from the newspapers interviewed us about 'the Mason County War,' as it had come to be called. We were supposed to stand trial in Austin, but then they transferred us to another jail in Lampasas County, just north of Burnet. Cooley had a lot of friends in that area, former comrades in the Texas Rangers, and so did I, parents of the kids I'd taught, as well as the kids themselves. We both had a lot of visitors, and one day I was visited by someone I'd been half expecting but didn't really want to see, at least not in that place."

"Are you well, John?" she asked as the deputy moved back out of earshot. She was dressed in mourning black.

"I've been better, Grace," he answered, feeling truly miserable as he remembered what might have been. It was something he'd been trying not to think about.

"I . . . we, Lisa and I have been so worried about you. It's been almost six months. Why did you leave us without even saying anything, not even good-bye?" There were tears starting in her eyes, and he could read in her expression the signs of a terrible hurt he had inflicted, a hurt that could only be the result of deep feeling. Finding it impossible to meet her eyes, he shut his own tightly and grasped the bars of his cell.

"Why?" she asked again.

"It was something I felt I had to do. The law wouldn't help. The Beards were my friends."

"But they're going to try you for murder, John."

"It wasn't murder. You've got to believe that."

"Did you . . . ? Did you kill a man?"

"Yes," he answered in a whisper, whereupon she gasped and turned away.

"I had to, Grace," he went on quickly. "They attacked us, over a dozen men against three of us."

"How could you?" she said, conveying so much revulsion as she asked the question that he was filled with self-loathing. He no longer saw any point in defending himself, no point in hiding anything.

"Because I'm the way I am, Grace." She covered her face and didn't answer. He went on. "Did you ever hear of Quantrill's Raiders?"

She nodded slowly, regarding him with amazement and dreadful expectation. He decided to hold back nothing. He said to her, "I was one of them. I was at Lawrence. We did everything they said we did. After the war was over, when I came here I thought I could be different. That business over in Mason County showed me I couldn't be any different. It's best you found out now."

The woman drew back, covering her mouth with her hand as though she were going to be sick, shutting her eyes and turning away. As the deputy let her out the door leading to the cells, Cooley sidled up next to him, uttered a brief, sniggering laugh and an appreciative lip smack.

"That's a mighty nice piece of ass, teacher. Wouldn't mind poppin' it into her myself. For sure I wouldn't. . . ."

These were very nearly Scott Cooley's last words. Had the deputy been twenty seconds slower in reaching the cell, John Ringgold might have faced a double murder charge. As it was, the deputy had to carry the unconscious Cooley to an adjacent cell and summon a doctor. John Ringgold was handcuffed to the bars of his cell.

He thought that he had seen the last of Grace Childs, but in two days she came to see him again. This time she was dressed in white. She had calmed down a great deal and even managed to smile as she greeted him. Moving close to the bars, to which the deputy had again handcuffed him, she reached out and stroked a bruise on his cheekbone inflicted by Cooley.

"I'm sorry I behaved that way," she said. "I believe that you're not a murderer. And what you did in the war was surely no worse than what a lot of other men did. You mustn't blame yourself. I know you, John. You're a good man."

If anything, he felt even worse than before. The healing balm of her forgiveness seemed to create an unbearable burning sensation as it flowed over him. For the first time since he lost Margaret in the war, he felt himself on the point of tears. For several moments he could not utter a word. When he finally managed to speak, he asked:

"How is Lisa?"

"She's well, John. She's terribly worried about you, though."

"Tell her not to worry. I'll be all right."

"No you won't, unless you let me help you."

"What can you do?" he said, then caught himself. "I mean, I'm mighty grateful, but there's nothing you can do."

"You're going to need a good lawyer. Those German people have witnesses who'll testify against you. Dave Wallace is the best lawyer there is between here and Austin."

"Wallace? He was your suitor before—"

She cut him off. "I know. It doesn't matter. He can get you off."

"Why should he? I can't even pay him."

"Don't worry about that. He'll be paid," she answered crisply.

"I didn't want Grace to be spending her money on a lawyer for me, and I told her so. She tried to reassure me by saying it wouldn't be costing her any money, but this didn't put an end to my wondering and worrying.

"Things became a lot clearer the following day when I was visited by Dave Wallace. We had met before, at school-board meetings and out in front of church on Sundays, and I had been duly impressed by his well-tailored suits and refined manners that seemed to go along with an eastern upbringing and education in the law. Now I learned that he could also be a blunt-spoken man."

"Ringgold, I'm here to save your neck," were his first words to the prisoner.

"Why should you?" John asked, even as he had asked Grace.

"Because for one thing, it's going to be damned embarrassing to the community back in Burnet if you swing for murder. You've been teaching their children."

"That's mighty civic-minded of you, counselor," the prisoner answered, sensing that this was less than a total explanation. They didn't like each other much, but there was a degree of mutual understanding. Wallace studied him a moment, perhaps wondering if John had guessed what he was going to say next. Then he came out with it.

"The main reason, if you have to know, is Grace Childs. I mean to marry her." At this John felt the same sickness he'd felt when she walked out of the jail the first time.

"What does Grace have to say about that?"

"She says she'll marry me," Wallace answered with a contemptuous half-grin. But then he added, "If . . ."

"If?" John echoed.

"If I get you acquitted of this murder charge. She cares for you, Ringgold. Damned if I can see why, but she does."

"How do I know you won't let them convict me? Wouldn't you rather just get me out of the way?"

"Frankly, yes. But Grace has told me she won't marry me if you're convicted. I also have my reputation to think about. Not one of my clients has ever been hung. That's a record I don't mean to spoil now."

It took John a second or less to make up his mind. Looking Wallace directly in the eye, he thanked him for his offer and his honesty but refused to be defended by him.

"There are worse things than hanging, Wallace. My own father was a lawyer down in San Antonio. He nearly got himself killed speaking out on slavery before the war. . . ."

"What does that have to do with . . . ?"

"Maybe nothing at all. My father wasn't a very successful lawyer. He didn't prosper. I guess speaking the truth mattered too much to him."

"What are you saying, Ringgold?" Wallace snapped in reply, anger showing in the perceptible reddening of his smooth dewlap and rounded cheeks. John Ringgold knew in his heart that the only reason he'd brought up his father and represented him in this misleading, idealized fashion was a desire to insult this complacent, well-fed advocate.

"Figure it out for yourself, Wallace. I'll defend myself and tell the jury the truth. It was self-defense. I don't need you to lie for me."

"Listen, you damned fool," Wallace snarled, his voice

rising. "That squarehead you shot had a lot of friends over in Mason County. Five of them are going to swear that they saw you shoot him down in cold blood. Without me to defend you, you're a dead man."

John Ringgold shrugged as he replied. "So be it."

He started to turn away and Wallace shouted, "If you don't care about yourself you might at least think about some of the people who do!" As John paused and turned his head to listen, Wallace went on. "The only reason Grace cares so damn much about what happens to you is what it'll do to her daughter. That girl worships you. What's it going to do to her when they string you up?"

Part of what Wallace said was obviously not true, and John was tempted to make another remark to the effect that lawyers were habitual liars who couldn't handle the truth without choking on it. But he knew that part of what Wallace said was probably true, and he remembered Lisa's eager, trusting expression as she brought him her poems. He shook his head and thought for a few moments.

"All right, Wallace," he said at last. "Have it your way. Get me off if you can."

Wallace uttered a triumphant laugh and said, "Don't worry, Ringgold, I'll get you off. I can't afford to lose this one." Not long after, John could hear his triumphant laughter out in the street.

Then the deputy came in and said, "You're a lucky man, Ringgold. Wallace'll get you off if anybody can. The last fella he defended was caught standin' over somebody with a smokin' hogleg in his hand. Damned if he waren't acquitted."

"Guess if he gets you off an' proves it was self-defense, he'll get me off too, teacher," Cooley chimed in from the next cell. John glared at him silently.

As it turned out, however, Attorney Wallace was to be deprived of his opportunity. Shortly after midnight that very evening, the jail was taken by a mob.

The sheriff and his deputy were aware that a number of strangers were arriving in Lampasas for the trial, and it was not hard to figure out that they were from Mason County, probably friends and relatives of the late Pete Bader. The sheriff was warned by a citizen who understood a little "Dutch" that the Germans were talking about "*das Tau*," meaning "the rope." Word had gotten around quickly that the renowned Dave Wallace would be defending the accused men in the jail. Indeed Wallace himself had been overheard in the saloon bragging that he would "win this one, just like all the others." At the bar, the Germans from Mason County could be heard muttering among themselves about "*Gerechtigkeit*." The Mason County War itself had begun with a piece of their wild "justice," and there was no reason to assume that their habit of taking the law into their own hands had been abandoned. The sheriff deputized four citizens for emergency duty, and he and his deputies armed themselves with shotguns. John Ringgold and Cooley were aware of these preparations, but the sheriff reassured them: "We ain't gonna have no lynchin' in my town."

Shortly after midnight, however, the two prisoners were awakened by the sound of a key in John's cell door. The sheriff was opening the door, and covering him was a bandanna-masked individual. Behind them were more masked figures with their pistols trained on the disarmed deputies.

"Hey, teacher, they're gonna lynch us!" Cooley said in a tremulous voice.

"Looks that way, Cooley," John answered wearily, almost indifferently. This would, he thought, take care of everything. It would certainly be better than having a jury convict him if Wallace failed to work his sophistic lawyer's magic and having to wait for the appointed day while a gallows was erected in the yard outside his cell window. At least Grace and his friends from Burnet wouldn't be feeling compelled to be with him in his last hour and watch him die. He stood up and faced the masked lynchers with a contemptuous expression.

To his utter amazement, one of them shoved a gun and holster into his hands and told him to "put this on." Then, having freed and armed Cooley as well, they locked the sheriff and his deputies in the cells and urged the two liberated prisoners out through the sheriff's office. As they passed near a table bearing cards and an oil lamp, John recognized one of the men, in spite of his bandanna.

"Dan—?" Before he could utter the last name, the man clamped a hand over his mouth, saying, "Please be quiet, Mr. Ringgold."

John chided himself for having blurted out the name. Of course it was Dan Fergus, Sammy's big brother. He hoped that the incarcerated lawmen had not overheard him. Looking around, he thought that he recognized some of the others, one overgrown youngster he had taught to read at eighteen and the father of two other pupils. Some of the other masked figures were Cooley's friends, two of them probably the ex-rangers who had visited him that very day.

"Hurry up, you fellows!" someone was yelling from the porch.

"Too late, dammit," someone else said. "Here come the Dutch."

Dan Fergus was apparently the leader of the rescuers. He turned to John and Cooley, saying, "There are horses waiting for you in the alley. Get moving while we hold 'em off."

Outside, raging cries of *"Wir wollen Gerechtigkeit!"* and *"Gebt ihnen das Tau!"* could be heard. Then the men on the porch began firing. John drew the pistol he had been given and started toward a window, but Fergus grasped him firmly by the shoulder.

"Please, Mr. Ringgold. Just run for it, will you? We'll hold 'em off."

John understood. Fergus and these other good citizens had risked their lives and their reputations for him, and it would all be wasted if he didn't escape. There was no time even to thank them. He nodded at Fergus, who directed him to a side window through which Cooley was already disappearing. As he slipped through the window, the justice-hungry Germans of Mason County poured a devastating fusillade into the front of the sheriff's office, and the rescuers replied in kind. John Ringgold could hear the cries of wounded men and hoped fervently that his deliverers were not among them.

He ran along the alley to where a man waited holding the reins of a fine big spirited horse. Recognizing John, the man held out the reins. He mounted quickly and spurred the animal down the alley away from the firing. As he passed in front of the brightly lit saloon, he saw that he was riding one of Dan Fergus's best breeding studs. Cooley was nowhere to be seen. Just as well, John thought. His ranger friends would be pretty disappointed if I killed him after they went to all that trouble.

3

He rode north from Lampasas, avoiding towns and set-
tlements. As he rode, he told himself that he ought to be
thankful. At least thankful to the good people who had
risked everything for him and thankful to the woman
who had offered him her love and the chance to be a
law-abiding, peace-loving family man. And yes he was,
to them, thankful. But toward whomever or whatever it
was that had ordered the fate involving them all in the
bloody affair called the Mason County War he was anything but thankful. For he saw now that he would always
be a homeless wanderer, a drifter. Reining in near daybreak beside a nameless muddy little creek that flowed
out of some low, mesquite-covered hills, he dismounted
and checked the saddlebags. Fergus had thought of everything. There was plenty of food, even coffee and
sugar and a bottle of whiskey. A full canteen was strapped
to the saddle horn, and there was a bedroll tied on
behind the cantle. He was outfitted for a long ride, and it
was clear that the good people of Burnet who had thought
well of him as an educator of their children and had gone
to the trouble of breaking him out of jail expected him to
ride far.

As he thought of the lonely miles ahead of him, the
lonely days becoming months and years if he lived that
long, John Ringgold felt the wearisome weight of the
gray dawn that always settles upon the all-night traveler,
felt it with the additional weight of hopelessness and
regret. Uncorking the bottle of whiskey, he drank deeply,
let the warmth of it soothe the aching inside him.

There was a chance, a very good chance, that a posse
would be coming after him. The least he could do in
gratitude to the people of Burnet was avoid getting himself caught and brought back again for trial. They would
probably look for him to double back and head south
toward Mexico if he didn't head up into the Nations. He
would therefore head northwest up into the Panhandle.
There were some big cattle outfits up there, so he'd
heard, and it was time for the summer drives to begin.
Driving one of those seas of living, lowing beef up the

trail to Dodge City required a large crew. Strangers were
welcome to sign on for the drive, no questions asked. It
was a good place to disappear for a while.

"So I signed on with John Slaughter, shortening my
name to 'Ringo' in the hope that I wouldn't be connected
either to my family or my past. I worked for Slaughter
for two years and was in on two drives up to Dodge City.
After my peaceful years as a schoolteacher, it was no
easy life. Eating dust day after day, getting by on four
hours of sleep a night, on the lookout for sudden death in
all the innumerable forms it can assume on a drive—the
flash flood in the arroyo, quicksand, the stampede, Indians who figured they had a right to help themselves to
our beef since we'd killed off most of their buffalo. You
worried especially when the 'Comanche moon' was up.
Comanches will attack at night, unlike most Indians, who
worry about their spirits getting lost in the dark if they
leave their bodies.

"By the time you reached the railhead at Dodge, you
were so damned thirsty you wanted to drink up the town.
Most of the fellows drank up or gambled away most of
what they'd earned on the drive. I drank right along with
them but usually wound up a little richer, being gifted
with an uncommon capacity for whiskey and a pair of
would-be surgeon's hands that worked well with cards.

"It was while I was with Slaughter's crew that I met
Curly Bill Brocius and some other fellows I was destined
to ride with again out here in Arizona. At first I didn't
take much to Curly, finding him a little too familiar and
talkative and full of practical jokes."

Such as the time he, Ringo, was coming out of a
barber shop in Dodge—freshly shaved, clipped and bathed
for the first time in weeks, savoring the taste of an
imported cheroot. Hardly had he puffed at the weed
before something whizzed most of it away, leaving a
truncated stub between his teeth. At the same instant, the
thunderclap sound of a .45 sent him whirling into a crouch
behind a porch post with his own weapon out and ready.

A loud guffawing from the burly marksman on the
porch, sitting with his chair tilted back against the front
wall of the barber shop, added instantaneous rage to his
amazement.

"What's the matter, cowboy? Can't take a little funnin'?"

Curly asked innocently when his guffawing had subsided to a deep-chested chuckle.

Ringo forced a smile as he holstered his own pistol, but there was an iciness in his blue eyes that Curly did not miss and that may have been the reason why the .45 remained trained on him.

"You owe me a cigar, Curly," he said, taking the stub from his mouth and flicking it at the man in the chair.

Laughing, Curly holstered his weapon, sat forward in his chair, and reached into his shirt pocket for one of his own cigars, whereupon Ringo's right-hand .44 came out of its holster and spit twice, smashing a rear leg of the chair and dropping Curly onto his backside on the sidewalk. Seeing what had happened, Curly guffawed as loudly as when he himself had been the pistol-wielding prankster.

"Didn't think you could move that fast, Ringo. Here, take your damn cigar and help me up."

From there they went into a saloon, and Curly began talking about Arizona.

"It's wide-open country, John. Ain't no law to speak of, 'sides the army, and they're so goddamn busy with the 'paches that you don't need to worry about them. A man can take what he wants, be somethin' he wants to be."

"I've been there. Passed through during the war. It didn't look to me as though the Apaches would let a white man be anything but dead."

"Depends on the man, John. A sure-enough man doesn't let a little redskin danger get in his way. It sure ain't stoppin' Slaughter. He's drivin' a herd out there and I mean to go with him. Once I get out there, I'm on my own, won't be punchin' cows for nobody but myself."

"Curly made himself my friend one night in Dodge," Ringo recalls, "when a fellow I'd cleaned out in a poker game tried to backshoot me in an alley. I heard a shot behind me and whirled around to find good old Curly standing over him with his hogleg out.

" 'It's okay, Ringo,' he said, laughing as though he'd just played another of his practical jokes. 'I never could stand a sore loser.'

"Marshall Ed Masterson, the brother of Bat, arrested Curly, but he was acquitted and returned to Texas with Slaughter's crew. I didn't return with them because I had decided that in spite of the sore losers who tried to backshoot you, the life of a gambler was a whole lot easier than that of a drover. So I hung around Dodge for a while and then began to follow the railroad west—first to Leadville, Colorado, then on to Las Vegas, New Mexico, where I arrived in the spring of 'seventy-nine.

"Las Vegas was a railhead of the Santa Fe and a place where a man with quick hands and card sense could prosper. I dealt faro and poker at the Buffalo Bar in the Exchange Hotel on the main plaza and managed to avoid any sort of trouble. It paid to be a good citizen in Las Vegas. There was a constant reminder of what could happen if you weren't right, outside on the plaza. An old windmill was kept standing there by the vigilantes for the sole purpose of stringing up 'malefactors'—meaning anyone found guilty of a serious crime or just being a damned nuisance. A couple of times I remember the Buffalo Bar being emptied as everyone went out to watch the vigilantes imposing law and order. Watching some poor devil strangle on that windmill took me back to when I was a kid in San Antonio and Asa Mitchell was dispensing the wages of sin with a Bible in one hand and a rope in the other.

"Aside from the vigilantes, Las Vegas was a pleasant enough place, at least as railhead towns go. Just a few miles north of it, at a place called Montezuma, are some hot springs, and I used to spend a lot of time there soaking my old wounded bones. It was there that I ran into an old comrade of war.

" 'Jesse?' I said to the spade-bearded man who had just eased himself into the steaming pool with me.

" 'I beg your pardon,' he replied rather stiffly. 'My name's Howard. Mr. Howard, from Tennessee.'

"Even hung over as I was, I knew I hadn't made a mistake. It was him all right. A spade beard hadn't really altered his appearance that much. But I was willing to humor him.

" 'Forgive me, Mr. Howard,' I said. 'You remind me a great deal of one of my distant cousins from Missouri. We served together in the war.'

"He looked around him then, saw that there was no one nearby and focused sharply on me as he said in a low voice, 'Ringgold? John Ringgold?'

" 'Yeah, it's me Jesse.' I hadn't seen him since 'sixty-four, when we took him to his mother's place badly wounded. From some of the accounts I read a few years later in the newspapers and the *Police Gazette* it was clear that he'd recovered. He and Frank, along with Cole and his brothers, had made names for themselves, hitting trains and banks from Kentucky to Texas. 'What are you doing here?' I asked him. He looked around furtively again before answering.

" 'Business trip. I was told about a young fellow named Bonney out here who might be worth recruiting for a little business venture I have in mind. Do you know him?'

" 'I've heard of him,' I said. 'They call him Billy the Kid. He was mixed up in that business down in Lincoln County last year.'

" 'That's right. He's the one. I met him yesterday at a cabin north of here, and we discussed the possibility of forming a mutually profitable association.'

"This was not quite the same Jesse I'd known in the war. Just as deadly with a gun or a knife, I had no doubt. His two shoulder holsters were within easy reach next to the suit he had removed when he slipped into the pool. But his speech was as discreet and proper as that of any churchgoing lawyer or businessman you might meet in San Francisco or New Orleans. His dark brown suit was immaculately brushed. He looked and sounded so sober and proper and serious that I couldn't help saying:

" 'If you and Bonney get together, you'll be fighting each other for room in the *Police Gazette*.' I laughed when I said it, and that didn't please him either. He looked around furtively again and then hissed at me:

" 'Will you be quiet! I don't want folks around here to know who I am.'

" 'Certainly, Mr. Howard,' I replied. 'Only I wish you'd enlighten me about one matter.'

" 'What's that?' he asked suspiciously.

" 'What the hell really happened up there in Minnesota? How is it that Cole and Jim and Bob are rotting in that Yank prison while you're out here free?'

" 'What are you talking about, Ringgold? I wasn't even there. Cole swore that I wasn't.'

" 'You can't fool me, Jesse—I mean, Mr. Howard.

Anybody reading the damn newspaper could see that he was covering for you.' As a matter of fact, it was one of Cole's sisters, Ida Mae, who told me in a letter about what really happened at Northfield, but I didn't tell Jesse that.

" 'All right, John,' he replied in a low discreet voice, 'I'll admit I was there. But there wasn't a thing Frank or I could do for Cole and his brothers. They chased us for nearly two weeks after we tried to hit that bank, posses from all over Minnesota. Cole had a bullet in the leg. Bob had his arm broken and was riding double with Cole. Jim was wounded in the jaw and couldn't even talk. Frank and I had to leave them if we were going to make it back to Missouri. You probably know the rest.'

"I nodded that I did, remembering my amazement that the Youngers had survived after their fight with the posse that caught them. According to the newspaper, Cole had eleven bullet wounds, Jim was hit four more times, and young Bob caught one through the right lung.

"Jesse shifted the subject. 'This Bonney is not what I'd call a serious young man. I'm not sure I want to go into partnership with him.'

" 'I don't know about that,' I replied, still wondering how Jesse could bring himself to leave Cole and the others for a posse. 'All I know is he tries to look after his friends. From what I hear, most of the people he killed down in Lincoln County were in some way responsible for killing a friend of his.' The anger I was feeling toward Jesse for abandoning our cousins finally got the better of me. 'If you go partners with young Bonney, you'd god-damn well better not leave him for any posse. He'll kill you for it.'

"At this Jesse's eyes flickered with sudden rage. I thought he might reach right out of that sulfur pool for one of his six-shooters, but he didn't. He said, 'Don't swear at me, John. I don't hold with swearing. . . .'

"Hearing this, I couldn't help laughing out loud.

" 'Pardon me, Mr. Howard. I'll try to be more proper in my speech. Here, have a drink,' I said, as I reached for the bottle of whiskey I'd set next to the pool and handed it toward him.

" 'No, thank you,' he said in sort of a prim way, then he went on. 'John, I've taken more out of you than I have from any man, mainly because you're kin and you helped save my life during the war. But I won't take much more.'

" 'You won't have to, Jesse, not from me. You've got your own conscience to live with.'

" 'Well, what about you?' he came back at me. 'You sound so high and mighty, but you don't look as though you live in what I'd call an upright manner.'

" 'Oh, I'm upright enough, Jesse,' I replied with a laugh. 'Most nights I'm upright at a cardtable till dawn. Then I generally pass out in my room in the Exchange if I can't make it out here to soak in the springs.'

" 'You can't live that way, John,' he admonished me. 'You need to settle down and make yourself a regular living. Haven't you ever thought of starting a family?'

"I wanted to laugh out loud, hearing this from him, but he was so obviously sincere in his concern that I restrained myself and said, 'I quit thinking about that and a lot of other things during the war. Do you have a family?'

" 'Yes, I do. A good wife and children. They're well provided for, thanks to my, uh, business ventures.' He regarded me thoughtfully for a moment, then he went on to add: 'If things don't work out with young Bonney, I might be willing to consider you as a partner.'

"As I took a long pull at the whiskey bottle, I thought about what he said, and I knew that I would never forgive him and Frank for deserting the Youngers. It also happened that I'd been hearing about the possibility of 'business ventures' out in Arizona. Curly Bill Brocius had sent me word that the opportunities for easy money out there were unlimited.

" 'Of course,' Jesse was saying, 'you'd have to consider changing some of your habits. A more sober way. . . .'

"Taking another long pull, I didn't hear the rest of what he said, but I already knew my answer.

" 'No, thank you anyway, Jesse. I figure to stay upright in my own way.'

"That was the last time I saw him. A little while ago I read in the *Tombstone Epitaph* about how Bob Ford shot him from behind in his own house in St. Joseph after living with him for several weeks. I guess he'd taken Bob and Charley Ford into 'partnership' with him, and they figured that the ten-thousand-dollar reward the state of Missouri was offering made killing him a more profitable 'business venture' than any train or bank job they might have planned together. Poor sonofabitch. A man's got to be damned careful about those he chooses to regard as friends. Real friends are so very rare that there is very little I wouldn't do for the few I've had. One of the problems I've had here in Arizona was determining who my friends really were. There were times when I felt a lot closer to some of those who were supposed to be my enemies. Doc Holliday, for instance. Even though we nearly killed each other and would do so again if we had the opportunity, there was a kind of understanding and mutual respect between us that the likes of Wyatt Earp could never grasp. I saw it the night Doc invited me to have a drink with him. . . ."

NINE

THE CHALLENGE

"Bring us another bottle, will you, Frank?"

"Comin' right up, Doc."

Buckskin Frank Leslie, small, wiry, lynx-eyed ex-Indian scout, sometime bartender at the Oriental Saloon, stepped lightly from behind the bar and brought them their second quart of whiskey. Killing off the first quart had taken them close to an hour, and they'd talked about everything from mutual acquaintances in Texas and New Mexico to the advantages of dealing faro in Prescott, but Ringo still hadn't figured out why Doc Holliday had invited him to have a drink. All he knew for certain was that Doc was in his own class as a drinking man. He watched the deadly doctor refill their glasses, noticing how he poured with the quickness of a bartender yet didn't spill a drop. Doc's hands were quick, strong and steady, the hands of a dentist turned gunfighting gambler, but, like Ringo's own hands, they didn't quite go with the rest of him. A sensitive-featured ash-blond man, he had a fragile, cadaverously thin, consumptive body that was wracked every so often by violent fits of coughing. It was, Ringo suspected, his consumption rather than the prodigious amounts of whiskey he put away that accounted for his flushed features and the peculiar spectral brightness in his gray eyes.

"Where was it you said your people live in Georgia?"

"Catoosa County. It's up—"

Doc interrupted him eagerly, though not rudely. "I know where 'tis, sho'ly. Up north, next to Tennessee." He was letting Ringo know, in the manner of well-bred southerners, that the county where his family lived was not unknown. It was the kind of gracious reassurance that was more commonly practiced by polite southerners before the war, when all the wealth was out in the country and the most prosperous families lived on plantations. A patrician like John Henry Holliday could identify himself and the rural neighborhood or county where he lived and be confident that both the neighborhood and the family name would be recognized immediately by members of his own class even several counties or more away.

"Ringo. Ringo. Let me see now," he reflected a moment. "I *have* heard of a family up there by the name of Ringgold. My daddy mentioned an officer by that name in his regiment, the Twenty-seventh Georgia Infantry, who was with him at Chickamauga. Must be fine people. I believe the county seat is named for them."

He paused a moment to let John Ringo reply, but Ringo only smiled a little and sipped his whiskey.

"I was too young for the war myself, sorry to say," Doc went on when he saw that Ringo wasn't going to reply, and Ringo replied instead to this expression of patriotic regret.

"You didn't miss a thing, Doc." Which, for all his wounds and what he'd come to know about himself didn't really express how he felt about the war, but he was being considerate of Doc's feelings.

"Yes," Doc replied, "well, that's what I've heard generally from fellows who were in it, my daddy included, but I'm not really convinced. There wasn't any fighting close by Valdosta, where I lived—"

"Lowndes County, down next to Florida," Ringo interjected. Though he'd never been in Georgia, he'd studied a map of it carefully more than once.

"Yes, that's right," Doc answered, obviously gratified. "We didn't see any fighting," he continued, "but we had a Federal garrison after the war was over. Nigra soldiers." He shook his head in disgust. "They made damn sure we knew they weren't slaves anymore."

"Can't say as I blame them," Ringo answered, and Doc looked sharply at him.

"Say, which side were you on?"

"Same side as your daddy, but not because I believed in slavery."

Doc regarded him curiously for a moment before replying.

"Well, I guess there were plenty of reasons for being a good southern man. A man sho'ly can have all kinds of reasons for choosing sides."

"That's a fact, Doc. Like maybe your own reasons for siding with the Earps." Doc's probing into his family background gave him the excuse he needed to do a little probing of his own.

The cadaverous doctor's only response was a laugh. He refilled their glasses again, and Ringo went on:

"You'd be a whole lot richer you sided with us."

"Maybe so, Ringo. But sometimes it takes more than money to make a man choose sides. You know that." When Ringo nodded in agreement he added, "Though I don't guess there'd be any other reason for you to throw in with Curly Bill and the Clantons. Way I hear it, Curly and that bunch couldn't do much without your brains."

"That's not true by a damn sight. But you're right about one thing. There's got to be more than money. Happens I enjoy the company I keep. You ought to join us. Way I hear it, you're not a man to let the law get in your way." He didn't really think he could persuade Doc, but it was worth a try.

"So Bill Leonard's been talking," Holliday replied with a chuckle. Leonard was an old friend of Doc's from New Mexico who had come out to Arizona at the same time. Now he was one of the "Cowboys," as the Clanton gang was called by its enemies.

"Not Bill Leonard. You're a man with a big reputation, Doc. We heard about you before Leonard arrived. That's why we wonder why you're with the Earps."

"Let's just say I enjoy the company."

At that very moment, Doc's chosen company, Wyatt Earp and two of his brothers, Virgil and Morgan, came into the Oriental. Blond, blue-eyed, powerfully built six-footers with leonine moustaches, they showed a strong family resemblance. Wyatt was in the lead as they moved toward the bar, and he halted the three of them abruptly as his lofty gaze swept across the smoky room and picked out Ringo with Doc. At the same moment Ringo saw him and saw that he looked puzzled.

"He wouldn't have been puzzled by the mere fact of my presence there in the Earps' own hangout, the Oriental. I'd been making it a habit, whenever I was in Tombstone, to drop by the place regularly of an evening, especially when the Earps were in town. It pleasured me to walk in and have a drink at the bar when they were all lined up there. My way of letting them know I was available anytime they wanted to settle our differences outright. Usually Doc was with them, and what had to be puzzling that smug sonofabitch Wyatt was the fact that Doc was drinking with me. As a matter of fact, I was still wondering myself why Doc had invited me to have a drink."

"Too bad we don't enjoy the same company, Doc," Ringo said.

Doc was prevented from replying at once by another coughing fit that seemed likely to be the end of him. His skinny frame was shaken so violently that it was painful to watch. Recovering, he wiped his mouth with a handkerchief, and Ringo, seeing the flecks of blood on the handkerchief, was reminded of the death sentence of his favorite poet, John Keats. As a matter of fact, Doc even looked a little like somebody's idea of a poet, a doomed consumptive coughing out his art. Holliday downed the rest of the whiskey in his glass and looked at Ringo with shining watery eyes.

"It is too bad, Ringo. Way I figure it, though, you're the only one around here who might have what it'd take to help me win a bet I placed with myself eight years ago." He paused for a moment, grinning across the table at Ringo like a man about to tell a good joke and barely able to restrain his own laughter. "Eight years ago I bet that a bullet would take care of me before tuberculosis did."

Ringo grinned back at him, appreciating Holliday's grim sense of humor.

"I'd be only too happy to oblige, Doc, and do the same for your friends over there, too."

"Would you now?" Doc replied more than a little sarcastically. He turned and waved casually at Wyatt Earp, as though there was nothing out of the ordinary in his drinking with the man generally recognized as the deadliest of their many declared enemies in the Arizona underworld. Earp nodded curtly in reply, ignoring Ringo, and turned to order a glass of wine, which, along with beer, was all he ever drank. Unlike Doc and Ringo, he worried about the effects of whiskey on his gun hand.

"You know I would, Doc. Anytime you boys feel so inclined."

Doc Holliday laughed easily, refilled his glass and started to refill Ringo's, but Ringo signaled that he'd had enough. It occurred to him that Doc might be trying to make him easy meat by filling him with whiskey, but he doubted that this was really the case. Doc was reputedly the gamest, most reckless member of the Earp faction and presumably not the kind to bother with any sort of calculated treachery. Presumably, when he was ready to fight, he would challenge Ringo, whether either of them was drunk or sober.

"Now that I think about it, it occurs to me that Doc and I had a lot more in common than southern roots, an uncommon capacity for whiskey and minimal respect for the law. Our friendships put us on opposite sides of the feud between the Earps and the Clanton gang, and we were both going to stay involved largely, I suspect, because it promised to turn into the best fight around. I see now that he invited me to drink with him and I accepted because it gave us a chance to take each other's measure, so to speak. You might say we were a little like some of those fellows who fought each other at Troy, not out of any personal animosity but because it was a way for a man to prove what he was—if he really was always among the best and bravest, with his head above the others, as the Poet says. Those Greek and Trojan spear throwers measured each other because it was one way to measure themselves. That's why a man would stop and listen to an enemy on the battlefield tell all about himself before he tried to stick a spear through him, and sometimes they'd even agree to avoid each other's spears. It was of course damned unlikely that Doc and I would ever avoid each other's spears, but we could share a bottle beforehand and find out something about each other before we met on any battlefields. I could tell that he envied me for having fought in the war, which did maybe give me something of an advantage in having less to prove. On the other hand, I regarded him as probably the most dangerous man I'd met since Quantrill, in spite of his looking like someone who'd just barely managed to crawl out of his deathbed. I'd heard about what he could do with a knife or a gun, just how damned quick his hands were. The Earps were mighty lucky to have him on their side."

His conversation with Holliday ended abruptly when Doc's woman, Big Nose Kate Elder, came over to their table. Marble-limbed, handsome, she moved across the room with long strides and an angry swishing of crinoline that was audible above the noise of the saloon. Pausing next to Doc's chair, she smiled briefly across the table at Ringo, then turned to glare down at her lover. Looking up, Doc saw first her big breasts and gleaming shoulders rising provocatively above her flame-colored taffeta gown, then her furious expression, green eyes alight with rage and lips curling scornfully.

"Damn you!" she hissed at him.

Doc greeted her with a not very convincing show of pleasure. "Good evening, Kate. You know Ringo, I believe."

"Miss Elder," Ringo said, getting to his feet and raising his hat. He stood because it was his habit to be courteous when he greeted any woman, but in this case he was also eager to excuse himself and avoid what any man could see was coming. Kate smiled at him, remembering the drinks he had bought her, then her handsome features turned angry again.

"You don't know how many times I've wished I'd let them lynch you back at Fort Griffin," she snarled in a low ugly tone that carried to the next table and caused a poker player to twist around and look at her.

"Now, hold on a minute, Kate . . ." Doc began, looking up at her with a pathetic expression.

"Be seeing you around, Doc. Thanks for the drink."

"So long, Ringo," Holliday called after him. This was followed by another coughing fit and a streaming torrent of sharp-tongued abuse.

". . . don't care about me, don't care about anybody but yourself . . . rotten, lying . . ."

Ringo chuckled to himself, pitying Doc but also envying him a little. In Las Vegas, New Mexico, Prescott, and other places, he had had his own mistresses to help him spend his money and attract players to the tables where he dealt. Possibly because of the whiskey inside him, he couldn't remember all of their names. One of them, Molly Larue, an olive-skinned girl from New Orleans who told him she was a fallen member of a wealthy Creole family, came to mind, possibly because she was as difficult a fury to placate when enraged as Doc's mistress and was also, like her, liable to air her grievances with him in the public forum of a crowded saloon. It could be a damned nuisance and even a little embarrassing. On the other hand, such relationships could relieve a man's loneliness for a few months or however long it took one of them to decide that the relationship wearied more than it satisfied. Since coming to Tombstone, the closest thing he'd had to a relationship was with Elena down at Irma's Place. He simply had no time for anything even temporarily more binding, involved as he was in planning and coordinating the activities of the Cowboys.

Now he moved toward the door, intending to leave, but the sight of the Earps lined up together at the bar stopped him. All three were watching him with identical expressions suggesting an attitude bordering on derision. As he returned their looks, Ringo's own bitter half-grin expressed his disdain unmistakably. Instead of leaving the saloon he walked slowly over to the bar and ordered whiskey. Along the bar between him and the Earps were three other drinkers, one of whom nudged the others, and the three moved away quickly toward the tables. Frank Leslie poured him a whiskey and left the bottle out alongside the glass.

"Haven't seen you in here for a while, John," he said, and Ringo caught the sideways flick of his eyes toward the Earps, who now began to move down the bar toward him.

"I've been away on business, Frank," he answered shortly. His own eyes did not leave the face of Leslie, a competent gunfighter in his own right who was apparently not intimidated by the possibility of winding up in the middle of an altercation between Ringo and the Earps. Leslie's narrow upslanting gray eyes were bright with anticipation.

"Ringo," Wyatt Earp growled after sidling down to within a yard of his enemy.

Ringo raised his glass and sipped before he replied with as much disdain as he could manage in two syllables: "Yeah, Earp."

"I want you to know something."

Ringo turned to face him squarely, straightening up to take full advantage of his two-inch superiority in height.

He was well aware that the speed of his hands was much less than it had been a short time before, before he began drinking with Holliday, but this did not alarm him. The readiness is all, he told himself. Whenever Wyatt Earp was ready for him, he was ready.

"I want you to know that I'm running for sheriff, and when I'm elected—"

"Who says you're going to be elected?" Ringo interrupted him with the sneering question. One of the things he loathed especially about Wyatt Earp was his insufferable self-assurance.

"I will be, don't worry about that. Folks around here have had their fill of your kind. And when I am, you'd best watch out."

The sneer did not leave Ringo's face, and he was ready with a reply that could have been taken as a challenge. But then it occurred to him that he really was in no condition to fight, that he was likely to succeed simply in getting himself eliminated as an obstacle to the Earps' designs to promote their own interests in Tombstone. Returning Wyatt's cold steady gaze, he burned with a hatred more intense than anything he had felt toward any of the numerous enemies he had confronted in a long violent career, and this, he would later reflect, was strange because Wyatt Earp had not really done anything to him or any of his friends yet.

"I can't say what it was, aside from the fact that he seemed so almighty sure that he was going to win out over us. And he looked so damned self-possessed and self-righteous. You could see it even in the set of his jaw. He was so different from Holliday, or even his own brother Morg, who was as hard-drinking and hot-blooded as Holliday. They were my enemies, too, but I didn't feel toward them anything like what I felt toward him. It was because I wanted so badly to kill him that I put off challenging the bastard until another time."

Having mastered the impulse to challenge his enemy then and there, Ringo snorted his contempt for the threat and turned back to the bar without replying. Morgan Earp started forward but was restrained by his brother.

"We'll take care of him soon enough, Morg," he said.

Ringo did not bother to answer or even look at the three brothers, but he watched them in the mirror as he finished his drink. Take care of me? We'll see about that, he told himself. The readiness is all, you bastards, and right now I'm just not as ready as I'd like to be.

Now Holliday came over to join them. Apparently unplacated, his furious mistress plowed her way through the crowd toward the door, nearly knocking one man off his feet as she went past him. Chuckling to himself, all the rage he had been feeling against his enemies temporarily gone out of him, Ringo watched her in the mirror. When Leslie reached for the bottle to refill his glass, he covered it with his hand.

"No more for now, Frank. I've got to be moving."

"O.K., John, but you know there ain't no bird kin fly on one wing. Say, did I tell you the one about the drummer who went to hell . . . ?"

"Yeah, you did. Last time I was in here." He grinned at Leslie and laughed a little, remembering the joke. Leslie had an endless store of them. When he was in the mood, Ringo would listen for hours to Leslie's jokes and funning. But now he was not in the mood. Suddenly being in the same saloon with the Earps was intolerable to him.

"I'd best be leaving now. *Hasta luego.*"

Leslie seemed to understand. His catlike gray eyes flicked sideways toward the Earps. As Ringo turned toward the door, he said in a low voice, "Come again soon, John. You're always welcome here when I'm tending."

Ringo waved his hand as he moved toward the door. Leslie was all right, he guessed. There were those who said he was capable of shooting a man just for the fun of watching him fall, but Ringo had never seen this side of him. Presumably it was self-defense and not any funning impulse that caused him to shoot Mr. Galeen between the eyes. Mr. Galeen, so Ringo heard, took a shot at Leslie one evening from a hotel balcony while Leslie was escorting Mr. Galeen's estranged wife home from a dance. Shortly after that, Leslie and the former Mrs. Galeen were married. Ringo had never asked Leslie if it was true that he made his new wife help him with his pistol practice by letting him outline her figure in bullet holes on the wall of their sitting room and not protesting too loudly when he shot tea cups randomly out of her hand. Some things you just didn't ask a man.

Outside the saloon, at the edge of the boardwalk, Doc Holliday's mistress was leaning against one of the porch supports. Seeing Ringo, she straightened up and smiled warmly.

"Hello, Johnny," she greeted him, as though it was the first time they'd met that evening.

"Kate," he answered, again tipping his hat.

"Going home now?"

Home? He almost laughed out loud. He hadn't had a home since he left Bexar County, Texas, but he answered her, "No, I'm not. There's a poker game down at Johnny Behan's."

"Nice night," she said, looking at him in a way that told him she wouldn't mind a little company, especially that of a man who knew how to treat a lady.

Ringo was not unaffected by the way she was looking at him, and by the ample, half-uncovered bosom she proffered. Her face wasn't pretty, but interesting: the bold prominent nose she was named for balanced by a strong chin and a high broad forehead. Like the tower of Lebanon—he remembered the biblical phrase describing the nose of a prince's comely daughter. The furies' rage was gone now out of her green eyes. Now they were soft and warm, but he knew that the rage was still there.

"It is that, sho'ly," he said. He grinned a little, still enjoying the way she was looking at him, even if she was clearly out for revenge on her lover.

"Guess a lady can't compete with a poker game," she said in a deep-throated purr that almost caused Ringo to forget his appointment at Behan's. But then, he reflected, it's a poor thing for a man to take another man's woman after they've drunk together as friends, even if they do happen to be enemies. Besides, if he had to fight Doc before he fought Wyatt and his brothers, he might lose and the Earps would reign in Tombstone unchallenged. Some things, he concluded, a man won't do, even to please a lady.

"A man can't always choose what'll please him, Kate. This is business and they're expecting me."

A shrewd businesswoman herself, she smiled understandingly.

"Some other time, Johnny."

He grinned and touched his hat brim. "Sho'ly."

Leaving the Oriental and moving past the other well-lit establishments on Allen Street, he turned down Safford and passed a series of vacant lots, some with tents on them, finally stopping before a small frame house that streamed light from every window. Judging from the number of horses tied out in front, he was one of the last to arrive. He knocked lightly at the door, and it was answered by Johnny Behan's fiancée, Josie Marcus.

"Good evening, Josie," he greeted her, experiencing as he did whenever he met her, a painful tightening inside because of her striking resemblance to Margaret Younger. Like Margaret, she was German and Jewish, and her large dark liquid eyes were like the eyes Margaret inherited from her Indian grandmother.

She greeted him warmly. "Good evening, Johnny. Come in. The others are waiting for you."

"I must apologize about my—"

She interrupted him, laughing. "About your hat. It's all right. I understand. At least you know what's proper, which is more than I can say for some men." She rolled her dark eyes sideways toward the entrance to the kitchen, out of which cigar smoke and the sound of men's voices were drifting.

Ringo chuckled a little, feeling foolish about the hat, which he had to wear whenever and wherever he played poker. It was a common superstition, one he shared with countless other gamblers, and he couldn't discard it.

As he started to follow Josie toward the kitchen, he was startled by the sudden appearance of a nine- or ten-year-old youngster in a nightshirt who sprang out of the bedroom and aimed a pistol at him.

"Hands up!" the child commanded, and Ringo obeyed at once.

"Albert! Don't you dare aim that at anyone!" Josie said, snatching it out of his hand.

"Curly says it won't shoot," the child protested.

"I know, Albert, but you remember also he told you it isn't a toy."

She handed the pistol to Ringo and shepherded the still protesting child back into the bedroom. He recognized the gun as one of his own, an old worn-out Navy Colt with a broken mainspring that Curly had asked for when he saw Ringo about to discard it.

"God, I hate guns," she said with a shudder as she reentered the room.

"I surely understand," he answered sincerely, remembering how he'd once felt about pistols himself. "Pretty hard to survive in this territory without one, though," he added. "Having a lawman for a husband will get you used to them."

He had intended to allude pleasantly to the marriage she and Johnny Behan had been planning for some months, and he was a little surprised to see her quickly drop her eyes and tighten her shapely mouth. Seeing by her expression that he had somehow unwittingly offended her, he was quick to apologize.

"Sorry, Josie, I didn't mean to . . ."

"It's all right, Johnny. Just that I don't know when we're getting married, or even if . . ."

"I always knew that Johnny Behan was a fool. It puzzled me some how he ever persuaded that lovely, intelligent, talented young woman from a good family in San Francisco to move in with him and look after his son and wait around until he happened to be damned good and ready to marry her. In the meantime he was spending all the money her daddy sent her on such things as that house that was supposed to belong to both of them but which he put in his own name so he could throw her out as soon as he'd gotten what he could out of her. He even got her to sell her engagement ring when he came up short on the house. The sonofabitch. I must admit I wasn't too sympathetic when Behan told me a few months later how Morg Earp beat hell out of him right in front of Josie the day he tried to throw her out of the house. By then, of course, she'd started seeing Wyatt. Now I guess she's still with him, up in Denver, so I heard. Near as I could tell, Josie's only flaw was her taste in men. But at least Wyatt's a sure-enough man and a gentleman. I hate the bastard, but I'll give him that. I hope he realizes what he has and treats her accordingly."

"Hey, Ringo, izzat you?" Ike Clanton bellowed from within the kitchen.

Ringo didn't answer. Josie smiled and stepped aside to let him pass, but he was reluctant to leave her. Suddenly he remembered that he had brought something for her, and reaching into his breast pocket he pulled out a small, slim volume.

"Thought you might enjoy this, Josie, being an actress." He handed her Byron's *Manfred*. "It's a play, the kind you just read. I sent all the way to England for it."

"How thoughtful, Johnny!" she exclaimed. Her delight was so gratifying that he would have been happy to let her keep the book, but she guessed that he was only loaning it. "I'll take such good care of it."

"Hey, Ringo!" Clanton bawled again.

"Keep it as long as you like," he said, smiling briefly as he moved past her and then reassuming his habitual saturnine expression as he entered the smoky kitchen.

"We've been waitin' for you, Ringo," Frank McLowry piped up irritably. He was a self-important little man who seemed to enjoy stirring up trouble with the bigger men around him. In the interest of maintaining a harmonious and profitable business relationship with the McLowrys, Ringo had put up with a great deal from him.

"My apologies, gentlemen," he said, taking a place at the large round kitchen table around which most of the leaders of the profitable association known derisively to its enemies as the Cowboys were seated playing poker with their host and ally, Sheriff John Behan. Behan was a little younger than Ringo, a carefully dressed man with spaniel brown eyes and a neatly trimmed black moustache. Like most of the others he wore a hat, but not so much because of superstition or cowboy custom as because he wanted to cover a large bald spot on his crown.

"We need your good advice, John, on a matter of concern to all of us," Behan began smoothly. "Deal him in, will you, Frank?"

Still looking irritable, the little man dealt Ringo a hand. He, Frank McLowry, looked even smaller at the moment because he was seated between two huge men, Curly Bill Brocius and Billy Clanton. Billy was only nineteen, but he was a seasoned gunhand who had been helping his brothers and his father move rustled cattle since he was old enough to ride. Ringo guessed that he had a good deal more spirit than his loud-mouthed brother Ike, who was in the habit of talking a good fight. On the other side of Frank, Ringo's oldest friend in Arizona, Curly Bill, winked across the table at him, a broad-

chested swarthy man whose dark complexion and perfect, accent-free command of Spanish had been real assets
to the gang during more than one foray into Mexico.

"You've heard about the holdup, or attempted holdup
of the Benson stage, have you not?"

"Yeah, I heard about it. Sounds like some fellows who
didn't know what the hell they were doing. I mean, if
you're going to stop a stage the first thing you do is . . ."

He started to warm to his subject, a subject about
which he was perhaps more knowledgeable than any of
them, with the possible exception of Frank Stilwell, whose
voice was as familiar to the Wells Fargo teams as that of
any of their drivers. Johnny Behan's spaniel eyes shifting
suddenly toward the door beyond which Josie might have
been listening alerted him to the necessity of being discreet.

" . . . shoot a horse, one of the leaders," he finished in
a lowered voice.

"What would you say," Behan asks him, "if I told you
that Doc Holliday was involved and was the one who
shot the driver?"

At this Ringo laughed out loud.

"I'd say your evidence will have to be damned convincing. Ol' Doc's got a better hand than that. He's no friend
of mine, but—"

Frank McLowry interrupted him, in effect giving him
the lie. "That why you were drinking with him tonight?"
Ringo fixed the little man with a cold killing stare and
was on the point of telling him that he'd be even less than
half a man when he lost his upper story, but Curly
intervened good-naturedly.

"Come on now, Frank. If John drinks with Holliday,
he's got his reasons. Give me two, will you?" He winked
again at Ringo.

"What's your evidence?" Ringo asked the sheriff.

"Testimony of an accomplice, Luther King," Behan
answered crisply, raising three fingers to the dealer. "Only
trouble is," Behan continued, "King escaped."

"How'd that happen?"

"It just happened. My deputy didn't keep an eye on
him like he should have. There was somebody waiting
outside with a horse. Probably Doc himself, I heard."

Behan was staring intently at his cards, and Ringo
knew that he was lying. He had heard the sheriff lie

before and knew that Behan had difficulty meeting the eye of one he was trying to deceive.

"Now you've got no witnesses against Doc?"

"Well, yes and no. Maybe you can help me in that regard. Frank here says that you were also talking with Doc's woman tonight."

"What about it?" Again Ringo glared at Frank McLowry.

"Take it easy. Just that I heard they had a falling out. That true?"

"What the hell does that—?"

"Easy, Ringo. Maybe nothing at all. Later on tonight I plan to meet with Miss Elder."

"I half suspected then," Ringo writes, "what that slimy little eel of a sheriff had in mind. After the meeting, he and Mike Joyce, the county supervisor, went over to the Oriental and found Kate in pretty much the same state as when I'd talked to her, only a lot less sober. They kept her glass full and gave her all the encouragement she needed to tell them what she thought of Doc. Then, when they had her in no condition to read, they put a pen in her hand and helped her sign a deposition to the effect that Doc was one of the men who tried to hold up the Benson stage. A real amateur job, that one. Two men killed and no strongbox to show for the effort. Hardly the kind of game Doc Holliday would deal himself into. I had to laugh at Johnny trying to make it stick. All the Earps had to do was sober Kate up and she admitted she didn't know what she was signing."

No more was said about the Benson stage holdup. Behan's reasons for wanting to implicate Holliday were clearly understood by everyone there. It would have been politically costly to Wyatt Earp in his campaign for the sheriff's office. While Ringo had little respect for Behan, he recognized his usefulness to the gang. On more than one occasion he had been a real obstacle in the path of the Earps, whose interests were tending more and more to conflict with their own. It was vital to their interests that he be kept in office. The thought of warning Doc, mentioning that Behan was sniffing around his woman, occurred to Ringo but was quickly dismissed. Doc was an enemy, albeit an enemy he respected. This two-bit reptile politician of a sheriff was their ally and as such deserved their support.

As the business meeting continued, along with the poker game, the Cowboy leaders discussed the next cattle drive up from Mexico. To an outsider listening, or Josie Marcus overhearing from the next room, it would not have sounded as though anything but a legitimate movement of livestock were being discussed.

"I was in a cantina down Janos way last month," Curly Bill remarked, "drinkin' mescal with a couple greasers workin' for the Obregon brothers. Passed myself off as a greaser and asked if they knew where a *vaquero* like myself might find work. They asked me could I shoot as well as rope. Seems the Obregon brothers have been havin' trouble with *gringos bandidos, ladrones de ganado*— what folks around here call rustlers—helpin' themselves to their stock. The Obregons mean to hire themselves enough guns to put a stop to it."

"Guess anybody goin' down there to deal with 'em oughta be prepared," Tom McLowry observed. He paused, then added, "For them *ladrones de ganado*, I mean," and the others chuckled knowingly. "You'll be ready for 'em, won't you, Ringo?"

"I guess. We'll be going down there soon as they finish their spring roundup. Any help you can give Curly and me with the drive will be much appreciated. Right, Curly?"

"Right enough, John," the big man replied, adding, "and you can tell any of your boys who might want to go down there with us that them Mex women still know how to treat a man right. Just ask John here." Curly's teeth flashed in a broad smile, and the others responded with knowing grins. Ringo himself grinned and flushed a little, remembering a night that had ended most pleasurably, though it began otherwise, when a man with a knife who claimed a proprietary interest in a friendly *ramera* had challenged him to a handkerchief duel. After the fight, the girl, who seemed to regard him as her rescuer, had been most skillful in dressing his wounds.

"Tell you the truth," Curly Bill continued, "every time I go down there I find it some harder to come back. There's a nice little spread just out of Hermosillo we ain't never visited on business. When I'm down there alone I always stop off for the night. Feller who owns it must be pushin' sixty. Nice old feller. Tells me he'd like to give up bein' a hard-workin' *ranchero* and spend the rest of

his days just sunnin' hisself in front of a little house on
the seashore at Guaymas, only he don't have a son who
can take over for him. He's got a daughter he ain't
married off yet. Looks like she ain't got a drop of Indin
blood in her. Looks whiter'n me by a damn sight. We
talk sometimes all nice an' proper with a old *dueña*
lookin' on. Her daddy's all but told me I'd be welcome to
settle down there."

"Why don't you?" Ringo asked him. He'd heard Curly
talk about his retirement before, and each time it sounded
a little more inviting. "Raise you twenty," he added,
pushing a double eagle out into the pot. All of the other
players had folded.

"See you an' call," Curly responded. Ringo had pairs
of tens and jacks, but Curly had a full house, queens and
sixes. As he raked in the pile of winnings with a big
brown hand, Curly answered Ringo's question: "Well,
John, like I told him, I got some business matters that
need tendin' up here. Maybe after the next drive I'll go
back down there an' stay."

"Speakin' of business, Curly . . ." Joe Hill left his
sentence unfinished, but Curly read his expression and
nodded.

"Guess we'd better be movin' out. Joe 'n me got us an
appointment." He stood up and filled a trousers pocket
with his take from the game. "See you boys around." His
flashing grin expressed his gratitude for their generosity.
As he started out of the room after Hill, he paused in the
doorway, which he nearly filled, and turned back. "Sure
you won't come with us, John?"

"I'm sure," Ringo answered shortly. After the two
men left, he wondered how many of those present were
aware that Curly and Joe Hill were on their way to hold
up the stage from Prescott. Did Sheriff Behan have any
suspicions? What would he have done if some informer
told him right out that two of his business associates were
about to commit armed robbery? Probably ask which
county they'd be in when the robbery took place. If it
was over in Pima County, he likely wouldn't concern
himself. Just as he wouldn't be bothered about the fact
that another large herd of rustled Mexican stock was
going to be driven up into Cochise County later that
spring. That was a matter for the *rurales* to handle, if

they could, before the herd crossed the border. Even the
fate of the nineteen Mexican smugglers over in Skeleton
Cañon last July, victims of the Cowboys, did not concern
him greatly. Ringo guessed that there wasn't much besides his own political survival that did concern Johnny
Behan greatly. He was definitely the kind of sheriff the
Cowboys needed in office, someone they could count on.

After the meeting he walked back through town along
Allen Street with Ike, Phin, and Billy Clanton and the
two McLowrys. All of them were staying at the Grand
Hotel, and as they approached the hotel Ike Clanton
suggested a drink at Bob Hatch's saloon and billiard
parlor across the street.

"Sure enough, big brother," Billy Clanton replied cheer-
fully. "And while we're at it I'll just have to whip you at
pool."

When the six of them were bellied up to the bar and
Bob Hatch himself had filled their glasses, Tom McLowry
turned to Ringo.

"You know, John, if our little friend the sheriff can't
help us out with them Earps, we're gonna have to help
ourselves."

Ringo looked at him quizzically.

"What do you have in mind?"

"Nothing yet, I guess," McLowry admitted. He was, in
the view of Ringo and others who knew him, a good
man, not at all like his quarrelsome strutting runt of a
brother. The two of them were southerners who'd come
to Arizona from Mississippi by way of Texas. When
Ringo was in charge of a cattle drive up from Mexico he
always aimed for the McLowry ranch in the Sulphur
Springs Valley, rather than the Clantons' ranch at Lewis
Springs or Joe Hill's place over at the San Simón Cienega.
He could count on Tom to get the best price for the
rustled stock from the ranchers who'd buy it. Tom was
also one of the best shots with either pistol or rifle in that
part of Arizona, the kind of man you'd like to have with
you if you were taking on all of the Earps and Holliday at
once.

"Well, you're right about our having to help ourselves,"
Ringo said, as he raised his whiskey. "There's only so
much Behan can do for us." Like Tom McLowry, he
hadn't thought of anything yet, but there was the germ of

an idea in his mind. He glanced over at the pool table,
where Ike and Billy Clanton were now chalking up their
cues. Phin Clanton and Frank had also moved over there
to settle themselves in chairs as spectators. Yes, he reflected, Tom McLowry is a good man, but what about
these others? Billy Clanton was plenty game, a tough kid
who was blessed with the same kind of disbelief in his
own mortality that Ringo himself had at nineteen when
he rode with Quantrill. What about Ike? He was fond of
talking about what he was going to do to Wyatt Earp
someday. When would that be? Ringo had the uneasy
feeling that Ike was a blowhard. About Phin he just
didn't know. He seemed to have more sand than Ike, but
Ringo had never seen him tested. There was always good
old Curly, at that moment presumably on his way to hold
up the stage from Prescott, but Ringo remembered how
Wyatt had "buffaloed" him, bent the barrel of his pistol
over Curly's skull when Curly accidentally killed Marshal
White. Why had Curly let that injury go so long unavenged?
Had Earp done that to me, Ringo was thinking, one of us
would have to be dead before the next sunset. He was
reluctant to suspect Curly of lacking nerve, and indeed
he had seen the big man acquit himself well in brushes
with the *rurales* down in Sonora, but the Earps and
Holliday were a different order of antagonist altogether.
The *rurales* were tough, but you could discourage them
with a few well-placed shots, make them keep their distance until you recrossed the border. The Earps and
Holliday, on the other hand, were, he suspected, not
unlike some of the enemies he faced in the war, the kind
who would keep on coming no matter what you threw at
them, like a charging grizzly with its heart shot away.
That kind of enemy was not to be confronted by anyone
who cared overmuch about keeping his hide intact. Curly
was a sure-enough man, whose friendship Ringo valued,
whose irrepressible good humor and funning could nearly
always draw Ringo out of his bitter moods. But it was his
very capacity to enjoy life, coupled with his hardheaded
common sense as a businessman who chose to operate
outside the law not because the risks alleviated the bore-
dom of living but simply because it was more profitable,
that made him doubtful as an ally in a head-on confrontation with the Earps. Gazing through the amber liquid in

the glass poised on his fingertips, Ringo wondered if in fact there was anyone on his side he could really count on in a showdown with that grim puritan of a deputy U.S. marshal and his brothers.

By now the whiskey haze that had clouded his thinking earlier had receded. He was beginning to see things clearly, and he remembered what Wyatt Earp had said to his brother Morgan, reassuring him that they would take care of Ringo "soon enough." "Soon enough" would be, Ringo guessed, when Wyatt became sheriff and had the full support of the law behind him. Then there would be no stopping him. In the name of "progress" and "decency" he would, as they say, sweep the streets of Tombstone clean. Like the Apaches under Cochise and Victorio, Ringo and the Cowboys would either surrender their freedom or face being hunted down like any other predators in the way of "progress."

He remembered the time he and Curly had helped some of Curly's friends down in Sonora rope an outlaw grizzly, a greedy cattle-killing behemoth whose jaws had snapped the necks of full-grown steers like matchwood and whose enormous paws could decapitate a strong man with a single sweep. Surrounded by laughing *vaqueros* whose well-thrown rawhide lariats did not leave a single foot free, it had gone down roaring like a fat man tripped up by small boys. While the riders held it immobile with their taut lariats, a small nimble *vaquero* with a pistol had dispatched it, and the magnificent silver-tipped hide had been peeled off to adorn a wall in the hacienda.

If Earp's going to nail my hide to a wall, Ringo was thinking, he's going to have to take some risks. I wasn't ready tonight, but then neither was he. If I wait until he's ready, chances are I won't like the odds much. I'll find myself cornered or treed by a bunch of yapping, sniffing curs who call themselves God-fearing, law-abiding folk, who can't hardly wait for their master's signal to tear my throat out. Once that bastard has his sheriff's star, they'll know their master. If I deal with him now, it's just a matter of a feud, not a confrontation between the forces of light and darkness.

Ringo made his decision. As though drinking to it, he raised his glass briefly before tossing off the rest of his whiskey, and Tom McLowry, noticing, regarded him curiously.

"You got anything in mind, John?" he asked, echoing Ringo's own question.

"Maybe."

McLowry didn't press him. When Bob Hatch reached for the bottle, Ringo shook his head and started to move away from the bar. He took some satisfaction from the fact that his head was clear, or nearly so, that the whiskey hadn't made his decision for him.

"Hey, John," McLowry called after him. Ringo halted in the doorway. "How 'bout we go on down to Irma's Place?" McLowry suggested with a grin.

Ringo grinned back at him.

"Not tonight, Tom. You go on without me."

It was just past noon. Ringo and the brothers Clanton and McLowry were lounging on the porch of the Grand Hotel, letting their breakfasts settle. In front of them the chalk-white dusty expanse of Allen Street was empty. Much of the daytime working population of Tombstone was beginning its siesta, while most of those who made their living at the cardtables had yet to rise.

The Clantons and McLowrys had risen just early enough to reach their ranches before dark. Unlike them, Ringo had nowhere in particular to go, but like them he had a purpose in rising earlier than usual. His head was clear. He hadn't had a drink yet, nor did he want one. Having come to a decision the previous evening he had slept better than he had in a long time. He felt alert and ready, wanting only the opportunity to act on his decision.

"Well, lookee here, will you," Ike Clanton sneered, and Frank McLowry spat out, "Bastards!" along with a stream of tobacco juice.

As though mysteriously summoned by his reflection that he had never been more ready for them, Ringo's enemies emerged from Bob Hatch's saloon. Wyatt, as usual, came out first, in conversation with the mayor of Tombstone. Then his two brothers appeared, and Morgan paused in the doorway to shout something back into the saloon. Apparently in response to Morgan's shout, Doc Holliday stepped out into the sunlight, stretched himself and then held up an arm to shield his eyes from the glare.

" . . . too damn early, you ask me," Doc protested,

and these were the only words that carried across to
Ringo. Laughing, Virgil and Morgan pounded him on the
back. Wyatt Earp listened attentively to Mayor Thomas,
a big round-faced man with a red dewlap rolling over his
collar who kept his thumbs hooked in the armholes of his
vest. The mayor was discoursing importantly about something, but suddenly his companion was no longer listening. All of his attention was focused across the street
onto the tall figure that had risen and stepped to the edge
of the boardwalk in front of the Grand Hotel.

Ringo said nothing to his companions, but seeing him
brush back his coattails to leave the ivory grips of his .44s
exposed, they guessed what he had in mind.

"Careful, John," Tom McLowry cautioned.

"I'm always careful," he answered, as was his habit
with well-intentioned cautionary advice he had no intention of heeding.

"We'll back you up, Ringo," Ike Clanton assured him,
and Ringo almost laughed out loud, reminded suddenly
of how a Trojan hero received a like reassurance from a
goddess disguised as his brother moments before the
invincible son of another goddess caught him in the neck
with a spear. Hector had nobody but himself to count on,
Ringo was thinking, but he died like a sure-enough man.
You die that way, pitting your manhood against an enemy that may be too much for you, and folks remember.
They might even forget everything else about you, all the
reasons they have to curse and revile you, if they see you
die like a man. That's your consolation if you lose. Then
there's always the chance you'll win.

He stepped down into the glaring dusty whiteness of
the street, and with a few long strides reached the middle
of it. There he halted, hands on hips and feet planted
wide apart.

"Wyatt Earp!"

Earp stepped to the edge of the boardwalk. Like Ringo's
companions, he seemed to guess what was in Ringo's
mind. His massive jaw and cold blue eyes reflected a
rigid unwillingness to tolerate any sort of cavalier frivol-
ity. At his side was the famous long-barreled Buntline
Special he used to chastise those who recked not the
lawful rod.

"What do you want, Ringo?"

Ringo hesitated a moment, not because of any second thoughts about challenging the man, but because he wanted to frame the challenge in such a way that it could not be declined. Having arrived at a state of readiness without the aid of whiskey, he would not consider the possibility that a duel would not take place.

"Earp, you know how it is with us, how we feel about your interfering with our business. If things keep on this way much longer, some good men on both sides are going to be killed. Before that happens you and I can settle the whole matter between us right here and now. Choose any weapons you like—knives, hoglegs, whatever. Just you and me. What do you say?"

For an instant, Wyatt Earp was speechless. His blue eyes were wide with amazement, and his mouth was slightly ajar, as though he couldn't quite believe what he'd just heard. He stared at Ringo as a man might stare at some aberration or freak that has affronted his sensibilities and thrown into question all of his perceptions of how things are or ought to be. Finally, he said:

"Ringo, you must be drunk. Either that or you're crazy. Well, it just happens I'm not either one. What's more, I'm running for sheriff. Do you think the people of Tombstone would vote for a man who fought a duel in the middle of a public street? If you think so, you'd damn well better sober up!"

With that, Earp turned on his heel and marched away along the boardwalk. Morgan Earp stepped forward, and for a second or two it looked as though he might accept the challenge his brother had declined, but then Wyatt stopped and glanced back over his shoulder. Morgan felt his brother's eyes on him, knew his will, and after fixing Ringo with a bitter stare that effectively expressed his longing to meet the outlaw in the street, he turned and followed Wyatt.

After Morgan and Virgil had gone after their brother, Mayor Thomas stepped forward to say something to Ringo. He reminded Ringo a little of Asa Mitchell, with the same frog eyes and wide fly-accommodating mouth, the same tendency to redden with indignation like raw beef. He started to say something but then clamped his mouth shut and followed the others.

With the challenge rejected, Ringo felt no exultation, no sense of triumph over the Earps.

Suddenly Doc Holliday moved out of the shadows toward the street, pausing with one foot on the boardwalk and the other down on the top step. He had his coat open, and beneath his pearl-gray silk vest a pearl-handled, nickel-plated .44 gleamed brightly. He looked at Ringo with a quizzical half-grin, and Ringo suddenly felt something incongruously close to gratitude toward this deadly enemy.

"How about you, Doc? They say you're the gamest man the Earps have." Ringo paused to jerk a linen handkerchief out of his breast pocket. "I don't need but a yard to do my fighting. Take an end." And he held out the handkerchief.

At this, Doc Holliday's half-grin spread with obvious delight. He stepped down into the street and moved rapidly with catlike springing strides toward Ringo.

"Thought you'd never ask, John. I'm your huckleberry, and this sho'ly is my kind of game," he said, reaching out to take an end of the proffered handkerchief. There was no need for either man to state the rules. Both had fought and survived this kind of duel before, either with pistols or knives. The first one to let go of the handkerchief was the loser.

As Doc Holliday grasped his end of the handkerchief he fixed Ringo with his bright, spectral stare. His taut-fleshed bony face was wreathed in the proleptic grin of a gladiator who has entered the arena so many times that he is more at home there than outside of it, living only for the moments of confrontation and deadly play. Meeting Doc's stare, Ringo had the sense that he had challenged not merely another deadly enemy but death itself. Fleetingly, he realized that fighting Doc would not settle the quarrel between the Earp faction and the Cowboys. Doc was not a leader of the Earps, nor, for that matter, a follower. He was his own man, an outlaw who happened to be a friend of Wyatt Earp. But it didn't matter. The business of settling the feud, worked out so clearly in his mind the night before, no longer mattered. All that mattered was what would happen in the next instant.

"You ever wonder what's on the other side, John?" Doc asked, as casually as if they were having another drink together.

Ringo didn't ask Holliday what he meant. He knew

exactly what he meant, knew also that Doc wasn't resort-
ing to that common device of gunfighters who seek to
give themselves a split-second edge by distracting their
antagonists.

"Yeah, Doc, I wonder," he answered, with the same
studied casualness. "Guess one of us is going to find out
pretty quick. Maybe both of us."

At this, Doc's sparsely fleshed grin broadened, en-
hancing the macabre illusion of a living death's-head. As
the two men sank into a bent-kneed crouch, free hands
poised above pistol butts, ready to claw downward, Ringo
was aware of the curious fact that he felt no animosity
toward Doc. At that moment he felt closer to him than
he had toward any human being for a very long time.
Conflicting allegiances aside, they were two of a kind.
Doc's disease was mirrored by his own spiritual pain. In
the next instant they would be brought even closer through
the shared fact of death.

"Hold it, you two!"

Mayor Thomas's shout effectively froze the two gunfighters in their attitude of poised readiness.

"You're not fighting a handkerchief duel here!"

The mayor had left the boardwalk and run into the
street. He snatched the handkerchief out of their hands
and stepped between them. Ringo was about to push him
aside and draw anyway, but he saw that Doc had stepped
back and apparently accepted the fact that it was over.

"Dammit, you two, this is a public street! If you want
to kill each other like a couple of savages, go out in the
desert and do it!"

Ringo straightened up and let his hands hang loosely at
his sides. He regarded the mayor with a bitter expression
but didn't reply. Seeing that Ringo too was resigned to
the fact that they wouldn't be fighting, Holliday said:

"Some other time, John, whenever you say."

When Ringo nodded silently, Doc flashed another
death's-head grin, turned away and set out at a brisk
walk to catch up with the Earps.

The mayor was about to say more to Ringo, but something in the outlaw's expression stopped him and no
words came out of his big flycatcher mouth. The mayor
nodded curtly and turned away.

As Ringo walked back to the porch of the Grand Hotel

he was so full of rage and frustration that he could hardly speak. His comrades in enmity with the Earps were on their feet to greet him, and he was amazed to see that they apparently regarded his defeat as a victory.

"Guess you showed them Earps, Ringo!" Billy Clanton exulted, clapping him on the shoulder.

"Yeah, you showed 'em we won't be pushed around!" Ike chimed in.

Ringo could forgive the ignorance of a nineteen-year-old, but the stupidity of an older man who should have known better irritated him.

"You're a fool, Ike!" he snapped furiously, causing all of their triumphant grins to vanish.

"You made Earp back down, didn't you, John?" Tom McLowry asked, bewildered at his rage.

"What the hell did that accomplish? The bastard's still alive, isn't he? As long as he is, we sure as hell won't have things our way."

Forced thus to look squarely at the facts of their situation, they all assumed sombre expressions and were silent.

Finally, Frank McLowry broke the silence with a characteristically sneering utterance:

"It surely surprised me to see you and Holliday squared off that way. Thought you two was *sech* good friends."

With difficulty, Ringo restrained an impulse to vent some of his rage and frustration by slapping a little respect into Frank McLowry. As he had many times, he reflected that Frank was not the kind of man you actually wanted to hit—just slap a little. But, still determined to beat the Earps, he would do nothing to weaken the Cowboy alliance against them. So he merely answered enigmatically:

"More things in heaven and earth, Frank."

At that moment, he saw a man he knew approaching rapidly along the boardwalk. On the man's leather vest flashed the star of a deputy sheriff. Cherub-faced, stocky, with round dark spaniel eyes like the sheriff's, Deputy Billy Breakenridge was another much-valued Cowboy ally. Right now he looked worried.

Ringo greeted him, noticing his worried expression. "Hello, Billy. How are things with you?" He was more than ready to be diverted by news of someone else's troubles.

The deputy hesitated, then blurted out apologetically:
"John, I got to arrest you."

"What the hell for? There wasn't any fight. Mayor
broke it up."

"It ain't that. Some fellows just put in a complaint.
They say you held up their poker game over at Evilsizer's
in Galeyville yesterday. Took five hundred dollars at
gunpoint."

"Damn!" Ringo spat out the expletive. Then he chuckled and grinned a little ruefully. "Guess those fellows
can't take a joke. No sense of humor at all. I'd have paid
them back sooner or later."

"We can get bail fixed and have you out in no time. I'll
send for Lawyer Goodrich, you want me to," Breakenridge
offered anxiously.

Ringo had not been in jail since the time he and Scott
Cooley shared a cell back in Texas, and the prospect was
less than inviting. If he chose to resist arrest, Billy
Breakenridge was not the man to stop him, but the last
thing Ringo wanted to do now was embarrass a friendly
lawman. So he rested his hand gently, reassuringly, on
the nervous deputy's shoulder and said, "It's all right,
Billy. I'll go with you."

He was suddenly awfully tired, having worked himself
into a state of total readiness for what had turned out to
be nothing at all.

He fell into step alongside Billy Breakenridge, and the
two of them tramped back along the boardwalk toward the
sheriff's office and jail. Neither man spoke. Ringo was already planning, and Billy Breakenridge was so relieved at
Ringo's lack of resistance that he remained silent for fear
of uttering anything that might offend the moody outlaw.

They had nearly reached the sheriff's office when the
sound of boots pounding along the boardwalk made them
stop. Turning, they encountered Ike Clanton, out of breath
after the unaccustomed exercise of running two blocks.

"Ringo, we got to do something," he gasped. "They're
gonna arrest Curly."

"Who? What the hell are you talking about, Ike?"

"Them Earps. Stilwell just tol' me. Curly an' Hill was
identified by a passenger on the stage from Prescott this
morning. Them an' Holliday is goin' over to Charleston
after 'em. What're we gonna do, Ringo?"

If there was anything more distasteful than Ike Clanton blustering and throwing his weight around, Ringo was thinking, it was Ike Clanton whining. Ignoring his question, Ringo turned to Billy Breakenridge.

"Earp doesn't have the authority to arrest them, does he, Billy?"

"Afraid he does, John. Same as with the Benson stage job, when he arrested Luther King. He's a deputy U.S. marshal, and those stages carry mail. It's gonna make Sheriff Behan look bad again an' help Earp get elected."

"Shit!" Ringo hissed under his breath. As he recalled the holdup plan, Curly and Joe Hill were going to intercept the stage about midmorning as it climbed up a steep sandy incline near Harmon Butte. If all had gone according to plan and they'd gone to Charleston with their take, they should be celebrating now. By the time the Earps and Holliday arrived later in the afternoon neither man would be in any condition to resist arrest. If they did resist, they'd be dead. What needed to be done was as plain as a doctored brand or a Comanche moon over Texas, if only he could get a little cooperation.

"Get Lawyer Goodrich for me, will you, Billy? Tell him to arrange bail any way he can as long as it's fast." Seeing the deputy hesitate, he snapped: "Go on. I'll be in the sheriff's office waiting for you."

As soon as the deputy left them, Ringo turned to Ike Clanton.

"Ike, I'm going to need a damn good horse—better than the one I'm riding. And a rifle. Mine's being fixed over at the gunsmith's."

"What're you gonna . . .?"

"Never mind. You just get a move-on. I'll take care of the Earps." Saying this, he was reminded of how his wartime commander, Quantrill, used to reassure his men when the odds looked doubtful. One of the many things Ringo had learned from him was how effective a show of confidence can be. Having been humiliated that very day by Wyatt Earp, he was in fact anything but confident in his ability to stop the posse, but Ike Clanton, who was obviously far from eager to take on the Earps himself, was easily taken in.

"Sure enough, Ringo," he answered and ran to do the outlaw's bidding.

Less than half an hour later, Ringo was leaving Tombstone at a dead run aboard Billy Clanton's Appaloosa mare, the fastest animal in three counties. In the saddle scabbard was Tom McLowry's brand-new repeating Winchester.

The Earp posse had nearly an hour lead, and there was little chance of overtaking them if he stuck to the main road. Cutting directly across country, however, appeared to be impossible. In every direction, high rocky ridges alternated with deep, brush-choked ravines. Between the ridgetops and the ravines the chaparral and scrub oak were so dense a man in chaps could crawl across their tops. He remembered what Buckskin Frank Leslie had told him some months ago, that there was a trail that ran from a box canyon near Tombstone to the crossing of the San Pedro River just outside Charleston.

"Far as I know, ain't no white man but me's ever been over it or even knows about it," the former Indian scout had said. "Only reason I found it was 'cause I was trailin' some bronco Chiricahuas for the army. I follered 'em all the way to the Pedro then sent one of my 'paches to fetch the soldiers. It ain't what you'd call a real accommodatin' trail. Fact is, I wouldn't recommend it to anybody but a Indin or a goat."

Remembering Leslie's directions, he located the canyon three miles from Tombstone. The mouth of it was barely wide enough to admit a rider, and having entered the canyon he wondered at first if maybe Buckskin Frank hadn't just made up his story and the trail as a joke. All around Ringo the towering vertical red-and-gold sandstone walls of the canyon appeared to be without enough of a break to accommodate a lizard—and the dim game trail along the creek at the bottom seemed never to have been traveled by man or horse. Cursing Leslie under his breath, he was nearly ready to retreat when his eye caught a place where a section of the canyon wall had separated itself from the rest during some primeval disturbance by the great cosmic prankster who overturns mountains by the roots. Circling around the boulder field below the break, he found what was left of a trail that had probably never been used much even when the Apaches were at their busiest. It zigzagged crazily across the cliff face like a knife slash and appeared to be broken in places. Still skeptical but realizing that he had no choice if he wanted to reach Charleston ahead of the Earps, he dismounted and began leading the mare up the treacherous path.

As he neared the top, the path narrowed dangerously above a straight drop of well over a thousand feet. Looking down at the boulder field far below, he wondered if thwarting Wyatt Earp was really worth putting himself and Billy Clanton's fine Appaloosa mare in this kind of situation. Not hardly, he decided, but then, he reflected, it wasn't so much a matter of getting in Earp's way as of saving Curly's hide. Curly was a friend, and John Ringo would never abandon a friend.

When he and the mare finally reached the top, he could see the San Pedro shining blue in the distance. Between the river and where he was were two high, timber-covered ridges. The trail, or what remained of it, led directly down a steep, rock-strewn slope into a ravine below the first ridge. He hesitated a moment, seeing what appeared to be an impassable obstacle below, then kneed the mare into a perilous descent that had her sliding at times on her haunches.

At the bottom, he was confronted by the obstacle, which looked no less forbidding than when he had seen it from above, an eroded gully over fifty feet deep extending the length of the ravine. The sides of this chasm were too steep to descend, but in places it narrowed to about ten or fifteen feet across. Riding slowly along the edge, he found, beside one of these narrow places, a relatively flat clearing that extended far enough back for him to put the mare into a run.

"Come on girl, show me what you can do," he urged softly, reaching down to pat and stroke her neck. "Billy says you're a jumper, too, not just a runner. Show this ol' cowboy."

Trembling from the exertion of the descent and perhaps in anticipation of what her rider would be asking, the mare whickered nervously.

For the first time since mounting her, Ringo used his spurs on the mare, and as he spurred her toward the edge of the chasm, he was exhilarated by a familiar sensation—a rush of energy through his loins and thighs that came only at moments such as this, when he had surrendered himself completely to action.

The rider's energy seemed to fuse with the power in the mare's driving haunches. At the edge of the chasm he rose in his stirrups and the two of them were borne away from the edge. Just for an instant, as they seemed to hover in midair above the yawning maw of the chasm, Ringo was granted an apocalyptic awareness of the world around him—trees, rocks, sun-bleached grass covering the ground across the chasm, which seemed unreachable. Then the earth received the mare's reaching hooves, and the rider was nearly thrown over her head. Recovering, he looked back across the gully, and it took him a moment or two to accept the fact that they'd done it, were not lying broken and bleeding on the rocks at the bottom.

"*Gracias, querida mía. Gracias, preciosa,*" he murmured softly to the trembling mare, falling naturally into the language of love he used with Elena and other generous ladies who had given him a taste of their warm south. Then, still charged with the energy that had flowed into the mare's haunches, he cupped one hand alongside his mouth and released a yell that echoed the length of the ravine, a yell that might have aroused the shades of Quantrill and Todd.

The remainder of the trail to the San Pedro was a little less challenging than the first part, but only a little. Every bit of Ringo's skill as a horseman was taxed. Fortunately for him, the mare was sure-footed—picking her way delicately among sharp boulders, threading the thick timber and chaparral like a deer. Near the ridgetops the trail ascended so steeply that Ringo had to dismount and lead her. Finally, as they started to descend the last precipitous slope above the San Pedro, Ringo was nearly knocked out of the saddle by an oak branch that tore off his Stetson and left a deep gash in his forehead. Plunging down the red sandy piñon-studded slope toward the river, he was dizzy and sick to his stomach.

Two hundred yards from the bottom, he reined up and paused to look west along the road from Tombstone. Less than a mile away he could see dust rising from what could have been a wagon but was, more likely, a party of riders. His head was still ringing from the collision with the branch, and now blood from the gash had begun to trickle down into his right eye. He untied the faded blue bandanna from around his neck and bound it about his forehead. Then he tapped the mare's flanks lightly with his boots and they completed the descent to the river. Having decided to make his stand on the Charleston side of the river, he rode across the bridge. Dismounting, he drew the Winchester out of its scabbard, then left the mare untied to crop the rich bottom grass beside the bridge.

In his haste to get here, he had assumed that Tom McLowry would not give him an unloaded rifle, and when he levered open the chamber he was relieved to find it full. Quickly he brought it up to his shoulder and sighted along the octagonal barrel at a ground-squirrel mound across the river. Then, pleased with the feel of the weapon in his hands, he hunkered down on his heels Indian-fashion with the rifle across his knees and waited.

His wait was brief. One moment he was hearing only the sound of the river gurgling about the bridge supports. A moment later he heard voices from across the river and the sound of hoofbeats. He rose quickly to his feet and brought the rifle up as a hunter would approaching a thicket within which his dogs had a quarry cornered. He needed only a fraction of a second to bring the weapon from there up to his shoulder.

As Wyatt Earp and his posse—consisting of his brothers and Doc Holliday—started to cross the bridge, they were halted by a familiar, hated sight—the tall, grim-faced outlaw who had put himself defiantly in their path so many times.

"Just keep coming, Earp," Ringo called. "It's a fine day for a swim."

Wyatt Earp was exasperated. He had been assured by the district attorney that Ringo would be held without bail for twenty-four hours. The news that Ringo was going to be arrested just as they were about to ride out after Curly had indeed seemed too good to be true. Now, either he had escaped or, more likely, Johnny Behan had released him without getting his bond officially approved.

"Do you think he means business, Doc?"

Doc Holliday chuckled at a question that hardly needed answering. The tall man with the rifle—dust-covered, hatless, with a bloody rag tied across his forehead—was obviously not to be trifled with.

"Yeah, Wyatt, I'd say he means business." Holliday

grinned across the bridge at Ringo, appreciating the humor of the situation in spite of the fact that a splendid opportunity to diminish the power of the Cowboys had now been lost.

Virgil Earp spoke up. "You know, Wyatt, if Ringo's here, I'll bet Curly isn't. Ringo must have warned him."

"I say we rush him," Morgan Earp growled. "He can't hit but one or two of us."

"Wouldn't count on that, Morg," Doc Holliday answered him. "That's a Winchester he's holding on us."

When all three had spoken, they waited for Wyatt Earp to decide what they would do. He was silent for a moment, bitterly regarding the man across the bridge. Finally, a brief snort of exasperated resignation escaped him and he said:

"Virg is probably right. We'll get Curly, and him too, another time." Then he yelled across the bridge:

"So long, Ringo. We'll be seeing you. Give our regards to Curly." He turned his horse away from the bridge and the others followed him, with Doc Holliday coming last. Just as his mount was turning away, Holliday looked back, still grinning, and waved a salute. Ringo, starting to grin a little himself, nodded in reply.

He allowed the Earps plenty of time to retreat toward Tombstone. Then he stepped slowly down off the bridge into the grassy depression where the mare was cropping the rich grass by the river. Thrusting the rifle into its scabbard, he grasped the saddle with both hands and leaned against it for a few moments. He was exhausted, felt so weak that he wondered if he could climb into the saddle, but as his sense of triumph grew, his strength began to restore itself.

"We did it, girl," he whispered to the mare. "By God, we did it!"

Riding into Charleston, he had no trouble locating Curly in one of their favorite saloons. He could hear the big man's laughter while he was still two hundred yards away. Before he went to the saloon, however, he left the mare at the livery stable with specific instructions for her care, including a rubdown and a long walkdown.

As he walked into the saloon, he saw the bar completely lined with drinkers enjoying Curly's generosity.

Joe Hill was being led up the stairs at the back by one of the girls. Curly himself was seated in a corner with a girl in each arm. Seeing Ringo, he bellowed with delight:

"Heyyy, Juanito! *Compadre! Hermano!* Thought you was back in Tombstone takin' things easy while the rest of us was out workin'. Come on over here an' have a drink with us."

Curly was drunk, but not so drunk that he couldn't see, even in the dim light of the saloon, the marks of the ride from Tombstone over Buckskin Frank Leslie's trail.

"Hey, *compadre*, what happened to you? Where's your Stetson? You look like you been buffaloed. You jest tell ol' Curly who the sonofabitch was an' I'll kill him. Was it that goddamn Earp with his big hogleg?"

Ringo grinned and shook his head but said nothing. Maybe later, after they'd killed a bottle, he would tell Curly about his ride and his stand—his victory—at the bridge. For now he was content simply to join Curly in his celebration. After his second or third whiskey, Ringo felt the familiar warmth spreading through him, along with something even more warmth-giving—the sense of victory. Maybe tomorrow would belong to the Earps. Maybe the Cowboys would be swept aside, trampled under or whatever in the name of Progress and Decency. Whatever will happen, he reflected, today is ours, ours to be savored like good whiskey.

"Where you been, honey?"

It was a girl he hadn't seen for a while, a bosomy, dark-eyed redhead who entertained him from time to time, whenever he visited Charleston. He wished he could remember her name.

"Me? I've been away. On business. How've you been?"

"Jest fine, honey. Looks to me like you're in a pretty rough business. How about lettin' Dory fix that head for you?"

Why not? She looked to be just what he needed to fix his head. Across the table, Curly's attention was being fought for by the two girls between their shrieking outbursts of laughter at his jokes. One of them had a pretty, intelligent face, with the most wonderfully inviting mouth he had seen in years, though she was a little on the thin side. The other had a less interesting face but the kind of figure that enters a man's dreams like a twining succubus

and makes him moan in the night. Before the night had
passed Curly would probably have both of them.

"Come along, honey."

The redhead, Dory, was drawing him out of his chair
to lead him away by the hand. Time to let the warm love
in, it would seem.

"Now, John there reads books," Curly was saying. "Ain't
nothin' in books, is there, girls?"

The two had not left off shrieking at a joke he had just
made. Without really hearing what the big man said, they
went on laughing and nodded their agreement. Ringo
joined in their laughter, and so pleasing was the sensation of victory that he too nodded in agreement. But as
the woman led him away from the table past the drinkers
at the bar he began to recite:

> *"She took me to her elfin grot*
> *And there she wept and sigh'd full sore,*
> *And there I shut her wild wild eyes*
> *With kisses four. . . ."*

The woman looked at him strangely, but then she
smiled and put her arm around his waist. As they started
to climb the stairs, she said:

"Sounds real fine, honey. A pome, ain't it?"

"A poem, milady," he answered, adding, "just like
you."

"That's nice," she said, laying her head against his
shoulder. "You're a gentleman, I can tell. Ain't many
come in here."

In her room she untied the bandanna and bathed his
forehead gently with water from a basin. Then she carefully disinfected the wound with whiskey, murmuring
sympathetically as the smarting made Ringo wince:

"Won't hurt long, honey. Dory'll make it feel jest
fine."

And before the smarting had passed they were in her
bed, and Ringo was rediscovering the wonder of a woman's body. No matter how many women he had enjoyed,
the wonder remained undiminished. Tonight there wasn't
enough whiskey in him to deaden his senses. Aroused as
they had been repeatedly that day by the proximity of
death, they bore him relentlessly toward the edge of

another chasm. The woman was ready to bear him across. Her driving haunches, firmly clasped in his strong, gentle hands, bore them away, over the chasm. Ringo was granted an apocalyptic moment—seeing the curve of her throat, feeling the hardness of her nipples against his chest, hearing the strange sad moaning from her parted lips. As he too moaned with his pleasure, she began to laugh and cry at the same time and to cover his face with her kisses.

"Oh my goodness, honey, ain't nobody ever . . . I mean I just never . . ."

"We did it, girl," he whispered, panting like a winded stallion.

"I'll say we did. You're really something, you know that? I just never . . ."

Remembering now, by his lonely fire in the Dragoons, Ringo chuckles to himself and pours more whiskey into his cup, half hoping it will deaden the effects of recalling that night—the burning ache in his groin, the throbbing erection. *Lente, lente currite noctis equi.*

But even as they had ignored the poet, the horses of the night refused to run slowly for Ringo. That night among others had passed quickly, making way for a day that belonged wholly to the Earps.

"Folks are starting to call it the Gunfight at the O.K. Corral, though I hear that's not exactly where it happened. I only wish to God I'd been there. They say it lasted only twenty seconds. Frank got it first—a bullet from Wyatt through his belly. I never liked him, but the way I hear it he died like a man, kept on firing back with that slug in his belly until either Morg Earp or Holliday finished him with one in the head. Billy took one in the chest from Morg that flattened him, but then I hear he got up on one knee and managed to wing Morg and hit Virgil in the leg. Then Virgil put another one into his chest, and that was the end of him. Poor Tom, the best shot in the group, didn't even get off a shot. Holliday had a sawed-off shotgun as well as his six-shooter, and Tom caught a double charge while he was trying to get Frank's rifle out of its saddle boot. Wouldn't you know the only one on our side who'd survive would be that big-mouthed gutless bastard Ike. And I hear it was Ike who brought on the whole thing when he got drunk and mouthed off about what he and his friends were going to do to the

Earps and Holliday. When the shooting started, he ran like a rabbit. If only I could have been there. The way I hear it, the Earps were in a hurry to settle the whole business their way while the rest of us were out of town. Smart sonsofbitches. Stilwell and Spence evened things out a little, I guess, by killing Morg Earp, but I don't hold much with that kind of thing—backshooting a man through a window while he's bent over a pool table. Far as I'm concerned, Stilwell deserved what he got when Wyatt caught up with him in Tucson and blew him in half with a shotgun. I only hope it's not true what they're saying, that he got Curly with the same shotgun over at Iron Springs. The last time I saw Curly was when Johnny Behan deputized the whole bunch of us to arrest and bring in the Earps and Holliday. Curly and I had some good laughs about that, being made deputies, especially when we found out that Wyatt was carrying warrants issued by the territorial governor for the arrest of practically everyone in the posse. So now it looks like maybe I'm the only one left. The Earps are gone too, but you'd have to be a damned fool not to see that they'll be replaced by more of their kind. This territory just won't be fit for a free man. Time to move on, I guess, but where? Mexico's a place where a man can still find a little room. Maybe that's where Curly went. I surely hope so. I'd like to think he made it back to that little place outside Hermosillo.

"Trouble is, I can't pass for a Mexican the way Curly can, and that woman I fought over down in Janos told me the *rurales* are looking for a red-haired gringo about my size. Maybe if I go far enough south—down into the Yucatán, say—I won't have to worry about their being told that this old gringo bandido is back in their country.

"Before I think about Mexico, though, I guess I'd better decide when, if, and how I'm going to get out of these mountains. I only wish that damned grizzly had found himself something besides my animals to chase. If he didn't kill the horse, it's probably back at the ranch I took it from, which is about ten long miles from here. Hell, I feel like a centaur with its legs sawed off. Ten miles. Afoot. It's going to be a while before I feel up to taking that little stroll. Besides, I'm nowhere near finished with what brought me in here.

"Looking over this scribbling, thinking about what I've recorded, I can see how I turned into Johnny Ringo, but I still can't figure out why. I've no one to blame but myself for the choices that made me what I am, but why did I make them? What is there inside a man like me that causes him to choose the things that are bound to defeat and destroy him? I'm wondering if it's an accident that I wound up on the losing side of every feud I got into, starting with the war. I always fought to win, but maybe somehow I always knew, even before I joined up with Quantrill, that I'd always be one of the losers.

"I can see how it is with Holliday. He chooses his destruction because it's a way of spitting in the face of death, showing his freedom as a sure-enough man. Someday he'll get himself killed by somebody with quicker hands before consumption has a chance to finish him. And maybe that's sort of how it is with me. I want to choose my destruction before whatever there is tearing away inside me has done its work and finished me."

On this thought, John Ringo sets aside his writing board and pours more whiskey. The moon has risen, silvering the tops of the bare peaks surrounding the one-time stronghold of Cochise. At his feet the burning chunks of scrub oak are still throwing off enough light to read by, and he remembers how, nearly thirty years before, back in a little farmhouse outside San Antonio, a young boy lay on his belly before the fireplace wide-eyed in the flickering light, struggling with Homer's lines. The man still reads by firelight, but tonight he will not read. He will instead simply listen to the sounds of the night. The wolves that den in the ravine off to the east of his camp will soon be loping across the meadow toward the stronghold's entrance on their way down into the Sulphur Springs Valley. Perhaps the grizzly will come again to make another try for the bacon suspended from the branch above the spring. He could wind up as either grizzly or wolf meat, he guesses, but the thought is not especially disturbing. The important thing is that he didn't wind up as meat for the Earps. As he sips his whiskey and feels its warmth spreading through him, he feels as well a curious, warmth-giving satisfaction when he reflects that Wyatt Earp's design of "cleaning out" southeastern Arizona—mandated by the governor himself, the Arizona Stockmen's Association, and the Wells Fargo Company—has been frustrated by his own continued existence. Ringo knows his enemy well enough to know that this profound disappointment must be gnawing at him. Maybe it will gnaw at him to the point where he will return to finish his work. Ringo would like nothing better. A chance to meet Wyatt Earp again is something worth living for.

Suddenly, somewhere over near the base of the conical peak, he hears a high, prolonged scream, a sound of suffering piteous and forlorn. One who believed in spirits might imagine that it came from the ghost of some wretched captive trooper dragged in here by the Apaches to provide amusement for their women, or perhaps a damned soul trying to escape infernal torments through the cave where the Apaches commune with the spirit of Cochise. Ringo doesn't believe in spirits, but this doesn't prevent a shudder from running up between his shoulder blades and raising the hair on the back of his neck. Again he hears the scream, and this time he is fairly certain that he recognizes it for what it is—the cry of a mountain lion. He has never heard it before, but he has heard it described, and he remembers the enormous cougar he saw during his ride into this place. The human quality of the scream is startling. The first time it sounded like a man being shorn of his manhood. Coming again, it was more like a woman screaming at the sudden recognition of an irreparable loss—the death of a child, perhaps, or the only lover who has ever meant anything to her. The sound effectively chills the man by the fire. In his hands the cup of whiskey reflects the dancing flames. He raises it to his lips and drains it.

TEN

THE HARDENED HEART

"Ringo? For Chrissake, izzat you?"

The man lying against the rock beside the dead fire starts to open his eyes, then quickly raises an arm to ward off the bright rays of the morning sun as they strike with painful force. His eyes close and then reopen as a dark figure on horseback interposes itself, momentarily blocking out the sun.

"Well now, I guess you're alive after all," the horseman says with a laugh. His voice is familiar, but with the sun behind him he is indistinguishable. The man on the ground sits up and raises his arm to shield his eyes for a better look.

"Leslie?"

He still can't make out anything but a formless black presence on horseback, but now he recognizes the voice.

"Yeah, John, it's me."

Gradually, as Ringo's vision clears, he perceives the laughing feline eyes of the little ex-scout beneath the wide brim of a snowy-white Stetson. The crown of the Stetson is ornamented by a band of silver conchas into which a small red plume has been thrust. The buckskin-fringed jacket he wears is elaborately decorated with the flowered beadwork patterns that Indians design for white men, reserving the geometrical patterns for their own people. On each hip, thrusting out from beneath the jacket, is the nacreous, nickel-plated butt of a six-shooter. His trousers are skin-tight, fawn-colored and thrust into the tops of high gleaming black English riding boots. Ringo remembers the first time he saw Leslie in his riding gear, when he took him for a tinhorn or maybe a pimp just off a train from the East. In fact, or so he has told Ringo, Leslie has never been further east than his native Kentucky, where he grew up among mountain

315

people who, in his words, "make their whiskey strong and keep their feuds alive."

"What are you doing up here?" Ringo asks, and is a little surprised by the less than friendly tone of his own voice. For some reason he can't quite pin down, he feels uneasy with Leslie here. Perhaps it's because he is conscious of his own seedy, unshaven appearance and how he must look lying against a rock with an empty whiskey bottle beside him. Or maybe it's because he has become so used to the loneliness of the place and wants no intrusion into his thoughts but the ghosts his memory summons. Maybe it has nothing at all to do with Leslie personally. But of course Leslie can only take it that way, and he replies with a short bitter laugh, saying:

"Well, I like that. A fellow rides forty miles into these damned mountains to rescue a friend and the friend asks him what he's doing."

"Sorry, Frank, I just didn't expect you. There's more whiskey in that pannier if you'd like a drink."

"Don't mind," Leslie says as he dismounts and stretches himself. Going over to where the pannier lies in the shade, he opens it and whistles as he sees the supply Ringo has brought with him.

"Damn good thing the 'paches don't know what you brought in here. God himself couldn't rescue you if they did."

"What's all this about rescuing? Who said I needed rescuing?" Hung over as he is and having been surprised in this less than presentable condition, he is especially annoyed because he himself realizes that he probably does look less than able to look after himself. Painfully, he forces himself to rise, then presses his hands into his aching back.

"Nobody said, John. But some of us—your friends—started wonderin' when that pack mule you rented come back to the livery stable. We figured maybe the 'paches got you." He raises a freshly uncorked bottle to his lips and takes a long pull. Ringo watches the Adam's apple rise and fall in the little man's leathery neck. Shuddering a little, Leslie continues: "Yeah, one of them chippies from down at Irma's Place, that little Mex cunt—"

Ringo cuts him off harshly. "Dammit, Frank, don't

you ever talk about a woman that way. Not around me anyway."

The crown of Leslie's white Stetson just barely reaches Ringo's shoulder. Startled by Ringo's harsh, menacing tone, he raises his eyes to regard the moody outlaw's face with a puzzled, resentful expression. Then he grins and nods, saying—

"Sorry. I forget you're touchy that way. Anyway, it was this Mex gal . . ."

"Elena?"

"Yeah, she's the one. She came into the Oriental an' tol' me about the mule. She ast me to track you down, said you mentioned something to her 'bout comin' in here."

Ringo cannot for the life of him remember saying anything to Elena about where he was going, but how else would Leslie know where to find him? He is still irritated by Leslie's presence, but he guesses he owes the little man some expression of gratitude.

"Appreciate your concern, Frank. Fact is, I could use a horse. A damn grizzly ran off both my animals."

"Sure enough, John. There's a little stick ranch 'bout ten miles south of here, belongs to a greaser. He had a couple o' pretty fair-lookin' ponies I saw last time I passed by there. I'll go fetch you one."

"I'd be grateful," Ringo replies, again forced to express a gratitude he doesn't feel much.

Leslie holds out the bottle to him, but he shakes his head, whereupon Leslie takes another long pull that sends another shudder through him.

"Yeah, we thought maybe you wuz fertilizin' an anthill after the 'paches got through takin' the spirit out of you."

"They've been here, Frank. Been here and gone."

"Chato and Nachite?" Leslie looks amazed.

"I don't know their names. No, not Chato and Nachite. Just some bucks from the reservation with an old medicine man. They came up here to talk with the spirit of Cochise in a cave over that way." He waves toward the ravine that leads to the sandstone wall.

"You don't say. Well, I guess you ain't heard about the big raid. Chato and Nachite brung their Cherry-kows up from Mexico to San Carlos an' rounded up over a hundred reservation Indins to take back with 'em. Nobody knows for sure where they are. Must be close to a thousand soldiers out lookin' for 'em. My guess is they'll foller the Gila over into New Mexico 'fore they cut south back acrost the border. It's been so damn dry this year there ain't hardly any water holes. They made the mistake of takin' along all their women an' kids, so they'll have to stick to the rivers."

"Do you know those chiefs, Frank?"

"Yeah, I know 'em both. Chato's a sure-enough Apache. Tough little sonofabitch. Got his face kicked in once by a mule. That's how come he's called Chato. Means Flatnose. He ain't real pretty like Nachite, but he's twice the leader, twice the man."

"Nachite's the son of Cochise, isn't he?" Ringo asks.

"Yeah, that's right. Ol' Mangus Colorado had a couple of real pretty daughters by a Mex woman he captured. His 'pache wives wanted her to be their slave, but he wouldn't have it. So they made their brothers challenge ol' Mangus to a knife duel, which turned out to be a mistake."

"I've heard that story. He killed them both, didn't he?"

"That's right. Anyway, that Mex woman must have been some to look at, an' he gave one of their daughters to Cochise. Nachite's one of the sons he had by her. He's real pretty to look at for a man, almost pretty as a girl. Has hands like a girl's. An' tall. Over six foot in his moccasins, like his granddaddy. The 'paches'll foller him 'cause he's Cochise's son, but the way I see it he don't have what it takes to be a real Apache leader."

"What do you mean?"

"Oh, he'd rather be enjoyin' female company an' drinkin' tulapai than ridin' the war trail. He needs women more than a sure-enough man ought to."

Ringo grins a little to himself, wondering if the little man is aware of how accurately he's describing his, Ringo's, own proclivities.

"Yeah," Leslie goes on, after another pull at the bottle, "a man gets hisself a woman, he's liable to lose hisself."

Ringo looks at the little man sharply, puzzled by the sudden bitterness in his tone but guessing that there must be some reason for his misogyny. Half suspecting that the

reason for this might also be one reason why the little
man has suddenly appeared in this lonely retreat, Ringo
asks—

"How's your wife, Frank?"

Leslie drops his eyes and looks into the ashes of the
dead fire for a moment before answering.

"She left me, John. Took the stage out to Yuma last
week. Goin' on out to San Francisco, I guess."

"I'm sorry," Ringo replies gently, though he suspects
that Mrs. Leslie had her reasons.

"Don't be. A fella can't live with a woman that don't
have a sense of humor an' can't take a little funnin'," the
little man replies gloomily.

Remembering the stories of how Mrs. Leslie had been
outlined in bullet holes in the wall of her parlor, Ringo
says nothing.

"Hey," Leslie says, suddenly cheerful, as though something has just occurred to him dispelling all the gloom
and bitterness, "how about you an' me tyin' on a good
one? I hear there's a new place over at Soldier Holes
where they pour the kind of whiskey I was brung up on.
We could start there, then move on to Antelope Springs.
They got some chip . . . girls over at Antelope that know
how to treat a man right, so I hear."

Ringo laughs and stretches himself, thinking of how
long it's been since he's had a woman. Long enough that
even this leering invitation from Buckskin Frank is enough
to touch off a response and start the sap moving. But
then he shakes his head.

"No, Frank, I've got business here."

"Business? Whaddya mean business?" Leslie sneers.
"Looks to me like all your business is pullin' corks outta
them bottles. You stay here much longer, you're gonna
be Indian meat."

Again Ringo is irritated, almost to the flashpoint of
rage. He wishes Leslie would leave, but at the same time
he realizes that the little man may have a more accurate
picture of things than he, Ringo, would like to admit.
What, after all, has he accomplished during his stay here?
For all his reflecting and remembering, has he come up
with any answers? He looks down at the pile of foolscap
next to the fire, pinned down against the wind by his

writing board. Where is all this scribbling going to lead him?

Leslie, too, notices the pile of scribbled sheets and asks with a laugh, "Hey, John, you writin' a book? Izzat your business?"

Ringo looks at the little man coldly, feeling exposed and vulnerable, as he did upon waking to find Leslie watching him. He is about to tell Leslie to mind his own business, but he replies instead, wearily, "You might call it that, Frank."

"Too bad you don't have somebody like ol' Ned Buntline to write one of them dime novels about you. Way I hear it, folks back east just can't read enough about the romantic"—Leslie savors the word, as though he's just learned it, pronouncing deliberately "roh-man-teek" —"adventures of famous gunfighters out here in what they call the 'wild west.' Ol' Buntline's makin' hisself a pile. Hey, you know what? I got one of his books in my saddlebag. You ain't the only one carries readin' around with you."

The little man sets down the whiskey bottle and goes over to his horse. Ringo watches as he draws from his saddlebag a tattered, coverless pamphlet and brings it over. The pages are deep yellow, almost orange in color, and ready to disintegrate, even though the printing date is fairly recent. On the front page, above the scene of a spectacular shootout in the false-front-flanked street of a western town, is the title WILD BILL'S LAST TRAIL.

"This about Hickok?" Ringo asks.

"That's right. It's about how he cashed in up in Deadwood."

"From what I hear," Ringo snorts skeptically, "that wouldn't even fill a dime novel. He was just sitting at a poker table with his back to the door, and some two-bit punk—"

"Jack McCall."

"That's the one. Came in and backshot him. Hickok was holding aces and eights at the time."

"Uh-huh. A dead man's hand, for sure," Leslie chuckles grimly. "Buntline dressed things up a little, tacked on a few adventures to fill out his yarn, the kind of things folks back east expect—wild Sioux Indins, pretty ladies dressed up like gunfighters—that sort of thing."

"Sounds to me like Buntline's a liar." Ringo's sour remark is prompted mainly by a recollection that Buntline and Wyatt Earp are friends. Earp's long-barreled Colt was a present from Buntline.

"Well," Leslie replies a little defensively, "I wouldn't exactly call him that. If he is, he's like those fellas who make lyin' a sure-enough art. Like in a braggin' contest. That's what folks pay for when they buy his books."

"You're saying that folks won't pay to read the truth about the 'wild west'?" Ringo asks, scornfully mouthing "wild west."

"No, John, I wouldn't say that. You remember the Younger brothers, the ones that rode with the James boys?"

Ringo is startled by the question. He has never told Leslie anything about his history prior to his arrival in Arizona, and he is not about to begin now, so he answers simply, "Yeah, I remember."

"Well, it seems they hired a fella by the name of Augustus Appler to write a book telling their side of things—how they got started with Quantrill during the war an' how the Yank authorities wouldn't let 'em settle down after the war an' be good honest Missouri farmers. A drummer from Texas told me about it, said he'd read it. I hear they're in prison up in Minnesota or someplace."

"That's what I hear."

"Yeah, well this drummer said it was a real interestin' story, made him kinda sympathetic toward the Youngers. I don't suppose it's all true either, any more than one of Buntline's novels, but it passes itself off as true and folks want to read it. I bet folks'll want to read your story," he says, nodding at the pile of foolscap.

"It's not for anybody to read," Ringo replies, "not anybody but me."

Leslie laughs. "Guess that means it's all true, then. A fella don't lie to hisself, does he?"

"I wouldn't say that, Frank," Ringo replies with a humorless chuckle, adding, "But, yes, I guess it's all true, whatever that means."

"You ought to pass it on to Billy Breakenridge. He says he's plannin' to write a book about what really happened in Tombstone. Says he's goin' to burn the Earps for sure. Plans to call it *Helldorado*."

"That so?" Ringo is mildly interested.

"Yeah, John, I bet he'll have plenty to say about you, an' Curly too. You're his friends. He'll do right by you."

Ringo smiles to himself, remembering the dying words of his favorite character in literature: *"God . . . what a wounded name things standing thus unknown . . . shall live behind me."*

"Wonder if Billy's book will change that any," he murmurs to himself.

"Whazzat?"

"Nothing, Frank. I was just thinking a little out loud."

"I bet you done a lot o' that out here. A man alone out in a place like this winds up talkin' to hisself. It's time we got you outta here. I'll go fetch you a horse."

"Thanks, Frank, but I'm not promising to leave here with you. Here's to pay for the horse, though." He pulls out of his vest pocket a small rawhide sack full of coins and tosses it to Leslie. "There're some double eagles in there." He is unused to paying for horses, having stolen every mount he's owned for the last three years or so. Perhaps because he is aware of this, Leslie reassures him.

"Don't worry, John. I won't let a greaser cheat you. See you later this evening."

"So long. And thanks again."

He is much relieved to see the little ex-scout depart. Not that he won't also be relieved to be mounted again, but he has no desire to leave this place with Leslie. He wonders what it is about the little man that repels him. Partly it must be because he himself is now sober. Back in Tombstone, where he is seldom entirely sober, he can spend hours listening to Leslie's jokes and gossiping, his homely good-old-boy-from-the-mountains philosophizing. That's the way of it when you're a drunk, Ringo reflects, one of the prices you pay. The company you enjoy with half a quart under your belt may not be tolerable when you're sobered up.

Ringo is entirely sober now. As a matter of fact, he reflects, with some satisfaction, he has drunk a good deal less since arriving in Cochise's stronghold than he has for a very long time. Drunk less and rested more, in spite of troubling memories and dreams. And, in spite of his seedy appearance, he feels stronger, both in body and what he hesitates to call spirit, that unseen something he feels at times that almost convinces him he can be more than what he has become. He looks at the bottle Leslie has left next to the dead fire, is tempted fleetingly to begin the day with a long pull at it—one way to deal with a hangover—but instead he simply picks it up and stashes it in the pannier. Then he sets to work rebuilding the fire.

In a little while he has reheated a kettle of beans and fried himself some bacon, the cowpuncher's rib-lining staples, which he washes down with some potent black coffee. By the time he is ready to settle himself with his writing board, he finds that his hangover is nearly gone. Maybe this evening he will try to leave whiskey alone altogether. Now he begins to write:

"Leslie talks about the risks of staying here, and I guess they're real enough. Nachite and Chato might take it into their heads to come in here and pay Nachite's daddy a visit so they can find out the best way to get back down into Mexico. Those reservation bucks I met will surely have passed on the word that some crazy white man has set up his camp right here on Cochise's doorstep. They'll be expecting to find me, and, as Frank says, I'll be their meat.

"In a way, I guess, it's like what old Paul says in the Good Book, about wisdom and foolishness. Whether you're wise or a fool depends pretty much upon how you look at things, what you value. If you see things the way Frank does, anything that helps you survive with your hide intact is wisdom. Survival, that kind, isn't all that important to me. Not that I'm what old Paul would call the spiritual sort. I'm about as carnal-minded as they come, a sure-enough 'natural man' who won't receive the things of the Spirit, not because he sees them as foolishness but because he prefers to walk after the flesh. I seriously doubt that any saint, maybe not even God Himself, could ever make me see how good it is for a man not to touch a woman. On the other hand, old Paul may be right when he says that you have to be a fool sometimes to gain wisdom. I have this strange feeling that if I'm fool enough to stay here, I may learn something."

He pauses in his writing, glances down and sees the Buntline novel. One by one, its yellowed pages are being turned by the morning breeze. He reaches over and picks

it up, wondering idly if it's like other Buntline novels he's
sampled. Though they are generally short, he has never
been able to get through one before setting it aside to
reach for Homer or Shakespeare. This one begins with a
conversation:

"Bill! *Wild Bill!* Is this you, or your ghost? What,
in great Creation's name, are you doing here?"

"Gettin' toward sunset, old pard—gettin' toward
sunset before I pass in my checks!"

The first speaker was an old scout and plainsman,
Sam Chichester by name, and he spoke to a passenger who had just left the westward-bound express
train at Laramie, on the U.P.R.R.

That passenger was none other than J. B. Hickok,
or "Wild Bill," one of the most noted shots, and
certainly the most desperate man of his age and day
west of the Mississippi River.

"What do you mean, Bill, when you talk of passing in your checks? You're in the very prime of life,
man, and—"

Ringo's hard-set mouth lifts a little in a half-grin as he
recalls Leslie's suggestion that he, Ringo, would be a
good subject for a dime novel. The more he thinks about
it, the more amusing it becomes. His half-grin broadens
as he imagines how Buntline might present him to his
eastern readers, and he can't resist an impulse to begin a
Buntline-type description of himself:

"This tall melancholy stranger was none other than John
Ringgold, or 'Ringo,' as he had come to be called, one of the
most noted hands with a gun or a knife and certainly the
most desperate outlaw of his day and age left in Arizona
Territory, being the sole survivor of a lawless element
that has been virtually eliminated by that stalwart champion of Law, Order, Decency and Progress—Wyatt Earp.
A native of Texas, brought up in a God-fearing Christian
household and with all the advantages of a classical education, Ringo aspired as a youth to the noble profession
of medicine. This aspiration was discarded during the late
War of the Rebellion wherein he distinguished himself as
a Confederate partisan ranger, or guerrilla, under the
black flag of the infamous William Clarke Quantrill, fight-

ing alongside his notorious kinsmen, the Youngers of Missouri. Thrice wounded in sanguinary contests with the northern enemy in Missouri and Kansas, Ringo was one of Quantrill's 'eyes,' a scout who narrowly escaped hanging on more than one occasion while gathering intelligence and lived to account for more than his share of the enemy, being especially savage in his dealings with the northern partisans known as Red Legs, whose scalps occasionally adorned his horse's bridle, after the barbaric fashion of the wild Comanche Indians of his native state. . . ."

Thoroughly enjoying himself, Ringo laughs out loud at what he has written. But then he reflects, a little sadly, that this description is probably fairly close to what will be said of him, how he will be remembered, even as Hickok and his old enemy Wyatt Earp will be remembered mainly as the heroic figures Buntline celebrated.

"Something too much of this, Ringo. You're starting to feel sorry for yourself. Buntline gives the easterners what they want—lawmen who are pillars of heroic virtue and outlaws who have just enough wit and sand to be worthy opponents in the great shootout between the big false fronts labeled Good and Evil. Easterners don't want to read about a wild west outlaw who's the outcast of his own dark mind, or one who has loved and been loved by good women, who will never allow a woman to be dishonored in his presence, who never forgives an enemy but never forgets a friend either. Maybe my story will be told someday. Maybe Billy Breakenridge will tell it. Or maybe somebody with a crazy name like that Gustus Appler Cole and Jim hired to tell their story will ride in here ninety years from now and find my recollections in Cochise's cave, where I intend to leave them. Maybe he'll tell the world what I can't seem to explain to myself— why I became what I am and why I can't seem to bring together what I think and feel and what I do."

Curious about how Buntline has garnished the simple facts of Wild Bill Hickok's death, Ringo turns to the last page of *Wild Bill's Last Trail*.

" . . . I'll break this bank to-night, or die in the trial!" cried Bill, defiantly.

"You'll die before you break it," shrieked out a

shrill, sharp voice, and the red-haired Texan sprang forward with an uplifted bowie-knife, and lunged with deadly aim at Bill's heart, even as the person we have so long known as Willie Pond shrieked out:

"Save, oh, save my husband!"

But another hand clutched the hilt of the descending knife, the hand of a short, thickset, beetle-browed desperado, who shouted, as he drew a pistol with his other hand:

"Wild Bill is *my* game. No one living shall cheat me of *my* revenge! Look at this scar, Bill—you marked me for *life,* and now I mark you for *death!*"

And even as he spoke, the man fired, and a death-shot pierced Wild Bill's heart.

The latter, who had risen to his feet, staggered toward the Texan, who struggled to free his knife-hand from the clutch of the real assassin, and with a wild laugh, tore the false hair from the Texan's head. As a roll of woman's hair came down in a flood of beauty over *her* shoulders, Bill gasped out:

"Jack McCall, I'm thankful to you, even though you've killed me. Wild Bill does not die by the hand of *a woman!*"

A shudder, and all was over, so far as Will Bill's life went.

Ringo's laughter startles several deer who have come to accept his presence and are used to browsing in the meadow in front of his camp. It subsides to a chuckle as he sets the novel aside, gets to his feet and goes to fetch his shaving tools from the tent.

"And why not a woman, Wild Bill?" he asks aloud, knowing instinctively that a man like Hickok would never have spoken the dying words Buntline gave him, with or without a bullet in the heart. "There's many a tall fella who's wound up in a box 'cause he stuck around when he should have left. Knowing that doesn't make women any less attractive in my eyes. Hell, I can see myself winding up in bed like the Assyrian king, shorter by a head, which some lovely little Judith has packed off to the Arizona Stockmen's Association to collect the two thousand it's worth. And why not? Better that than being cut down in the street by some big-balled lawman or hung by vigilantes or rotting to death in prison. Not that how you die isn't important. People remember that more than how you lived. But I wouldn't mind being remembered as a man who died at the hands of a woman, providing, of course, that she made it worth my while beforehand. The head she turns in for the reward surely ought to have a big, contented smile on its face."

As he sets a pan of water on the fire and peels off shirt and underwear from his upper body, he muses upon how Buntline might represent his death for the entertainment of eastern readers. Maybe having one of his famous confrontations with Wyatt Earp turn into something, with more lead flying than filled the air at Gettysburg and himself finally going down with one in the heart but enough breath left to fling eloquent imprecations at his stalwart slayer.

"Or maybe someplace down in Mexico," he mutters aloud. "Up to my ass in *rurales*, going down with both hands full and a goddamned Bowie knife clenched between my teeth."

Reluctantly he goes over to the tree upon which he has nailed a steel mirror. Having felt the hard stubble sprouting along his jaw and from his chin, he is half prepared for what he will encounter, but he still receives a shock.

"Jesus, Ringo, you look awful," he tells the deeply lined angular reflection, whose hard flat planes and bony prominences of nose and cheekbones seem to have been cast from metal or chiseled out of rock. Some color is starting to flow into his face, but the graying stubble that covers his lower features, matching the streaks of gray in his auburn hair and the silvering mat on his chest, reminds him depressingly of the faces of the insensate human wrecks he occasionally steps over in the alleys outside the Crystal Palace after an all-night poker session. No wonder Leslie had trouble recognizing him at first.

As he sets to work with soap and razor, his spirits are lifted a little by the feeling that he really has regained some of the strength he gave up as irretrievable during the years of ceaseless submission to a routine of unrestrained dissipation. Not that he hopes to regain the sort of strength he had once, when he could straighten a horseshoe with his deceptively delicate hands. But he knows that he is stronger than he has been for a long time and is mildly astonished at the resiliency of his own nearly forty-year-old body.

"Almost enough to make a man believe in God," he says aloud.

And surely enough to make him feel ashamed, he reflects silently as he scrapes away the graying stubble.

Evening. Leslie is as good as his word. He rides into Ringo's camp leading a horse, but the animal—a short-legged, ewe-necked, hammerheaded buckskin stallion—is less than pleasing to its new owner's eye.

"Twenty dollars!" Ringo exclaims, when Leslie tells him what he paid for the horse.

"He's worth it, John. The greaser told me this fella's the leader of his *remuda*. He didn't want to sell him, wanted me to buy another animal."

"Why didn't you?" Ringo asks, unable to conceal his disappointment as he walks over to examine his new mount.

"I know he ain't real pretty to look at, but he's a good mountain horse. No windsucker, for sure. He's the kind can get you out of a tight spot in a hurry."

"Well, I guess I'll just have to find that out next time I get into a tight spot," Ringo replies with a shrug as he begins to examine the stud more closely. The short legs and disproportionately large body could be deceptive, he sees now. Maybe Leslie is right. The animal has a murderous rolling eye.

"The Mex said he's a little on the feisty side, havin' growed up as a mustang. I'll take the ginger out of him in the morning if you like."

"Teach your grandmama to suck eggs, Frank," Ringo answers with a grin. It's been a while since he's peeled a bronc, but with his sense of newly restored strength he welcomes the challenge.

"I'll help myself to some of your whiskey, you don't mind," Leslie says with a questioning look.

"Have all you want," Ringo replies shortly, still determined not to drink any himself this evening. More than ever he wishes that Leslie had not come, even if it had meant walking ten miles to get himself a horse. For the first time, what he is writing is starting to make some

kind of sense, but he needs time to work out the meaning
of it all. If he could just keep on writing a little longer,
uninterrupted. . . .

Leslie goes over to the pannier and pulls out the same
whiskey bottle he had uncorked that morning. Then he
turns to Ringo and in a casual manner remarks:

"Oh, by the way, John, guess I neglected to mention
that I ran into Curly over at Galeyville last week."

Ringo is so startled that he whirls to face Leslie, as
though the little man had just cocked a gun behind him.

"Curly? What do you mean 'Curly'? He's dead. Earp
shot him over at Iron Springs. If he isn't dead, he's down
in Mexico."

Leslie uncorks the bottle and shrugs as he raises it to
his lips.

"Well, John, all I know is what I seen. Curly himself
bellied up at the bar in Evilsizer's. Said he'd just come up
from Mexico with five hundred head. Wondered what
had happened to you."

Ringo doesn't believe him, is certain the little man is
lying.

"Yeah, he told me to tell you if I seen you," Leslie
continues, hunkering down before the dead fire, "that
he'll be takin' things easy for a spell 'fore he goes back
down into Mexico. If you don't find him at Evilsizer's,
he'll likely be at Soldier Holes or Myers Cienega. He said
he needs you real bad to help him with something."

Ringo stares at the little man, still certain that he is
lying but unable to figure why he would be.

"You *sure* it was Curly?" Ringo says, knowing that
Leslie will insist that it was, wishing that he could beat
the truth out of him, wishing that the little man hadn't
put him in his debt by fetching that damned ugly crowbait
stallion.

"Yeah, John, it was," Leslie answers softly, raising
feline eyes that have widened a little with innocence real
or feigned and a grin that seems to express good-natured,
patient acceptance of a friend's momentary unreasonable-
ness. When Ringo says nothing in reply, Leslie grasps the
bottle by the neck and holds it out to him.

"Here, have some of your own pizen."

Ringo shakes his head and turns away, unwilling to
share with Leslie his thoughts or even what his eyes

might reveal. Why he is so suspicious of the little man, so unwilling to believe what he says, is not at all clear to Ringo. Leslie has, after all, been acting like a friend. Maybe he is telling the truth. Maybe Curly, his only real friend in this damned territory, really is back, and what Hill and the others said about his taking eighteen buckshot in the chest was just a story to keep the bounty hunters off his trail.

There's only one way to find out. But when Ringo thinks about leaving this retreat with Leslie, he feels strangely apprehensive, as though he will be leaving behind something of value. But what? Whatever it is, it will have to wait here for him until he finds out what his friend Curly needs. That is, if Leslie really had talked to Curly—

"It was Curly, all right," Leslie repeats, interrupting his thoughts and then, as though somehow he can hear Ringo thinking, "Said you're the only real friend he's got in the world. Said he needed you for something important."

Ringo glances over his shoulder at Leslie. The little ex-scout is still hunkered down before the fire ring Apache-fashion with the whiskey bottle in his hands. He looks up at Ringo with that same innocent good-old-boy-from-the-mountains-you-can-trust-me grin and again holds out the bottle. Next to where Leslie is squatting, Ringo's manuscript pages are fluttering in the up-canyon breezes from the stronghold entrance. For a moment or two, during which he feels a terrible, unexplainable pang of sadness, Ringo looks at the fluttering sheets beneath the writing board. Then he turns and walks over to take the proffered bottle.

2

Because of the Apache danger, they avoid the ridgetops and follow arroyos wherever they can. Normally during mid-spring the arroyos in this desert have rivulets and there are little tanks in the places where the sandy bottoms have become hollowed-out sandstone shelves. But during this abnormally dry season, there are no rivulets.

"The troops of Tema looked, the companies of Sheba waited for them. What time they wax warm, they vanish," Ringo mumbles to himself. They are walking their horses along the bottom of one narrow arroyo between red eroded walls that confine the heat like an oven, and Leslie glances over at him.

"Whazzat?" he growls.

"Nothing. Just something Job said about dried-up arroyos. They're like friends who let you down."

"Zat so," the little man replies without interest.

"Yeah, they let you down when things get hot," Ringo goes on, using up a little more valuable energy and tongue moisture, even though he's feeling terribly worn out and thirsty, having desiccated himself with whiskey the previous evening. The more you drink the thirstier you get, he reflects, for possibly the two millionth time. Whiskey is like one of those arroyos Job talks about, like one of his friends he can't count on.

He would like to take a pull at his canteen, but he knows that he will be even thirstier later in the afternoon. In this heat a man can empty his canteen in a few minutes. He has whiskey in his saddlebags, more than enough for what he's estimated is a two-quart ride, but whiskey doesn't go down well in this kind of heat. At times like this he wishes that he had developed the Apache art of handling thirst in the desert. One of their tricks is to put a pebble under the tongue to keep the saliva running. Ringo considers trying this but decides that he doesn't have the energy to climb down and get a pebble.

Even Apaches must get pretty thirsty on a day like this, he is thinking. Then they come around a bend in the arroyo that is partly shaded by a big lone cottonwood with exposed roots that reach down over the edge like grasping fingers.

Because they are in the shade, hunkered down while one of them burrows in the sand like a badger, looking for water, Ringo does not see the little brown men with their bright bars of white face paint until Leslie shouts:

"Hostiles, John! Look alive!"

There is barely enough room in the arroyo to wheel their horses about, and they do not manage to get themselves moving back the way they came before the Apaches open fire. Along the walls of the arroyo ahead of him

Ringo sees dust puffs thrown up by rifle slugs. Indians can't shoot worth a damn, he tells himself, even though he's been told that some Apache marksmen are notable exceptions to that rule.

Leslie was right about the qualities of the animal Ringo is riding, and as the two men emerge from the arroyo onto a flat, sandy, alkaline plain, Ringo moves well ahead in spite of his greater weight. Behind them the Apaches are yelping eagerly like wolves closing in on a hamstrung elk. He feels confident, though, that their horses are strong enough to outrun Indian ponies, and there doesn't seem to be much sense in doing anything but running. But then he hears from behind him, above the bestial, demonic howling, a cry of terror, pathetic and rending, like that of a climber losing his hold on a mountain crag face, or an ocean swimmer seized like a piece of floating bait by something, or that cougar he'd heard screaming in the night:

"Ringo, for the love of Christ!"

Glancing back, he sees Leslie on the ground scrambling on all fours toward the horse that has been shot out from under him, reaching for the carbine in its scabbard. The mounted Apaches, seven of them, are moving toward him fast. Ringo spurs the buckskin for another two hundred yards toward the cover of some trees, then, with a hard yank on the reins he halts the animal and pulls its hammerhead around. He is among the piñons and cedars that surround the plain on three sides, and the Indians probably have not seen him stop, probably cannot imagine a lone white man with a chance to save himself doing anything but that.

Now he sees Leslie down on his belly behind his dead pony, with his rifle laid across its flank and the Apaches nearly on top of him. Reaching him, the warriors divide so that three of them pass on either side while the remaining man tries to force his pony against its natural inclination to jump over the dead animal. At the last instant, the Indian pony swerves to avoid the obstacle, and as the warrior passes within two yards of Leslie, he pays for his daring. The little scout rolls over on his back and fires with the sure, deadly instinct of a snake striking, and the bullet catches the Indian squarely between the shoulder blades, tumbling him lifeless a few yards away.

Having ridden past Leslie, the other Apaches separate to form a wide circle around him just out of rifle range. Once they have him encircled, they can either wait for nightfall to move in stealthily or stay where they are with the limitless patience of their kind, waiting for the white man to make a reckless attempt to escape. For the moment all of their attention is on Leslie, and they seem to have forgotten about the other white man now watching them from a screen of piñóns and cedars.

Ringo has dismounted and tied the buckskin's reins to a cedar branch. Having drawn his newly repaired Spencer carbine out of its saddle scabbard, he levers a bullet into the chamber. As he plants the metal butt plate against his shoulder and sights along the octagonal barrel at the closest Apache, who is over two hundred yards away, he realizes that he is going to need some luck. The Indian too has dismounted and has made himself an even smaller target by squatting on the balls of his feet in that cramping posture an Apache can maintain for hours with his carbine planted upright on the sand in front of him. For several long moments Ringo tries to steady the wavering muzzle and keep the sights on the tiny brown figure squatting like a prairie dog by its mound. He aims for the man's body, but as he squeezes off the shot and feels the buck of the rifle against his shoulder, the Indian leaps up like a released spring, grasping what is left of his head with both hands, then falling back onto the sand, where he writhes for some moments like a headless snake and then is still.

"Should have sighted this bastard in when I got it back," Ringo mutters. "Gunsmith must have monkeyed with the sights."

A prudent man in Ringo's position would simply stay where he was, keeping the other Apaches at a distance and covering Leslie's escape. But his pounding heart and the hot, furious blood coursing through his limbs will not let him do what he knows a prudent, sensible man would do. Yanking the buckskin's reins loose from the branch, he climbs onto the animal and spurs it out onto the plain, at the same time uttering a Missouri rebel yell.

Seeing the lone white man emerge from the trees, hearing the strange high prolonged war cry that breaks from him, the remaining five Apaches are surprised but not intimidated. They recover from their astonishment with the quickness of seasoned fighters and turn their fire on him from five directions.

Unwounded, Ringo spurs his mount toward the nearest Apache. The man hesitates a moment before scrambling onto his pony's back. Once again the white man utters that strange war cry, and the Apache responds with his own defiant battle shout. The two men are carried by their ponies toward a near collision, and as they are about to pass within a few feet of each other both fire their rifles almost simultaneously. Ringo feels a sudden burning sensation just below his ribs and knows that he has been hit. As he passes the Indian and looks back, he sees the man drop his rifle and slump over his pony. Glancing back again, he sees the pony running on riderless and a brown figure rolling on the sand.

Ringo no longer feels the burning along his side, but when he looks down he sees some tiny spots of blood on his shirt. A crease. Nothing serious, he reflects, but he'd better get it patched before he loses enough blood to notice.

Now two of the remaining four Apaches are lashing their ponies across the flat toward him. Suddenly one of them straightens up with his hands reaching and falls backward, shot from behind by Leslie. The other man comes on toward Ringo. Fifty yards away, he resorts to the Comanche trick of sliding down the offside of his mount so that nothing but his moccasin is visible on the horse's back. With one hand he clings to the horse's mane, while with the other he fires his rifle from beneath the animal's neck.

Ringo halts the buckskin and levers in another bullet. Aiming carefully, trying to allow for the alteration of his sights, he manages to bring down the oncoming horse, which screams piteously and falls, carried by its momentum into a near somersault that leaves the rider pinned beneath it.

There are only two Apaches left in the fight now. Prudently, one of them holds back, perhaps intending to leave the field to the crazy white man who seems possessed by what they call in their own language the *hesh-ke*, or killing frenzy, but the other man comes on. Ringo attempts to lever another bullet into the Spencer's cham-

ber, but it jams. Cursing the gunsmith, he spurs his horse
toward the Apache, with the rifle raised above his head
like a club. The man reins in his pony for a steady shot,
and when he fires, it is close enough to lift Ringo's hat
from his head, but apparently it is the Indian's last shot.
He raises the empty weapon, intending to ward off the
blow of the white man's rifle, but it passes beneath his
raised arms, catching him across the midriff. While the
Indian is bent over, Ringo wheels the buckskin like a cow
pony and clubs him again with terrible force across the
back of the head.

As he looks about for the remaining Apache, Ringo is
suddenly grabbed from behind. He tries to pry the muscular brown arm from around his neck and to keep off
the knife he knows the man must have, but the man's
strength and weight are too much for him. The two of
them fall together on the sand, then roll apart. As they
scramble to their feet, facing each other, Ringo's attention is caught by the weapon the Indian holds, an agency-
issue butcher knife with a blade as long as a Bowie's.

It would be a simple matter for Ringo to draw one of
his .44s and finish the man off, but instead he draws his
own knife, and the two of them begin circling each other
in the wary half-crouch of gladiators waiting for an opening. The Indian is about eighteen or twenty and large for
an Apache, close to six feet. Also remarkably handsome,
in spite of the wide bars of white paint across his nose
and cheekbones. Except for his breechclout and moccasins he is naked, and his smoothly muscled brown body
gleams with a healthy sweat. He will be difficult to grasp
when they close together, Ringo thinks. Fleetingly, he
wishes that he too were naked, and twenty years younger.

"Use your hogleg, John. Shoot him!" Leslie shouts.
Having clubbed to death the Apache who had been pinned
under his horse, he is running to help with this last man.
His suggestion is prudent and sensible, but Ringo snarls:

"Stay out of this, Frank!"

"Don't be a fool, John. That's Nachite's son. He'll kill
you."

"Back off! If he kills me, you can have him."

At the mention of his father's name, there is a flicker
of recognition in the young Indian's eyes, which are large
and dark as polished obsidian or those bits of volcanic

glass called Apache tears. In the fineness of his features, Ringo can see the youth's Mexican blood, and the way he moves his splendid body leaves the outlaw no reason to doubt that Nachite's son has inherited other gifts from his Apache forebears, one of whom was renowned especially for his skill with a knife. Leslie is right. He is being a fool, and he can't really understand why he doesn't heed the little man's sensible advice. To make matters worse, the midday sun on his bare head and the bleeding bullet crease across his side are making him light-headed. He must move in quickly before he loses any more strength.

As Ringo moves in, Nachite's son dodges nimbly aside but manages with astonishing quickness to slash Ringo's left forearm. Only the tough gray fabric of the outlaw's old jacket prevents the blade from going all the way to the bone. At the touch of the steel, Ringo springs back.

"That's one for you, sonny," he says with a grim laugh that causes the youth to look at him strangely, perhaps with a little of that awe Indians are said to feel toward the insane. Like an echo of this thought, Leslie yells:

"You're crazy, Ringo! For Chrissake, use your six-shooter!"

Ringo ignores him and continues to address the young Indian, switching to Spanish:

"*Vuelva usted. Vuelva, cachorro,*" he beckons, grinning coldly in the manner of his old enemy Doc Holliday.

A flash of anger in the youth's black eyes reveals that he understands, is only too ready to "come again" and sink his knife in the crazy white man who would presume to call him a puppy, but he is also smart enough to see that the older man is tiring, that if the fight goes on much longer, he will surely win. As the two warriors circle each other, just out of knife reach, Ringo lets his wounded arm hang limply by his side, as though the blade had indeed reached the bone, cutting through the vital sinews. The young Indian watches him warily, keeping his distance, not wholly convinced that the arm is useless, even though the sleeve is blood-soaked and blood is trickling down the white man's fingers. Then suddenly Ringo seems to stumble, is off-balance for a second. Instantly the youth is upon him, slashing upward in an attempt to open the white man from belly to brisket. Just barely, Ringo manages with his blood-covered hand to grasp the Indian's wrist. At the same time, Nachite's son grasps the wrist of Ringo's own knife hand. For a few moments the two of them are motionless, panting in each other's grasp, and the young Indian glares furiously into the eyes of the white man who has tricked him. Then Ringo, remembering a wrestling trick he learned from Cole Younger, drops suddenly into a half-crouch, pivots sharply on the ball of his left foot and thrusts his hip into the young Indian's lower belly. At the same time he drives his right leg between the youngster's legs, throwing the boy over his hip. Nachite's son lands squarely on his back with Ringo on top of him.

In the process of throwing the young Apache over his hip, Ringo loses his Bowie knife, but he manages to stun the youngster with a fist to the temple. Nachite's son relaxes his hold on his own knife and Ringo twists it out of his fingers. Then he manages to pin the young Indian's knife hand beneath his knee. Recovering from the fist blow, Nachite's son reaches up to ward off the descending knife. He catches the white man's wrist, but as he feels Ringo's strength, he must realize that he can only hope to slow the knife's descent, not stop it. His large dark eyes reveal no fear, only a determination to oppose his strength to that of the white man for as long as he can.

"Finish him, Ringo!" Leslie is shouting. "Cut the bastard's throat!"

Ringo has been determined to do just that, but the sound of Leslie's voice causes him to hesitate, with the tip of the knife blade less than two inches above the young Indian's throat. His hard blue eyes and bony features are set in a pitiless deadly attitude, but he hesitates.

"Lemme help you, John!" Leslie offers.

"Get away, dammit!" Ringo pants.

Looking down into the eyes of the young Indian he is about to kill, he is strangely reminded of a moment in the war, a moment he recalled in all of its unforgettable terror only a few days before. He remembers a smoke-and dust-filled ravine that was a circle of the damned, in which the only sounds were the bestial snarls and groans of men clubbing and stabbing each other like warring troglodytes. He remembers an eighteen-year-old Confederate guerrilla, lying helplessly pinned on his back beneath a huge blue-uniformed enemy determined to smash his skull with a rock. More strangely, he also remembers a child who has now become a man, the son Lucy McMaster bore him in the name of another man, the young man who has gone off to Harvard College to become a preacher of the Word. He and Nachite's son must be about of an age.

Still, in spite of these distracting memories, Ringo is about to finish the young Indian, but he hears once again at his elbow the sound of Leslie's voice, insistent and profoundly irritating.

"Kill him, for Chrissake!"

To his own amazement, Ringo suddenly jerks his wrist free of the Indian's grasp and tosses the weapon as far as he can. Then he quickly rolls free of his young enemy and stands up.

"What the hell, Ringo!" Leslie exclaims in disbelief. "You had him. What're you gonna do now, fight him again?"

He ignores Leslie, focusing all of his attention upon Nachite's son, who has not moved since Ringo released him, except to raise an arm to shield his eyes from the sun. Expressionless, he regards the tall white man who has spared him. Then slowly, with a kind of defiant dignity, he rises to his feet and confronts Ringo, as proudly erect as if he were the victor in their combat. Though he knows he is still in the power of the white man, could be cut down instantly by one of his six-shooters, there is no apprehension in his dark eyes. He is simply, defiantly ready for whatever the white man has in mind, whether it is some exquisite form of torture to rival the hideous pain-inflicting crafts of his own people or whatever.

The young Indian's splendid physical presence stirs within Ringo a painful mixture of feelings—envy and a hopeless longing for the lost beauty and strength of innocence, an equally hopeless yearning to see his own son, but also a proud, heartening recognition of what he shares with the young Apache. "You and me, youngster," he wants to say, "we're the same really. A couple of obstacles in the pathway of Progress. The goddamn blue-bellied pony soldiers and the big-balled Wyatt Earps are going to see to it that we don't hold up Progress for long. We can't beat the sonsofbitches. They'll have their way, and when they've hunted us down and cornered us, they'll peel away our hides. But by God they'll remember us. Anybody who's ever fought us will sure as hell remember us." He wants to say all of this to the handsome young warrior, but instead he simply gives a quick sideways jerk of the head and a command:

"*Vaya!*"

At first, the young Indian stays where he is, looking puzzled, wondering perhaps if the white man intends to play the game of letting the captive run for his life, a game not unknown to the Apaches. Clearly the white man is in no condition to run him down, but then of course there is no need for the white man to run when he can simply draw one of his six-shooters and send a bullet in pursuit of the fleeing captive.

"*Vaya!*" Ringo commands again.

The youngster nods grimly, as if to acknowledge that while the odds of outrunning a bullet are not good, they are better than what he faced with the knife at his throat. Suddenly he whirls and sets out at a run in the direction of the ravine, giving no sign that the fight has tired him in the slightest. With his long blue-black hair flying and the sun on his gleaming sweat-polished body, he is a magnificent figure to watch. Like a god, Ringo is thinking, one of Homer's gods down from Olympus. He himself is trembling with exhaustion, starting to feel the loss of blood from his wounds, ready to drop.

"Tough kid," he whispers aloud, more to himself than Leslie.

"You're not lettin' him go!" Leslie gasps in astonishment.

"Yeah, I am," Ringo answers wearily.

"Well, I'll be damned if I'll . . ." Instead of finishing his sentence, the little man levers a shell into the chamber of his Winchester and raises it to his shoulder. Just in time, Ringo whirls and grasps the barrel of the weapon, jerking it downward like a pump handle, so that Leslie's shot plows the sand less than ten feet in front of him.

"Dammit, Frank, I said I was letting him go!"

But the little man isn't listening. He glares at Ringo with an evident desire to make his next shot count at Ringo's expense. As he struggles to tear the rifle free, Ringo suddenly releases it, but at the same time he backhands Leslie across the face with enough force to stretch the little man flat on his back in the sand.

It takes Leslie a second or two to recover from the blow. Then, with the quickness of a tripped springe, he scrambles to his feet, levering in another shell as he rises. But his rescuer, whom he now yearns to kill, is ready, and Leslie finds himself covered by a .44. When the little man raises his eyes to Ringo's face, he encounters the same baleful expression that Nachite's son had encountered before Ringo was moved mysteriously to spare him.

"Jesus, Ringo, don't . . .!"

"You little backshooting sonofabitch, I saved your ass. Guess maybe that was a mistake."

Deliberately, Ringo cocks the hammer of his pistol, fascinated by the range of expressions he is seeing on Leslie's face—murderous rage and hatred, along with naked fear, revealing themselves like exorcised demons— and none of these much disguised by a nervously assumed good-old-boy grin.

"The only reason I wanted to shoot him was so he wouldn't get back to the main band an' bring more of his friends after us. Please, John. . . ."

Strangely, considering that nothing can be more foolish than one man turning on another when both are threatened by a common enemy, Ringo finds it much harder to hold back from killing Leslie than it was to spare Nachite's son. And again, as though he possesses a preternatural faculty enabling him to eavesdrop on Ringo's thinking, Leslie echoes this thought.

"Hey, look, John, we're white men. Ain't this silly as hell, two white men fightin' each other over a goddamn Indin an' God knows how many others nigh about?" He laughs nervously at the absurdity of it.

Seeing the fear of death in Leslie's eyes above the nervous grin, fear that had not been in the young Indian's eyes as he watched the descending knife, Ringo despises Leslie but also begins to feel something akin to pity. With an enigmatic nod at the cringing little man, Ringo lets down the hammer of his .44 and holsters it. Then, without a word, he turns his back on Leslie and begins to look for his mount. If Leslie wants to backshoot him in the fashion of Jack McCall, he is welcome. He,

Ringo, is all fought out for this day, and a strange, unnameable instinct is making him aware that this will probably be his last fight ever.

"Godalmighty, John, you scared the shit outta me. Ain't no way to treat a friend, is it?" Leslie yells after him.

Ringo doesn't answer. He has located his ugly but reliable crowbait stallion cropping grass in the cedars three hundred yards away. Crossing the three hundred yards of sand to reach the animal requires more of an effort than it took to overcome Nachite's son. When he reaches his horse, Ringo grasps the saddle with both hands and rests his head on the seat. Then he pulls a bottle of whiskey from the saddlebag, intending to use it to clean his wounds but instead raising it to his lips for a drink that, given his condition and the midday sun hovering overhead like a great blazing buttock, could be the end of him.

"To hell with it," he mutters, gulping greedily and then coughing painfully, like his consumptive enemy Doc Holliday. "To hell . . ."

Leslie is at his elbow cautioning him. "Guess you earned yourself a drink, John, but I'd take it easy if I was you. We'll get you on to Antelope Springs. Ain't but ten mile from here. I know a gal there who'll take good care of you. Patch you up an' . . . Hey, Ringo!"

Leslie jumps aside as the outlaw suddenly falls backward, measuring his length on the sand.

"What'd I tell you, Ringo?" he says with a laugh. Hooking his thumbs into his belt, he regards the sprawled figure at his feet with what was probably the attitude of bow-bearing Paris over the fallen Achilles, a mixture of amazement at the ludicrous vulnerability of the mighty and amused, cringing contempt.

"You're hell on wheels, big man, but you sure can't handle your whiskey," he says sneeringly, reaching down to take the bottle from the unconscious man's grasp. Much of the liquor has already drained into the sand, but Leslie, having wiped away the sand from the bottle's mouth, finds enough remaining to enjoy several long swigs. Then, for another whole minute, he looks down at Ringo, rubbing the cheek that still feels the impact of the outlaw's hand. His narrowed feline eyes reveal the thoughtful attitude of a man confronted by equally attractive alternatives, and one of them manifests itself in a movement of his hand toward the butt of his holstered .38. The movement is arrested, however, and he says to the man at his feet:

"Naw, you ain't ready to die yet, big man. Not *yet.*"

Then he sets to work reviving the unconscious Ringo.

3

"Another bottle, if you will, Mrs. Patterson."

Widow Patterson hears John Ringo's order but doesn't bother to look up immediately. The open novel in her lap has drawn her into it, into a fabulous world two thousand miles to the east, where all the rooms have teak and mahogany paneling varnished to catch the brilliant light thrown by candelabras or crystal chandeliers, where gentlemen in frock coats and brocade vests sip port wine and smoke cigars, where satin-gowned women are ladies because gentlemen see to it that they have nothing else to worry about besides being ladies. Still unready to withdraw from that world, still dreaming herself a part of it, she rises from her chair beneath the one window that admits enough light to read by and walks across the room very slowly, like a great lady summoned from a drawing room somewhere in New York City or Baltimore. As she reaches behind the bar to draw out a quart bottle of her next to cheapest whiskey, she pauses, straightens up and looks closely at the man who has spoken to her. Unlike the small man slouching in the chair across the table from him, he is sitting rigidly erect with his hands on the edge of the table, as though to steady it. His dark, bloodshot eyes regard her steadily, sadly out of cavernous hollows. He hasn't had much sleep, she guesses, what with stumbling around her kitchen in the middle of the night in his underclothes, pawing through the cupboards after something to drink. A few whiskeys for breakfast have brought some color back into his face, but he still looks like a man more ready for death than anything else.

"Sure you want another bottle now, Mr. Ringo?"

"Sure enough, Mrs. Patterson." He smiles gratefully at what he takes to be concern for his health, when in fact she is mainly worried about what he might do to her little drinking hell if he puts away more than he can handle. Hardly a week seems to go by at Myers Cienega that some thirsty cowpoke or freight hauler doesn't fill his skin a mite too full and then try to take the place with him. Usually there are other fellows around to put an arm on the hell raiser before he does too much damage. Now there is nobody around to subdue Ringo but that little devil he's drinking with, Buckskin Frank Leslie, and she doubts that he would get in Ringo's way. Nobody, she has heard, gets in Ringo's way, except maybe Doc Holliday or the Earp brothers. A mighty dangerous man, so she's been told. But from what she can see, he is also something like a gentleman, not like most of the ignorant, boozing riffraff that draw rein here. A different, more gentlemanly sort of drinker he seems to be, not mouthing out a lot of filthy nonsense or letting the devil that's inside every man come out to play, but staying real quiet and looking sort of sad, even when he is laughing at something Leslie says. Looking into those mournful, tired eyes, she guesses that he will behave himself, as long as his thirst doesn't wake him up again in the night with no whiskey in reach.

She brings a fresh bottle over to the table and Leslie pays her. As she takes his money, she notices a wide stain on the floorboards around his chair. Been spilling his liquor, it looks like, can't hold it any better than Ringo, she thinks. But then she looks more closely at him. He is talking loud, the way a drunk will when he can't hear himself too well, and laughing a lot, but there is something about his drunken manner that doesn't seem quite real. She has the feeling he is trying to look and sound a lot further gone than he really is. It's his eyes. Sharp gray, hard as glass, they are fixed on Ringo in sort of a hungry way, like those of some animal, a bobcat or a snake maybe, getting ready to strike its victim. She doesn't like Leslie much, having heard about how he frightened his poor wife out of her wits by shooting teacups out of her hand and making her stand against a wall while he outlined her figure in bullet holes. No wonder she divorced him, though maybe it served her right for marrying the man who killed her first husband. . . .

Suddenly Leslie looks up, fixing that same hard gray gaze on her. Like a bobcat or a snake, she thinks again, not the sort of man a woman could trust a whole lot, or a man either. She wonders if Ringo knows what he is doing, getting so helplessly drunk that way with a man like Leslie. Not that it matters much to her what one murdering scoundrel does to another. Still, she shudders a little as she turns away from them and goes back to her book. Leslie watches her cross the room, then he speaks.

"Where do you want to go next, John?"

Ringo thinks for a moment, gazing steadily into his lifted glass before he tosses it down. From across the room, Widow Patterson notices how he wipes the escaping drops from around his mouth with a handkerchief, like a gentleman.

"Hell, maybe."

Leslie guffaws loudly at that and refills his companion's glass. He fills it quickly without spilling a drop, like the bartender he is at the Oriental Saloon in Tombstone, but he pours a good deal more than a shot and leaves his own glass empty.

"Hell, Ringo? We've hit every hell between here and Tombstone. . . . Soldier Holes, Antelope Springs. . . . You want to go back maybe?"

"Go back . . ." Ringo echoes, without really hearing what Leslie has said. His hand slides deliberately toward the brimful glass, lifts it carefully between thumb and forefinger, turns to let it poise for a moment upon his fingertips. Light from the single window across the room shoots through the amber, giving it a dark bronze, almost golden hue.

"Like a little chalice," he mutters. *"Hoc est corpus meum . . ."*

"Whazzat?" Leslie asks, his voice suddenly thicker, more nasally drunken-sounding.

"I said, '*Nunc est bibendum, nunc pede libero, pulsanda tellus . . .*' "

Leslie scowls for a moment, as though he is wrestling out a translation of what he has heard. Then he chuckles.

"It sure don't sound much like Apache, and it ain't greaser. Izzat some Comanch' you learned back home in

Texas? Or izzat something outta one of them little books you carry around in your saddlebags? If it is, then you better say it in American for the benefit of us simple mountain folk."

Ringo sips a little of his whiskey before replying.

"It's part of a poem by Horace. He says that now's the time for drinking."

"The hell he does!" Leslie exclaims with a laugh. "Well now, I guess I know what you find in them books, just a little more encouragement to go on and do what you're going to do anyway."

"There's a lot more to the poem, Frank. It's mostly about a woman named Cleopatra. Quite a woman she was. Even Horace had to admit it." He raises his glass. "To Cleopatra."

Leslie reflects a moment.

"Yeah, seems I heard something about that gal. Wasn't she the one who had all them conquering heroes for lovers? They'd take over her country, then she'd take them over. She was a trap they didn't have enough sense to walk around. Just like all women. Any woman's a trap if you take her seriously."

"Can't agree with you there, Frank." Ringo finishes his glass. "A good woman can save your soul."

Leslie snorts his amazement and contempt.

"If that's a fact, Ringo, then how come you never let your own soul be saved?"

Ringo smiles wearily as he murmurs, "Maybe I don't think it's worth any good woman's trouble."

Leslie chuckles mirthlessly as he refills both their glasses.

"Mebbe you don't need a *good* woman. Mebbe what you need is another night with Lupe. You want to go back to Antelope Springs?"

Ringo shakes his head slowly, smiling a little as he remembers the night with Lupe at Antelope Springs. Funny, he thought at the time, how she'd been there in his room above the Cantina Estigia waiting for him to come upstairs from the poker game. Nothing mysterious really, as it turned out. Leslie had arranged the whole thing, though why he still isn't sure. *"Que quiere usted, Señor Reengo?"* At first he thought he'd gone into the wrong room. *"Quiere Lupe?"* Then he saw his coat draped over a chair, where he'd left it earlier. It was his room and she was sitting on the edge of his bed, showing more than a little of her brown nakedness beneath the Indian blanket draped about her shoulders. *"Quiere Lupe?"* she asked again, her voice strangely husky, rasping. There was a warning there if he wanted to heed it, but John Ringo had never been a man to hold back from danger to either body or soul. The sound of love's disease in her voice actually drew him to her, fanned into glowing life the embers of passions he had thought to have all but drowned long since in bottles beyond counting. *"Qué hombre,"* she rasped appreciatively, her almond eyes feverishly alight with her pleasure. "You like Lupe?" For an answer he plunged himself even further into her hell, willing his damnation, willing the exquisite torments of the waiting demons. As her hard muscular thighs worked him deeper and deeper, she fastened her lips to his mouth, licking across the roof of it like a torch. His naked sweating chest was impaled upon glistening pointed breasts as hard as polished bronze. When she finally managed to suck forth his spirit, he was utterly desiccated. "You like Lupe?" *"Consummatum est,"* he whispered in reply, to himself, and though she couldn't have understood him (or could she?) her triumphant whore's laughter rang out across the desert night.

"Time to go, John," Leslie is saying.

"A damnably hot little demon she was, Frank. Why'd you send her up to my room? A joke? Some joke. She had something inside her, and now I've got it. Nice work, you little backshooting sonofabitch. If she had what I think she had, then I'd better not let too many years pass before I put a bullet through my brain. While I've still got one." He wonders why Leslie continues to grin at him through the haze that has settled over their table. Then he realizes that he hasn't actually said a word, and Leslie is speaking again:

"I said it's time to go, John."

"You ever shoot a man facing you, Frank?" Now he has managed to speak, for he sees Leslie's grin disappear. A threatening frown passes quickly across Leslie's face, then he laughs expansively.

"I take a man any way he lets me, John. My wife's first husband was pumping lead at me from a balcony, and I let the moon shine in between his horns. But it's not been often I give a man that much chance, you're right. Partly it's how I was raised. Back in Kentucky folks shooting at each other are mostly involved in feuds, and if you don't pick off your enemy when he gives you the chance, there's no telling how many of your kin he's liable to rub out. It was the same when I was scouting for the army. You don't think about giving redskins a fair chance. That's the *last* thing you think about. And I still see it that way. You take your man any way you can, and don't take no chances you don't have to." Leslie pauses a moment and regards Ringo closely before he goes on: "I must admit, though, that I fair admire the way you used to handle yourself with the Earps and Holliday."

"What are you talking about?" For an instant, memories of his various run-ins with the Earps and Doc Holliday swim together confusedly—challenging Wyatt Earp to a duel in the middle of Allen Street, inviting Doc Holliday to grab the end of a handkerchief and draw against him (guns or Bowie knives, it didn't matter), standing them all off with a rifle at the San Pedro bridge the time they were on their way to arrest Curly.

"I mean," Leslie is saying, "the way you used to stroll up and down Allen Street in front of the Earps, and the way you'd just walk right into the Oriental and have yourself a drink while they were there leaning on the same bar. I was tending bar a few times when you did it, and that's when I decided I had to get to know you better."

"That was just a lot of show-off stuff, Frank. I never did accomplish anything that way."

"Whaddya mean, Ringo? You've got some reputation now, no question about it, and now your enemies is all gone. How does it feel?"

How does it feel? Damned lonely. Because it isn't just his enemies who are gone. Nearly all of his friends as well, and mostly rubbed out by the damned Earps. Both McLowrys and Billy Clanton at the O.K. Corral, and not long after that, or so he's been told, Wyatt Earp claimed he put eighteen buckshot into Curly Bill's chest while Curly was trying to bushwhack him at the Iron Springs water hole. Some of the men with Curly confirmed Earp's story. But why didn't they bring Curly into Tombstone for burial? They had to know that Curly was the sort

who'd want to be laid out properly, with a dark suit on at
least, and maybe a quart of good whiskey in the box
beside him while his comrades stood around and paid
their last respects. As he recalls, the fellows with Curly at
Iron Springs were pretty vague about the whole business,
and the possibility that Curly was still alive, hadn't been
shot after all, occurred to Ringo even before Leslie claimed
to have seen him in Galeyville. True, the only one besides Leslie who claims to have seen Curly recently is
Lupe over at Antelope Springs, a girl he trusts about as
much as he trusts Leslie. But it is still just possible that
the big man is alive, has gotten himself set up on that
little ranch down by Hermosillo and now maybe wants
Ringo to help him stock it with some good Arizona beef
from Colonel Hooker's Sierra Bonita Ranch or one of
the other big spreads. It would make sense for him to let
the word go around that Earp killed him, seeing as how
he, like Ringo himself, has a price on his head that the
Arizona Stockmen are eager to pay any bounty-hunting
sonofabitch who can collect it. It would make all the
difference if Curly were alive. Curly is a friend, and
Ringo would do anything to help him out.

He hasn't answered Leslie's question, and now Leslie
is grinning at him in that good-old-boy-from-the-mountains-
you-can-trust-me way he has, which Ringo has come to
see for the mask it is. He remembers how the little man
looked when he stopped him from killing Nachite's son.
Now, just for an instant, the little gunman's eyes show
Ringo something that doesn't go with the grin. It comes
and goes so quickly that he can't really be sure, what
with the whiskey haze that has settled between them and
the dim light of the place, but just for an instant, Leslie's
hard gray lynxlike eyes darken, actually seem to bar like
a cat's. At the same time they are filled with a strange,
inhuman light. Ringo has seen paintings of the *santos* in
little mission churches down in Sonora—on their knees,
haloed, their eyes illumined by an unearthly vision. The
light he catches now in his companion's eyes is like that—an
unearthly illumination—but it seems to emanate from
whatever is opposite to the hope and joy of salvation.
The light of pure undiluted malevolence. Ringo hasn't
seen anything like it since the last time he blew the head
off a rattlesnake. "Now you're seeing him, Johnny. Don't

trust him." Who said that? A woman's voice, it seemed to be. Ringo looks around, but there is no one else in the room, no woman except Widow Patterson over by the window. "He's a tinhorn backshooter, you know that, just like the devil himself. You're a damned fool if you put yourself in his power," the voice goes on urgently, insistently. "But John's already put himself in my power," Leslie is saying. Ringo hears his voice clearly, answering that other voice, even though Leslie's lips are closed and fixed in that you-can-trust-me grin. "You've drunk your way into my power, John, and now there's no turning back. You were right when you told Lupe, 'Consummatum est.' I don't read much Roman poetry, but I do read the Good Book—mostly to pick out verses I can use—and I must say I fair admire the way you mocked the Man Himself, using His words to tell us you were finished. Course we already knew you were, soon as you laid down with Lupe. You like Lupe? Kee-air-ray Loopay?" Leslie mimics and then guffaws loudly. The sound of his laughter so enrages John Ringo that he reaches for his right-hand .44 and would blow the little man out of his chair. But there is no gun at his hip. His two ivory-handled pistols are upstairs in his room, along with his saddlebags and rifle. A good thing for both of us, he thinks, and his rage begins to subside, for he can see now that the infuriating laughter he hears is not coming from the little man across the table. It is coming from within his own brain, and it seems the only way he can shut it off is to use a gun on himself. "Do it, John." Leslie's voice again. "The Earps and Holliday are gone now. They won't do it for you. Put a bullet through your brain." And Ringo sees then that the Leslie across the table is in fact speaking, but he is saying something else.

"Time to go, John."

Ringo pushes back from the table and stands up, straightening to his full six feet two inches. Then he begins to sway, and Leslie, nimble as a cat, is around the table instantly to grasp his elbow and steady him. Ringo shakes him off.

"Get away from me, you little Satan."

Leslie shrinks back in amazement. For a moment he looks frightened. Then he begins to grin again and finally manages to force a laugh.

"Hey, John, what the hell are you saying?"

Ringo says nothing more, as he brushes the little man aside and staggers purposefully toward the stairs. Grasping the pine-log banister, he begins to work his way up a step at a time. Leslie calls after him:

"What the hell's got into you? I'm your friend. I'm here to look after you."

Ringo does not hear him. He hears only the sound of his own steps, the slow heavy steps of a big man alone in darkness climbing toward the door at the head of the stairs. There is someplace he has to go, but he can't quite figure where. If Curly has gone down into Mexico, then maybe he ought to go down there and find him. Or maybe he ought to head out toward California. One of his sisters, Mary, whom he loves more than all the world, lives near San Jose now. She has never stopped writing to him, has begged him to come out there again and again. Does she really believe what he's told her, about being in the cattle business? She probably does, in spite of rumors that might have drifted out west, about the bad men who rode with Curly Bill, preying on Mexican smugglers, stages and cattle herds on both sides of the border. Some cattle business. Yes, she probably still believes him, and even if she found out the truth, she wouldn't stop loving her big brother. But he would die before he'd willingly let her know the truth. Maybe if he died soon she would never know. "Why do you have to die at all, John?" That strange, oddly familiar woman's voice again. "There's nothing to keep you dying here in Arizona. Why can't you listen to those letters you carry around in your breast pocket? Go to the people who love you before it's too late." "Too late already, John," rejoins that other familiar voice. "Too late . . ." he whispers to himself as he reaches the door at the head of the stairs.

In the darkness of the room he shared with Leslie, he manages to find his saddlebags, rifle, ammunition belts and his two six-shooters, which he belts on first. Buckling on his two ammunition belts, he fails to notice that one of them, carrying extra .44 cartridges, is upside down, and the shells begin to drop out of their loops. He does not hear them striking the floor, for there is another sound filling his head, that same obscene familiar laughter that is Leslie's. And when that familiar laughter subsides, he is hearing Leslie's voice again: "Time to head out, John, like I been telling you. You've dealt your last hand and left me holding all the aces. You're on the out trail now. Riding out dead drunk, but you'll have one helluva long time to sleep it off."

Emerging from the dark room, he seems to leave that Leslie behind, chuckling over its infernal witticism, but the other one is waiting for him at the foot of the stairs as he begins his slow, difficult descent.

"Just take it easy, John. I've got your horse saddled outside. Thought we'd be riding out 'fore now."

Ringo does not reply, being wholly preoccupied with finding the steps beneath his feet. As he comes to the bottom, Leslie starts to reach out a steadying hand but draws back as he sees the look in the big man's dark blue eyes.

"What the hell *has* got into you, Ringo?"

"Hell maybe, and if it's all the same to you, I'll just ride on in there by myself."

"You ain't makin' sense, John. You better let me go with you."

Ignoring him, Ringo sets down his rifle and saddlebags and, without too much difficulty, walks over to the window where the Widow Patterson, having put aside her novel, is knitting. Lost in her lonely abstraction, aware of little besides the clicking of the needles, she has not heard the exchange between the two men. When she looks up, Ringo is standing over her, just removing his big white felt hat. He stands there for a moment, smiling shyly, apologetically as he tries to find the words he needs. Then he says:

"Mrs. Patterson, I'm grateful for the hospitality you've shown me, and I want to apologize for disturbing you last night."

He is a gentleman, sure enough, she decides, and a fine figure of a man still, in spite of all his hard living. She finds, though, that she cannot look into his eyes. The sadness they reveal, some unutterable misery of his heart, is more than she can bear. She lets her eyes drop to her knitting needles before she replies.

"It's all right, Mr. Ringo. You weren't yourself last night."

"No excuse. I have no excuse. A man is what he is.

Drunk or sober he's . . ." He is still too drunk to make her understand what he means, what he wants to say. After a moment of trying to find the words, he gives up. Reaching into a trousers pocket he fishes out a twenty-dollar gold piece and hands it to her. "Here, ma'am, for any damage . . ."

Widow Patterson's mouth drops open in astonishment as she stares at the gleaming double eagle in her palm.

"You didn't do any damage, Mr. Ringo," she protests, in spite of a well-nigh irresistible cupidity aroused by the rich beauty of the coin.

"No matter. You keep it. I have all the money I'll be needing." Awkwardly, he reaches out to pat her shoulder. She has to look up then, and as she meets his eyes again, her heart is wrenched by their terrible sadness. He may be an outlaw and a killer, she thinks, but my God he's suffering and I pity him. For a few long agonizing moments he holds her with his suffering, and she can almost feel the bitter grief and despair that has, like trickling acid, etched those deep lines in his still handsome face.

Finally he releases her and, drawing a silver watch out of his shirt pocket, he announces:

"Close to twelve. Guess I'll be moving on now."

She wants to say something to let him know she understands his need of her sympathy, pities him in his lonely suffering, but she is afraid that his man's pride will make him scorn what a woman can put into words.

"You be careful, Mr. Ringo," she calls after him, but he doesn't seem to hear her.

With his saddlebags slung over one shoulder and his rifle cradled in one arm, Ringo makes for the door. Another .44 cartridge falls from the nearly empty belt he has buckled on upside down, and Leslie, following after, stoops to pick it up.

"Hey, gunfighter, you're losing ammunition," he says sneeringly, not quite loudly enough for Ringo to hear as the big man pushes through the swinging double doors. Laughing humorlessly to himself, the little man follows only as far as the doorway. Holding the swinging doors still in his hands, he peers over them after Ringo, his sharp-featured visage set in a wry, oddly quizzical smirk.

Ringo's ugly buckskin mount is saddled as Leslie said.

As he steps off the porch and approaches the animal, Ringo throws his arm across his eyes to protect them from the dazzling glare of the midday sunlight upon the chalk-white dusty ground. The terrible heat through his blue flannel shirt nauseates him, and he has never felt less like riding, but he knows that no matter how crapulous his condition, he has to leave Myers Cienega at once. Where is he going? He has no idea, but he senses that there is someplace he must be, if only he can figure where. Perhaps he can think more clearly in the saddle, when the midday heat has sweat some of the whiskey out of him.

He ties on his saddlebags and tightens the cinch around the stud's belly. Pausing for a moment before he swings into the saddle, he looks back toward the doorway of the Widow Patterson's saloon. At first he can only make out Leslie's small white knuckles upon the tops of the doors, but then he sees the little man's face framed by the darkness behind him. Again, while he can't see clearly enough to be certain, he seems to encounter that same malevolent expression in the eyes, the look, he thinks suddenly, of a rattlesnake that has managed to corner its prey and is readying itself to strike. Again it passes quickly and Leslie smiles good-naturedly as he says:

"Take care of yourself, John. See you in Tombstone."

"Don't follow me, Frank, I warn you."

"I won't, don't worry, Ringo," the little man replies with a bitter chuckle. "I only come this far with you on account of you asked me to keep you company after I brung you into Antelope Springs to get patched up."

Which is true, Ringo has to admit, and now he wonders why he ever asked the little gunman to ride along with him. It wasn't as though he owed Leslie for reviving him and helping him to reach Antelope Springs. He had, after all, gotten himself cut up and shot in the process of saving the little man from the Apaches. Was it because, starting with that first long pull at the bottle from his saddlebag after the Apache fight, he had drunk himself into a mood to welcome Leslie's company? Was it like other times, when he had just enough whiskey warmly numbing his brain to let him enjoy Leslie's mountain humor, his jokes and stories, which are not unlike what he used to hear as a boy in southwest Texas? Maybe. He hasn't had a good laugh since Curly disappeared. But that doesn't explain why day after day he has let Leslie prod him on to drink himself nearly insensible. And sick. God, he is sick now. Swinging onto the buckskin, he nearly falls off. And why he let Leslie and his little friend Lupe make him sick that other way too. . . . Christ, he might as well ask the little tinhorn, backshooting, pimping bastard to put him out of his misery. Maybe that was what, why . . .

" . . .'less you want my company. I don't ever ride with a man 'less he invites me along." Leslie has stepped out onto the porch and is standing there with his hands on his hips just above his gun belt. With an experienced gunfighter's eye, however blurred by sun and crapula, Ringo notes that the little man's holster is tied down and the hammer thong that holds his .38 in the holster for riding has been slipped off.

"I don't plan to give you my back, Frank. You have something in mind you'd like to try, you'd best try it now." He holds his reins in his left hand, leaving his faster hand free. "I mean maybe you're going to get me anyway, but I've got enough pride left I won't make it easy for you."

Leslie's face suddenly becomes, Ringo thinks, a very convincing mask of amazement. Wide-eyed, open-mouthed, he seems to be rendered speechless by a sudden grasp of Ringo's monstrous suspicion.

"You can't be thinkin'. . . . What do you take me for, John?"

Ringo's only reply to that question is a short scornful laugh. He turns his horse away from the porch and begins to move off at a slow walk, twisting himself in the saddle so as to keep an eye on Leslie until he is nearly out of pistol range and can barely hear the little man calling after him:

"You're crazy, you know that, Ringo? So drunk you're crazy. . . ."

And maybe he's right, Ringo thinks, as he spurs his mount into a lope that will put some distance between himself and Myers Cienega. But his sickness will not let him maintain the lope, and after a mile he slows the buckskin to a walk. Soon he comes to a fork in the road and, without really thinking about it, turns east toward Galeyville, onetime headquarters of Curly Bill.

"Yeah, maybe he's right," he mutters to himself. "I'm plenty drunk now. Maybe I'm a little crazy, too."

It is because he is hearing voices again, women's voices. One of them is the voice he heard back at Widow Patterson's, saying something he can't quite make out. But there is another one he recognizes, though he hasn't heard it for many years. It seems to be coming from a great distance, from far away back in Texas even, from a grave he has never visited.

"Don't let your heart be hardened, John," it pleads, faintly but urgently. "The Lord punishes hard hearts."

"I won't, Mama," he murmurs, wanting to reassure and comfort her, even with a promise he knows he can't keep.

It is the least he can do in return for all she did for him—loved him, gave him a good Christian upbringing, taught him how to read the Good Book, so that he knew that "the wages of sin *is* death" and that you don't have a chance if your heart is hardened.

She also, he remembers, gave him, unintentionally, a little exposure to what some call the True Faith when she paid Padre Garcia to tutor him in Greek and Latin. The good old man couldn't help teaching him something about his religion, even gave him a copy of the Good Book in St. Jerome's Latin, which he still carries in a saddlebag with his favorite reading.

"It is never too late, Juanito," the padre told him more than once. "One can always repent." Even then the boy John Ringgold wished that he could believe him.

But somehow what his mother and her vigilante-leading, damnation-preaching friend Asa Mitchell said always made more sense. Especially after the boy became a man with a heart hardened by the war. Having Quantrill as your leader in that war was like having the devil himself guide you into the bowels of hell. If that didn't harden your heart, nothing would. Surviving in that inferno, you knew you were either a fiend or one of the damned. So that when the war started all over again back in Mason County, Texas, he was ready. The man with the hardened heart was ready. He knew what the wages were, and in the hardness of his heart he accepted them.

And it still makes sense, what his mother taught him, to the veteran outlaw who became Curly Bill's lieutenant. He remembers the good times with Curly and the others, times when the furies of guilt and despair seemed to have left him and he could lose himself in activity—planning a foray down into Mexico to rustle cattle or waylay a smuggler train, driving a horse herd away from an army post, reliving the exploits back at Evilsizer's or Roofless Dobe Ranch. But there were the other times, when he caught himself actually envying the men he rode with, envying their apparent incapacity to feel any sort of guilt, which was itself a kind of innocence. The big outlaw chief himself was the pattern for all of them, wearing always a cherubic smile on his round, swarthy face, even when he was dealing death from the hip. He enjoyed life more than any man Ringo had ever met, and he was the only one who could lift Ringo himself out of the abyss of melancholy that always seemed to yawn whenever he slowed down long enough to think about what he had become. Seeing Ringo in one of his somber, reflective moods, he would not rest until he had coaxed him out of it. "Dammit, Ringo," he would say. "You've got more brains, and guts too, than the rest of this outfit put together. I won't plan anything without you. But I'm damned if I'll let you spoil our fun. Either you drink up and start laughing with us or you fight us."

Stay with Curly and you had to share his fun. His infectious good humor was irresistible, and Ringo would find himself laughing uproariously at the outlaw chief's crudest witticisms. But there was more to sharing his fun than laughing at his jokes or his pranks, such as having him surprise you by shooting a cigar out of your mouth. You had to be ready for anything, ready to act with less conscience than the devil himself. And Ringo had been under the illusion for a time that he had managed to silence his conscience, or had perhaps even assumed the demonic innocence he envied in his comrades. He was able to maintain this illusion until a July afternoon in 'eighty-one, when he shared Curly's fun at a place called the Devil's Kitchen in Skeleton Cañón.

"Jest a bunch o' greasers," Curly said of the nineteen Mexican smugglers they cut down there. "Help me finish 'em off." And Ringo helped, stepping among the brown-faced corpses to find and finish the living. One he found half floating in a pool of the creek, his face a mask of terror. *"Madre de dios! Cristo mío, socorro!"* the man gasped, crossing himself with a blood-covered hand as Ringo raised his pistol. For some reason, he lowered it again, was unable to fire, and simply stood where he was on the creekbank looking into the man's enormous terror-filled eyes. Suddenly a .45 roared beside him, a hole appeared in the brown forehead, and the pool went red. Ringo turned to find Curly regarding him quizzically, the ever-present cherubic smile playing about his lips. "Takes care o' that. Now let's go find them mules," he said, holstering his .45.

When they rounded up the smugglers' mule train, it turned out that the animals were carrying close to $75,000 in Mexican silver in their bulging *aparejos*. Curly and his men rioted for weeks around Galeyville and Charleston, drinking, whoring and gambling all of it away. For some reason, Ringo alone couldn't seem to help keeping his share nearly intact, even increasing it substantially later with what he won from his comrades in the endless poker games back at Roofless Dobe Ranch. So drunk that he could barely make out the cards, he played recklessly, actually trying to lose but unable to stop winning. His mood was deadly somber, and for once Curly left him alone, left him to reflect that it took a friend like Curly to show a man what he really was. Not that he'd had many doubts in that regard.

In the year that has passed since the massacre, his thoughts have returned often to Skeleton Cañón. He heard that the bodies were left unburied, left for the animals to tear, and he thought of that bloody hand moving between the points of the cross. Now, riding eastward from Myers Cienega, the memory of that day is more than his insides can endure. Reining in beneath the shade of a giant oak, he slides out of the saddle, drops to his knees and vomits. When his guts are empty he goes on retching, endlessly it seems, as though he is trying to heave up the whole past. When he finally ceases his heaving, he can barely manage to stand up. Luckily, the buckskin has not moved, and he pulls himself up by a stirrup. Then he stands for a moment with his head resting on the saddle, which he clings to with both hands.

He is utterly exhausted, must find a place to sleep. Looking about for a rock-free shady spot to lie down, he suddenly notices the oak tree itself and its peculiar formation. It has a short thick base, out of which rise five other trunks, each as thick as a full-sized tree. In the palm, as it were, of this giant hand lies a large flat rock wide enough for a man to sit on and lean back against one of the trunks. The tree is actually a favorite lunch and siesta stop for lumber haulers driving between Tombstone and a sawmill some ten miles away. Ringo has noticed it before but has never rested in its shade. Now it beckons him to rest.

He leads the buckskin over to the tree, sits down on the rock and pulls off his boots. These he ties to the saddle. Then he winds an end of the buckskin's tie rope around one of the trunk fingers and returns to the bench. Most of the whiskey seems to have been sweat or vomited out of him, but he is trembling and shivering with chills in spite of the heavy afternoon heat. What he needs is a drink. There is a bottle in one of his saddlebags, but he simply doesn't have the strength to get up and fetch it. He needs a little rest before he tries to move again at all.

Leaning his head against one of the thick black fingers, he drops off quickly, plunges into an abysmal dreamless slumber from which, it would seem, nothing less than an angel's trumpet can arouse him. For a little while he remains there, like a man in a coma. Then, still totally immersed in darkness, he finds himself on his feet groping toward a tiny distant light, like a firefly in the night on the other side of a swamp. All around him a moist, swampy darkness is alive with gliding things and fixed things that reach out to grasp him as he passes. He hears strange mournful cries, birdlike but more forlorn than those of any nightbird, and once, off to one side of him, a gibbering that sounds almost like articulate human speech. He moves ahead toward the light, but his progress is arrested suddenly by a cold, foul-smelling substance that rises lapping about his waist and begins to draw him down like sucking quicksand. As he is being drawn down, he is aware that the light is growing larger, moving toward him. Terrified, hoping that the bearer of the light will hear him, he cries out in a manner as unfamiliar to him as the devouring terror itself:

"Holy Mother of God!"

His cry, it would seem, awakens him, for he finds that he must throw up a hand to protect his eyes against the searing brightness of the sun at midday. The sun, it would seem, has not moved since he left Myers Cienega. Opening his eyes again, shielding them against the excruciating brightness, he beholds a vision whose reality he cannot at first accept. When, after considerable hesitation, he does accept it, he is filled with a sudden joy that is nearly unbearable, that is more painful than sadness.

"Hello, Johnny, it's about time you woke up," she says, chiding him playfully in a way he remembers. "I never knew *you* to keep a lady waiting."

"Are you . . . ?" he begins in a near whisper. "You can't be . . ."

"I'd better be, Johnny Ringgold," she says, laughing. "I'd better be."

"I thought I'd lost you."

"Never, Johnny. You can never lose me," she says, not laughing anymore but with the old mischief still in her dark eyes.

Now his throat is tightening so that he cannot speak, and he feels the beginning of tears.

"Come here," she commands gently, "and don't look so sad."

He rises immediately to obey, not even bothering to pull on his boots. She is mounted on a big sorrel, very like the high-spirited stallion Blaze that Harry Younger had given him twenty years before. When he goes over to her, she gives him a stirrup, and he swings up behind her. Then he puts his arms around her, and she takes one of his hands, pressing it to her breast while she leans her head back against his shoulder.

"Hold me, Johnny. It's so good to have you holding me . . . again."

As he kisses her smooth dark-bronze hair and she strokes his hand upon her breast, tears begin to course down the harsh lines and angles of his face, like life-giving rivulets in an unforgiving desert landscape.

"Will you come with me now?" she asks.

"Surely," he whispers hoarsely.

She touches the sorrel's flanks with her spurs, whereupon the animal lunges forward like a bronc coming out of a chute, but instead of bucking it settles into a bounding gallop unlike that of any horse he has ever ridden. It occurs to him fleetingly that the fastest animal he has ever ridden would be unable to stay close to this creature, would be like a draft animal trying to catch a thoroughbred. Trees and rocks move by them on either side in an indistinguishable blur.

"Take the reins, Johnny," she calls back to him.

He reaches around her and takes them with one hand. With the other arm he encircles her slim, taut-bellied waist. Without any apparent awareness of rein or riders, the sorrel plunges ahead, and soon Ringo is able to make out in the distance the dim shadowy shape of what must be a mountain peak. It must be a mountain, for he can even make out patches of snow just below its summit. But Ringo knows this country well, and he knows that the mountain has no business being there. There isn't a mountain that high south of the San Franciscos or north of the Sierra Madres. There isn't supposed to be anything there but a few desert buttes. Where are we? he wonders.

Were it not for the presence of the woman, he would be anxious about being unable to say where he is. As it is, he is content, holding her before him, breathing the fragrance of her hair blown back against his cheek and feeling the warmth of her body against his. As they draw closer to the mountain and it rises before them higher and darker and the snow fields crowning it catch sunlight like the mirrors of an Olympian heliograph, Ringo's heart pounds with a tremendous excitement. With all his being, he yearns to ascend the mountain with this woman whom he loves with all his being.

But as they draw near the base of the mountain, he is startled to see that the very earth before them has moved apart, has opened into an enormous yawning chasm that blocks their path to the mountain, slashing across the land as far as the eye can see in either direction. It is like the great gorge of the Rio Grande as he saw it once up in northern New Mexico, uncrossable by any wingless creature. And he is afraid. In spite of the power he feels surging through the flanks of the Pegasus beneath them, a power that is somehow one with the love flowing into him from the woman, he is afraid.

"Hang on, Johnny!" the woman calls back to him.

And he responds by tightening his arm around her waist while looking anxiously ahead, beyond the abyss, to where the great eye-filling mountain beckons and defies. Nearing the edge of the abyss, he still clings to the woman, but he is afraid, and his fear drains the strength from his arms. As the driving haunches and reaching forelegs bear them away from the edge, he lets go of her. "Johnny!" Margaret screams, reaching back for him. But in less than a second he is well beyond her reach. "Johnny!" he hears her calling down to him as he begins falling headlong into the abyss. Far below, as though stirred by Leviathan, who maketh the deep to boil like a pot, white waters are boiling around and around sharp upthrusting rocks like the jagged teeth of some primeval chaos monster. Eagles circling above the water are like tiny black specks of whirling ash. Shutting his eyes, he relinquishes himself to what he cannot resist.

While Ringo slumbers in the palm of the great oaken hand, two riders encounter each other a few hundred yards away. One of them, a blond muscular six-foot man with a leonine moustache, regards the other, a smallish fellow, whose elaborately beaded and fringed buckskin jacket appears to be designed for someone's Wild West show, with a grin of mixed amusement and contempt.

"Who's tending bar back at the Oriental, Frank?" the blond-moustached man asks.

"Not me, Wyatt. Guess you can see that. What're you doing out here, if you don't mind my asking? Thought you'd left these parts for good."

"I will be, Frank," the other answers, "just as soon as I finish my work here in this territory." As he says this, he nods toward the tree in which Ringo is sleeping and his grin disappears. "That sonofabitch," he mutters.

"Now's your chance, marshal. He's so drunk he won't give you much of a fight."

"I thought you were his friend," Earp replies, a quizzical expression in his ice-blue eyes.

"Not hardly. Not no more anyway," Leslie answers with a bitter laugh.

"Well then, you won't mind staying out of the way while I attend to my business. Or I'll put it another way. You make one move to help him and you're a dead man."

At this Leslie laughs again and draws back in an exaggerated gesture of fear. "He's all yours. It's thanks to me, though, that he's not in any condition to give you a fight."

"I won't count on that," Earp replies. "I've never seen him not ready to fight, drunk or sober. He has sand, I'll give him that."

"You're right, Wyatt," Leslie agrees ingratiatingly. "Best not take any chances with him."

Earp looks at the little man with curiosity and contempt. As he knees his horse into a slow walk toward the tree, he keeps Leslie in sight. Reining in a few yards away from the sleeping man, he rests a hand on the butt of his long-barreled Buntline Special and waits for the man to awaken.

Expecting to be devoured by the boiling waters of the abyss, Ringo is suddenly conscious of the fact that their roaring, a dim sound from far below that becomes deafening as he plunges toward them, has ceased. And when he dares to open his eyes again, he is lying on soft grass beneath the still unmoved midday sun. Getting to his feet, he finds himself standing in the middle of the broad meadow that stretches between the tumbled boulders at the foot of the tall cathedral rocks that form the Devil's Kitchen above the creek winding its way among the oaks and sycamores along the bottom of Skeleton Cañon. The meadow is full of flowers—wild roses, paintbrush, lupine, daisies. Scattered among them are small, shapeless white objects, which at first he takes to be bleached rocks. Looking down between his feet, however, he recognizes the top of a skull and knows that he is among the remains of his victims. Drawing his right-hand .44, he walks over to the creek, stepping carefully among the scattered bits of bone. He finds the pool without difficulty where it swirls beneath some overhanging willows, and there, as he expects, is the wounded man. Only it isn't the smuggler. It is a brown-robed figure whom he has not seen since he was a boy. When he looks up at Ringo there is no terror in his eyes, only pity. "My son," he says, raising a bloody hand, "it is never too late. You will be forgiven, if only you will ask."

Ringo looks into the old man's eyes, then down at the

weapon in his hand. He is about to replace it in its holster, but he is suddenly filled with an overwhelming revulsion, like a man who finds himself grasping a poisonous reptile by mistake. Drawing back his arm, he throws the pistol as far across the meadow as he can, even as he had thrown away the knife when he chose to spare the Indian boy and ignore Leslie's urging to cut his throat. Looking back into the pool he sees the bloody hand again raised and moving between the points of the cross.

Without the weight of the pistol, either in his hand or at his hip, Ringo feels something like the relief of a prisoner unshackled. His left-hand .44 is still in its holster, and he draws it out and tosses it into the grass next to the pool. Next he discards his Bowie knife and the hideout knife on its lanyard. When he looks again into the pool, the bloody figure is gone. There is only the clear swirling water.

Freed of the steel bondage of his killing tools, he begins to feel a sense of elation of a kind he has not known since he was a boy, when he mastered a lesson fully and won the good old padre's approval. And this sense of elation is enhanced enormously by an inexplicable sense of Margaret's presence. He cannot see her, but he can feel her near him.

In this strange state of elation, unaffected by the crapula of the morning, he awakens to find himself still resting in the great handlike tree. He realizes that he has been journeying in a dream, but he still yearns to maintain his sense of well-being and the feeling of Margaret's nearness. Perhaps if he can bring himself to heed the lesson of his dream. . . . His weapons are still in their places, ready for use, and as he starts to rise, he reaches for his right-hand .44, intending to leave it, along with his other weapons, on the seat in the tree. "Never keep a lady waiting," he whispers to himself and starts to smile.

"Look out, marshal, he's drawed!" comes a shout from a few feet away.

Ringo does not have a chance even to turn toward the voice before he is deafened by the roar of a gunshot, accompanied, it seems, by a woman's scream. For a fraction of a second he is vouchsafed an apocalyptic vision of the shining mountain beyond the abyss. Then the darkness closes in.

"That's some shooting, Wyatt," Leslie remarks with an appreciative whistle.

The blond man does not answer. He dismounts and walks over to where Ringo has fallen back into his seat in the oak tree, the .44 still in his hand.

"If somebody was to fire that hogleg he's holding, it'd look just like he done it hisself. Want me to do that for you, marshal? That way nobody'll ever suspect. . . ."

"Do as you like," Earp snaps in reply. Without another word, he turns back toward his horse, mounts and spurs away at a swift, businesslike gait just short of a gallop.

Leslie watches Earp's rapid departure for a few moments, then he turns back to the figure in the tree. The .44 is still firmly grasped in the right hand, and for a second Leslie is terrified by the thought that Ringo might be still alive, in spite of the ghastly wound in his temple. With an instinctive cunning and quickness, his mind formulates a lie to explain why he didn't warn Ringo of Earp's approach.

But the lie is not needed. Ringo has been killed instantly by Wyatt Earp's bullet. Leslie sees now that one reason he thought that Ringo might still be alive is the incongruous expression he is wearing. With a wound like that, a man's face should be twisted in a painful grimace or frozen in an attitude of rage and hatred toward the antagonist inflicting the wound. Ringo's lean, bony features are strangely relaxed, and his hard mouth even appears to show the beginnings of a smile. He looks much more like a man enjoying a peaceful dream than an outlaw who had died with a gun in his hand.

Ringo's expression exasperates Leslie. He tries to shrug it off as the effect of drink transporting the moody outlaw away from the troubles of this world into a world of dreams. But if this was the case, then why did he draw against Wyatt Earp? The little man is baffled and so irritated by the expression on the dead man's face that for a moment he considers firing Ringo's own pistol into his temple. There are, after all, no powder burns, as there would be if it had been suicide, but mainly, another bullet might somehow change the dead man's expression. Then he realizes that an overly large wound in the temple might arouse suspicion that Ringo's death was not suicide, and it is, for reasons he cannot fully grasp himself, important to him that Ringo's death be thought of as a suicide. So he merely fires the .44 in the dirt and then replaces it in Ringo's hand. After that he steps carefully around the tree to make sure that he has left nothing to evidence his presence. Finally he tears off a branch of the tree with which to wipe out his footprints. But first he addresses the dead man:

"You'd've done it yourself sooner or later if Earp hadn't done it for you. An' I was just helpin' you along, like you wanted me to if you really stopped to think about it. You were dealin' your last hand, and you give me all the aces to help you cash in. Guess you might wonder what I get out of it, and I don't know as I can answer that. Mebbe it's like when the 'paches capture a good man and torture him till he's just got nothin' left. Them red devils really believe they can appropriate his spirit, what it was that made him a strong fighter. Mebbe I was after your spirit, John. Question is, did I get it?" He regards the dead man curiously, as though he actually expects an answer. And perhaps it is because none comes that Leslie's habitual good-old-boy grin is replaced by a strange look of disappointment. But then he laughs aloud and sets to work brushing out the footprints that would give him away.

Buy them at your local

bookstore or use coupon

on next page for ordering.